Thistle in Her Hand

THE ROMAN

Thistle in Her Hand
by
Margarita Thompson Diddel

WINDSWEPT PRESS
INTERLAKEN, NEW YORK
1988

Copyright © 1988
Margarita Thompson Diddel
All rights reserved
This book may not be reproduced, in whole or in part, in any form (beyond that copying permitted by Sections 107 and 108 of the U. S. Copyright Law and except by reviewers for the public press), without written permission from the publisher.

Cover illustration by Norman Fortier; courtesy of The Whaling Museum, New Bedford, Mass.

Additional copies of the book may be ordered from:
Windswept Press
P.O. Box 299
Interlaken, NY 14847

Dedication

To the memory of my grandmother, Maria Tobey Hamblin, whose stories of her life as the whaling wife of Captain John Hamblin inspired the writing of *Thistle in Her Hand*.

I wish to express my profound gratitude to Arnold Murray, my creative writing teacher at Lindsey Hopkins **Adult Education Center, Miami, Florida,** for his patient encouragement and valuable counsel.

And special thanks to the retired Senior Curator of the Old Dartmouth Historical Society, New Bedford, Massachusetts, Mr. Philip S. Purrington.

I would also like to thank my daughter, Rachel May Diddel and my son Andrew and his family, especially my granddaughter Katha Diddel Warren, for their efforts to get this novel published.

MARIA TOBEY HAMBLIN

Foreword

Thistle in Her Hand was written from what my grandmother, Maria Hamblin, had told me of her experiences at sea aboard *The Roman*. *The Roman* was a sperm whaler that had to go to the Indian Ocean and the South Pacific, as sperm whales were getting scarce near home and were extremely important during the American Civil War. My grandmother kept me entertained with stories about *The Roman*'s trip home and how they miraculously escaped *The Alabama*. When *The Roman* finally entered the Cape Cod waters the ship was at first considered a phantom ship as it had been thought to be lost.

The voyage home was to have been completed two years earlier but the home office ordered the experienced Captain John Hamblin to continue whaling and to send the oil home as the Union desperately needed it to conduct the war.

We still have an embroidered hassock made by my grandmother on this voyage, amongst many other treasures collected by the Captain and his young wife. She spent many an hour with her embroidery, trying to submerge her fears, especially for her two children born on the four-year voyage. My mother, Henrietta, was one of these two children.

I heard so much about whaling days and experiences from my grandmother and others living in the Cape Cod area at the turn of the century. At that time, there were many whaling people, whaling wives and whaling men alike. I was particularly impressed with these whaling tales because I had spent my youth in the subtropics. My father had gone to the Yucatan as American Counsul and archeologist in the Mayan field. I had very little experience with the ocean except for one traumatic experience with sharks that left me with a horror of the sea. I could never understand or imagine how my grandmother could ever have been willing to go off to sea!

Many years later I wrote my book based on the knowledge given me at my grandmother's knee; the book was, however, not published at that time and I put my manuscript away and somehow lost the box. It wasn't until 1963 when I retired and had time for creative writing classes that I decided to write again about the whaling wives' story. Having lost the original manuscript, I could only write from memory, imagination, and research on the general topic.

Late in the 1960s I completed my novel of life aboard *The Roman*. I did not at that time get around to publishing the story. Now, however, I have a special interest in doing so because people seem to have lost touch with that phase of our history.

—Margarita Thompson Diddel

Chapter 1

On the warm mid-afternoon of July 19, 1859, comely seventeen-year-old Maria Tobey gathered the voluminous skirt of her spriggy muslin frock and descended lightly from the stagecoach that had brought her to the Cape Cod village of West Falmouth, Massachusetts, from Monument Beach, her home town, farther up the Cape.

The burly grayhaired driver had already brought down her portmanteau from the top of the stagecoach and set it down at the open front gate of the yellow picket fence. He smiled at her as he turned to climb back to his post.

'I declare, seems like yesterday you was a skinny little girl I was bringing to Cap'n Tobey's home for your summer visit to your Uncle Asa and Aunt Eunice, and look now what a purty young lady you've got to be, Maria. I reckon next year you'll be a missus.' He nodded his head as he looked at her again.

She was delicately built and slightly below average height. Her face was oval and her chestnut-brown hair, smoothly drawn on either side of a middle part, lent

character to her young face. The apple-green lining of her straw bonnet made her hazel eyes fairly dance with green highlights. Though summer was half over, her creamy-white skin had just enough color to suggest good health. She carried her shoulders well, and her green sash showed her waistline fashionably tiny.

She waved him a smiling goodbye and for a moment watched the coach, like a big bumblebee, disappearing in a cloud of dust. 'Yes, Seth Gifford, you are so right—next year by now I'll likely be a missus—Mrs. Gordon Crothers.'

Then she turned briskly. Picking up her portmanteau, she started up the flower-bordered walk leading to the comfortable two-storied, clapboard house. Eagerly she glanced around for any changes in the familiar scene. The petunias along the walk were the same riot of colors, but the house had had a new coat of yellow paint with brown trim since her last visit. Everything looked spick-and-span as ever. That's the way their home would be—Gordon's and hers. Maria's face flushed as she thought of the surprising news she had for her uncle and aunt. 'I can just see Aunt Eunice's face, all smiles—Gordon is just the kind of person she would like me to marry,' she mused as she went up the granite front steps.

As Maria reached for the polished bronze knocker the door swung open. Without warning she was gathered to the ample bosom of Aunt Eunice and greeted with a hearty, 'We're so glad you could take time from your social life this summer to visit us. From all accounts you're the belle of Monument Beach. Let's have a look—why, you're prettier than ever. But land's sake, let's go in out of the hot sun and rest a bit in the parlor. I want to hear all the news. First, how's the family?'

'Stepmother is still ailing,' Maria reported as she sat down by her aunt on the horsehair sofa in the cool parlor. 'Papa and the boys are well. Lisha likes working with Papa in the shipyard. But David spends every waking moment on the water, on his beloved dory. He's only eleven but he can handle it like an experienced sailor. Papa says he is a born seaman.'

Then Maria, a troubled expression in her eyes, turned to her aunt: 'David is disgusted with me. I won't even step into his boat; but, Aunt Eunice, as you know, I still am terrified of the sea. When I go to the beach with my friends, I get so scared I can't even put my feet in the water. You should see how they laugh and tease me. I just can't help it. My stomach tightens up on me.'

Eunice Tobey rose and went to the lace-curtained window and lowered the shade against the sun. 'Maria dear, you always were—even as a child. Your dear mother was, too; maybe you inherited her deep fear of the sea. She loved the land—gardening—just as you do. I do, too.'

'I reckon some people are born for the land, others for the sea—like David and your Uncle Asa. I am sure if Asa had not lost his leg on that whale chase, he might be out awhaling now. Horrible—I might be out there with him.'

'How's Uncle Asa?' Maria asked with that sad feeling that came over her when she thought of her tall, lanky uncle with his kindly light blue eyes and graying whiskers—her beloved Uncle Asa—stumping around painfully on the wooden leg that reached halfway to his hip.

'Asa's tolerably well. Keeps busy—every day, rain or shine, he harnesses Queenie to the buggy and drives to Falmouth to his gear shop. He doesn't talk about it, but

Thistle in Her Hand

I know he still thinks of his whaling days, hankers for the sea. Dearie, do you know what he's got now back in the marsh? A whaleboat? Sometimes when it's high tide he sculls around in it and probably dreams he's back on the ocean.' Aunt Eunice shook her head and sighed.

'But why did a smart man like Uncle Asa have to go whaling and lose his leg in that fight with the bull whale? If he was so crazy about the sea he could have sailed on a clipper ship—got to be captain of one maybe . . .' Maria spoke up.

'I reckon whalemen are a breed of their own,' said Aunt Eunice, as if thinking aloud. 'They love the open seas and the excitement of the whale chase. And your uncle is of that breed.'

'Land's sake alive!' she exclaimed, looking at the Seth Thomas clock on the mantle. 'It's most four o'clock! Let's skedaddle to your room and I'll help you get settled before the company comes.'

'Company? Who?' Maria asked as she picked up her portmanteau and followed her aunt up the green-carpeted stairway.

'A whaling captain,' Aunt Eunice answered over her shoulder. 'A Captain John Hamblin. He's been coming to your uncle's shop for whaling gear for his ship. Seems he's sailing soon for the South Pacific—sperm whaling—a good three- or four-year voyage. Your uncle thought it nice to invite him for our Saturday night baked beans and brown bread.'

'And, I hope, your apple pie,' Maria added, eagerly.

'Oh yes, your favorite pie—I've made it extra fancy for you,' Mrs. Tobey laughed as she led her niece into the guest room.

With a sigh of contentment Maria looked around the room. How friendly this bedroom was! She had known it most of her life. So cheery with its yellow flowered wallpaper, its bird's-eye furniture and those new braided rugs! Aunt Eunice must have just finished the rugs. Maria's eyes went fondly to her aunt, who was busily fluffing out the feather puff and adjusting the counterpanes—colorful like the petunias on the front walk—on the fourposter bed, as if to give it extra comfort.

Aunt Eunice, in her gray percale dress and white starched apron, had not changed—a little stouter perhaps and her dark hair had silvered about the temples, making her soft blue eyes a little bluer. She looked up with a twinkle in her eyes.

'What's this I hear about a young man—a summer visitor—getting ahead of your other beaux?'

Maria's face flushed. 'I was going to surprise you with the news! Gordon Crothers is my beau—real beau. The Crothers are from Dorchester—been coming summers for about three years—and come to church regularly—like it was their church.'

'I have never heard you speak especially of him,' Aunt Eunice interrupted.

'Because he's never paid attention to me—says he'd thought of me as one of the kids until the Strawberry Festival at church in June.' Maria giggled and felt the heat rise to her face. 'I like him better than anyone else. And I've decided to say yes!'

'You will like him, Aunt Eunice. He is away this week working in his father's hardware store, but he will be back Saturday in time to take me to the garden party his mother is giving. I'm making the prettiest dress—a flouncy dimity...'

Aunt Eunice was listening, her face beaming approval, when suddenly she remembered that the company was due soon and there was the pot of beans in the oven to check and other things to do. 'That's wonderful, Maria,' she said, and gave her niece a hearty hug. 'I want to hear everything, but I must go tend to my cooking. We'll have a chance to talk when we are doing the dishes and the menfolk are in the parlor yarnin' about their whaling experiences.'

She stopped and added, 'Maria, you've such a knack with fixing bouquets—after you get settled, will you go into the garden and pick posies for the table?'

'Oh, I'd love to, Aunt Eunice! I'll hurry and be ready in a jiffy to pick the flowers and help with dinner.' Maria opened her portmanteau and started to get settled as she had done so many times every July at Uncle Asa's for years. She took out the new green gingham plain housedress she had just made and exchanged it for the fluffy 'Sunday dress' which she hung in the lavender-scented closet.

As she deftly emptied the contents of her portmanteau, she thought about the coming party on Saturday when she was sure Gordon would propose. She suspected this party was to be in her honor; she knew his parents liked her and her folks liked Gordon. She knew she would be happy with him. And if he got to be manager of the branch store his father was planning to open in Falmouth, maybe they'd live in one of the lovely homes on Elm Street. How happy Aunt Eunice would be if that happened!

Yes, Saturday he'll propose, she thought happily as she stepped to the washstand and tipped the white porcelain pitcher, pouring water into the bowl. 'Probably have the diamond ring,' she said aloud as she washed her warm face and hands and dried them on the linen towel from the rack. For a moment she clasped her hands to her mouth and dreamed of the wedding. 'At church, of course. Next June when Gordon graduates from college. That will give me more time to fill up my hope chest and make my trousseau. My underwear will be of fine linen...'

'Good gracious,' Maria interrupted her reverie disgustedly, 'here I am daydreaming and the company will be here before I get those flowers picked.' She hastily adjusted the hairpins in the figure eight at the nape of her neck and left the room.

A few minutes later she stood in the garden at the side of the house absorbing the colorful mid-summer beauty around her. Summer had come early this year with August flowers already blooming. Those sunflowers along the fence looked like golden sentinels, she thought. Then she bent and deftly snipped rich red zinnias, yellow calendula, and orange marigolds with the garden scissors.

'Now a border of sweet alyssum,' she murmured as she stepped to the sundial around which the dainty white flowers grew in profusion. She paused on hearing the clack-clack of horse's hoofs and saw a smart rig stop at the side gate. A tall, bearded man alighted and hitched his horse to the hitching post. Maria watched him as he turned in at the side gate and strode up the gravel walk. A seafaring man by the slight roll in his gait, but no ordinary seaman by the way he carried himself. And his clothes, Maria noted, were well cut from fine material. A peaked cap rested on one side of his sunbleached, reddish gold hair. And his fine long beard also showed much exposure to sun and salt water. Must be thirty-five, Maria thought, with growing interest.

He caught sight of Maria and smiled before he spoke.

Thistle in Her Hand

Maria liked his smile and his deepset eyes, blue and steady, with sun crinkles about their corners. He was younger than her first glance had led her to believe, but had a look about his face that showed he had borne heavy responsibilities.

'Excuse me, ma'am, but is this Cap'n Asa Tobey's home?' His voice was deep and assured.

'Indeed it is, sir.'

He approached the sundial, cap in hand, bowed slightly and said, 'I'm John Hamblin.'

'Oh, my aunt is expecting you. I am Maria Tobey, Captain Tobey's niece, here on a visit.'

And Maria put out her hand. Her fingers seemed to tingle when they touched his, and when their eyes met she had a nice warm feeling, as if they had known each other for a long time.

'I'm proud to make your acquaintance, Miss Tobey. Your uncle invited me to come to taste his wife's good baked beans and brown bread, but he never mentioned his charming niece. Maria! What a pretty name!'

'Pretty?' She shook her head. 'I've grown so tired of hearing my brother and others sing:

> *Maria, Maria—sits by the fire*
> *And watches the flames*
> *Go higher and higher.*'

The captain laughed heartily. And Maria, realizing her childish outburst, tried to hide her embarrassment by reaching down and pulling strongly on a weed at her feet.

'Oh, watch out, Miss Maria! That's a thistle. You'll prick your hand.' Captain Hamblin leaned across the sundial in concern.

With an amused laugh, Maria extended her hand and firmly closed it on the thistle, then opened it again. 'See? There isn't a scratch. Long ago Uncle Asa taught me how to handle a thistle weed. He says it's like life—grasp it firmly and it won't hurt you; handle it gingerly and it will prick you in a thousand places.'

She stopped suddenly and asked, 'But where is Uncle Asa?'

'He'll come later. His horse went lame in one hoof and is at the blacksmith's getting a new shoe. The captain asked me to come ahead and let Mrs. Tobey know before she starts worrying.'

'Then we'd better go in, Captain Hamblin.' And Maria led the guest to the honeysuckle-covered side porch just as her aunt appeared, a puzzled expression on her round face.

'Aunt Eunice, this is Captain Hamblin—Uncle Asa's friend you're expecting. Seems Queenie had trouble with a hoof and Uncle has her at the blacksmith's getting her a new shoe. He asked Captain Hamblin to come ahead and tell you before you start aworrying.'

'Captain, I am glad you did. I hope Asa won't have to stay long and make supper late. Let's sit here a while. There's a nice breeze from over Buzzards Bay.'

She pulled three chairs together, then added with a smile as she sat down, 'Somehow I expected an older man.'

'I reckon you'd call me an old timer in a whaling way! I'll be twenty-eight come November but I have been whaling since I was fourteen—and a captain going on three years.'

Maria, realizing that she must put the flowers in water before they started wilting, reluctantly excused herself and went into the house. She wanted to listen to him talk, much as she disliked his subject. But as she stood by the dining room sideboard arranging the bright blossoms in the azure-blue Sandwich glass bowl, she could hear through the open window the young man's pleasant voice as he told her aunt about his recent return from a two year's voyage to the Arctic, whaling for whale oil and 'bone.' The ship was The Congress and it was his first captaincy. He then told her of his new appointment as Master of The Roman.

'It is a fine ship—one of the best in the New Bedford whaling fleet. It is now being made ready to sail from New Bedford for the Indian Ocean and South Pacific. It's sperm whaling this time. Tougher but brings more money.'

'Leaving soon?' she heard her aunt ask.

'In less than five weeks—August twenty-third.' Maria detected great pride and joy in his voice.

What a pity, she thought. Such a nice man with that awful love of the sea—just like Uncle Asa. 'Yes, what a pity,' she whispered to herself, feeling a real regret, a strange sadness.

The flower arrangement was finished but Maria lingered beside the sideboard mirror, surveying herself critically, tucking a stray lock here and there, tidying the tatting lace around her collar, as she continued to listen with interest to her aunt's questioning.

'I'd always hankered to go to sea, and when I was fourteen I asked my father's permission to go. He refused, wanted me to be a doctor like himself. He was Dr. Benjamin Hamblin of Sippewisset. The village being so near here you've probably heard of my father, Mrs. Tobey.'

'Oh, yes, I've heard of him. He was interested in studying the herb medicines the Indians around here use; he was sure the medicines were Nature's cures for many of our ills. He died before he could prove it. As for you—I can guess, Captain Hamblin. You did what so many boys are doing even now—shipped on a whaler just leaving from New Bedford.'

'Yes, Mrs. Tobey.' He answered slowly as if on a sigh, 'It grieves me that my parents died before they had a chance to see me captain; it would have pleased them—making up for the worry I caused them by running away to sea.'

'Asa did the same when a boy—and, like you, got to be captain, only to lose his leg on a whale chase and put an end to his days at sea. But in his heart he is still a whaler. Why, out in the marsh—'

Just then Maria, the folds of her dress adjusted, the tatting on her collar patted into place against her throat, and the stray locks of hair tucked in, stepped back onto the porch. John Hamblin looked at her with open admiration, then politely turned to his hostess.

'Ma'am, you just mentioned about the marsh. Cap'n said he had a surprise for me out in the marsh. If so, maybe I'd better see it before it gets dark. Would you show me your uncle's surprise, Miss Maria?'

Aunt Eunice chuckled, 'Yes, we know what he's talking about. Maria, you take the captain to it. Meanwhile, I'll finish setting the table. Your uncle'll be along soon, I expect.'

As she opened the door to enter the house, the tempting aroma of beans baking in the rich molasses and salt pork drifted across the porch. The visitor sniffed appreciatively. 'Smells mighty good, Mrs. Tobey,' he said as he followed Maria down the porch steps.

Maria led the way past the barn with its row of stately

hollyhocks, their red and white and pink blossoms standing out against the yellow wall, and on through the open gate and down the worn narrow path between masses of wild rose bushes with some of the delicate pink roses still in bloom. She picked her way out of the reaching brambles as she chatted about the unusual luxuriance of the flowers this summer.

'Look over there—near that pond—the marshmallows are starting to bloom,' she remarked over her shoulder, smiling at him. He smiled back but hardly gave the flowers a glance. He was looking at her with a pensive, sad expression in his eyes.

Oh, that awful voyage is on his mind, she decided, and wished he would forget it for a while and be as happy as she felt walking along with him. For some reason the sky seemed especially blue and everything around looked so beautiful; she felt very much alive. Her heart felt gay.

'Do you know my father, Elisha Tobey of Monument Beach?' she asked the captain, hoping to get him into a conversation.

'I haven't had that pleasure, but tell me about him,' he answered as he reached down and removed a bramble from Maria's path.

'Papa is not at all like his brother, Uncle Asa; he's a landlubber and book lover. He's memorized most of Robert Burns' poems. He is always repeating, "A man's a man for all that," when he talks about slavery. He's an Abolitionist and is working hard to stop slavery in this country.' Maria, usually shy before strangers, found it easy to talk in the captain's presence. She told him of her mother's death.

'I was only six and my brother Lisha was three. Davey was a baby. Lisha and I are landlubbers like

Papa but Davey is like Uncle Asa—loves the sea.'

Just then Maria, puzzled by his silence, turned with a smile. 'We're almost to the surprise. Be ready.' She was startled by the strange look on his face—there was a look of firmness about his mouth as if he had been thinking about something and had come to a decision. But when he said, 'Good, I am glad,' he looked at her with a special warm, personal look. She felt excited, anticipating his look of surprise at seeing a whaleboat in the marsh. It would probably put him into a jovial mood.

'Here we are,' Maria called gaily as they approached a clump of tall slippery elm saplings on a rise of ground at the turn of the path. Now they could see the marshy land spreading far out to the green-covered sand dunes along the horizon. A creamy cut in one of the dunes showed a bit of Buzzards Bay, blazing in the light of the lowering sun.

Stopping on the knoll, Maria and John lifted their faces to the fresh breeze blowing in from the water, enjoying for a moment its brisk pleasantness after a sultry day. Then, with a ripple of laughter, Maria pointed across the marshes below to a narrow wooden pier where a boat rocked gently all its long length with the incoming tide.

'There's the surprise—a whaleboat—imagine it—a real whaleboat in those narrow marsh streams! When it's high tide Uncle Asa sculls around in it some days—probably dreaming he is going out to sea—going out awhaling.'

Maria looked up at John and started to explain that, as she had on her good shoes, she did not want to walk to the boat in the dank marsh grass, especially with fiddler crabs swarming around and crunching underfoot. John did not take his eyes from hers.

'They're gray green—flecked with gold—sort of hazel aren't they?'

'What are you talking about, Captain Hamblin?'

'About a pair of lovely eyes I want to remember and think about when I am away at sea,' he said gently. He reached for her hands and held them in his own.

'Oh, you are making a collection of memory pictures of your lady friends to recall when you are at sea?' She slanted her eyes toward him coquettishly while half-heartedly trying to free her hands. Surprised at herself, she found she liked his masterful grasp of her hands.

'No, Maria. It is only my future wife's eyes that I wish to recall,' he answered quietly. He tightened his hold on her hands. 'Maria—dear, what do you say to that?'

'Good gracious! Supper's probably on the table—the beans will be getting cold.' With a quick, firm movement Maria freed her hands and ran lightly toward the house. John followed her with long, easy strides. Neither spoke.

A few minutes later they walked up the side porch steps and directly into the dining room. The table gleamed with white linen, silver, and cut glass. The blue bowl of flowers glowed in the center. Aunt Eunice, coming from the kitchen with a glass dish of piccalilli, beamed. 'Oh, there you are. Supper's about ready. Asa's home—and washing up. Well, Captain, what do you think of Asa's surprise—the whaleboat out in the marsh?' She set the dish of pickle relish on the table and, looking amused, waited for his answer.

'The boat? Oh, yes, a good boat...I guess.' John Hamblin was obviously startled and embarrassed that he had not noticed anything incongruous about a whaleboat in the marsh.

Eunice Tobey looked at him, then at Maria's flushed

cheeks, and shook her head slightly as she turned to go back to the kitchen. Just then the tall, bent form of Uncle Asa, towel in hand, appeared at the kitchen doorway. He was chuckling and his blue eyes twinkled under their heavy grizzled brows.

'I didn't tell you about the real surprise, Cap'n—meeting my favorite niece, my brother Elisha's daughter. She's nothing like her old uncle, though. She's a landlubber for sure—scared to death of the sea.'

They sat down to a steaming platter of brown beans edged with golden slices of salt pork. Another platter nearby held the rich dark brown bread gleaming with moist raisins.

Later, when Maria had removed the last empty dessert plate from the dining room and placed it on the kitchen table, her aunt turned from the piles of dishes she was stacking ready to wash, and faced her. Maria stared back, troubled: Aunt Eunice's face was no longer the smiling, genial countenance, but a somber one, with a drawn expression. When she spoke the tone of her voice was sharp, even frightened.

'The captain could hardly eat for looking at you. He's really smitten. Whaling men make up their minds mighty fast and do fast courtin'. And you are taken some with him. Oh, Maria, he's a fine man—anybody can tell that—but don't go marrying a whaling man. Sometime he'll expect you to go to sea with him—you know how fearful the voyage will be for you. Or if you stay home with the children, like I did, it means nights of walking the floor with worry—and he can't be with you when you need him most—'

'Oh, Aunt Eunice, don't fret yourself sick. I'll never marry a whaling man, even if he takes my fancy.'

And Maria put her arms around her aunt. She knew

what was going through her aunt's mind—her three golden-haired boys taken in one week by the killer disease, diphtheria, while Uncle Asa was at sea. Maria was a little girl at the time. 'I'm practically engaged to Gordon.' And as Maria talked about the coming party on Saturday and about Gordon, she lightly dismissed Captain John Hamblin from her mind.

Later, when the captain was taking his leave, Maria tried to make her farewell remarks casual but in her heart she felt a reluctance to see him go. And later as she lay in bed, wide awake, trying to think of Gordon and her plans to marry him, thoughts of John—as her mind now persisted in calling him—would take over.

'Oh fiddlesticks! Tomorrow I'll have forgotten him and have my peace of mind back,' she muttered, giving her pillow a vigorous punch and settling down to sleep. 'I'll concentrate on Gordon.'

The next morning, as Maria adjusted her skirts about her in the Tobeys' church pew, a tall figure slipped into the pew beside her with a 'May I?' She felt a sudden lift of her heart and knew it was John Hamblin. She gave him a swift glance and then, blushing in confusion, searched for the hymn number just announced. Gently he took the book from her hand, found the correct number, and whispered, 'May I share yours?'

For the next hour, as the service went on, Maria's thoughts whirled with confusion. She thought she had dismissed John from her mind to concentrate on Gordon, the man she was going to marry; but try as she might she could not focus Gordon's image in her mind. Why not? She was in love with Gordon, but what was this warm, sentimental feeling growing in her heart for John? She couldn't be in love with two men at the same time!

She tried to keep her hand from trembling as she held

her half of the hymnal for the closing hymn. 'Rock of Ages, cleft for me,' John's rich baritone soared above the others. The small boy in the pew turned to look at the newcomer admiringly.

After the service the Tobeys hurried out but John stopped to speak with the preacher.

'That was a good sermon this morning,' declared Uncle Asa as the three walked slowly homeward. Maria smiled dreamily. All she remembered was the happy feeling that had stayed with her all through the service as she sat at John Hamblin's side.

'I am sorry I was late to church,' John said as he joined the group, 'but when I found you folks had already gone, I just hitched the horse to your post and hiked it over here. If I had known you were walking to church, I would have brought the buckboard and taken you home,' John said, looking with concern at Captain Tobey's apparent painful walking.

'Cap'n Hamblin, my husband insists on walking to church and no help, no sirree,' Mrs. Tobey said in a tone of resigned annoyance. Then she and Maria exchanged surprised looks and concealed smiles as they saw Asa Tobey accept the younger man's arm to lean on.

'It's that blame missing leg that's giving me a mite of trouble,' he said, jocularly.

'Cap'n Hamblin, come in and have baked ham and potato salad with us. It's ready, as I don't cook on the Sabbath—just warm the vittles I cooked on Saturday,' Mrs. Tobey said with a cordial smile. Maria knew John's kindly gesture had pleased her aunt.

'Well, Ma'am, I'm afraid I'm imposing, but I will accept before you change your mind,' the captain said with a grin.

Thistle in Her Hand

It was a hearty meal and a merry one with much laughter. The two captains vied with each other in relating sea yarns until Aunt Eunice and Maria shook with helpless laughter.

Wednesday morning as the stagecoach rumbled homeward toward Monument Beach, Maria tried to put her meeting with Captain Hamblin out of her mind. But, try as she would, she could not forget his eyes, his smile, his voice, his hearty laughs at Uncle Asa's quips, and most of all, his unanswered proposal.

'He wants to marry me,' sang the wheels of the coach! 'He loves me,' cracked the driver's whip! 'But he's a seaman. No! No! No! Marry a whaling man? Never, never, never. I must forget him.'

As the stage rumbled along the dusty white road, Maria stared at the pine trees bordering the highway, but she stared without seeing. Her thoughts were back at Uncle Asa's home, reliving those last moments alone with John in the hall when he was about to leave for Sippewisset. 'It's still the Hamblin home. My aunts are living there. I mostly stay there between voyages,' John told her as he took his scarf and black derby from the hat tree.

Then he sighed as he murmured, 'I sure hate to leave—but I have to be in New Bedford early in the morning—important changes are being made on The Roman and I as captain must be right there for the next few days. When I'm finished, I'll write you for permission to call on you at your father's home.'

Before she could answer, he grabbed her hand, drawing it to his lips for a second, then dashed out of the door.

Perhaps he'll forget, she told herself as the coach

came to a stop before a two-storied, weather-beaten shingled house with a spacious veranda across the front. It was Maria's home in Monument Beach. In her heart she was hoping John would not forget.

As she arrived home and stepped from the coach, her little brother Davey, his face all smiles, was waiting for her.

'You ought to see my dory. I painted it a bright blue,' he told her as he picked up her portmanteau.

'Oh, Davey—you and Captain Hamblin. All you think about is boats or ships.'

'Who's Captain Hamblin?' Davey asked, eagerly.

'Oh, a friend of Uncle Asa's who came to dinner Saturday. He's going sperm whaling to the South Pacific . . .'

'Jiminy Crickets! I wish I'd been there and heard him,' the little boy said, disappointed.

'You may hear him yet, as he may come here before he sails.'

Maria tried to speak nonchalantly but she wasn't fooling herself. Just talking about John started her heart pounding.

At that moment the door opened and her father, followed by her brother Lisha and her stepmother, stepped onto the porch smiling their welcome.

'We were waiting until you arrived to have dinner,' said her father, giving his daughter a hug and a kiss. And for the time being John was forgotten in the talk of home and the plans ahead.

Chapter 2

On Thursday morning when Maria went to the combination store and post office there was a letter from John, asking permission to call on her Friday afternoon. Indeed not, she said to herself, I shall write him that I shall be too busy. She tried to feel firm about it, but she was conscious of regret. Silly!

But that afternoon, as the clouds began drawing to themselves the sunset colors, he came in a smart buggy drawn by a black horse. Maria saw him from her windowseat where she sat putting the last stitches into her party dress. For a moment she couldn't move. He tied his horse with a flourish to the iron horsehead post and started for the house.

Indignantly she said aloud, 'I will refuse to see him. I will have Mother say I have a headache—anything.'

Then her heart began to hammer and, without so much as a glance at the mirror, she was running out of her room, across the living room, and down the front hall. She opened the door and John took her hands in his. His deep blue eyes claimed hers, held them, and the world around them for a moment ceased to exist.

'Maria, my darling!' he said, huskily. 'I couldn't wait—I had to come today.'

With an effort, Maria pulled her eyes and hands away from him. 'Come to the sitting room and meet Mother,' she said, trying not to appear flustered. 'She's probably in the kitchen.' Maria turned toward the sitting room and John followed.

'Please sit down,' Maria said, pointing to a comfortable upholstered chair, and quickly left the room before John could speak. She soon returned with her stepmother and David. When she had made the introductions, she said, 'Papa and Lisha, my other brother, haven't come home from work. Lisha works at the shipyards.' Maria's face was still flushed but she tried to speak in a matter-of-fact manner.

Mrs. Tobey sat down and conversed for a few minutes, then excused herself to go to the kitchen. 'We'd be happy to have you to stay for supper, Captain Hamblin. We're just having a boiled dinner—corned beef, cabbage, and taters.'

John, a pleased smile on his face, said, 'It sounds mighty tempting, Mrs. Tobey, and I accept with thanks.' He then turned to the bright-haired boy who had thrown himself on the floor at his feet. 'Well, young man, tell me about yourself. I hear you have a dory and are quite a seaman.'

'Aye, aye, Sir. I aim to be. But I want to hear about you. Sis told us you're getting ready to go whaling as Captain of The Roman. You must have whaled a lot and had lots of adventures. I'd like to hear some,' he finished hopefully. 'I want to be a whaling captain someday.'

'Yes, Captain Hamblin, tell what whaling is like—the cruel hard life part as well as the funny or exciting stories,' said Maria, suddenly bitter. 'Then maybe David will stop wanting to go to sea. Meantime I'll help Mother with the dinner.'

John nodded and smiled, 'I promise to tell this skipper.' As Maria left she could hear him talk about the hardships of whaling; but she could see that David was half listening, as if he had other questions of his own to ask.

She shrugged her shoulders in resignation. But her mind turned to the captain himself and her own desire to linger near him. She hurried out of the room, her lips set. I am not going to let him hypnotize me, she resolved as she set the table with an extra place for John.

Presently her father and Lisha came in from the shipyards.

'Whose rig is out front?' demanded Maria's sixteen-year-old brother as he pumped up some water and washed his perspired face and grimy hands at the kitchen sink.

'Shh!' whispered Mrs. Tobey. 'He's the whaling captain Maria's told us about. She met him at Uncle Asa's.'

A few minutes later the other two male members of the Tobey family were gathered around John Hamblin in the living room and, from the kitchen, Maria heard them discussing ships and the seven seas as if they were old friends.

On a trip to the dining room with a dish of currant jelly, she peeped through the bead drapes separating the rooms. David listened, his hair like a golden brown curly cap on his head, his face tanned a golden brown, his chestnut eyes slightly tilted at the corners, giving them a smiling look. Like Mama's, Maria thought, recalling her gentle mother who had died when Maria was only six and David a toddler.

She watched her usually lively, slim twelve-year-old brother sitting back on his knees, close to John, his elbows propped on an arm of John's chair. His eyes were glued to the visitor's face, drinking in every word John was saying.

Maria looked then at her father's face, and at her brother Lisha's—so much alike—round, tanned. Lisha's was freckled, fresh, and young; her father's careworn, framed in light, thin hair, white about the temples. Lisha's hair was a darkening tow, cut short, like a brush on his head. They, too, listened with deep interest. Their gray-blue eyes held dreams, too, but Maria knew their dreams were landlubber dreams, less dangerous than David's. He looked so vulnerable at this moment, dreaming of adventure on the high seas. Oh, those terrible seas! How could anybody stand the thought of going to sea!

Maria, deep in thought, was startled by her stepmother's voice asking, 'What'll we have for dessert?' She noticed a touch of vivacity on her stepmother's pallid face under her neatly drawn up hair, formed into a knob on top of her head. 'The captain seems like a very nice person,' the older woman added.

Mother must like John, Maria thought as she answered, 'Nothing special. Cookies and tea are plenty good enough. After all, he came uninvited.'

Trying to harden her heart against their guest, she only succeeded in bringing a flush to her face. Her stepmother stared at her in surprise.

When the meal was over, Maria stayed in the kitchen helping with the dishes as long as possible before joining the group in the sitting room.

It was not long before John rose to leave. 'I have a

long drive to Sippewisset ahead of me. Our family home is there—my aunts are living there and keeping it the home I go to whenever I am not on a voyage.' He then shook hands with everyone except Maria, and waited expectantly for her to go to the door with him.

In the hall he caught her hands in his own. 'May I see you tomorrow?'

'Tomorrow? Oh, no. David and I are driving to Pocasset in the morning to see Aunt Abby—spend the day there.'

'Must you go?' John put as much feeling as possible into the question.

'Decidedly. She and the family are expecting us.' There was a silence.

'Aunt Abby's like a second mother to us. We lived with her for several years after our mother's death,' she explained.

John's hold on her hands tightened. 'Saturday, then?'

Maria shook her head. 'I've a garden party Saturday.'

'Very well, my darling. Sunday afternoon at two. And I refuse to take another no.'

Maria thought a moment. If she let him come on Sunday, she could tell him about Gordon—that they were engaged. She could show him the ring, and that would put an end to it.

'All right, Sunday.'

'Sunday at two.' He repeated happily. Then he bent and kissed her hands and went out quickly. She stood for a minute looking at the closed door and feeling the imprint of his kiss on her hands. 'I shouldn't have seen him again. He . . . oh, what does he do to me?' she said.

Her father was sitting alone when she returned to the living room. He looked up from his reading. Then Maria was on his knee, her head on his shoulder.

'What is the matter with me, Papa? I was so sure I

wanted to marry Gordon. I know he is going to ask me Saturday. His letter today even hinted he'd bought a ring. And now, I don't know. Papa, I'm in love with John! What shall I do?'

Elisha Tobey patted his daughter's shoulder. 'My dear, life's full of surprises. All I can say is to take a long look ahead. Let your mind guide your heart—if you can.'

Maria sat up. 'If you can,' she echoed. 'I must, Papa. I'll think hard. And pray hard.'

'And let me warn you, Daughter, that whaling men are known to do fast courting.' Then the father added with a troubled look, 'And Captain Hamblin tells me he now owns considerable stock in The Roman—and if a captain owns much stock in a whaleship, he has the right to take his wife on a voyage—'

'Well, Papa, that settles it. I go on no whaling ship even if I am crazily in love with the captain,' Maria declared as she kissed her father on the forehead and hurried off to bed.

Chapter 3

NEXT morning as young David was harnessing Selim to the buggy and Maria was in the sitting room wrapping her new party dress in protective brown paper to show to her Aunt Abby, there was a clatter of horse's hooves on the street and then a sudden silence.

'A buggy is stopping here! I wonder who—' Maria's stepmother put down the ball of string to be used in the wrapping and started toward the front hall door.

Maria breathed a deep sigh as she thought, 'It's John—I know it's John Hamblin. Oh, why did he have to come here again?' She tried to feel annoyed, but the blood sang in her veins.

Quietly she waited for his voice to answer her stepmother's cordial 'Oh, good morning, Captain Hamblin. What brings you so early?'

'Good morning, Ma'am. I remembered an errand I had to do in Pocasset this week so I decided to go today and save Miss Maria that long drive.'

'So? That was thoughtful of you.' Maria smiled at the irony in her stepmother's voice. 'But you'd better speak to Maria about it. She's in the sitting room.'

Maria's knees felt suddenly weak as she heard their approaching steps. She summoned all her strength to refuse him.

'Miss Maria,' John cried out gaily as he swung his hat, a bowler, in a wide bow, 'may I offer my services to Pocasset? I have a fine steed outside, prancing to go.'

'No. Well, yes...' Maria heard herself giving in. 'David must go along, though. Our cousin Amasah is expecting him.'

'And Mrs. Tobey, too, if she wishes,' John responded, undaunted. 'Plenty of room. I have a surrey.'

'Oh no, thank you. I didn't plan to go.' Mrs. Tobey turned away to hide a smile.

In a moment John was on his way to the barn to help return faithful brown Selim to his stall. Maria had on her bonnet when they came by the kitchen. David was hanging on John's arm, his eyes full of anticipation.

Out in the street, John handed Maria up into the front seat of the smart-looking surrey. She slipped to the end of the seat and motioned David to sit beside her, thus putting him between her and the captain. John said nothing, but started the spirited roan with a touch of the whip and a click of the tongue. Before Monument Beach had been left behind, he was deep in a whaling adventure for David's delight. Maria, too, listened, absorbed.

'Did you ever see a real sea serpent—like the Chinese serpent?' David asked when John paused.

'I have seen sea snakes in the Indian Ocean, but never a serpent. But that doesn't mean there aren't any. David, my lad, there must be many creatures in the great deeps that've never been seen by man, or so seldom no one knows if they're real or some sailor's imagination. Some day man will invent a contraption that will help us find out what is at the bottom of the ocean.'

John sighed as if wishing that contraption would come in his time, Maria thought as she noted that momentarily he had a far-away look. Oh dear, how could a person be interested in the horrible creatures in the ocean! She gave a little shiver just thinking about it.

David, too, had been thinking as John talked. He suddenly sat up and burst out, 'Golly, Captain Hamblin, I can't wait until I'm old enough to sign on a ship. Especially on a whaler with you.'

'Oh no, Davey mustn't!' Maria pulled her brother toward her as if to remove him from contagion.

'Could we hurry a little?' she asked. 'Aunt Abby will be wondering.'

'Of course.' John slapped the reins on the back of the horse and it broke into a trot. David pointed the way as they came into Pocasset and presently they drew up in front of a Cape Cod cottage of weather-beaten silver grey shingles, surrounded by late blooming annuals—asters, cosmos, petunias, and marigolds. It was on a slight knoll and the flower gardens sloped away on all sides, giving the cottage the appearance of a posy-bordered, floppy-brimmed hat. A boy of about sixteen was weeding among the flowers.

'Hi, Amasah!' called David, as soon as the horse stopped. 'Come see who we brought!'

'This is Amasah, our cousin,' Maria said to John as a gangly tall youth with a mop of sunbleached blond hair ran to meet them. 'Amasah, this is Captain Hamblin—'

'And he's a whaling ship captain,' interrupted David.

Maria spoke quickly to Amasah, 'Will you and David take care of the captain's horse?'

'I expect he's ready for his oats, boys,' John said as he helped Maria down and Amasah took his place.

As the boys drove around the rear of the cottage toward the barn, Maria and John walked slowly up the rose-bordered walk to the front door. Maria glanced at John, who looked so much younger in his straw hat rakishly tilted to one side. His well-cut alpaca gray suit and bow tie gave him a trim look. 'Aunt Abby will take it for granted I have brought Gordon,' Maria thought. 'What will she think when she finds out he is a whaling captain? How shall I explain?'

Just then Aunt Abby appeared at the door, smiling in welcome as she tied a freshly starched white apron over her neat black and white checked dress.

Abby Godfrey was small and spare, her skin tanned from many hours spent in her garden.

'My mother's sister,' Maria said as she started the introductions.

'No doubt of the kinship; there is a strong family resemblance. And both have a right pleasing look and manner, Mrs. Godfrey. Only your eyes are not green flecked with gold, hazel, like your niece's.'

And John's eyes, alight with warmth and admiration, rested on Maria's face. Maria blushed and her heart began beating with a strange exhilaration. She hoped Aunt Abby had not noticed. Oh, what a ninny she was—gone crazy in love with a man she scarcely knew— and a seaman, at that!

Would she come to her senses after he had gone to sea? These troubled thoughts raced through her mind as she was about to finish the introduction, presenting John. But before she could utter a word, her aunt spoke, her voice lilting with happiness.

'Well, now, it's right nice that you brought your

young man...' she began. But she was stopped by Maria's raised eyebrows and warning look.

'Aunt Abby, this is Captain Hamblin, a friend of Uncle Asa's I met when I was visiting in West Falmouth. The captain had an errand to do here in Pocasset and kindly brought David and me here. Saved me the long drive.'

Maria tried to speak with all the dignity she could muster. In her heart she knew she was not fooling her keen-sighted aunt, but she counted on Aunt Abby's quick mind to react wisely. And she was not disappointed.

'I am so glad to meet you, Captain Hamblin,' her aunt said cordially. 'Do sit down and rest a minute.' She led them to the parlor. 'I've apple dumplings baking in the oven and they'll be ready after a bit, and then we'll sit down to eat. I know you folks are hungry. Oh, don't worry, Captain; I have plenty. I always make a few extra. Amasah likes them even cold and I warm them over for my husband when he comes home.'

'How is Uncle Josiah?' Maria asked quickly.

'Fine. Too bad he's not here to meet you, Captain, but this week is his run with The Mary Jane.'

'The Mary Jane is the coastal ship between Boston and Newport. Uncle Josiah is her captain—has been for years,' Maria explained.

'Captain Josiah Godfrey—indeed I've heard of him and hope to meet him soon,' John said with a smile. He said 'soon' with some emphasis. 'I wonder what he is planning?' Maria thought. But her attention was brought back by her aunt's questions about the family.

'You know, Captain,' Aunt Abby turned to John, 'Maria and her brothers are like my own children; they lived with us after my dear sister, their mother, died.

We missed them so after their father married again and took the children away.'

Maria nodded. Fleeting, sweet memories came back to her in a powerful surge. The first sad days after Mama's death and the comfort of Aunt Abby's understanding love—the dozens of fat gingerbread raisin cookies she baked, her private cure-all for children's disappointments and hurts; the happy times when Uncle Josiah, shortish, stout, and jolly, had been with them, the snow fights with the three boys and some of the neighborhood children, the huckleberrying and picnics on Telegraph Hill in summer.

The back door slammed. 'That's David and Amasah coming in, hungry as bears. I'll get dinner on the table in a jiffy,' said Aunt Abby. And she whisked out of the room.

'And I'll go and help my aunt,' Maria said quickly. She picked up the stereoscope and a batch of its picture cards from the lamp table in the center of the room and handed them to John as she started to leave. 'These will keep you entertained for a bit.'

'Maria, darling...' John said quietly, his blue eyes warm and smiling. 'Thank you, but I don't need these; I have my own pictures to think about. About a girl I'm in love with. About you...'

Maria fled to the kitchen without waiting to hear more. The nerve of him, she said to herself, trying to feel anger. Instead, a happy feeling tingled in her chest, almost making her breath come short.

'Aunt Abby,' she whispered hurriedly when the boys were occupied washing their hands at the kitchen sink, 'I didn't ask Captain Hamblin to come with us. He just appeared this morning with the surrey and insisted. I only met him last Saturday at Uncle Asa's. Uncle had invited him for a baked bean supper. Next morning he came to church, and Aunt Eunice, of course, asked him to stay for dinner.'

Aunt Abby's dark brown eyes snapped with interest. 'Go on.'

'And yesterday he showed up at home just before suppertime.'

'Hm... Sounds like a hungry young man!'

Maria ignored this and hurried on, 'Oh Auntie, I know now that he is serious. And I seem to have taken a fancy to him. Oh, I'm so mixed up. Here I am practically engaged to Gordon. He is away in Boston with his father but he will be back tomorrow in time to take me to his mother's garden party. I know he is planning to propose to me there. He practically said so in his letter yesterday. But I still promised John—Captain Hamblin—to see him Sunday afternoon. I couldn't say no. Then he came today and I fully intended to say no to his invitation to drive us here but, as you see, I accepted. Why am I suddenly such a ninny?'

'There, there, now, Maria dear. Don't get worked up. Tomorrow you will see Gordon, and after that the captain and your plans to see him Sunday will be forgotten in your new happiness. We'll have lunch now and then I'll see your dress and we'll talk about Gordon.'

In a few minutes John and the family sat down to thickly sliced roast beef, freshly baked bread, and homemade relishes. By the time the baked apple dumplings were served, Amasah had become another admirer of the captain.

'Gee, I'd like to be sailing with you, Captain Hamblin,' he said. 'I've promised my father I'd finish school before I do anything about it, but I sure want to go to sea.' His young voice broke in its intensity.

The captain nodded. 'Your father's right.' He looked at David especially as he continued, 'Get lots of education. You'll be needing it. The whales are smartening up these days. It's getting harder to hunt them down.'

'When are you sailing, Cap'n?' asked Amasah, fork poised in mid-air.

'August twenty-third, barely four weeks away.' The captain looked pointedly at Maria. She dropped her eyes quickly.

'And when will you get back?' David asked, all eagerness.

'In about three years, God willing.' And Captain John Hamblin sighed as he spoke.

The spoonful of crusty dough and apple dropped from Maria's hand to her plate with a clatter. The color left her face. Her aunt looked at her sharply.

'Suppose you three gentlemen go out on the porch while Maria and I tidy up here,' she suggested, rising quickly.

'Good,' said David. 'Cap'n Hamblin, tell Amasah of the time you almost got left on a cannibal island...'

Now alone, Aunt Abby confronted her beloved niece with a serious, almost frightened face. 'Maria, you looked so stricken when the captain spoke of the long time he would be gone. I realized you are falling in love with him. Nip it in the bud, darling. Don't give up marriage with Gordon and the kind of life you should have for the life of a whaler's wife. You know what marriage to a whaler means. It is bad enough to marry a seaman on a clipper ship, but those ships at least go directly to big ports. A whaling ship just wanders in far-off seas, with maybe a stop now and then at some God-forsaken port or heathen island.

'The only mail a whaler gets is maybe at those places or what some other whaler brings, and likewise the only mail the family gets is what some whaler brings back from a chance meeting of whaleships somewhere on some ocean. And the wife waits aworrying for the loved one that never comes back, or comes back too late.'

Aunt Abby wiped her eyes with the edge of her white apron and continued without giving Maria a chance to speak.

'Cousin Melissa—the pretty black-haired cousin who used to come to your house when you were little—remember her, Maria?'

Maria nodded; she remembered the gay little person her mother called her twin cousin as they were just the same age.

'Well, Maria, she nigh wore out the widow's walk atop her house in the Vineyard waiting for her husband who was mate on a whaler. She got sick awaiting and aworrying, and when her husband finally got home after four years all that was left of her was under a tombstone. Sometimes the captains come back "princes of finance," as your uncle puts it, but most of them come back poor after a bad luck voyage, or come back broken, crippled, like your Uncle Asa. And if you ever go with him, Heaven forbid, it will be misery for you with your fear of the sea and smelly small quarters. Oh, Maria, let your head guide, not your heart.' And Aunt Abby, strongly moved, wiped her eyes again as she drew her niece to her bosom.

'Don't worry, Aunt Abby,' Maria said, her own eyes teary. 'I will do just that—let my head guide me and not my silly feelings.'

Later, when they were heading for home, David spoke up with concern, 'Captain, you forgot your errand in Pocasset.'

'Errand? Oh, that. It can wait for another day.' He

changed the subject quickly. 'I like your folks. A child couldn't help growing up to be a fine person in a home like the Pocasset one, and yours in Monument Beach. Many such kinfolk.'

John smiled down at David at his side and then at Maria. She had insisted on the same seating arrangement in the rig as they had had that morning on the way to Pocasset.

John said as he tipped the whip to speed up the horse, 'My own family is small now. There's Aunt Hannah and Aunt Sarah in Sippewisset. They're my father's sisters. And there's my sister Louise. She's married to Sam Holman, a successful whaling broker and insurance man in New Bedford. And, of course, Milly, their five-year-old daughter. That little niece of mine looks like a beautiful living doll and is as sweet as she looks.' John Hamblin's light tone became serious as he turned to Maria, his eyes ardent.

'The Holmans always see me off when I leave on my voyages. Perhaps this time...' he stopped, his thoughts unfinished, but Maria knew that he hoped she would be at the wharf to bid him goodbye. She wouldn't be, of course, but why did the thought of his sailing away forever from her life give her heart such a tug? Oh, her foolish heart again. 'Aunt Abby, I will have my mind guide me,' she said to herself with such determination that she almost whispered the words.

At home again, John handed the reins to David and, after bringing Maria down easily with his strong hands about her waist, led her to her door. He took both her hands in his as he said, 'Thank you for allowing me to be with you today.' His blue eyes burned into hers. 'You're sure you won't change your mind about tomorrow?'

'Quite sure,' said Maria. But her fingers trembled in his grasp. 'Mrs. Crothers would never forgive me if I didn't go, especially since it's her son I'm . . .'

'It's her son I heard you're going with,' finished John, unsmiling. 'I see.' He dropped her hands and turned to go, then faced her again. 'But you will see me Sunday, Maria! I'll be here at two.'

Maria nodded, unable to speak. She watched him get into the surrey, and after David had jumped off he started the horse off at a trot.

'Oh, dear. I should have told him I couldn't see him Sunday, since I am practically engaged.' But Maria knew in her heart it wouldn't have made any difference. He would have appeared at two just the same.

'But Sunday, when he sees the ring on my finger and I tell him I'm betrothed, it will make a difference. John is like that. I can see him leaving immediately, the courting over.' Maria gave a sigh of pride. She was letting her head guide her!

She went to her room, unwrapped the party dress from its brown paper, laid it on her bed and stood looking at it. Suddenly, for the first time since she had met John, she could recall exactly how Gordon looked— his dancing brown eyes, his thick hair with its slight wave, his tallish good figure, his carefree laugh. And young, just two years older than she. And, in a way, it was exciting that he should pick her out for his girl— she a village girl—when he must have met many attractive city girls. It was good his family liked her. Life took on the rosy hue it had had before her visit to Uncle Asa's!

Saturday afternoon, as Maria and Gordon walked slowly along the familiar streets to his home, her arm in his, he talked enthusiastically about his prospects. 'Father's about decided on having the store in Falmouth, a sort of subsidiary to his Boston store. And I am to run the Falmouth store after I graduate from Tufts in June.'

'Yes, this is what I want,' Maria thought. Aloud, she said, 'That's really wonderful news.' She tried to feel as enthusiastic as she had felt before when they had discussed this possibility. She had felt so excited then, but not now. What was the matter with her? She felt like dough with the yeast left out.

Gordon was in buoyant spirits and full of talk about his plans and she listened attentively until they came to his home. The garden was already alive with people. A long table was festive with flowers, pitchers of lemonade, plates of cakes, cookies, and bonbons. A silver service stood at the end of the table for those who preferred tea.

After exchanging gay greetings with the family and friends, Gordon led Maria to a bench under the sugar maple and said, 'I'll get some lemonade and cake for us. We can sit here and talk.'

And he hurried away.

Maria watched the familiar faces passing to and fro. Well-dressed young men and girls in pretty dresses passed with a gay 'Hi, Maria, where've you been keeping yourself lately?' or 'Oh, Maria, don't forget, you and Gordon are coming to our clambake next Saturday.'

Maria answered their greetings, saying the right things and trying to show the right feelings. She began to be uneasy and wished Gordon would hurry.

'But this is what I want,' she assured herself. 'Then why does everything, everybody seem so flat, so meaningless?' her heart questioned.

Thistle in Her Hand

'Did you miss me, Maria? There was such a line-up at the table I decided to load our plates with cakes, cookies, and candy. I'm starved and I hope you are, too.' Gordon put a glass of lemonade at either end of the bench and beside it a plate of cakes and other delicacies.

Maria studied the young man beside her as he ate hungrily, talking gaily between mouthfuls. Her own appetite had vanished. She nibbled and looked and listened.

'You're mighty quiet tonight, sweetheart. But I guess I'm not giving you a chance to say a word.'

Maria nodded. 'My mind's wandering.'

Sauntering about later with Maria, Gordon led her to the vine-covered summer house at the far corner of the garden.

'Good. It's empty. We have a chance to be alone,' he said as they entered and sat down on the willow settee.

Maria's heart was beating fast. 'Gordon is going to propose and everything is going to be right again,' she thought.

But instead of saying a word, Gordon impulsively put his arms around her and drew her close and their lips met. Maria's kiss was perfunctory but Gordon made up for it as, with extra warmth, he pulled her closer, kissing her brow, her cheeks, her thinly covered shoulders. Maria sat perfectly still, searching her heart. Why didn't she feel romantic?

'Whatever is the matter, Maria? Don't you love me? I thought—that is, I wanted to ask you—even brought the ring.' His finger slipped into his vest pocket and for a second she saw something glitter in the sunlight that streaked through an opening in the vines. 'I've never seen you like this before.'

'I don't know what's come over me, Gordon. I'm so mixed up. Please don't ask me—anything.' Her voice trembled and broke.

'Of course. I didn't mean to rush you,' he said. 'Only this afternoon seemed the perfect time and I thought you felt the same as I do.' His face was sober, a puzzled frown on his forehead.

'Gordon, please take me home now.'

'So early? But of course, if you wish.' Gordon sounded hurt.

'We could slip out this way, couldn't we, without disturbing the party?' Maria pointed to the gate that led to the side road. 'I'm feeling sort of sick. I don't know what ails me.'

She rose and hurried ahead of him, her thoughts in a tumult. 'Oh, why doesn't Gordon make me answer him? Why is everything so different from what it should be? Why? Why?' The questions jumbled through Maria's mind as they walked homeward in silence.

'Can it be because I'm thinking of the meeting with John tomorrow? Yes, that's it. Once I tell him—once and for all—that I am going to marry Gordon and cannot see him again, my mind will unjumble.'

The new resolution cleared her mind, so she smiled and acted more like her usual self as they came to the door of her home. Gordon was about to bid her goodnight.

He cautiously slipped an arm about her waist and gently pulled her to him. 'I'm sorry it didn't turn out as I hoped. But I'll see you tomorrow after church.' He reached for her lips, but she turned her face and the kiss fell on her cheek. He released her quickly and with a short 'Goodnight, Maria,' he left.

She closed the door softly and ran through the sitting

room to her own room. There she threw herself on the bed and sobbed.

Her father, in his big leather armchair in the sitting room, was startled by his daughter's actions and went to her room to investigate.

'Papa,' Maria told him between sobs, 'I know now I don't love Gordon. I love John. But I will not marry a seaman, a whaling man—not while he's a whaling man. I will not marry a whaling man. I will stop seeing him.'

And Maria sat up, wiping the tears from her eyes. 'Yes, Papa, and that is settled.'

Chapter 4

MARIA held to her resolution to stop seeing John until Sunday afternoon when, from her bedroom window, she saw a smart looking black horse and buggy draw up to the house and stop. It was John, coming at two o'clock as he had said.

A minute later she saw David run out to meet him and begin talking to him eagerly while the bronzed young sea captain secured his horse to the hitching post and started for the house. She heard her father's cordial welcome and their voices in a pleasant interchange in the parlor. It was hard to listen because her heart was beating so hard against her ribs and her blood was racing and singing through her veins.

Oh, dear! His deep modulated voice with its quiet assurance did that to her. She mustn't let it. She must be firm and dignified when she told John she could not see him anymore. She must let her head guide her and ignore her silly dancing heart. She must think of the future and act sensibly, not rashly. She looked at her mother's daguerreotype on the wall, her sweet gentle mother, and said aloud, 'It's what you would advise me to do. And I'll do it right now, Mama.'

But still she hesitated, smoothing the lavender-scented folds of her Sunday blue and white dimity. She opened her handkerchief box and selected a fresh handkerchief, lacy and fragrant. Then she tucked a soft curl into the well-netted roll at the back of her neck. Finding no other excuse for hesitating, she squared her slim young shoulders and drew a long breath as she went into the sitting room and on to the parlor.

With a firm step she crossed the room to where John was seated on the sofa. John rose and held out both his hands. She saw her father slip out of the room, taking David with him. Without meaning to, she extended her hand and it was caught in both of his strong hands and carried to his lips.

'Maria, my dearest,' he breathed, his eyes shining. 'Let's go for a ride out in the country. It is such a beautiful day.' She withdrew her hands.

'Captain Hamblin,' she began, but the words she had rehearsed would not come out. Maybe it would be a good idea to go for the ride; it would be easier to talk to him when he was busy with the horse, the thought flashed through her mind.

'All right. I'll get my bonnet,' she said, turning and hurrying out of the room.

'And your shawl,' he called after her. 'There's a touch of pre-autumn in the air.'

John chose a shady wooded road. He allowed the horse to set its own pace and they looked at the birchwood, sugar maples, and dogwood trees in their rich green foliage.

John pointed to a clump of sumac and said, with a sad note in his voice, 'In just a few weeks that will be flaming red and those trees beautiful yellows, golds, and browns—in just a few short weeks, when I am out at sea.' Then he remained quiet for a few minutes, his face serious. Maria, too, was silent as she reflected that in a few short weeks he would be gone for a long time—maybe gone out of her life. She felt strangely depressed, her heart heavy.

They came to a sunny clearing and John turned the horse toward it and halted. He faced Maria.

'Maria, look at me.' And he untied the blue ribbons of her bonnet and removed it. Then with one finger he gently lifted her chin and looked into her eyes. 'I love you. Will you marry me, Maria my darling?' His voice was husky with emotion.

Maria felt herself, her will to resist him, being drawn into the quicksand of love in his deep blue eyes. She tried to say no, but couldn't form the word while he held her gaze. Her bonnet dropped to the whip socket and hung there at a crazy angle until a sudden draft carried it to the moss below.

John continued to hold her eyes while his arms slipped around her. Slowly Maria felt herself yield to his arms. Her mind made one last effort to warn her. Beware! Take care!

But the voice grew fainter and her whole being responded to the strength of his arms, the tenderness of his kisses on her hair, her forehead, her cheeks. She had a warm feeling of belonging to him, of their belonging to each other. Just being close to John, the man she loved, was all that mattered now.

The thought that she had never experienced this feeling with Gordon flitted through her mind; she liked Gordon, but she did not love him. Gordon—he deserved being loved as she loved John.

'I'm waiting for your answer, Maria dear,' John said softly in her ear. He picked up her limp hand and held it to his lips.

'I don't know. Oh, I don't know! There is so much to

consider. But I do love you, John.' Her confession came out against her will.

With a low cry of triumph, John guided her trembling arms to his shoulders and his own hands went around her waist, pulling her close in an embrace that left her breathless. Then his lips were on hers and she was conscious of a current of deep love racing through her veins.

The misgivings about the future were forgotten. It was a moment of ecstasy, with John's face so close to hers, the tingling of the hairs of his moustache and beard on her skin, breathing the familiar scent of castile soap, Bay Rum, and the clean 'new' smell of his worsted jacket that was the masculine aura of the man she loved.

The world around them had taken on a strange and beautiful look. The canopy of green leaves above them showed a patch of brilliant blue sky—bluer than she remembered seeing it before. The sound of the breeze through the trees, the rapid chirping sound of the early cicadas, the twittering of birds in the trees. It was all part of a beautiful world. It was like a lovely dream, but it was real, real—a real world of love.

'My darling,' John said, still holding her tight in his arms, his cheek on her forehead now as he spoke, 'we must start back home because it will soon be dusk. And I have a duty to perform, to ask your father's permission to marry you, especially as you're not eighteen yet. Maria, if he consents, will you marry me and come with me on this voyage? There'd be rough times living on a whaleship, but there'd be pleasant times, too and I will look after my wife mighty well. What about it, dear?'

Maria turned a serious face to him and answered, 'It isn't the hard life I fear. Goodness knows I've been told enough about it, but it is my horror of the sea that would keep me from going on your voyage. John, it isn't a natural fear; it's a horror, a terror, a nightmare that I guess I've inherited from my mother. I could not stand it. I would sicken and die.'

Maria hesitated, and lowering her head said softly, 'If Papa consents, I will marry you soon—before you sail, and be waiting—'

And she looked at him with her mouth half open in a tender smile.

'My beloved,' John drew her close to him, pressing his lips hard on her soft parted lips. Then the lovers were lost in a long and passionate kiss, Maria bringing to it a fervor she did not know was in her. Their moment of ecstasy was broken when the horse, nibbling on grass, was startled by a rabbit jumping near his nose and suddenly reared. John had some busy moments calming the horse and retrieving Maria's bonnet which had narrowly escaped the wheels of the buggy. When he returned to his seat, he took the reins and started the horse trotting homeward.

Then he turned to Maria, who had been sitting quietly admiring the efficient way he had handled the emergency. Probably as a captain he had to handle many emergencies and she knew he dealt with them all efficiently, like this one. And the thought gave her a feeling of security about his coming home safely from his voyage.

But he would be gone so long! And suddenly she found herself on the verge of tears.

'My darling,' John said. Holding the reins in his right hand, he drew her to him with his left and kissed her quivering lips. 'Time is so short,' he went on, 'I want you with me every free moment, awake or asleep, before

I sail. If your father consents, will you marry me this week? And be with me in New Bedford these last weeks, when it is absolutely necessary I be there until sailing day? Until August twenty-third?'

'But there'll be no time for a wedding, even a tiny one.' And Maria disengaged herself from his embrace and looked at John with dismay. 'Reverend Jones, our pastor, is away in Ohio visiting his sick mother. Just students from the seminary in Boston are supplying the pulpit.'

'Maria, beloved, we would do what is customary among whaling folks—just drive to the nearest city, look up the minister we prefer, and get married in the parsonage. I kind of like the idea, keeping the marriage personal and private, don't you, sweetheart?' John said, looking tenderly down at Maria.

She was now smiling up at him as she cuddled close to him. 'It's a new idea, but we'll wait and talk to Papa about it.' She then changed the subject and asked, 'What is being done to The Roman?'

She tried to listen to what John was telling her but her thoughts wandered to what was ahead when they got home. Would Papa consent to her marriage before the voyage? She wasn't sure. Usually he allowed his children to make their own decisions, 'as long as it is honorable, not too dangerous or farfetched,' he would say.

Would he consider farfetched her decision to marry a man she had known less than two weeks? A whaling man at that? Oh, but John was not any man, and she felt she had known him a long time. And her heart sang with joy as she listened to his beloved voice talking about tackles and davits, whatever those things were.

Thistle in Her Hand

When Maria and John stepped into the house no one was about, but by the sounds the family was already at the supper table. 'I'll step into the parlor and wait. It's better, because the talk between your father and me will be personal.'

'Of course, John dear.'

Maria looked at John in amazement. For the first time he appeared nervous, and his hands as they clasped hers were perspiring. John, who could be cool and calm in great danger, was nervous about this meeting with her dear Papa. She understood why he felt this way but she was too happy now to be nervous about Papa's decision.

So Maria, face rosy and eyes sparkling, went into the dining room and breathlessly said to her father, 'Papa, John has something important to ask you. He is waiting in the parlor.'

Elisha Tobey jerked his head up and looked at his daughter in troubled surprise, then said slowly, 'Is it something agreeable to you, Maria?'

'Yes, Papa,' she replied, smiling.

'Very well, daughter,' he said wearily, slowly untucking the napkin at his collar as if trying to delay an unpleasant task. Placing it neatly on the table, he rose and walked out of the room with a heavy tread.

Her stepmother and two brothers, Lisha and Davey, were still staring at her in stunned surprise. All eating had stopped.

'Maria, is it what you really want, or have your senses gone giddy?' her stepmother asked in a sharp tone, her thin face and dark eyes, even the knot of black hair on top of her head, indicating disapproval.

Maria, her face still radiant, remained standing facing

the door, waiting for her father and John to appear. She turned her head as she answered, 'Yes, Mother. John is the man I love and want to marry.'

Davey broke the somber spell with a whooped 'Gollee! You mean Captain Hamblin, a real whaling captain, will be in our family? Can I call him John?' Lisha and Davey asked Maria other questions which she answered in monosyllables, as if only half hearing them.

As dusk set in, her stepmother brought in a lighted whaleoil lamp with a pink glass shade and set it in the center of the table, from where it cast a glowing circle of light on those in the room.

'Maria, sit down and have a bite to eat,' her stepmother said kindly. The woman's look of disapproval had given way to one of sadness.

'No, Mother, I'm not hungry,' was Maria's answer. She was not smiling now but looked worried, a troubled frown between her eyes. Why were they so long in coming back? The fingers of her dainty small hands twined and intertwined nervously, pressed against her chest.

After an interval her father and John appeared at the door. Whatever had passed between the two men, Mr. Tobey looked happier. He went to Maria, and lovingly putting his hands on her shoulders, said, 'Daughter, you and Captain Hamblin have my consent to your marriage, and my blessing, if your decision, Maria, is your true decision. Therefore, I ask you to delay your answer to John's proposal until Wednesday when he is to come for your answer. The captain—John—has promised not to write you or come until then. That will give you time to search your soul and pray for guidance in making the right choice, the most important decision in your life.'

Her father's voice became stern as he said, 'And I

insist that you, and you alone, Maria, decide without consulting anyone, family or friend.' Mr. Tobey turned and gave his wife and sons a meaningful look. They silently nodded assent. Then he faced his daughter again. 'Are you willing to comply with my wishes, Maria?'

'Yes, Papa, but I am sure now,' Maria answered, smiling through tears. She reached out her hand to John and he took it, pressing it to his lips as he looked at her, obviously trying to keep his own composure. Maria and John, for a fleeting moment, were gazing into each other's eyes, oblivious of those around them.

Mr. Tobey shook his head, then said in brisk, ordinary tones as he took his place at the head of the table, 'Now I know we are all hungry, so let's sit down and enjoy Mother's fine stew and hot biscuits. Maria, take your place and John, here is your chair.'

'Thank you, Sir, but I think I'd better go. I'll get a fresh horse at the Wareham Stables and head back to New Bedford tonight,' John answered.

With a slight bow to Mr. Tobey and the family at the table, he left the room. Maria, her hand still in his, accompanied him to the hall door. For a moment he held her close and sighed as he said, 'Until Wednesday, my darling.' Then he kissed her quickly and hurried out of the house.

Maria stood at the door until she could no longer see the buggy. Then she closed it softly, went to her room, threw herself on the bed and cried out of lonesomeness for John. Soon, emotionally exhausted, she fell asleep.

Her stepmother slipped in later with a tray of supper. Seeing Maria in a deep sleep, she quietly placed the tray on the night table and tiptoed out of the room. The tray remained untouched while Maria slept on through the night.

Margarita Thompson Diddel

Maria was surprised as she went about her work the next day that, with John away, her mind was freer to consider what was best for the years ahead. When she was with him her heart took over and her mind had no say.

Now Aunt Abby's words were coming back to her. 'If you marry Captain Hamblin, oh dear, he will be gone three years or more to the other side of the world, and you, not eighteen yet, will no longer be the belle of Monument Beach, enjoying a carefree girlhood. You will be a lonely woman pining for the husband that might never come back. Dear niece, knowing you, when there's a storm at night, you'll worry yourself sick thinking of him in such a storm. Don't marry a whaling man. Decide now before it is too late. I know these would be the words of your dear Mama.'

And Maria would stop whatever she was doing—dusting or ironing or some other chore—and moan softly, 'I love John, but I don't want to marry a whaling man. I must stop my marriage plans before it is too late.'

Then her thoughts would dwell on John and she would be submerged in melancholy. Many times during the next two days, Maria, pale and distraught, still unable to come to a decision which was hers to make and no one else's, would slip up to her room to pray for guidance, for some sign to guide her. But no sign came.

On Tuesday night, as she lay in bed tossing and turning in the throes of indecision, the windows of her bedroom rattled in a sudden gust of wind followed by a spatter of rain against the panes. The wind drew the soft curtains through the open window and stood them out like clothes on a clothesline. As Maria was closing the windows, a flash of lightning illuminated the front yard.

Thistle in Her Hand

She stared. The trunk of the big maple tree looked stark—like the mast of a ship. Then came a driving rain and the tree was blotted out. The hurricane winds, torrential rains, thunder and lightning of a sudden Nor'east squall engulfed the night.

Maria shivered. Soon John will be out at sea, at the mercy of a storm like this, the ship tossing on a wild sea, maybe sinking. A spasm went through her body as the picture passed before her eyes, terribly clear. She had to sit down, weak and sick, in her little rocker. Clutching her head in her hands, she tried to blot out the vision. 'I can't stand it! I can't stand it!' she cried in despair. The words came back to her, '...you'll worry yourself sick thinking of him in such a storm...'

Suddenly Maria stood up straight, eyes wide with wonder. The Lord had answered her prayer, had given her a sign to help her make the right decision, had shown her what would happen to her if she married John. She knew now what her decision must be.

Better for John, too, she thought, remembering the terrible nightmare of suffering she had just experienced. Many such worrisome nights and she would sicken and die. John would come home and find her under the tombstone as had the husband of Cousin Melissa on the Vineyard.

Maria clenched her hands together as she half-whispered in a determined voice, 'I will be strong and turn back before it is too late. Tomorrow I will tell John, and knowing John...' her lips closed almost on a sob as she thought, 'Yes, knowing John, he will leave, silent, grim-faced, but he will respect my decision and leave.'

The squall passed, leaving peace and serenity once more. Maria felt a peace of mind and serenity, too, after the agony of indecision of the last two days. She went back to bed and fell into a deep sleep and did not awaken until late next morning. When she came downstairs, dressed in a starched, high-necked, white-with-black-sprigs percale dress, her freshly combed hair in a black silk net, she found her father and brothers already gone, and her stepmother out in the vegetable patch gathering string beans. Maria briskly helped herself to a baking powder biscuit still warm in the oven, and poured a cup of tea from the brown teapot at the back of the stove. She was glad to be alone and not tempted to discuss her decision with anyone.

Suddenly she put down her cup, spilling some of the tea in her haste to set it in its saucer. The biscuit rolled off the saucer onto the floor, but Maria did not stop to pick it up in her hurry to go to the door. She had heard the sound of the double clip clop of horses' hoofs and buggy wheels stop in front of the house. She knew it was John. He must have come with a span. Stepmother said whaling captains liked to drive spans of horses, she thought incongruously as she opened the front door and saw John hitching two lathering black horses to the iron hitching post. He then bounded up the stone steps and into the house.

Without a word said she found herself in John's arms. He was holding her so close that she had trouble breathing, but she didn't mind because now her arms were around him tight, too. Then he was saying, so jerkily that it was hard for her to understand at first, that he would have come Monday, captain duties or not, but he had promised her father to wait until Wednesday—today.

'Oh, my darling, my darling, I've been nigh crazy these two days. I can't sail away and leave you. Maria, say that you will come with me. I will take good care of you and you will get over your fear of the sea. We will be together. Will you come with me?'

'Yes, John, I will go with you. I couldn't stand staying home without you,' she answered him, laughing and crying at the same time. She knew then it was her true decision at last. 'I didn't know it, but the Lord guided me last night with the storm.'

John had let her go as she talked, but now he caught her in his arms again and was kissing her lips, her face, her hair, punctuating the kisses by words such as 'happiest man alive,' and talking about their life together on the whaler.

'Darling,' and John became serious and practical as he took Maria by the hand and led her to the sitting room. He sat down in Mr. Tobey's big leather chair and pulled Maria onto his lap.

'Remember, my love, what I said about an early marriage—my having to be in New Bedford every day until we sail? Will you agree to our going to another town, say Bridgewater, and being married in the parsonage? We can have two days to ourselves at the Inn there and then go on to New Bedford.'

'Yes, John, if Papa agrees, I am willing. But what about my clothes for around the Horn?'

'You can get everything you need in New Bedford. The emporiums there have been fitting out whaling folks for years—I expect the whaling wives, too. Louise says she will help you shop. She has a friend who has been on whaling voyages, a Mrs. Snow—'round the Horn and all—and can advise you. And Louise says...'

John was interrupted by Mr. Tobey coming in. Embarrassed, the two young people jumped up and went to the sofa.

Mr. Tobey smiled wryly, 'I came home early to find out what your decision was, Daughter, but I know now.' And he walked over to his chair and sat down, a look in his pale blue eyes that was not so much sadness as patient resignation.

'But Papa...Papa,' Maria spoke up, breathless. 'Something more—with your permission, I am going with John. I love John and I know now I can stand the terror of the sea—even the storms—better than being separated from him.'

Maria's father rubbed his hand over his mouth as he always did when disturbed. Then he regained his self-control and said, quietly, 'Maria, to my thinking, you have made the right decision. A wife should go with her husband. And as for your terror of the sea, you are a grown woman and must confront that terror and trust in the Lord.'

'Sir, I shall take good care of Maria and see no harm comes to her. That terror, Sir...?'

'John, it started before Maria was born—four months before. On July Fourth. The Sunday School had a clambake on the beach. I wasn't there or this would not have happened. Some young people in a dory coaxed my wife—Maria's mother—into taking a sail around the cove. It was a clear day and the water was not rough. Suddenly a squall came and my wife nearly drowned. After that came nightmares, oh Heavenly Father, what nightmares! And Maria was born with that terror.'

'Thank you, Mr. Tobey,' John said, holding Maria close, protectively. 'Now, Sir, we want to speak about the marriage.' And John related the conversation he and Maria had just had.

Elisha Tobey repeated John's words, 'Go to Bridgewater Saturday and be married,' as if trying to adjust to the impact of the information. Then slowly, as if measuring each word, he answered, 'Well, Maria and John, in the circumstances it is about the only thing you can do.'

Maria's stepmother, who had come to the sitting room door in time to hear the conversation, spoke up. 'Oh, but we can't let Maria get married without some fuss. I couldn't bear the thought of it. At least we can invite some relatives and friends to come here and bid them Godspeed as they leave on their wedding journey. And I will do just that.'

Chapter 5

THE news of Maria's decision to marry a whaling captain and accompany him on his coming voyage to the South Pacific—Maria with her horror of the sea—caused much excitement among the young people of the community, and consternation and shaking of heads among the older members. Aunt Abby was stunned when she first heard the news from Elisha Tobey, who had driven to Pocasset to tell her personally. After shedding some tears, however, the spare little sun-browned woman rallied gallantly, as she had rallied to other crises in her life. She started laying out flannel on the dining table, 'to make nightgowns for Maria's nights 'round the Horn,' she told her brother-in-law, with determined gaiety in her voice and tears in her soft brown eyes.

Young Lisha, sent by his father to break the news to Aunt Eunice and Uncle Asa, brought back the report of their reaction. 'Aunt Eunice just sat, her face grayish and her lips set tight, never saying a word. Uncle Asa looked flabbergasted for a moment, then started beating his real leg with his two fists, the way he does when excited. Then he said, with a smile, "Waal, I'll be hornswoggled, spunky little Maria has steel in her backbone! She'll weather the storms! And she's marrying a mighty fine man."

'Then he got up and tapped his corn-cob pipe on the porch railing. Patting his wife on the shoulder he said, gentlelike, "Don't fret yourself, Eunie. Time flies and before we know we'll be seeing the Jones Co. and Roman flags on the staff on Telegraph Hill yonder, telling us the Woods Hole lookout has seen The Roman heading for New Bedford. And Lisha, you'll be seeing it on your Telegraph Hill. The news travels in minutes, I hear tell, along the Telegraph Hills on the King's Highway to Boston. It did that when my ship came in—when any whaler comes in. Remember, Eunie? I sailed away and before you knew it, the flags told you I was home."

'Aunt Eunice,' Lisha continued, 'just looked up at Uncle Asa with that sad look in her eyes she has sometimes and said, "Oh, Asa, to me it seemed you'd been gone a long time, a lifetime."'

And Lisha looked at Maria, a slight quiver in his own lips. But Maria was too busy packing her small leather hobnailed trunk to pay attention then to what Lisha had been reporting.

Friends and relatives flocked to the house with gifts, but only those gifts made of sturdy cotton and wool went into the little trunk. Those of delicate material or silk were fingered regretfully and laid aside. Everything had to stand the rigors of sea travel. Into the trunk went clothes for hot weather or for Antarctic cold when the Horn was rounded, clothes to last the many months the ship would be far from civilization; for its quarry, the mighty leviathan, rolled his island bulk in lonely seas remote from the haunts of men.

Thistle in Her Hand

Maria's personal medicine chest carried home remedies collected for many needs not cared for by the ship's chest. Into her chest went hamamelis, smelling salts, and Bay Rum. John's aunts brought packages of dried herbs good for ague and other possible ailments. Maria's father contributed several jars of Arabian Balsam.

'Here is your balsam, Daughter, reputed good externally, internally, and eternally,' he chuckled. 'Probably The Mayflower women had it on that good old ship.'

Uncle Asa brought Maria a sea chest of sturdy oak with many partitions and a drawer at the bottom. 'This is your work chest for all the sewing you will be doing, Maria,' and he was silent for a moment, as if pondering what was to be expected of his beloved niece. 'A lot of fancy work material, I reckon, will go into it, but prepare for a lot of darnin' and patchin'. Whaling life is hard on clothes.'

Aunt Eunice, her serenity restored, had gone to work making a heavy woolen robe, gray with pink piping around the ruffled cuffs and neck, 'for the days round Cape Horn,' she said with a smile as she handed Maria the garment. Maria flung her arms around her aunt and for a moment tears came to her eyes. But her aunt said jokingly as she patted Maria's shoulders, 'I had to use a red hot needle and burning thread to get this finished in time. And the love that has gone into it will help keep you warm.'

Blushing, and with dreamy eyes, Maria packed the portmanteau she was taking for their short honeymoon in Bridgewater. Into it went the exquisitely embroidered underwear and nightgowns she had made for the big hope chest of walnut, hand-carved by Uncle Asa years before. And the soft sky-blue satin robe and the matching half slippers with perky bows Aunt Eunice had given her the Christmas before that she, Maria, had put away in the chest for her dream trousseau. Maria sighed because most of these lovely things would have to come back home after her stay in New Bedford. Together with the rest of her best dresses and bonnets they would be packed away when she sailed. She would keep only two or three of these dresses for use on the occasional visit to a port.

Since there was no time to make a dress for her wedding, Maria and her stepmother decided on the golden brown taffeta with a plaid of thin stripes of lavender, black, and white, and a black silk fringe on the sash. Maria had made the dress in the early summer to be her fall Sunday dress. She sighed as she thought of the beautiful trousseau she had dreamed of through her girlhood years, and of the beautiful wedding that was not to be. But then, she was marrying John, her beloved.

When John was not with her and her spirits were low, the old terror of the sea would come back and with it the old throes of indecision. 'No, I can't marry John and go on that terrible ocean. I can't, oh, I can't. I will tell John so tomorrow,' she would murmur, wringing her hands, then add in misery, 'But I love him so.'

Even on her wedding day the terror came as she stood before the mirror in her bedroom while Aunt Abby arranged the folds of her wedding dress. On the colorful counterpane of her cherrywood spindle bed lay her black velvet cape lined with pink satin, and beside it her black velvet bonnet with delicate pink rose buds around the face. Suddenly Maria left the mirror and stood at the window, staring unhappily across the fields toward the brooding Buzzards Bay.

'I don't know! Oh, I don't know if I want to marry

John and go to sea,' she cried, but she obediently accepted the bonnet from Aunt Eunice and pulled it over her softly parted hair until it rested on the braids at the nape of her neck. Aunt Abby handed her the dainty black silk gloves and gently turned her toward the door.

In the parlor, the freshly laundered whiteness of the heavy lace curtains contrasted with the blue figured wallpaper, the polished dark furniture, and brightly shaded whale oil lamp. There were John and the small company of relatives and close friends who had been invited to bid the couple Godspeed in their life's journey together. John, tall and stiff in a black broadcloth suit and mulberry satin vest embroidered in white, stood by the unlighted fireplace, his back to the white marble mantle. His eyes, intensely blue today, were on the doorway where shortly Maria would appear. Across the bay, trim and freshly painted, The Roman, one of the finest vessels of the New Bedford sperm whaling fleet, was almost ready for sailing. But today John was not Captain John Coquin Hamblin, master of The Roman. He was only John Hamblin, a bridegroom waiting for his bride.

Maria walked slowly across the sitting room toward the parlor. Once more, frantic indecision gripped her heart. On the threshold of the parlor she stopped and murmured desperately to Aunt Eunice just behind her, 'Oh, I must turn back. I don't know if I want to marry John and...'

But just then John stepped forward, his eyes alight with love for his little bride. He crooked his arm gallantly toward Maria and, with a rustle of taffeta, she was by his side, her small gloved hand on his arm and her face turned up to him, smiling tenderly. Thus, oblivious to the rest of the world, they walked to the fanlighted front door and to their new life together.

Outside in the shade of the maple tree was a smart-looking buggy, shiny brown with yellow wheels. Sitting in the buggy, holding the reins of a roan restless to get going, was Lisha, his freckled face beaming. Next to him sat David, a happy smile on his golden tanned face and his brown eyes shining. He was wearing the captain's cap John had given him. It was slightly tilted as John often wore his cap.

David jumped down from the buggy and, turning to John, said respectfully, as a seaman speaking to his captain, 'Sir, I put Maria's portmanteau next to yours, back of the seat.'

'Thanks, little brother—Captain,' and John gave the young shoulder an affectionate tap. 'We'll be seeing you fellows in New Bedford before we sail?'

'Aye, aye, Sir,' David answered quickly.

'And me, too, Captain,' Amasah spoke up as he got up from sitting near the tree trunk, a broad grin on his freckled face.

Lisha got down on the other side of the buggy, still holding the reins of the prancing horse until John had lifted Maria into the seat and tucked in her skirts before springing into his place beside her and taking the reins.

'Could we go now?' John whispered in Maria's ear.

Maria's heart missed a beat. This was the moment she dreaded—the final cutting off from old ties. But she obediently began her goodbyes to the guests now gathered on the lawn shouting, 'Godspeed,' and 'We'll be waiting for you after a fine voyage.'

John and Maria, with upraised hands, saluted the company and tried to be gay as they drove away. Maria then waved, leaning over the side of the buggy, and continued waving until a bend of the road hid them from sight.

Thistle in Her Hand

Feeling childish but unable to stop herself, Maria began to chatter about the details of the morning, the guests, the preparation for her leaving. John listened quietly for a while, then shifted both reins to his left hand. With his free hand he put a finger on her lips.

'Maria, darling, let's talk about us.' His arm went around her and he pulled her close.

Maria felt her shyness evaporate in the warmth of his embrace. There was safety in John's arms. Here she could forget her fears of what lay ahead.

John outlined for her his plans for the remainder of their time ashore. 'We'll have all tomorrow to ourselves at the Inn,' he began, 'then Monday morning back to New Bedford to my captain duties. I'm glad that Louise and Sam invited us to stay with them, as I shall have to be gone from you much of the time and you might get lonely.'

'One of my duties is to make sure there will be plenty of citrus fruits, especially limes, on board.'

Maria sat up and looked at John in amazement. 'Limes!' And her laugh twinkled in amusement. 'Sour, puckering limes.'

John's face showed delight that Maria had lost that somber look. 'Yes, my darling, it's important to keep the crew from having scurvy. I learned that from the maritime news. The British vessels keep plenty of limes aboard. I reckon that's why the English sailor is called "limey,"' John laughed.

Then, drawing Maria back into a tighter embrace, he said tenderly, 'And I want to look for delicacies for you, my love. You will miss many foods you are used to.'

'I won't mind, John. I can eat anything.' Maria felt that she spoke the truth.

'Even whale blubber and hardtack?' John teased.

'If there's plenty of strong tea,' she giggled.

Thus they chatted until they entered the busy city of Bridgewater with its tree-lined streets, comfortable homes, and its teachers' college campus. John drew up before a neat gray-shingled house next to the Methodist church and shortly they entered the parsonage. There they were married in a simple ceremony with only the minister and his wife for witnesses.

'John and Maria,' the white-haired, tall, thin Reverend Brown said, holding their hands in his after the ceremony, 'now Mr. and Mrs. John Coquin Hamblin, you are embarking on the sea of matrimony, an uncharted sea for both of you. Let me give one piece of advice from what I have learned as a pastor over the years. You will weather the storms on it, this sea, the trials and tribulations, sorrows and tragedies that may come, if you always hold each other dearer than any other, dearer than self, until death do you part.'

'And even after that, Pastor, for if I die before Maria, I shall be waiting for her on the Other Side,' John declared, smiling down tenderly at his wife.

'And I will be waiting for you, John. Death will not part us,' Maria said, tearfully, as she smiled into his eyes.

And thus absorbed with each other they left the parsonage to go to the Inn and their honeymoon tryst.

Maria had visited Bridgewater in the past, but today as she sat close to John in the buggy on the way to the Inn, she looked as in a dream at the houses and shops, the trees and flowers along the way. Even the people looked like figures in a dream. There was a soft glow of unreality about everything. She could not talk but sat hugging John's arm to her. He, too, was not talking,

Thistle in Her Hand

just glancing down at her from time to time, smiling happily, his eyes shining bluer than she had ever seen them.

Still he kept an eye on his driving, down the busy street with its many horsedrawn vehicles. It was Saturday afternoon when farmers from all around came to the city with their families for shopping and diversion. Many tourists were here also for a weekend vacation.

As the rig pulled into the yard of the Inn, Maria straightened her bonnet and smoothed her dress. The setting sun bathed the familiar lines of the hostelry with a rosy hue. John spoke to the liveried man for a moment; then he jumped down and lifted Maria to the ground. Her hand on his arm, they went up the steps into the Inn's reception room and lobby. He led her to a red plush armchair, saying in a low tone as he gave her shoulder a loving tap, 'Sit down here, dear, while I register at the desk. I have made reservations. The liveried man will bring the luggage to you.'

Maria, still floating in a dream cloud, was looking around the room. It featured red plush upholstered furniture, heavy cream lace curtains and red velvet drapes contrasting with the soft gray wallpaper. People came and went, some into a dining room off the reception room. Suddenly she was brought back to reality by the nasal voice of the man with the luggage.

'Ma'am, are you Mrs. Hamblin?' He was trying to hide a grin as he set down the brand new luggage, obviously belonging to honeymooners. And the wide gold wedding band on Maria's left hand shone bright.

Maria, who had been Maria Tobey only two hours ago, felt her cheeks grow pink. She tried to look at the man coolly and to make her voice sound matter-of-fact, but when the words came out they sounded hurried, above a whisper.

'Yes, I'm Mrs. Hamblin.' There it was, a reality. Since Wednesday she had often said to herself, 'Mrs. Hamblin, Mrs. John C. Hamblin.' But it was all part of the dream world she had floated in—the hurried preparation for the marriage, leaving home and loving people, the marriage ceremony in the cheery parsonage parlor with the vases of garden flowers put there by the pastor's sweet, silver-haired wife who had been advised by John of their coming. 'We wanted to make the parlor as homey as possible for the ceremony,' she had whispered softly.

Then the marriage ceremony, John putting the ring on her finger, and signing the marriage certificate. All those things seemed part of the climax of being Maria Tobey. But now that she had said, 'Yes, I am Mrs. Hamblin,' it was a fact before the world. She knew now that she was married.

She looked at John, his back to her, writing in the Inn's register. There were other men at the desk, too, but she did not look at them, only at John's tall figure and good shoulders in his well-cut, black broadcloth suit, his hair shining red gold under the brim of his black bowler. Her heart gave a little jump, and she felt suddenly shy. And when she saw him talking, smiling politely, to the clerk, an utter stranger, it came over her that she did not know John at all. He, too, was a stranger.

And here she was in a public place, at an inn. There was no familiar atmosphere of family life for her to retreat into now. Suddenly her heart began to palpitate and her hands grew wet with perspiration. She felt her family had abandoned her, letting her go out alone into life with a stranger.

Just then John turned, caught her eye, and smiled. Suddenly all her panic left her and she hurried to him, putting her hand on his arm. She allowed her fingers to press his forearm and felt them hugged tight against his ribs and she thought she could feel his heart thumping inside.

The respectful clerk nodded to a sleepy-looking porter who picked up their luggage and led them upstairs to a pleasant corner suite facing the water.

'The W. C. is at the end of the hall,' he said and added proudly, 'Just installed last month. This place is real modern.' He put their bags inside and turned, 'If yeh want hot water or anythin', pull the bell rope.' He waved a hand toward the red satin tassled cord.

When they were alone, Maria removed her bonnet and placed it next to John's hat on the closet shelf. As she turned to fluff her hair in the mirror, John caught her in his arms. Watching him in the mirror, she saw the look of ardent love in his eyes.

'My dearest love. My own dear wife,' he spoke softly in her ear.

Silently Maria turned and nestled against his breast.

'Speak to me, my dearest; tell me what you are thinking.'

Maria wished she could express the jumble of thoughts running through her mind, but she could only manage, 'I do love you, John dear, and I am proud to be your wife. I only hope I won't disappoint you at sea.'

'You won't. Not at sea or ever. Down under that softness there's a woman with grit. The sea brings out the best and the worst in us. Believe me, I've seen it both ways.' He held her close, then changed the subject abruptly. 'Are you hungry, dear?'

Maria admitted that she was. 'I was too excited to eat at the house.'

'Then we'll freshen up a bit and go down to the dining room and see what they have to offer before...'

Maria's heart missed a beat. Tonight was the dreaded first night. A strange feeling of fear, panic, began creeping over her, but she forced herself to be calm.

The dining room was partly filled with vacationing guests and overnight travellers. The waiter led them to a secluded table and discussed the menu with John.

'No seafood,' John said firmly. 'We'll have plenty of that later.' They settled on roast lamb with parsleyed potatoes and green peas.

John ate leisurely and talked of the strange and exotic places he meant for Maria to see. She listened and watched his face, discovering that a well-worded question would send him off on another tale, and delay going up that stairway. A couple of hours passed and the dining room emptied.

Suddenly John said, 'Enough of story-telling for now. It's getting late.'

When they were in their rooms again, they found them aglow with the lighted whale oil lamps, the big one with the ornate red shade in the living room and the small one with a delicate pink shade in the bedroom on the night table next to the bed. And the bed had been neatly turned back, with the pillows fluffed invitingly. The commode had fresh towels and face cloths on the rack and the porcelain bowl and pitcher and the chamber below were shiny and colorful with painted wild roses. John had made reservations for this, the bridal suite.

Thistle in Her Hand

John and Maria opened their luggage, her portmanteau and his valise, and Maria arranged her few articles on the dresser while John put his on a small table. He kept up a pleasant conversation about the good service they were receiving, so different from what he had found in some other hotels, but Maria was silent; the words would not come out of her throat. After she finished arranging her things she just stood still, unable to move.

In the mirror she watched John take off his coat and vest and hang them in the closet. She saw him glance at her, then hesitate before removing his boots. Still she could not move.

Then he was beside her and his loving arms held her. 'May I help with those buttons, hooks, or whatever you call 'em?' He gently unfastened each one, then kissed each soft shoulder. 'Now I'll leave while you get into your nightgown. I'll finish undressing in the other room.' Then, taking out his nightshirt and other items from his valise, he went into the sitting room and she heard him whistling to himself.

Suddenly Maria came alive. She hurriedly took off her dress and hung it up in the closet. Then she hurried out of her two petticoats, corset cover, pantalets, and whalebone corset and put them neatly on the chair. Next came off her bow-tied black slippers and black lisle stockings. She reached for the daintily embroidered nightdress, the loveliest one in her portmanteau, and for her blue satin slippers and robe. She put on her slippers and stood up to put on her nightdress. Then she glanced at the bed with its turned-down covers and remained standing, trembling with sudden panic.

Just then John knocked gently. 'May I come in?'

At her faint 'Yes,' he entered, eyes full of love. He stretched out his arms and Maria, her panic gone, ran to him like a child going home. John picked her up in his arms and her own arms went around his neck, and her face against his chest. She murmured, 'Oh, John, I am glad we are together. I am not afraid of anything with you.'

'My darling,' he whispered huskily and their lips met in a kiss full of love and passionate yearning. Then, with Maria still in his arms, her slippers still on her feet, their bows standing out like blue angels, John strode to the lamp on the little bedside table and put out the light. Enveloped in the soft velvety darkness of night, John and Maria, still embracing, turned toward the bed, and the slippers fell with a gentle thud on the carpet. Tonight was to be their very personal and private part of the marriage rites, the physical consummation of their marriage. And tonight was to be their first night together, first of many nights in the years to come.

Chapter 6

It was Monday noon, and Maria looked around as they drove into New Bedford. New Bedford! Even the name had a new and frightening connotation to Maria. This was not the New Bedford she had known on the rare visits the family had made to this city, shopping trips mostly. The hotel where they had lunch, the cozy little shops; the bookstalls where her father browsed while she and her stepmother went shopping. This New Bedford of the sea and the wharves was so...so male. The maleness was the feeling that had both attracted and repelled Maria when she had first met John. Even the sea here had a different odor than it had on her own Cape Cod. Maria tried to analyze the smell as the horse clip-clopped along the cobblestone roadway. There was the permeating odor of hot tar and creosote, the slightly sweet odor of whale oil freshly spilled from a damaged cask, and even the tangy smell of old rum casks. And strange, heavy sounds assailed her ears, such as when a drayload of empty oil casks came rumbling noisily down the street.

She snuggled closer to John, nuzzling her face into

the heavy broadcloth coat that he wore. She trembled involuntarily. So much had happened in just a little over two weeks. She, Maria, had met John, had fallen in love against her better judgment, and finally had married him. Married! The word was so new and yet so final. She, who had spent so much of her life in a woman's world, in innocent, almost childlike parties and flirtations, was now a married woman. It was a feeling not a few days away from innocence, but a lifetime. She closed her eyes to hold back the tears.

She felt John's arm draw her to him as he reined the horse to the side of the road. 'Maria, darling,' he murmured in a troubled voice, 'you're trembling.' He gently lifted her face with his forefinger and kissed her tenderly on both her closed eyelids. 'Don't be frightened. Nothing is going to hurt you. Nothing.'

Maria opened her eyes, now bright with tears. 'I know, John dearest. When I'm with you I'm not really afraid. I'm terrified of the sea, and here I am married to a sea captain and going to live on the sea. But with your love,' and she smiled up at him, her hazel eyes warm with love, 'I know I won't have the same fear. Maybe I'll even get to like the sea—when it's calm, anyway.'

John smiled back at her as he said, slowly, 'That's my reckoning, too, Sweetheart—Wife.'

Evidently her last remark surprised and delighted him, as she could tell by his eyes. They always lighted with a fascinating little twinkle when he was pleasantly surprised. 'What a deep blue they were! Almost violet,' Maria thought. 'That's because he is happy, very happy. He is back in his own world, going back to the sea. Papa would say that's the Viking in him.' Maria sighed as she looked at him, her heart almost bursting with love for her husband.

Thistle in Her Hand

John took up the reins again and flipped them to get the horse going. 'Dearest, I brought you this way along the wharves that line the Acushnet River so you could get used to the huge size of the whaling business,' he said, proudly.

'That's Long Wharf over there. The Roman is moored at the far end; you can't see her from here. A lot of wharves, eh, Dear? And all with ships coming or going.'

Maria looked, more in confusion than astonishment. There was a veritable forest of masts jutting into the bright mid-morning sky. And sails of different sizes! And the colorful figureheads of some of the ships!

'There are more whalers with the stern showing the port of New Bedford under the American Eagle,' John continued, 'than any other port in the world. There must be three to four hundred ships and over ten thousand seamen who go out from here.'

There was no mistaking the pride in John's voice, and Maria smiled, not wanting to cast any reflection on John's other love.

They were heading now toward the residential area, toward the Holman home, and Maria felt another little twinge of shyness or timidity about meeting John's relatives. She felt she already knew John's sister Louise, her husband Sam, and their five-year-old daughter Milly. But knowing them through John's eyes and meeting them in person were different things. Maria busied herself arranging her bonnet and tucking in her hair that was now falling down around her shoulders.

It was a warm day and Maria was wearing the same straw hat with the apple-green lining and the same dress with spriggy, tiny pink flowers with green leaves on a white background, that she had worn on her trip to

Margarita Thompson Diddel

West Falmouth the day she met John. She hoped the family would like her outfit as much as John had.

'You look fresh as a daisy and more beautiful,' he had said that morning as they started out from the Inn at Bridgewater.

Supposing they don't like me, Maria thought uneasily. Louise probably had had someone else in mind for her handsome brother. Some society girl from Boston or New Bedford. Not just a Cape Cod village girl. And the marriage had been so sudden. Would Louise think...?

Just then the buggy drew up under the big shady elms of a stately colonial home. It was painted soft yellow, with long white shutters matching the white columns at the entrance.

'Oh, how beautiful!' Maria exclaimed, forgetting her thoughts of the moment before. 'How beautiful everything is. The lawn like velvet...the lovely big garden...and that darling arbor with the red rambler roses...'

Then the door flew open and a pretty, blond woman rushed down the steps, followed by a shorter, portly, dark-mustached man.

'Louise and Sam, here we are!' John called out as he reined the horses to a stop.

'Oh, John,' Louise exclaimed, kissing her brother.

Then, turning to Maria, she held out her arms. 'You must be Maria,' she continued warmly, kissing her, too. 'I'm so glad you came to us, we've loads of room. I can't stand hotels myself.'

Then Sam puffed up beside his tall, slim wife, and gave John's hand a hearty handshake. 'John,' he boomed jovially, 'you're always surprising us, but this is the nicest surprise of all. Welcome to the family, Maria.' And he gave Maria a bear hug and a smack on her cheek.

There was no mistaking the welcome and real friendliness in both Louise and Sam, and Maria's shyness melted away.

'Where's Milly?' John asked, looking around.

'Here I am, Uncle John!' shouted a shrill, excited young voice. And a small duplicate of Louise came bounding around the corner with flying pigtails and flung herself into her uncle's arms, burying her face in his shoulder.

John carried her to Maria. 'Milly, here's young Aunt Maria.'

Milly peeked out from John's shoulder and gave Maria a broad grin, showing none of the shyness small children usually have. Then she held out her hands to the newcomer. With a thumping heart Maria gathered the little girl into her arms and held her tight. For a moment all she could think about was this darling little girl, maybe like the one John and she might have. The little arms went tight about her neck, and Maria could smell the fragrance of Milly's hair, the freshly laundered aroma of her dress, and even the slightly sweet odor of perspiration from her flushed face.

Then Milly was out of Maria's arms and bounding up and down around the four older people, who now moved toward the house.

Maria drew a breath of delight when they entered the hallway with its tall mahogany hatrack and settee polished like satin, and the green-carpeted winding staircase. An elaborately carved grandfather clock stood at the first landing of the stairway. The ornate candle chandelier on the hallway ceiling shone with prismatic jewel droplets. These reflected the colored etched panes of glass on each side of the doorway.

Sam led the group into the parlor—drawing room, he called it. Maria looked around with admiration. A luxurious room indeed, with satin-striped light gray wallpaper and mahogany Chippendale furniture upholstered in blue damask, the dainty white net curtains and satin drapes of the same powder blue color. Her eyes feasted on the elegance and beauty, the square piano in the corner, the portraits in their gold frames. The large mirror on one wall reflected the rich beauty of it all. Maria turned and smiled toward Louise and Sam. 'I am storing all this in my mind to think about—sort of mental pictures—later.'

'And when you come back I'll s'prise you when you hear me play real pieces on the piano. I am going to take lessons in September,' Milly said as she shyly took Maria's hand.

Maria bent down and gave Milly a hug and a kiss. 'And I'll be waiting for the s'prise.'

'And so will I,' John said as he, too, bent down and kissed the top of the little girl's head.

'And don't be surprised if the piano is in a new room off this room—a music room we're planning to build,' Sam said as he affectionately tousled his little daughter's hair.

'What say we go upstairs to your quarters,' Louise suggested with a smile, 'so you folks can get settled before dinner.'

'Fine,' John agreed. 'I'll get our luggage from the buggy and bring it up.'

'I'll go with you, and get Manolo—that's our stable-boy, Maria—to take your rig back to the stable,' Sam said as he followed John out of the room.

Thistle in Her Hand

Maria felt a sense of contentment as she and Louise went up the broad stairway. Milly had darted ahead and was calling them from the balustrade of the hallway upstairs, 'Aunt Maria, just wait and see your bathtub. It's be-ooutiful.'

'Yes, the new wing that will be your private domain, yours and John's, has a bathroom with running water. We have a special tank up near the roof and water pipes down from there and pipes out to a sewer. Milly is excited about the bathtub. It's enameled tin with roses painted on the outside. But Sam will not be satisfied until he can get a porcelain tub,' Louise laughed, amused. 'Sam would like to make this place as beautiful as Versailles in France. He went there once on a clipper ship and has talked about that place ever since.'

She led Maria into a light and airy room with blond wood furnishings, a sitting room with daffodil yellow curtains and a bowl of yellow and white flowers on the small table.

'Oh, it's so lovely,' was all Maria could say as she looked around at the desk and other furnishings.

'Amanda, she's the chambermaid, you'll like her, will bring you breakfast here. You'll have all the privacy you folks want, but we'd like you to eat dinner and supper with us. We can visit before you go,' and Louise looked away toward the window facing the ocean in the distance. The smile left her face and her eyes had a sad look.

'Time goes so fast we'll be back before you know it,' Maria found herself quoting Uncle Asa. Somehow Maria was in a dream world and her feelings were no deeper than what she was seeing and hearing.

'You're right, Maria dear,' said Louise, back to her cheerful self as she led Maria and John, who had just appeared, luggage in hand, to the bedroom.

Margarita Thompson Diddel

'This is the cheeriest bedroom I've ever seen,' Maria declared ecstatically as she looked around the big room. A large dormer window had dainty white lawn curtains and a pink and white chintz valance, and the same gay chintz was on the bed canopy, chaise longue, and upholstery of the little rocker and armchair. The bed had a dainty pink and white spread and pillow covers. There was a delightful fragrance of roses coming from the large cut glass bowl on the table at the window, and Maria ran and buried her face among the pink blossoms.

'Oh, so lovely!'

'Yes,' John answered, looking at her with adoring eyes, 'Like my wife, for instance.' He dropped the luggage on the chaise longue and took Maria into his arms in a passionate embrace and kiss. Louise, a bit embarrassed, made a hasty exit, taking with her Milly, who had been flitting around the room like a yellow hummingbird.

'Remember, dear lovebirds, the dinner bell will ring in half an hour,' Louise called back merrily as she and Milly started down the staircase. 'And, John dear, remember Lizzie is a wonderful cook, but with a temper like her carroty hair if we are late.'

John laughed as he let Maria go and they got busy transferring their clothes to the closet, the new French chiffonier, and the bureau. As they worked John told Maria about Lizzie, the cook, and her husband, Patrick, who had charge of the stable and garden. 'They're from Dublin. Irish as the shamrock and both with hearts of gold. They've been with the Holmans since long before Milly was born. They have a cottage near the stable and it's surrounded with flowers like your Aunt Abby's place.'

For a moment a stab of nostalgia went through

Thistle in Her Hand

Maria's heart at the mention of her aunt, but her thoughts were diverted by the tinkling of the bell downstairs. She hurriedly put the last items left in her portmanteau into the bureau drawer, and snapped the portmanteau shut.

'Oh, that's the first bell, the "get ready bell," ten minutes before the dinner bell,' John smiled as he took Maria's hand. 'But I think it will be a good idea if we go down ahead of the others and I'll introduce you to Lizzie and Amanda, who will wait on the table. Amanda and Manolo, who helps Patrick in the stable, are Portuguese. They're brother and sister and their family lives here in New Bedford. So after a quick washup, let's start down.'

No one was in the dining room when they arrived and Maria looked around with delight at the beautiful room with soft red wallpaper with silver scrolls in panels, and on one wall a painting, a Delft blue bowl overflowing with colorful fruit. The sideboard, the leather-covered chairs, and all the furniture were beautifully carved dark walnut. The dining room table was set with gleaming silver and crystal on the immaculate damask tablecloth. Beauty-loving Maria sighed a sigh of contentment, as would a master artist sigh when viewing a picture that filled his soul with joy.

Just then a trim, swarthy young woman dressed in a maid's black uniform and immaculate starched apron entered with a tray of condiments. And Maria met Amanda who waited on the table and was also chambermaid. John's deep voice reached Lizzie's ears in the kitchen and she came out all beaming and wiping her floury hands on her apron to greet John's bride. To her he was not captain, but a beloved member of 'her folks' family,' as she explained to Maria.

'And now you are, too,' she added.

Lizzie had prepared a regular feast, with a fancy wedding cake at the end.

'We're having the wedding feast we missed, John,' Maria said, wiping her eyes. John nodded and kissed Maria.

'And this calls for a toast,' Sam said, motioning Amanda to bring in the bottle of sherry and pour it into the small wineglasses.

Sam stood up, wineglass in hand, and smiling toward John and Maria said, 'John and Maria, you are facing life together bound not only by the bonds of matrimony, but by the even more important bonds of love. May you always face life, its troubles as well as its joys, together. God knows it helps, as well I know, as Louise and I have done. God bless you, Louise.'

And Sam, carried away by his emotions, could say no more, but sat down, wineglass filled with wine still in hand.

John, noticing the solemn faces around the table, and especially Milly, who sat very silent and wide-eyed, arose, and in a pleasant, semi-jovial voice that Maria now recognized as one he used when a situation was getting tense, answered the toast by thanking Sam for his wise advice. He assured his brother-in-law they would keep it in mind, and smiling down at Maria said, 'Not so, my beloved wife?'

Maria smiled back, holding her own emotions in control, 'Yes, John. Yes, Sam. Yes, oh yes.'

Then, raising his wineglass, John said, 'Now let's drink to Sam, Louise, Milly, and to Lizzie and Amanda and to Patrick and Manolo, who are making our stay here so happy. Maria and I are sorry we have to leave so soon—in a few days—but the sooner we go, the sooner we'll get back. And if we are to get back sooner, I'd better hustle back to the wharf and to my job.'

'Goody, goody!' Milly clapped her hands in obvious delight. 'And I have to go to tell Patrick that you are coming back sooner. He's in the garden!'

She dashed out of the room.

Louise laughed as she explained to Maria that ever since Milly could toddle she had joined Patrick in the garden. 'Those two have a running conversation. They talk to each other and to the plants.'

After John had left to resume his duties as captain, Maria went up to their bedroom to rest and to unpack the valise that had been delivered earlier along with the other luggage for the voyage. This valise held the clothes that she would use during her stay in New Bedford but would return home along with anything else that would not do on the voyage. As she handled these dainty clothes, reality came back to her. She became pensive, aware of what lay ahead when she was far from shore, from home and loved ones. For some reason, when she thought of loved ones she thought of Milly.

'I wonder if she is still there with Patrick in the garden,' Maria said aloud, going to the window and looking down. 'There she is, the darling,' she whispered as she spied the little figure crouched next to the stoutish old man in work clothes.

'I'll remember this when I'm out at sea. I'll remember this day. A lot of beautiful pictures will come to mind,' she thought aloud as she continued to gaze down.

'Yes,' she mused to herself, 'I'll never forget the first sight of this beautiful, elegant home and the grounds around it, the lawns like velvet carpeting. And Louise and Sam coming down the steps with such welcoming arms. And Milly.' Maria looked down at the little girl now playing hide and seek among the rose bushes with a gray cat, and she smiled tenderly as she turned back to her chore of getting settled.

'Yes, I'll recall all this to cheer me up when I get into the dumps,' she murmured.

Chapter 7

NEXT morning John was already dressed to go to the wharf and his captain duties when there was a gentle knock on the bedroom door and Amanda's sweet voice announced breakfast was on their sitting room table. Maria quickly got out of bed and after a quick washup at the bathroom basin put on her white lace morning cap and blue satin robe and slippers and joined John at the daintily set table with white linen, shiny silver, and delicate flowery chinaware. A platter held a golden brown omelet circled with small sausage links. Amanda had slipped away and they were alone.

'Oh John,' Maria exclaimed softly with sheer delight as she sat down, 'this is a feast for the eyes. And what a breakfast! Those hot biscuits hidden in that napkin, strawberry jam in that lovely crystal jam dish.'

'Lizzie has gone all out for us. Probably churned the butter for us this very morning,' John said with a grin as he poured Maria a cup of tea from the colorful teapot.

Then he added with a sigh, 'We'd better enjoy her fine cooking while we can. Doc, the cook aboard ship, and Henry, the steward, will do their best, but nothing like this.' He served Maria and started his own breakfast.

Maria bowed her head as she had done all her life while her father asked the blessing. But another thought intruded in that religious moment, the old nightmarish realization that so soon she would be on that awful sea for a long time. For a second a chill went over her.

John noted her blanched lips and reached across the table and caught her hands in his. 'What is the matter, Dearest?' he asked in concern.

'For a moment, that old bugaboo, that fear of the sea and of going away got me,' she confessed, 'but it's gone. When it comes again,' and Maria, now smiling, disengaged one hand and made a tight fist, 'I'll give it the "Thistle Treatment" Uncle Asa taught me. Remember my crushing the thistle the first time I met you at Uncle Asa's?'

'Do I remember?! That was the moment I fell in love with you. How well I remember!' And he looked into her eyes with great tenderness.

'Maybe I fell in love with you then, but didn't know it,' she laughed and put her hand back in his. And for a moment John and Maria lost themselves in each other's ardent gaze, only to be brought back to reality by the deep tones of the grandfather clock on the stairway striking the hour of eight.

'Good gracious, time to get going,' John said as he hurriedly poured himself another cup of tea. 'And I hear you and Louise have a busy day ahead shopping.'

'She's decided that first we are going to visit a friend, Mrs. Snow, who can advise me what to get since she's been on four voyages—twice around the Horn. She's invited us to tea this afternoon.'

Thistle in Her Hand

'Good idea, my love. The Snows are mighty fine folks. They both come from a long line of Nantucket whalers from the days when Nantucket was the hub of the whaling industry. Captain Snow has been one of the very best, most successful New Bedford whalers. He's retired now.'

And John, obviously pleased with Maria's plans, gave her a quick hug and kiss and hurried away.

That afternoon Maria, dressed in her wedding outfit, even the black velvet cape, since the day had turned chilly, took her place beside Louise in the phaeton that the stable boy had just brought to the front steps. Louise and Manolo looked admiringly at a smiling Maria, dark-lashed hazel eyes alight with pleasure, cheeks a delicate pink and lips a darker shade of pink, quite a different Maria from the pale, frightened girl who had worn this wedding outfit the Saturday before.

'You are riding in a phaeton this afternoon. I use this rig when Milly and I are doing errands or going not far from home, like Fairhaven where we are going today,' Louise said.

'But where is Milly?' Maria asked in disappointment.

'I persuaded her to stay home and help Patrick make a lovely bouquet for the supper table. Our call at the Snows' is going to be really a business call, as we have so much to discuss about the clothes you will need to buy and I know she has valuable advice to give you from her long experience as a whaling wife,' Louise said as she took up the reins and started the sturdy gray pony on a good trot.

'You and Mrs. Snow will like each other. And you will like the captain. He has been a big help to John in whaling matters. Captain Snow was a smart whaler and had "greasy luck," that is, brought back a full cargo of sperm oil on his last voyage, so he could retire to a good life. They bought a nice home in Fairhaven. Wait till you see how beautifully it is furnished. But they themselves dress very simply because they are Quakers.'

As they approached the fine verandah of the two-story house, gray-shingled with white trimmings, blooming pink hydrangeas at the gate of the white picket fence around the spacious grounds, Louise said with a deep sigh, 'I hope and pray that your voyage will have such greasy luck that you folks can settle here in a lovely home like this. John can go into business with Sam. His marine insurance business is expanding very much, with New Bedford getting bigger and all that. How Milly would love having you here! We would all love it.'

'Oh, Louise, you have no idea how I would love it. It is so alive here, with such fine churches and stores, so much activity. And we'd have lively times, especially Milly and I,' Maria said gayly. For the time being Maria was feeling light-hearted and optimistic about the future.

Maria and Louise walked up the flagstone walk bordered by late blooming rose bushes and were welcomed at the door by Mrs. Snow, a stoutish lady primly dressed in a dove gray gown with a white fichu at the neck. Maria had visualized her as a white-haired lady with the drawn look she had noticed on women's faces who had been long at sea. Instead she saw a middle-aged woman with a soft, smooth skin and twinkling light blue eyes. Yet Louise had told her that Mrs. Snow had spent some twenty years at sea, borne two daughters, one aboard ship in the Mozambique channel. Both daughters were now married to college professors.

'A special welcome to thee, Maria Hamblin, who is

going to sea as a whaling wife as I did about your age, and as the dear bride of John Hamblin whom we have known for many years and love as a son,' Mrs. Snow said as she took Maria's hand and led her into a parlor richly furnished in mahogany and red satin upholstery.

Exquisite figured cream lace curtains covered the tall windows of the room and whale oil lamp chandeliers glistened above, reflecting the glow of the briskly burning pine wood fire in the big fireplace. Portraits in gold frames adorned the walls, and against one wall stood an elaborately carved ebony whatnot filled with exotic-looking shells, and coral and jade figures. The kind of home I hope John and I will have, Maria thought as she looked around the room. There was an air of hospitality about the place and the singing of a canary in the sitting room nearby added a sort of joyousness to the surroundings. Maria had a feeling of delight, well-being.

As soon as the women were seated comfortably, Mrs. Snow tinkled a silver bell and a maid in black uniform and dainty white apron brought in a black lacquered Chinese tea tray with the tea things. And while the women sat around the tea table having tea and crumpets, Maria had many questions to ask and the friendly little Quaker lady had much to tell her. At first their subject was clothing to be purchased for the whaling voyage, especially things needed when rounding the Horn. Then Louise asked her friend, 'Martha, have you, as a wonderful whaling wife of the past, advice to give to this whaling wife-to-be?'

Mrs. Snow was silent for a moment. Then, leaving her chair by the tea table, she went and sat down on the sofa by Maria.

'Yes, Maria Hamblin, I want to give thee one

valuable bit of advice thee must never forget. Thy husband is a good and loving man, but remember, on the ship he is two men—your husband and the captain of the ship. Thee can dictate to your husband, but never, never to the captain of the ship. To be captain of a whaling ship he has to be a strict man, and can be a hard man. I know after voyaging with a man like him, my husband Seth.

'And when necessary, he uses language and severe measures that shock you, but as master of a whaling ship with its motley crew, rough, undisciplined, some murderers, he has to be a hard man to survive. John already has the reputation of a man with steady eyes who will stand no nonsense, but he also has the reputation of being able to exercise authority without bullying. By this quality, as well as by his position, he commands respect and gets it. A captain's word is law, even as to life and death, and no one must challenge it, not even you, Maria. Remember, you are not the captain's wife. You are John Hamblin's wife. If thee ever goes up on deck—and I tell thee from my own experience—and dictate to the captain, thee will be shocked by the stern look and sterner words thee will get, furious looks and words, maybe.'

'Oh, Mrs. Snow, I'll never, oh never, forget your advice,' Maria said in a solemn, shaken voice.

Mrs. Snow took Maria's hand between her own hands and said, gently, 'Another bit of advice, one hard to follow, as well I know, is to keep aloof from the crew and even from the mates. Remember, thee is one woman, a young attractive woman, among twenty-three or more men. Thee must never forget thee is on the captain's level and must keep, ever keep, on that level for the sake of discipline.'

Thistle in Her Hand

Mrs. Snow sighed and continued, 'The going will be hard at times, but there are good times, too. Just keep thy Bible handy. Repeat the 91st Psalm when in trouble, and sing some of the beautiful Methodist hymns thee knows well. All this will help thee keep thy peace of mind.

'And don't forget when thee is cooped up in thy stateroom for days in stormy weather and the air thee breathes reeks of smelly oilskin coats and other odors, and thee despairs of ever breathing real air again, remember the human body can stand much, especially when young, and that good air will come again.

'Yes, we whaling wives suffer much for the love of the one, but I have never regretted it, and thee will not, either. But now, my dear, I shall ring the bell for fresh tea and let us talk of more cheerful things than advice.'

The days that followed the visit with Mrs. Snow were busy ones, with shopping for the journey and social events at church and at the homes of friends. Then there were rides in the phaeton with Milly snuggled against her Aunt Maria.

On one of these rides Louise pointed out a somber gray building and said, 'That's the Bethel Chapel seamen go to before a voyage. John used to attend, but he says that this trip the chaplain is going to The Roman along with some of the owners of the company. Some whaling captains are doing this.

'The pilot boat, a tugboat, takes them to the river where the ship has been moved earlier to wait the right tide to get going. Then the pilot tugboat pulls the ship, with the help of the outgoing tide, along the dangerous shoals until the Vineyard is reached thereabouts, and then there is a short service—putting the voyage ahead in the hands of the Lord. Sometimes this is followed by a collation in the saloon, tea or lemonade, food and cake. Then when the pilot boat is ready to leave the job of piloting the ship, the visiting folk go back home in his boat. Sam, as broker for the whaling company and now in the work of whaling insurance, is supposed to go on these farewell parties. But the poor dear gets so seasick on the water that I have to take his place. I was on the water so much as a girl, a tomboy, I'm afraid, that I am at home on boat or ship. I'm a regular sea dog. You may be sure I'll be on The Roman.'

'Mama, I want to be there, too,' cried out Milly, sitting up straight, eyes alight with eagerness.

'Not now, since no children are allowed, but when you are older, you shall, my darling, my—our Milagro,' Louise said as she leaned over to kiss the top of the blond head.

'Milagro? How came that new name?' Maria asked in puzzled amusement.

Louise laughed. 'That was what Sam wanted to name her when she was born. It is the Spanish word for "Miracle" and that was what her coming meant to us after ten years of hoping and praying for a baby. Since "Milagro" was too foreign sounding we settled on the sweet name of "Milly" for our sweet little daughter.'

'Aunt Maria, when you come back from your voyage, will you and Uncle John pray for a baby? I'll help you take care of her.'

'Indeed we will, my darling,' and she looked at Louise and her eyes smiled tenderly from a blushing face.

The time was drawing near. On August twenty-third, when The Roman was due to sail, still Maria had not visited her future home.

Thistle in Her Hand

'Wait, my love, until it is ready for inspection, which will be the day before sailing,' John would always say when Maria and Louise suggested a visit to the ship. 'I want The Roman to look her best when you meet her,' John would add, with a twinkle in his eye. 'Besides, the wharves are a madhouse just now with so many ships coming and going. Ships—whalers, especially—going around the Horn or Cape of Good Hope are leaving now to take advantage of the winter that is summer Down Under, since the crossing is less stormy.'

One afternoon after tea, Louise suggested that Maria, Milly, and herself go up to the cupola at the top of the house and Maria could get a panoramic glimpse of what was going on about the wharves.

'I expect Milly and I will spend much time there when the company tells Sam it is time for you to be coming home. I'm going to tell John that if Sam is away when The Roman docks, he should get someone to bring you folks here and he can leave you and go back to the wharf to do what he has to do,' Louise said over her shoulder to Maria as they trudged up the narrow stairway to the cupola.

And Milly, between Louise and Maria, turned around and grabbed Maria's hand in happy excitement, 'And I'll hurry and pick you beautiful bouquets, Patrick and I, and I 'speck Maggie will hurry and cook the chicken the way you like it and Amanda will get the house extra clean and we'll be all ready. And will I be happy to see you!'

'And will I be happy to see you,' Maria said and gave the little hand a kiss. For a moment Maria was caught up with the illusion of the quick passing of time and the homecoming.

When they reached the glass cupola Maria stared

unbelievingly at the panoramic view of the waterfront. Ships and boats of all descriptions were coming or going or docked at the several wharves.

'You can always tell a whaling vessel by the many boats hanging to the sides and its tubby look. Oh, look at the clipper ship just sailing out! Doesn't it look trim? Streamlined, as Sam describes them. It's the fastest merchant vessel there is. Faster than the new-fangled steamers that are starting.'

'Louise, I hear merchant vessel captains don't take their wives along, since a woman on merchant vessels brings on bad luck,' Maria said, a troubled look on her face. 'Why is it not the same with whaling captains taking their wives?'

'My dear, a whaling vessel is not a merchant vessel. It's like a farmhouse on a prairie sea. It settles on the lonely seas. The men hunt the whale and bring it in where it is cooked out into oil, and the spermacetti from the head—if it's a sperm whale—is brought back for our lamps and candles at home, and to lubricate our machines. If it's a "bone whale," the whaling vessel brings back the whale oil which is not so good as sperm oil for making a good lamplight, but it has the bone from the sieve in its mouth. The bone is for so many things—the bone in your corset and the stays in your high collars, and the ribs in our umbrellas.'

Louise patted Maria's shoulder as she continued, 'Martha Snow tells me the crew likes to have the captain's family on board. It gives them a feeling of home on the ship. They like to see a child's wagon or other toy on the quarterdeck. And if the wife is on board the men feel the captain will be easier on them. And believe me, Maria dear, Martha says the crew act more civilized in the way they live.

'But now let's take a walk out on the widow's walk

around the cupola. We can see better, especially with the spyglass.' Louise unlatched a door that led to the narrow fenced-in walk and soon Maria was gazing in rapt amazement far off at the Vineyard Islands and on toward the horizon at what appeared to be little feathers or plumes against the sky.

'I suppose that is a whaler headed for the Horn,' she said with a shiver. 'I fear the Horn, the terrible cold, but I couldn't bear it if John were on that ship and I at home. I think my spirit would fly out to him,' Maria added slowly in a low, pensive voice, her hazel eyes dark as she gazed after the disappearing vessel.

'How John would like to take you by the way of Good Hope—it's not so bad—but the company has set this route and it can't be changed at this late date. You are coming back by way of Good Hope. And you will have our prayers, dear.'

'And I will have Papa's prayers. He is such a good man. He loves God so devoutly and tries so to help his fellow men that I think he has close communication with God. He is sure it is God's will that we come back, and I take great comfort in that.'

'I hope your father comes on the twenty-third when your brothers and your cousin Amasah are coming to spend the night and be there to see you off. I am sorry the others—your mother and relatives and our aunt in Sippewisset—do not feel they can come. There's plenty of room in the house to "sleep" all of them.'

'The boys are probably counting the hours until they get here. To see me, yes, but mostly to see The Roman. You know, Davey and Amasah are planning to sail with us on the next voyage, but like you, I hope and pray that this voyage will be so successful that we'll settle down here.'

Little Milly, who had been so engrossed with the

scene on the water that she had not listened to the conversation between her mother and aunt, caught Maria's last words and said in great earnestness, 'Please tell Uncle John to hurry up and come home 'cause I'll be missing you so much.' Maria picked her up and gave her a reassuring hug.

The day before sailing there was much activity in the Holman household. John had decided that it would be best to have Maria spend the night before sailing aboard The Roman to give her a chance to get used to the ship and the swinging bed while the ship was docked. So Maria had packed and was ready. Meanwhile Louise and the servants were busy getting ready for a garden party that afternoon as a gay send-off to John and Maria.

The party was indeed festive and colorful. It was a warm afternoon of Indian Summer and the ladies wore billowy gowns of many hues, and fashionable leghorn hats that were like bouquets in themselves. The men in their white trousers and dark coats added contrast to the light colors.

It was like a beautiful painting, Maria told herself, a beautiful picture she would think about later. She made herself chat and smile, but underneath there was a melancholy she could not throw off. She wondered whether all this gaiety was a brave attempt on the part of the guests to cheer Louise and Sam especially, and her heart warmed with gratitude at the thought.

Maria's attention was diverted by a glimpse at the driveway of Selim drawing the family buckboard with three beaming youths, her brothers and cousin Amasah in it.

'Where's Papa?' she asked anxiously.

Thistle in Her Hand

'Mother's having one of her bad spells and he couldn't leave, but like as not if she's better he'll be here 'fore you sail tomorrow,' Lisha said.

'You boys drive to the stable yonder and Manolo will help you unhitch. Then go to the house and spiffen up after your long drive, then come to the party—the farewell party the Holmans are giving for John and me.'

As Maria was starting back to the party Sam came up with a very attractive, dark-haired, plumpish young woman. 'Maria, I want you to meet my cousin Cornelia who's come up from Savannah for a visit. She's from these parts,' Sam added with a teasing smile, 'but she's turned Southerner after marrying a true Southerner, Charlemagne, a descendant of the French Huguenots. And they have twins, fine lads, Carl and Charles. I want you to meet them. Oh, here they are.' And Sam beckoned them to his side and introduced them to Maria.

Maria noted they were about Amasah's age, fifteen, but tall and dark with aristocratic bearing. When she told them that her younger brothers and cousin had just arrived and were putting up the horse and buggy, they excused themselves and ran to join the boys. Their southern drawl sounded musical to Maria's ears and she turned to their mother with a warm smile, 'You must be proud of your sons.'

'Proud? They are her jewels, as were the sons of the other Cornelia of Roman history, mother of the Gracchi,' Sam spoke up before his cousin could answer.

Cornelia laughed and gave Sam's arm a good-natured slap. 'Sam! Still as crazy about history as when we went to school. But he's right. The boys are our pride and joy. We dread the time when they go away to college, to Harvard. Then I expect we'll be up here half the time.

Who knows, we may be here when you get back from your voyage, and Sam and Louise may have a welcoming party for you and John. We can meet again right here under this maple, by the birdbath. Will you plan one?'

'Fair lady, you may consider it already planned,' Sam smiled and waved his arms. 'But now let's go to the lemonade and fancy French cakes on the table,' he added.

John came after the party had been in progress for two hours, and expressed regret at being late and at having to go back immediately, taking Maria with him. The Roman was to be moved from its berth to the river earlier than planned and it was urgent that he be back at the wharf.

Louise excused herself to accompany her brother and Maria. Sam decided to drive John and Maria in his roomier surrey so that Louise and the boys could visit the ship. There was room for Milly and for Cornelia because Maria's brothers and Amasah chose to 'hoof' it over. The Savannah youths decided to join them.

As Sam's surrey passed along the streets to the waterfront, Sam pointed out to the women many of the buildings connected with whaling—copper shops, spar yards, blacksmith shops for making harpoons, lances, and whaling gear, rigging lofts and sailing lofts.

'Maria, sweet Maria,' Sam turned to Maria, 'these words are just words to you now, but when you get back they'll have a real meaning to you.'

Maria nodded as she gazed with amazement at sights so new, yet now of great interest to her. 'Everything for whaling,' she murmured, 'I never believed...'

John, sitting in front with a now sleeping Milly on his lap, laughed and reached back to squeeze her hand.

'This part of New Bedford is a hive of industry centered around whaling,' he said. 'The world whaling center is our New Bedford town.'

The surrey now passed the big Wilcox lumber yard and moved along Front Street and the wharves, where rows and rows of barrels were visible under a protective covering of seaweed.

Sam then diverted their attention from the oil barrels. 'My whaling insurance office is over there,' he pointed with his whip. 'But that business is not very flourishing. People are always going to buy insurance tomorrow, when it may be too late.'

The next turn led to the docks. 'There she is,' John spoke with pride. Maria could see two wharves, at the end of which loomed a ship.

'Which is The Roman?'

John pointed it out, remarking that the other visible one was The John and Edward, just returned to port, her hold filled with whale oil and bone. 'She's been in the North Pacific,' John explained.

'Oh, how I wish we were just returning, rather than starting out,' Maria thought fervently, as she was helped out of the surrey by Lisha. The five youths had taken a short cut and were already on the wharf admiring The Roman, newly painted in black, the portholes white. Some ran to help Maria with her bundles, others clustered around John while Sam hunted for an unoccupied hitching post for his horse.

'Remember, we're going with you next voyage, John,' David said, his arm in his brother-in-law's. 'Amasah's goin' in the fo'c'sle and I can be cabin boy. We're both heading for being captains like you.'

'We'll see, David. But meantime, as I said before, get a lot of education. More and more whales are smartening up, too.' And John fondly tousled the boy's smooth golden brown hair. He turned to the Georgia youths, who were looking at him attentively, dark eyes alert.

'Do you fellows aim to be whaling captains, too?'

The youths saluted and Charles spoke for both, 'No, sir; we aim to be clipper ship captains. Our father has promised us each a berth after we finish training.'

Maria and Louise came up to them with Milly holding onto her mother's hand, and they all started toward The Roman. They had to be wary as the way was teeming with activity.

John was stopped from time to time by some of his own crew for orders or directions. Maria regarded Lisha, walking briskly ahead followed by the other four, who loped along with that awkward grace of youths who had grown too fast. Boyish David kept up with them at a trot.

Her precious little brother, she had held him close in her arms, little girl arms, when Mama had died. 'Little Davey will be a tall, slim youth when I see him again; and the others will be young men,' Maria thought, and her hand went to her throat as if to hold back a sob. Resolutely, she turned her attention to the vessel they were nearing. The others had gone ahead, but she lagged behind, her spirits dragging.

David came back to his sister, pointing excitedly to the three tall masts. 'Sis, the one at the stern is the mizzenmast, the middle one is the mainmast, and the one at the bow is the foremast. That's the one that goes down into the forecastle where the ordinary crew live, only it's called the fo'c'sle, saying the word real fast. I know all about whaling ships. Gollee, I wish I was going. Isn't she a big whaler?' And David squeezed his sister's hand in his admiration for The Roman, and ran up the temporary ramp to the middle of the ship where John was talking to the other boys.

Maria stood and gazed at the ship with mixed emotions. Though she had lived in a whaling area all of her life, and some of her relatives had been whaling folk, she was only now aware of whaleships. In her childhood she had stood on the sand dunes and watched them in the distance crossing Buzzards Bay on toward Vineyard Sound. Now Maria felt she was seeing a whaleship for the first time. This would be her home for the next two or three years—this ugly, blunt-nosed cumbersome vessel!

Just then Sam, his horse finally tied safely amidst the hectic traffic of the docks, came up puffing and out of breath to her side. He took her arm and led her up the ramp onto the ship. She stopped before the gangway and looked up to the bustling deck, where men scrambled among the ropes and crates, whaling ship stuff strewn about. The masts were like steeples piercing the sky; and there were the ugly brick stoves, the tryworks where they fried the oil out of the whales. She put down her head and covered her eyes. It was like a strange nightmare. It was all so foreign to her.

Sam gave her shoulder a soft pat. 'Buck up, sweet Maria, all this does look so strange to me, too. Being a lan'lubber myself, I can sure sympathize with you, but I'm sure you'll be glad you went. Why, you will have so much to tell us when you come back!'

Sam leaned down and added softly in her ear, 'And you are going with John, the man you love. And you couldn't love a better man.'

Maria, ashamed of giving way to her emotions before Sam, raised her head to thank him for his kind concern. As she did so, she caught sight of John standing in the waist of the ship surrounded by boys all badgering him with questions. She felt her heart leap with joy and wanted to go to John and touch him—to put her hand on his arm.

She sighed with relief. Just being with John was all that really mattered. Her moment of panic gone, Maria smiled at Sam and took him by the arm toward the gangway so they could get on The Roman to listen to the conversation between John and the boys.

'I'd better listen and learn about my new home,' she whispered to Sam with a wry smile.

'I reckon you should, honey,' he responded with a serious nod as they started up the swinging gangway. Suddenly glancing beyond her careful footsteps she saw the water churning down below them. Her grip tightened around Sam's arm and her thoughts began to swirl like the water. Sam quickly grabbed her around the waist and guided her up onto the deck. Maria battled the fear that gripped her chest and the weakness in her limbs. Her pink cheeks drained their color as she felt the slight give of the vessel underneath her small, leather-tipped cloth shoes. Once on the ship her panic subsided, but in the pit of her stomach there was a slight sensation of nausea.

I must get used to this, she told herself fiercely. I won't be a sissy and give in to it now with the ship still tied to the dock. She straightened her back, and, smiling to reassure the worried Sam, led him behind where John was standing with the youths so they could listen.

'I hear tell that whalin' ships are built by the mile and cut off any length you want,' quoted Lisha firmly.

'Well, this one was cut off at exactly 109 feet, 4 inches,' replied John with a twinkle in his blue eyes. 'And not only that, Lisha, she's 27 feet, 8 inches wide

Thistle in Her Hand

and 13 feet in depth. Oh, she weighs just about 375 tons.'

Lisha gazed at the ship with the eyes of a youth already well-apprenticed in ship building. 'She's no beauty. No clipper ship for sure, but I can see she's good and solid—well built.' The other boys were silent, their eyes on John, awaiting his answer.

'It had better be to last our long voyages,' he replied while his keen eyes investigated an uneven section of the copper sheathing visible above the waterline. 'These ships are built for utility, not for line.'

'Capt'n Hamblin,' squealed one of Cornelia's boys, who, like Maria, were visiting a whaling ship for the first time, 'a whaling ship sure doesn't look like any other ship I have ever seen.'

'You're right, Carl,' John agreed, ruffling the young boy's bushy locks. 'It is built not only for riding the waves in chase of the whale, but also for cutting up the whale, turning the blubber into oil, and storing the oil to bring back for people like you and me to light our lamps, or lubricate our machines and bicycle chains. Your mama even uses it on her sewing machine.' The boys all listened to every word in awe.

'So you see, my friends, this big clumsy vessel may not be as finely lined as a clipper ship, but it is a hunter, factory, and storage house all rolled into one ship! And what would civilization do without the whaling ship in this day and age?' John concluded proudly to the beaming youngsters.

Just then John noticed Maria standing by Sam and his face lit up. Turning to Maria, he took hold of her hand and stated, 'Now we'll go to the stern of The Roman to see your quarters, since I know you're anxious to see them first.'

Maria smiled and blushed, pleased that John's

attention was focused on her now. She didn't notice that her husband's voice was purposely cheerful as he quickly led the way toward two narrow shelters, separated by the wheelhouse, but all covered by a single wooden roof.

'These are the afterhouses,' he explained. 'In one we keep some of the whaling equipment, and for the time being some extra provisions like those you see here. In this other one is the companionway or entrance to the Big Cabin below. Here is where we store our signalling flags like the waifs and other office flags. And here is the wheelhouse where you see the wheel the man uses to pilot the ship.'

As Maria listened to what John was saying her eyes kept straying to the strange sight about her. The Roman seemed bristling with boats.

'Why so many boats?!' she asked, pointing to five boats up on cranes on the bulwarks nearby.

'Those, Maria, are the whaleboats or "whalers," and we have a lot more than five. Look up, there are some more stored up in the skids above us.' John pointed to the wooden framework attached to the side of the ship. 'A whaleboat looks like a long rowboat, but if you look closely you'll see that it is pointed at both ends, designed so that it can turn and move swiftly.' Maria was looking about somewhat confused, but trying to absorb all she was hearing and seeing amidst the chaos of the ship.

'This part of the quarterdeck we call the skids.'

'And remember, dear sister,' Lisha interrupted in a stern voice full of concern, 'Mrs. Captain Hamblin, the quarterdeck is your yard and don't you stray beyond these skids.'

Lisha held his sister by her shoulders as he spoke half

Thistle in Her Hand

in fun, half in earnest. 'And that is what Uncle Asa told you so many times. He said no matter what, you can't go on deck unless John is with you.'

'Oh, Lisha!' Maria snapped back, pinching her brother and then, stepping back, embarrassed at her childlike response in front of all the people, added in a more serious voice, 'Don't worry, I know all that.'

'You're very right, Lisha,' John quickly confirmed without smiling, 'Maria and I will go over a few of these rules later.'

Noting Maria's dismay at his comment he quickly changed the topic. 'But now I want you to look at our new galley or kitchen.' And John pointed to a small, boxlike building next to the afterhouse on the quarterdeck.

'Here's where Doc will prepare the meals for us and the men on the ship.'

'What!' Maria burst out in amazement when she looked into the tiny room where meals would have to be prepared for so many people three times a day. Every bit of space was utilized. The big wood burning stove occupied much of it and the sides were lined with utensils, each fastened firmly in its place. The walls were covered with kitchen cutlery, each piece pegged down with a clamp.

'And here's Doc!' John called to the grizzly haired seaman who approached with a well-defined limp. John gave his shoulder a friendly pat and smiled as he said, 'He was our cook on my last voyage, and a very good one, too. We call the cook on all of the whaling ships "Doc" because he takes care of the men's ordinary cuts and bruises.' John's eyes shone with pride as he introduced Maria and the Old Salt to one another.

'Doc,' Maria addressed him, her face alight with

admiration and interest, 'how many people do you cook for? Do you have help? And John, I mean the captain, said you were such a good cook. Who taught you to cook?' Maria had found an area of the whaling life she could understand and her curiosity came out in a barrage of questions to the old man.

John explained to Maria how busy Doc was and that there would be plenty of time for him to answer all of her questions later. Then he excused the old sailor to continue his work. But Doc, flattered and amused at the interest the captain's young wife showed in his job, gave a quick answer to her questions first.

'I cook for thirty-seven men on the ship, ma'am, making up I figur' 'bout three meals a day. Can't say my cookin' is as good as the capt'n 'as told ya, that's fo' sure. But, anythin' I learned my Ma taught me. When I'se a boy I he'pped her in 'er eatin' place in Nantucket. Fine meetin' yer, Ma'am,' he finished with a friendly nod as he limped into the galley.

'And what's this building?' Maria asked, pointing to a smaller boxlike building in the skids nearby.

'That is to be your sitting room, Maria, after the vegetables and fruits that now fill it are eaten. We have to use every available space on the ship for food storage right now, but it won't be too long before it's eaten and the building will be yours.'

'Oh, this is the charthouse that the women told me about! John, I am so glad you had one built for me. They said that if The Roman had one I could sew and iron in it!'

John beamed at Maria's pleasure and interest. He had indeed convinced the owners of The Roman, The Jonathan Edwards Company, whose flag waved atop the mast, to have a charthouse built aboard the ship since his wife was to be on the voyage with them.

'And it's good for more than chores, my darling!' he said proudly. 'You can sit and see the way the ship is heading and feel the good sea breeze.'

A carpenter was putting the finishing touches on the small building and John introduced him to Maria. She could tell by John's manner that he had high regard for the man.

'Pleased to meet you, Mrs. Hamblin,' the tall, thin, weather-beaten man said. 'Just call me Chipps, ma'am. They all do.'

'Very well, Chipps!' Maria responded happily. She was so glad this kindly man was on the voyage and prayed there were others like him. She had heard of strange characters that signed on for the long whaling voyages. Her father had described them as the 'flotsam and jetsam of society.' She shuddered to remember some of the stories she had heard from the boys and others about the rogues on whaling ships—debtors, thieves, even some murderers escaping from the law and prison.

One thing for sure, she'd never go beyond the skids unless John was with her. She had been warned enough by Uncle Asa and the whaling wives she had met. 'Especially for a pretty, young girl like you,' they would add. She became aware that the seasickness was returning, but tried to ignore its presence.

Just then Maria and John noticed that Sam and the five boys, who had wandered off from their company at the galley, were over by the middlemast jabbering and pointing up to the crow's nest.

'That's something you'll never see on a clipper ship, but it sure is important on a whaler,' John told them. 'That tiny platform is about a foot wide on each side of the mast. Those things that look like huge spectacles above the foothold are padded hoops secured just a little higher than a man's waist.'

'How does the man get up there?' one of the twins asked.

'Oh, he goes up the mast on the footholds or the wooden or iron cleats, climbs onto the platform through the hoops, and rests his arms on them, standing comfortably and gazes around, hopefully awake, and looking for whales. There are generally two men up at a time.'

Maria was staring up to the crow's nest, her eyes squinting and her lips pursed. 'John, that's so dangerous. One man's son in Falmouth was nearly killed getting down. He lost hold of the mast.'

John nodded his head sadly. 'I know, my love. But we remind the seamen at all times that one hand must always be touching the ship.'

Maria's glance went up again to the ship's masts that stood up like broomsticks, bowsprits soaring at an angle. For some reason fear tugged at her throat as she looked at them and saw in her mind's eye the great sails they would soon support. Men were busy everywhere. Some furling sails, others making them. She could hear an animated symphony of sound—sounds of carpenters at work, pans crashing in the galley, brushes scrubbing against wood, and the whang of anvils.

'Where are Louise and Cornelia?' Maria asked, looking around and realizing that she was the only female anywhere to be seen. More than once she had felt uncomfortable upon catching a sailor staring at her or others apparently talking about her. Not knowing quite what to do, she could feel the heat rise to her face and turned away, hoping neither John nor Sam would notice.

Sam laughed and looked mysterious as he answered

Thistle in Her Hand

her, 'Just you wait. They're prowling around in the Big Cabin. Louise is checking on things. You know what a meticulous housekeeper she is!'

It was a good feeling to know that they were on the ship with her. The ship, the men, the life seemed so male and rough to her. To admit that her legs still felt a little weak, that the roll of the ship made her stomach queasy, that she felt so frail and untrained next to John and the others was something she would only divulge to them. She did not want to disappoint John, to tell him she understood none of it, not even the galley, and that perhaps she did not have the strength or inclination to be an old sea wife, to stay in the small quarters, to have no women friends, no softness, and no more Monument girlhood of flirting and smiles and lace...

'Yes, the Big Cabin. I expect our Maria wants to see that most of all. This, my love, will be home.' John sent Maria a fond smile as she, leaning on Sam's arm, drew up the rear.

'What say, my fair lady?'

Before Maria could answer, Amasah spoke up. 'Capt'n John, where will I bed down when I sign up come next voyage?'

'It depends how you sign on. The ship is divided into sections according to use. The quarterdeck, above and below, is for the officers. Next forward is the steerage, where live the cook, the steward, the cabin boy, the boatsteerers or harpooners. In the waist, or middle of the ship below deck is the blubber room, where the blubber is cut up before it goes to the tryworks, and the big space called the hold for the oil, whalebone, spermacetti, or whatever the catch may be. The entrance is that hatch. Up forward is the door that leads to the fo'c'sle where you will go as an ordinary seaman.'

'That will be me, like you when you started, Cap'n,' Amasah said, touching his forehead in salute. 'Sailing before the mast.'

'Sure will be, Amasah my boy, for the foremast starts below in the fo'c'sle—miserably tight quarters,' John said, shaking his head gloomily.

'I'm going down to see my quarters,' laughed Amasah.

'Me, too,' shouted David and ran after his cousin.

'Below all the living quarters from bow to stern,' John told Maria and the others remaining, 'extends the hold for barrels of oil, storage, necessities for the voyage, extra whaling gear, lumber, and so forth. By the time we start for home, if we are successful, most of the hold will have barrels of greasy gold and spermacetti. Now let's go down to the captain's quarters where Maria and I will live.'

And John led them down the companionway which was hardly more than a steel ladder into the low-ceilinged dining room or forward cabin. At that moment he was called away and Sam took over and started to explain that the raised table 'plumb against the mizzenmast was the dining table.'

'But where are Louise and Cornelia?' Maria asked, looking around.

'Oh, you'll run into them soon,' Sam said with a mischievous grin, then continued, 'and these rails on the edge of the table are to prevent the dishes from sliding off when the ship's in rough water.' He pointed to the pewter whale oil lamp with a tin reflector but no glass which was fastened to a small stand clamped to the mizzenmast. 'That lights the room at night. In the daytime the skylight lights this room and the next room, the Captain's Big Cabin it's called. In the corner of the skylight is the compass, the barometer, and the ship's clock the man at the wheel up there in the wheelhouse goes by in steering the ship.'

Maria listened, but found herself too confused to comprehend. It was all so new and strange and for a moment she panicked wondering if she could stand living for long in such small ugly quarters.

Just then a heavy-set, grey-bearded man well past middle age, came down the companionway and introduced himself as the mate, Mr. Richards. He showed them his cabin, a cubbyhole off the saloon. It had a bunk, a chest, and a sort of desk where he kept the ship's log.

'It's the first mate's chore,' he said. 'Also watch the ship's tell-tale to be sure the steerer is on the job. The captain and I take turns, Mrs. Hamblin,' he said making a slight bow to Maria. Again she felt she was meeting another good person to have on the voyage and her spirits rose.

Mr. Richards then pointed forward to a cabin with two bunks for the second and third mates. He smiled as he pointed to a small closet-like room on the port side of the dining saloon. 'That's the pantry, where Henry, the steward, prepares food brought from the galley. You and the captain, Mrs. Hamblin, will eat in the saloon. We mates also, taking turns so one is always on deck. Oh, here's the captain and Henry now.'

John was back with a companion, a tall negro dressed in spotless white, a genial smile on his face. He spoke only a few words, but Maria wondered whether he could be an escaped slave. If so, her father, a strong Abolitionist, might have had a hand in his escape.

'Human slavery is an abomination in the eyes of the

Lord.' How many times had she heard her father utter those words in the past ten years? And sometimes he was away from home—on an errand of mercy, the children were told. For a moment Maria had a wave of homesickness as she thought of Papa, gifted with words and fired with ideals, the home, family, and friends she would not see for such a long time. Suddenly she stopped, annoyed at herself for being such a homesick ninny. Smiling at John she said gaily, 'I'm dying to see our abode,' and waved her hand.

'This way, my lady,' he said, and taking her hand led her into the next small room, the captain's Big Cabin or office. It was at the stern of the ship with two portholes over a rise of structure which must cover the rudder, Maria thought as she looked around. The rising was utilized for a closet. A horsehair sofa was against the back wall. She was glad, since it gave the room a homey touch. She noted the big captain's desk against the partition to the next room.

Then her eye caught her own little bedroom rocker with its gay chintz cushion and with a cry of delight she ran to sit down in it. As she did so she heard a merry laugh, Milly's, in the next room. Maria ran in all excited. The others, John, Sam, Lisha, and the twins, slipped back on deck for lack of room in the little cabin or stateroom—the only real personal home of John and Maria.

'Welcome to your house,' cried Louise and Cornelia in unison.

Speechless, Maria looked around a room not much bigger than Selim's stall back home, with the gimbal bed taking much of the space. Dainty white curtains were over the porthole or window. And the bed, bulging with a feather mattress, was neatly made up with a bright star quilt for a spread. The colorful rag rug covered the small space by the bed. And a small shelf-like table with Maria's beloved Bible, her mother's, was near the head of the bed. Everywhere there was evidence of the women's handiwork, a curtain over where the trunk was nailed to the partition and all the things brought from the house neatly put into the many new drawers lining the partitions.

'We had to work fast to get everything in place! And how Louise got to finish the curtains...' Cornelia chuckled.

Maria shook her head, smiling through happy tears.

'Oh, Aunt Maria, come see your funny water closet,' squealed Milly as she led her aunt up a couple of steps to an alcove where there was a toilet seat with two apertures, one larger than the other. 'You don't pull any chain. The water goes below by itself. It's the ocean water shushing by.' Milly's blue eyes were large with the wonder of it all. Maria looked down into the dark green water below in dismay.

'Louise, what if a shark nips me?'

'Don't worry. It's too high up. But folks, we'll have to go because it's suppertime. The boys are probably starving. And Maggie has sent a hamper with good things for the steward to serve you and John for supper.'

Together the three women, Maria, Louise, Cornelia, and Milly left to join the others on deck.

Amasah was telling John, with the others listening, of the visit to the fo'c'sle. '...bunks so crowded, especially those at the bow that come to a point. Such noise! Men hammering down their sea chests and yelling at each other. Rough looking bunch, most of them. There's a character calls himself a pirate from Key

West. He looks like one. Wears an earring in one ear and a bandana as headgear. He plays the harmonica.'

'And makes nice music,' David put in. 'He played "Yankee Doodle" for us and told us how he got away from some cannibals.'

John laughed heartily. 'Davey, if he's a good yarnster and can make music, I'll never be able to get rid of him no matter how shiftless he turns out to be. The crew will stand up for a man who entertains them when there's no whale to chase and makes life lively.'

David spoke up again. 'There's one that's mean. Name's Portugee. At least that's what I heard someone call him. When he came aboard I saw the mate who had charge make him lay his sheath knife on the deck. Then the mate broke off the point, and explained why. It made Portugee mad—he got a mean, bad look on his face. I'm afeared of him.'

John looked very serious as David told of the seaman Portugee. 'I am glad you told me, Davey my boy. I'll talk to the mate about him.'

'Uncle John,' the twins approached the captain. 'We noticed on your desk the American flag folded with the stars showing on top. We counted thirty-three! How or why so many, sir?'

'We are flying that new flag tomorrow. Thirty-three stars for our thirty-three states. Last year Minnesota came in as a state, and this year, 1859, Oregon has come in.'

'Sir, how can our President, James Buchanan, take care of all those states?' David, suddenly interested, asked.

'He could take care of this country if the states would stop fighting each other—the slave states wanting to secede. Our fifteenth President is a fine man, a smart man, but some say we need a stronger man. They talk of Abraham Lincoln. We'll see, David. You boys are going to hear plenty of political talk.'

Just then Louise came up and asked John again if he and Maria couldn't come home for supper. John shook his head regretfully, and his sister hurried the boys, Cornelia, Milly, and Sam homeward, occasionally stopping to wave back.

Maria and John stood hand in hand and waved until all were back in Sam's carriage and gone out of sight.

Chapter 8

AFTER the company left, Maria hurried John back to the stateroom to show him what those dear women, especially Louise, had done to fix it up and surprise her. Then they went back to the Big Cabin and Maria sat down in her little rocker in delight.

'John, how did you get it here without my knowing?'

A smile flitted across his face as he answered. 'Your father sent it by stagecoach to the wharf. Notice the hooplike contrivance over the rockers? That's to hold it on the floor during a storm. Everything has to be ready for those storms that plague us.' He went over to his desk and showed her the clamps on every drawer and in the medicine chest back of the Big Chair, as the captain's chair was called. John changed the subject quickly, noting the look of panic in Maria's eyes. He reached over and passed a caressing hand over her cheek as he pointed above to the compass in the ceiling.

'It's not the compass itself,' he said as he sat down in the Big Chair. 'It's the telltale compass or the underside of the compass itself. I can look up from my desk or over the partition from the bed and tell whether or not the man at the wheel is steering right.'

'Isn't that a lamp under a sort of hood close to the compass?'

'Yes, my darling, you are seeing the light that illuminates the compass at night for the helmsman and me. It is called the gimbal light because it is set in gimbals, a heavily weighted contrivance that keeps swinging upright, no matter how the ship rolls. The barometer and clock by it are set in gimbals, too. And so is our bed, for that matter. The light has a real glass chimney and see how shiny clean it is? That's one of Henry's jobs to keep it like that. It is very important that the helmsman have a clear view of compass, barometer, and clock when he looks down into the skylight.'

Maria looked at the skylight overhead. It was boxlike, with a grill to protect the glass. It lighted the Big Cabin from the sofa to the table at the mizzenmast. She could see the wheel under the protecting roof. The man at the wheel, in turn, could look down into the skylight frame and see the compass, the barometer, and the clock.

As Maria gazed upward, she saw a man's hand reach over and yank a rope which rang the ship's bell twice.

'Two bells. That's supper time,' John said, holding Maria's hands to help her up. 'Bells are struck for changing of the watch. We haven't set up the watches—that comes tomorrow—you'll enjoy watching the procedure. You'll get used to telling time by the bells, Maria.'

Maria and John were the only ones in the saloon and the steward served them a delicious supper from the hamper Maggie had sent: biscuits and creamed chicken with peas fresh from the Holman vegetable garden, with other dishes which Maria did not even notice—she moaned softly as she was fighting a queasiness in her

Thistle in Her Hand

stomach and the sight of food was making it worse.

'It's the constant motion of the ship on water, even when docked,' John said, comfortingly. 'Just take a little food and a cup of hot tea and we'll go up on deck. The fresh air will perk you up. You'll get used to it all and not even notice it.'

Just then the second mate, Rogers, an illiterate but good-natured Irishman with a brush of carroty red hair on his round head, joined them at the table. Following him came the third mate, Agrimonte, a tall, lean mulatto from the Cape Verde Islands. He looked like a field hand and spoke broken English. After the introduction the men asked John about some ship matter. Maria watched them as they talked and was proud to see in what obvious respect they held John.

In the back of her mind there lurked a small worry—those rough men in the fo'c'sle Amasah and David talked about. She hoped no one would start a fight that ended in someone getting hurt. She remembered David's fears. Often her little brother's observations were discerning and his opinions wise.

Shortly afterward, John led her up the companionway to the narrow deck at the stern of the ship. It was night now. The fresh air made Maria feel much better and they stood for some time at the quarterdeck rail looking out over the city. 'It seems as if every house is brightly lighted,' Maria said in marvelling tones.

John, holding one arm around Maria's waist, waved the other toward the higher part of the city, the residential part, as he spoke. 'There are many festivities tonight. New Bedford is now a city of wealth and society. Many ships have come in this week, so there is much celebrating. The offices on Water Street are full of whalebone, and casks of oil are covering the wharves, as you saw today. No wonder New Bedford is getting the name of being the best lighted city in the United States. With so many ships bringing in sperm oil, it has the best illuminant to use.'

'John, what will happen when the whale has been hunted down and there is no more oil? Remember once we had plenty of whales around Buzzards Bay and the Sound? Many were killed off, especially the sperm whales, and now you whalers have to go to the ends of the earth to hunt the sperm whale.'

'Don't worry your dear head. Something else will be found. I'm hearing rumors of petroleum being refined to make a fine illuminant called kerosene—said to give a better light than even sperm oil. But it's too costly to refine much just now.

'But, my dear, it's bedtime. Time to go to the stateroom and learn to get into the gimbal bed. It's tricky until you learn to climb into it.'

In the saloon as John and Maria descended was a fat boy, Timmy the cabin boy, waiting for them with a lighted lantern because the table light at the mizzenmast had been extinguished. He had a broad smile as John introduced him and proudly led them with the lantern to the stateroom, and hung it on the proper peg.

'I am glad to see you, Timmy,' Maria said warmly.

The boy grinned some more and mumbled, 'Yes'm. Thank ye,' and hurried away.

'You'll be seeing much of Timmy, because his job is to look after things around the Big Cabin—help Henry. Henry sees he doesn't laze around,' John said with a laugh.

John and Maria spent some time and much laughter as she tried to get onto the elusive bed. Finally, John picked up his primly nightgowned little wife and placed

Thistle in Her Hand

her in the middle of the bed and soon they were in each other's arms. For the time being they were John and Maria, still on their honeymoon.

Maria awoke next morning to the noise of a busy port—bells, the distant clang of hammer on metal at the anvil, the rumbling of drays along the cobbled streets, and the shouting of men.

'Good gracious! What a racket and it's hardly daylight,' she murmured sleepily and reached out her hand to touch John. His place was empty. She remembered him saying before they went to sleep, 'I'll be up very early—better stay in bed until after the ship is warped to the river.'

Maria sat up, fully awake. 'Today we sail! I must get up and dress. Maybe I'll have a chance to talk to the folks at the dock before the ship is moved. I must tell Davey not to go out too far in his dory,' she whispered to herself as she started to get out of the swinging bed. Just then there was much commotion, yelling of commands, and other noises and the ship started jerking. 'She's moving,' groaned Maria, feeling suddenly dizzy, nauseated, having to lie back in misery.

After a while The Roman stopped moving and there were different sounds, especially the creaking of chains. 'Must be the anchor being let down. And soon the pilot tug bringing the company will be here. I must get dressed,' Maria thought as she left the bed and started to get dressed. But the slight motion of the boat was making her stomach queasy. 'Maybe if I put on my wrapper and morning cap and go for tea I'll feel better,' she decided, forcing herself to put on stockings, slippers, and wrapper.

John came in then and noting her blanched lips, helped her put on her morning cap. 'You will feel better after a cup of tea and some fresh air on deck, my darling,' he said as he put his arm around her and led her to the saloon. A solicitous Henry had tea and biscuits on the table in a hurry.

'The sea is like glass,' John told her as she sipped her tea, 'and many people are already at the dock waiting to see us off. You will be surprised how the fresh air and the excitement of it all will settle your stomach. I'll help you dress, and up on deck we go,' he said.

It was as John predicted. As she stood beside John at the quarterdeck bulwarks where she could get a full view of the wharf crowded with family and friends she forgot about her queasy stomach and started excitedly waving both hands. Scarves, handkerchiefs, and hats were now waving, and sounds of voices came indistinctly.

'John, there's Amasah and Davey and the twins up on that piling of boards—and I see Papa standing with Lisha by the piling. Oh, John,' and Maria squeezed his arm in her excitement. John smiled and patted her hand; the color was back in her cheeks and the nausea forgotten. 'John, Papa made it—he made it,' she said, tears running down her cheeks. 'And there's Milly on Sam's shoulders. She's wearing the red dress and red bonnet I like so much.'

'Milly! Milly!' Maria shouted at the top of her voice, forgetting those about her. John held her close, fearful that she lean too far over the bulwarks. 'Oh, John, she's heard me...'

But John's attention was diverted by a boat rowing toward the ship. The men at the oars were rowing as if their lives depended on getting to the ship.

'My God, the tugboat's started. They'd better make it

before it gets here,' John muttered with a nod of his head indicating a direction far from the wharf.

The crew at the rail hurried back to their work posts to be ready for The Roman to be pulled out as soon as the guests disembarked from the tugboat and came on board. The tide was turning and there was not a moment to lose. No delay would be permitted.

John's thick brows made a straight line on his forehead as he anxiously watched the progress of the boat. 'My God, it's Smitty,' he muttered under his breath. Maria was breathlessly watching the boat, which now battled some rising waves.

'Smitty's one of my best men,' John told Maria. 'He went with me on The Congress voyage. Mr. Richards just told me he is not on board—can't understand.'

Just before the arrival of the tug, the boat reached The Roman and soon a ruddy-faced, tousled-haired young man came over the bulwarks and staggered wearily toward John. He saluted John and gasped out, 'Sorry I am late, but my baby was born this morning. Sir, a fine girl—Christina, my mother's name. Sir, I am a papa now,' and he beamed with pride. 'And Agnes, my wife—fine.'

'Mighty glad to hear that,' John said heartily. 'Go report to Mr. Richards.' Then he turned to Maria with a grin, and started to say, 'He just made it,' but in alarm said, 'You're sick.'

'Yes, John, I feel so sick.' And without hearing more, John took her in his arms and carried her to the stateroom and laid her on the bed. He poured water from the flagon of water on the chest of drawers and gave it to her. 'I must get back on deck. I'll send Louise down to help you.'

After he left she drank the water and managed to get off the bed and crawl to the toilet seat where Louise found her retching. Maria felt too sick to notice the green water below.

'Oh, Louise, I know seasickness is the worst sickness there is,' she moaned when she was able to speak.

'John says it was your watching the water. He blames himself for not warning you,' Louise said soothingly as she helped her sister-in-law get back to bed and get comfortable. Henry appeared at the door with a bowl of hot chicken soup that Maggie had sent. Also a tightly corked bottle of hot water wrapped in a towel to put against her stomach. Maria drank the soup at Louise's insistence and felt a little better. Louise left, assuring Maria that she would look in on her from time to time.

Maria lay quietly in bed, furious with herself for not being up on deck with the guests since she knew it would mean so much to John. Services started. Maria couldn't hear the chaplain's words, but there was some singing and then it was quiet on deck as the mates chose their watches.

Then she heard John talking to the men, telling them what he expected of them. She could not catch all his words but his voice was not that of John—it was that of the Master of the ship. She could recall Martha Snow's words, 'Remember, my dear, John is both your husband and the Master of the ship. Never, oh never, interfere with the captain in dealing with the crew. A whaling ship captain has at times to use certain language, certain acts of discipline. If you interfere, the captain will look at you with fury. I know whereof I speak.'

Maria put her head into her pillow. Never, oh never would she risk that look. Never. Never. And gradually

Thistle in Her Hand

Maria, weak and tired, dozed off into a fitful sleep only to be awakened by Louise standing by her bed holding a bright geranium in a gayly decorated earthen pot.

'I hated to waken you but the service is over and the tugboat is to go back. Milly wanted me to give you this geranium to be your pet, to keep you from being lonesome. All the guests send greetings—John will tell you. They will be at the dock when you return. Chipps is going to set it in the skylight where it'll get plenty of light.' And with a quick kiss and an attempt at gaiety, 'Remember, if Sam is not at the wharf when you return, John is to bring you right to the house. We'll be waiting for you.' Then Louise left hurriedly to join those returning to land.

Soon after there was a great commotion on deck as sails were unfurled and the ship forged ahead on its own power.

Some time later John came and there was a jubilant note in his voice as he said, 'Well, the mates have chosen their watches and now the voyage has really started.'

Maria sat up. 'I feel better and must get up and see land while I can.'

'I'll take my spyglass since we are already a long way from New Bedford, but you'll see some of the Vineyard Islands,' John said, picking up her slippers to put on her feet.

At that moment the mate came into the captain's cabin and called John. 'Cap'n, I need to speak with you, Sir.' There was urgency in his voice and John dropped the slippers and hurried out. Maria listened with alarm, her sickness momentarily forgotten.

'Cap'n,' she heard the mate say, 'there's smoke over New Bedford way.'

'Smoke, Mr. Richards? Must be from those new soft-coal burning schooners. I'll go up and take a look with the glass.'

John returned in a few minutes and Maria heard them discussing the suspicious smoke. She heard John say, 'We are already late in sailing. We'll have to go on. We are not justified turning back on just a suspicion.'

'You're right, sir, but there'll be many worrisome moments until we hear. The men on my watch have been so busy I don't reckon they noticed.'

'Good. And we'll say nothing more about it, Mr. Richards.'

'Aye, aye, Cap'n. But we'll do a lot of praying about it,' she heard the mate answer with a sigh.

'That we will, Mr. Richards. That we will.' And she could tell John was indeed worried as he left again without saying a word to her.

Maria could not help wondering why John and the mate were so concerned. It's just one of those newfangled ships with belching smoke, she assured herself. She was more concerned with the conversation she overheard a little later in the cabin between John and the second mate Rogers when they came down from the deck.

John was speaking. 'I see you have Portugee on your watch. What do you think of him?'

'Cap'n, he's a seaman, and smart. I think he'll make a good harpooner, for sure. He's a stranger round these parts—says he's from Maine. Why the hell did he sign on for this long voyage? Can't help feelin' he's arunning from the law.'

Maria remembered what Davey had said about a mean man named Portugee and how angry he got when Mr. Richards made him lay his long sheath knife on the deck and have its point broken. For a moment fright gripped her as she thought of him in the forecastle—maybe with another sheath knife hidden. A man like that would be a danger to the other men in the crowded quarters. Her concern was particularly for Smitty with a new baby back home, Christina, and his wife Agnes.

She tried to hear more but the urgent need to go to the toilet diverted her attention. She looked longingly at the two steps to the toilet seat in the nearby alcove. She could call John to help her, but a feeling of shyness held her back. She must make it alone.

She managed to get off the bed and started to take a step when an attack of dizziness sent her down on her knees. Determinedly, lips set and blinking back the tears of self pity, she crawled to the toilet seat and, not allowing herself to look at the rushing waters below, sat down. For some moments she remained seated, feeling not only relief but exultation. She had done it! She then looked at the little iron washstand with its pewter pitcher and white enamel basin, the small mirror above it, and on the shelf her comb and brush and a bottle of toilet water by it, and soap.

'I must be a sight. I'll wash up and comb my hair,' she said aloud and started for the washstand only to have a sudden wind send the ship rolling. Maria fell in a heap. John heard her scream and came running. He picked her up and carried her to the bed.

'Oh John, I thought I was so smart,' she whimpered as her worried husband passed a towel doused in hamamelis over her pallid face.

'It is good to try to walk, get used to the roll of the ship, but only when I am with you,' he said, tenderly. 'Lie still now, and this evening when the wind dies down, I'll take you up to the deck.' Then, gently pushing her hair back from her face, he leaned over and kissed her on the forehead and hurried back to the deck.

Maria lay there, still feeling miserable but glad to be prone on the bed as the ship was now swaying violently. Must be a squall, she surmised, since there was so much commotion overhead, much running and sounds she guessed were of sails coming down. And so much yelling of commands! She was shocked to hear John use strong language she had never heard him use. She put her hands to her ears to drown out the sounds and she mumbled, 'That is not my John. That's the captain of the ship and his concern is the safety of the ship and its people. Oh, I must never forget that.' And Maria, with her forefingers pressing her earlobes down to dull her hearing, buried her face in her pillow and groaned, 'Will I ever be able to stand it all? I can't. I'll die and never see home again.' Sobs shook her for a while and then she dozed off into a troubled sleep.

John woke her up some hours later and made her drink a mug of hot chicken soup. 'The last of Maggie's soup with a hard biscuit floating in it. This will give you vim and vigor.' And to her amazement her stomach accepted the food and she felt better all over. And to her further amazement, the ship was barely rocking.

'Now, dearest, put on your wrapper and slippers and come up on deck. The fresh air will do you good and there's a surprise for you,' John told her.

It was already dusk when, with his protecting arm around her, Maria stepped on deck. Wide-eyed, she looked around on a strange world; there was nothing but the vast deep about them—as far as the eye could see there was nothing but sky and water.

'Oh John, just the ocean and our ship. No land or

other ships. We are so alone on the ocean.' She trembled, feeling they were waifs in another world, a weird, watery world.

'Maria, soon you will get so used to this scene you will not be frightened anymore.'

He smiled down cheerfully as she turned her face and, looking up into his eyes said, 'I'm not really frightened. I guess it's because I am with you, John.' As she said this, a warm feeling came over her, the realization that all that mattered in her life was to be with John.

Chapter 9

FOR a while, one day was like the next for Maria, who spent much of her time in the gimballed bed except for the times when John came and insisted she go to the saloon and try to eat.

'Make the most of the food we have on the table; after a while we'll run out of the good eatings we stocked up on from shore and then there'll be ship fare. Doc can make it good and tasty, but you may not find it to your liking.'

Maria could tell his firm tones came from concern for her health, and she forced herself to eat some meat, summer squash, and Indian pudding. Henry, the steward, hovered about her like a mother hen trying to bring something that would tempt her appetite.

'Missy Hamblin,' he told her when the captain and the second mate had left, 'you look awful weak and sicklike.' He shook his head, a troubled look on his kindly black face as he poured more tea into her dainty teacup from the red lacquered teapot John had bought especially for her use. 'My captain is mighty worried, I can tell.' Maria noticed he always referred to John as 'my captain,' and in a way was more concerned about his beloved captain than about her.

'Don't worry, Henry. I'll be all right once I get used to the rolling ship. By the way, how are the poor men on the crew who've been so sick, like me, not used to the sea? Poor men! Sick in that awful fo'c'sle?'

Henry gave a low chuckle, 'Missy, them's likely now working. The mates, especially mate Rogers, the one with the red hair and bad temper—what a bad temper!—gets them up and goin', sick ones and all. Uses the end of the rope likely. They've no time to pay attention to stummic miseries. The mates are hard men. Yes, mebbe they have to be. Thems that are still sickly and puky, well, Mr. Richards leaves them at next port. Says their mothers have spoilt them and never let them get guts. Guess that's so—only men with guts can work on a ship, 'specially a whaling ship, that's for sure.' And Henry went back to the pantry and his work.

Maria made her way back to the stateroom and tried to pick things up and make the room neater but soon had to give it up and return to the bed as the miserable sickness came back. Probably the seas were rougher and rocked the ship more now.

John appeared a while later, announced that the squall had passed and suggested Maria go up with him and watch from the quarterdeck something interesting: the mates were going to choose the men to man their whaleboats.

'Tomorrow we start whaleboat practice and soon we'll be whaling,' John said, and there was an exuberance in his voice. 'And, you, my darling, will be catching on to walking with the roll of the ship, but it takes practice. So up, Maria, and I'll help you.'

For a moment a wave of resentment went over her. He's being cruel like the mates with the greenies, she thought. But she got up even though her stomach was still growling, and holding on to John's arm went up on deck. She was surprised how the fresh air revived her.

Still clinging to John with one hand and the gunwale with the other, she watched the mates take turns picking out their men from the line of rough-looking men, some mere youths. The second mate was having his turn. She heard the mate say 'Portugee—harpooner,' when he called his name. Maria noticed that Mr. Richards had already chosen Smitty and the Pirate; they were standing by his side. She turned to ask John something but the seasickness was coming back. John, noting her greenish pallor, quickly led her down the companionway and, picking her up, carried her to the bed.

'Don't get discouraged, Maria, one of these days you'll be walking with a sailor's roll like the rest of us,' he said cheerfully.

'Discouraged?' Maria moaned bitterly. 'Maybe I'm like the sickly, puky men Henry talked about. I've been spoiled, overprotected, and have no guts. Can I ever get that horrible word "guts" that one needs to live on the ship?' Maria shut her eyes to keep back the tears.

John gently smoothed back her hair as he talked in a quiet voice, a serious voice. 'Maria, don't worry about "guts." That's for men. You have plenty of courage, darling, but you need to grab at it, hold it like the thistle. Remember?'

And he added with a chuckle, 'When I first laid eyes on you at Uncle Asa's and lost my heart to you.'

Maria reached up and caught his hand, bringing it to her cheek as she looked up and smiled at him. 'Yes, I remember. I can just see you walking up the path. I think I took a liking to you then and there.'

John leaned down with an affectionate pinch on the

cheek and a 'must get back on deck.' Then he was out of the stateroom and she could hear him leaping up the companion ladder. Unconsciously she shut her hand as if grasping the thistle. 'Yes, I will get over this seasickness and I'll start now.' With determination she got off the bed, but had taken only a few steps when the seasickness drove her back again. Disconsolately she sobbed into her pillow, 'Will I ever get over being seasick?'

As the ship made its way eastward, carried along by the westerlies, the seas became less rough and Maria found it easier to get about, to adapt to the roll of the ship. Even more to her amazement, she found herself hungry, even for the simple fare of 'salt horse,' salted dried meat, boiled potatoes, and hard biscuits.

But whenever certain winds came and the ship started going this way and that, the old seasickness came back and Maria had to take to the bed until the ship stopped its 'gyrations.' At such times that was what the ship seemed to do, gyrate.

She would ask John why later, she thought. For now she was grateful to lie on the swinging bed and clutch the pillow to help her stop the dizziness.

'Yes, the ship gyrates because sometimes it is caught by cross winds,' John explained to Maria later when it was calm and they sat in the Big Cabin, he at his desk and she in her small rocker darning John's socks.

Winds, ocean, I hate it all, Maria thought, but said nothing to John now engrossed in making notations in his personal log book. She glanced affectionately at his bent head, thinking the poor dear was having problems enough now, especially with some of the greenies not able to learn the ropes. Sometimes Maria felt John slept with one eye to the ceiling, to the telltale compass,

Thistle in Her Hand

going up on deck in the night to help the mate with some bungling greenie, or other difficulty.

Funny thing, Maria mused, John still seemed content with his lot and when alone with her in the stateroom was usually a dear, loving husband. And busy as he was, he took time to give her pleasant surprises.

One morning after part of the night on deck he came down at dawn and got her up to watch the sunrise. A startling sight: a big ball of gold on a sea of sparkling golden waves.

'Nowhere but on an expanse of ocean like this can you see such a sight,' John told her, holding her arm tight to his side. 'God in his firmament,' he whispered reverently.

For days she could hear sounds of great activity overhead all day long, but she had felt too miserable to care what was going on. But one morning she decided to go up to the quarterdeck and see for herself. It was a day when the sea was quiet and she felt able to get about.

She was amazed to see so many men working, and at so many things. It seemed like a great many shops combined—coopers, carpenters, blacksmiths, and sailmakers. She watched the last with special interest, being a needlewoman herself.

'What heavy iron thimbles they have to use!' she remarked to Doc, who came out of the galley to join her. His thin, sun-browned face was wrinkled in smiles to see the captain's little lady getting used to sea life. And Maria smiled back; she liked this oldish man who John told her had been a whaler until an accident crippled one leg, and who now continued sea life as the ship's cook and first aid man.

'The sailmaker is very important on the ship,' Doc

said in his downeast drawl. 'He's kept busy all the time because sails tear and even break, if the man at the wheel don't turn the sail right. But, s'cuse me, Ma'am, I must get back to my pots an' pans.' And with a friendly bob of his head Doc hobbled back to the galley.

For a moment Maria stood, fascinated, watching the sailmaker working on a piece of canvas, manipulating the heavy shears, then she turned to go down the companionway. As she did so, she caught sight of a swarthy man by the tryworks grinding on a piece of metal. He stopped his grinding and stared at her in open admiration. There was an insolent air about him which alarmed her and she hurried to the companionway. That looked like the man Portugee. Silly to be so alarmed, but after this she'd better go on deck with John.

One day John told Maria that there would be some excitement on deck. That afternoon Maria hurried up to watch. It was quite calm and Maria felt quite alive and active. John had told her they were going to practice taking the ship—managing the sails to change the course of the ship. There was much excitement with the officers giving orders. The men tried to obey them, but many had not learned the names of the ropes the officers called out and they made many mistakes.

'I am afraid I should be a dull scholar at learning all the names of the ropes,' Maria told John that evening. 'I can't get the time the different bells ring. Let's see—at twelve noon and midnight, twelve bells, and twelve-thirty, one bell. At one, two bells and at one-thirty, three bells.

'Then at four, eight bells and at four-thirty, one bell, and the routine starts again. At five, two bells—the supper hour for the men. Ours is five-thirty, three bells.

It goes on to eight o'clock when it is eight bells again and so on.

'Will I ever learn all that, and the times the different watches go on?' Maria was now feeling the need to know and John grinned.

'Maria, my sweet chickadee, you'll know so much about the ship one of these days you'll be ready to take a turn at the wheel.'

'How my brothers would be surprised to hear you say that,' Maria giggled, then suddenly tears welled up in her eyes.

'Oh, John,' and Maria threw herself into his arms. 'When are we going to get letters from the family, from home?'

'When we get to the Azores—maybe, if a clipper ship has gone there lately. If not, when we get to Buenos Aires, for sure. That is our first official stop. The Company mail goes there.'

'I hope so. It seems so long since I have seen or heard from the family, yet it hasn't been two weeks,' Maria said. Then noting John's somber look, she added, 'But I am glad I am with you. And you'll see me get guts, and make a good sailor.'

'What?' John drew away from her, shocked.

Maria, now laughing, told of her conversation with Henry. 'And I want to start by helping you do the washing out under the skids.' It had worried Maria to have John and the cabin boy take the tubs out, hang a line, and John scrub the clothes and help the boy hang them on the line, tying the clothing on or using strong iron clips to keep it from being blown away.

Fortunately there had been much rain, so soft water was no problem. Maria had washed her own underwear whenever she was not seasick—washed it in a bucket and hung it on a line John had put up for her in the stateroom. With the porthole open enough wind entered to dry the clothes. Now she wanted to do the laundry as at home, and hang it on the line to dry in the sunshine.

John shook his head, 'We'll wait a while, my darling washerlady, until you are surer on your feet. Besides, in case we raise a whale, the skid space will have to be cleared immediately for the extra boats to be brought down and readied for emergency, and the clothes and lines will be piled in a heap in a hurry.' He talked in a quiet voice, a serious voice.

'Maria, as I said before, don't worry about guts—that's for men. You have plenty of courage. It'll be there when you need it. I know now it was selfish of me to let you in for this rough life, but how glad I am you are here.' And John leaned over and pressed his lips hard on hers and she wound her arms around his neck to hold his face closer to hers.

'We are now in the haunts of the sperm whale,' John told Maria as they took their evening walk on the quarterdeck. 'Two men are now on watch in the main crow's nest, and one in the foremast crow's nest during the day. We're more than ready for whale hunting business to begin, I'd say.'

'I hope the greenies are ready to prove themselves,' Maria said with a sigh of resignation. Every evening at sunset she had watched as it was 'all hands shorten sail!' The constant drills rapidly drilled into even those inexperienced and clumsy landsmen how to find their way aloft with ease, and how to do something else besides hold on for their dear life once they got there. Maria recalled that they seemed to learn very fast under terrible cursing and a storm of blows from the tough mates, especially the cruel redheaded Irish mate.

And then there was one full day of tedious boat drills. The boats were lowered and manned, and the 'greenies' had their first practical lesson in the business of whaling. Maria had watched, fascinated by the precision and efficiency of the entire crew in this ordeal.

The very next morning came the call from aloft: 'blackfish!' The officers were pleased. The men would now have a real test and trial of the skills before the real whaling began. John and the mate hurried from breakfast up to the deck.

Maria, curious, went up to the charthouse to find a comfortable seat among the vegetables and sacks of potatoes and observe the action on deck and in the boats. She could see in the distance numerous large blackfish cavorting about and enjoying themselves. But she grew anxious as she watched the boats full of excited seamen being lowered away and leaving the ship for the hunt.

Doc, watching the scene from the door of the galley, came over to Maria, 'Good, good practice for the real whalin', Mrs. Hamblin!' He said, his voice resounding with pleasure.

'What do you mean, Doc?' Maria questioned.

'Well Ma'am, there's 'bout fifty of those blackfish just waitin' for our men to git 'em. Then all hands will turn an' flench 'em, that is, strip 'em of their nice black skin, then try-out the blubb'r to make a good many casks of that fine oil!'

'But Doc,' Maria protested, 'those fish aren't whales! Why do the men have to kill them?'

'Why those gambolling blackfish are small-toothed whales, Mrs. Hamblin!' Doc chuckled, explaining. 'Jist like a miniature cachalot 'cept that its head is rounded at the front and its jaw is bowed. Why they'se 'bout ten or twenty feet long and weigh anythin' from one to three tons! Best of all, those frolicsome critters have heads full of oil—at least one or two barrels for us from each.'

'Oh no!' groaned Maria in sympathy with the fish as she watched the men plunge their lances into the animals and the injured fish try to flee. 'It's plain carnage, that's all! I am not going to witness it any more!' she declared, leaving the deckhouse and hurrying down to the cabin in anger. She threw herself onto the bed in disgust.

Later that morning as she was doing some chores she felt the ship heave to once again. Looking through the porthole she saw that chain-slings were being passed around the one...three...five bloody carcasses of the animals that were just shortly before gambolling playfully about in their schools like porpoises. The men heaved away cheerfully, probably using the tackle rope and windlass as John had described, lifting the monsters right on deck. After eight bells rang, apparently giving the men a short break, Maria went up on deck to see the carnage for herself. There they lay, a mountainous pile of lifeless blubber! She looked over at the trypots readied with wood underneath to be lighted after lunch to render the harmless animals into oil.

Maria began to cry. She turned slowly and proceeded down the companionway to the Big Cabin. She no longer wanted to eat lunch or talk to anyone, even to John. She sat down in her rocker and immersed herself in her mending.

Soon afterward she heard John's steps bounding quickly toward the cabin. She cringed, knowing he was coming to share his excitement over their day's conquest with her. Now he burst into the room, but finding that Maria was visibly upset he walked up to her and took the mending out of her hands. He took her hands in his and looked straight at her. She averted her eyes, trying to keep John from seeing the tears swelling in her eyes by turning her head away. But his firm hand rested against her wet cheek and made her face him.

'I'm sorry this bothers you, this killing of the blackfish, Maria. This is our life on a whaling ship, this is our business, and this is our means to get back home.'

Maria sat quietly and looked down at the floor. It was hard for her to accept this and she wished John did not realize it, but he did.

John gently lifted her chin, smiled at his sad little wife, and brushed away her tears with his handkerchief.

'Buck up, my darling! You'll be a fine seaman and captain's right hand lady and...I'll need you.'

Maria returned John's smile. It was a wan smile as she wiped her nose.

'Yes, I will.'

That afternoon and the entire next day were spent by the men flenching and trying-out the blackfish catch. Even though only five fish were captured and nine barrels of oil rendered, the men had to toil and sweat through this, their first exercise in working together and on The Roman. Maria remained below deck throughout, except for the dinner hour when the men went below to eat and she could walk alone with John on deck for a half hour before they ate their dinner. Smoke and an awful stench filtered into their quarters, but Maria tried to ignore it and to quietly go on with her work. She knew that these few days of discomfort were only a prelude to what lay ahead with the processing of the sperm whales. She listened to the activity on deck, occasionally catching John's voice barking out commands to the toiling seamen. But most of her hours were spent alone, buried in thought.

With the first few barrels of oil in the hold, The

Roman sailed without event for the next few days. The air cleared and the ship life relaxed. But one stiflingly hot afternoon, when Maria was sitting in her rocker mending a tear in John's jacket, using every wile at her needle's command to make the mend invisible, she suddenly stopped. Laying aside her fine work she walked restlessly about the small quarters in her wrapper and thin muslin underskirt. John was making the usual ship inspection.

Did she imagine the ship was beginning to roll more than usual? She went to the porthole in the stateroom and saw the waterline rising against the glass. Yes, the ship was rolling considerably, long, slow rolls. The sea covered the porthole for a while and then it cleared, enabling her to see across a wide expanse of water, smooth, oily looking water. Why then was the ship rolling? A vague uneasiness enveloped Maria.

Instinctively, she began picking up loose articles and putting them in the safety of the clamped drawers of the chest. She wished John would come and tell her that everything was all right and no stormy weather was ahead, but he did not. The ship now began to dip and turn, and the creaking of the ship's timbers increased. The old nausea was coming back. She fled to the swinging bed and secured herself inside of it.

The ship tossed and rolled in the violent waves, the sea crashing against its timbers. The water rushed by the porthole, covering it entirely. The winds howled outside and the rain poured down in torrents against the ship. She gripped the sides of the bed as it rolled and rolled, but always kept level with its gimbals underneath.

Maria was terrified, she was certain The Roman would sink and they all would drown. Where was John?

Thistle in Her Hand

Why couldn't he come down to be with her? She cried out only to be answered by the waves and the wind crashing against the ship high above the porthole. It had come on so quickly. No one had even warned her. She started to repeat Psalm 91 as Mrs. Snow had told her to do when she was alone and frightened, repeating and repeating the words, never letting go her grip on the sides of the bed nor taking her eyes off the porthole.

She did not know how much time had actually passed in what seemed an interminable anguish, but she was startled to look out and see the sun shining down upon a wide expanse of smooth, oily water. The ship no longer tossed, but was rolled gently with the thick, undulating waves. Thank the Lord for taking care of them in this awful storm! Her whole body eased with relief, and she found herself smiling when John appeared by her side.

'Oh John, are you all right? That was an awful storm. I prayed and prayed...'

'Oh no, my dear,' John interrupted, 'that was no storm. That was just a short squall. A bad one while it lasted, but it didn't even last two hours. I'm afraid, though, that that powerful little squall threw the ship off course. Maria, you will surely know when a storm comes!' And, firmly, he took her hand in his.

'Oh yes,' Maria answered, 'I was a silly ninny to be so scared by only a squall! Why, I was almost angry that here we were going to drown and you were not down here with me! I was sure we were all going to drown.' She felt a little foolish now that all was so calm and John was there beside her.

John chuckled and looked at his wife. He had never imagined that even a short squall could terrify her so. How selfish, indeed, he was to bring her along. And how courageous she was to come. He did not want her to detect his concern, but what would happen when the real storms came?

'Let's go up on deck and get some fresh air, my lady. You can see how quickly the men do their repairs after a wind blow.' He pulled her up off the bed and brought her into his arms, giving her a strong hug. The two walked up on deck. Maria was so absorbed in her thoughts that John's voice startled her.

'There now, looks like the gale yesterday moved us from our noon position of yesterday.' He then took out his personal logbook from the desk and entered his findings in it. 'I'll have to adjust the ship's clock to the correct present noon position. Yes, my lady, and you shall see me do it!' he said teasingly as he lifted her chin and kissed her lightly. He was happy to hear Maria's gay little laugh again. For so long she had been pensive and tearful.

He then took the quadrant out of its mahogany case in the lowest drawer of his desk and started for the deck, followed by curious Maria. He was soon setting up the quadrant, pushing slides, and doing some squinting at the sun high over the mastheads.

Maria looked around the peaceful ship. She was amazed to find everything so quiet and orderly, as if there had not been a destructive gale the night before. All was quiet as the men on watch busied themselves at their tasks. The others, below, rested, waiting their turn to help run the ship. Chipps, the ship's carpenter, was busy making repairs on a whaleboat; the sail-maker wore his funny big thimble. The cooper worked on a barrel he was making in preparation for the whale hunt they were all expecting. Still, everything remained peaceful and subdued.

Suddenly she heard mate Richards call out to the

helmsman, 'Eight bells!' With that call the quiet ship awoke to instant life and stirred into activity. Maria saw the helmsman reach for the bell cord and ring eight lusty peals. One seaman grabbed a belaying pin and began beating a tattoo on the fo'c'sle hatch with a hearty call of 'Eight bells!' The words resounded in the fo'c'sle and steerage. 'Eight bells! Eight bells!'

The watch below turned out with a rush of feet. Delegations for dinner supplies appeared from the steerage and forward and Doc ladled food into their wooden 'kids' and 'kegs' as fast as they could move. This was the high point of their day when no whales were around.

Maria knew that the cabin folk would be served a half hour later. Suddenly, for the first time since they had sailed, she felt hungry and rejoiced with the men that it was the dinner hour.

She turned her head toward the weather side of the quarterdeck where John stood, his eyes glued to the telescope of the quadrant which he held in his hand. It was high noon and the tall captain, his red-gold beard and thick, bright hair, bleached by sun and spray, was intent on 'shooting the sun' to help him find the exact position of The Roman. Maria watched him move the index arm of the triangular frame until the mirrors reflected the image of the sun on the horizon. All the time he was explaining each step to his curious wife.

'Next I'll teach you how to compute a ship's longitude and latitude,' he said, giving her cheek a loving little pinch. Maria smiled in return. This part of whaling life she certainly did enjoy, imagining herself doing this for the captain sometimes once she knew it well enough.

'Now we'll go down to the cabin and check the

chronometer,' said John, starting toward the afterhouse and down the companionway.

'I must adjust the chronometer to the new noon position,' he explained as he worked with what they often called the 'jewel of the captain' on a whaling ship. Maria admired the exceptionally precise timepiece.

'We have moved many miles from the noon position of yesterday, and the clock upstairs is a little off in sympathy.'

Maria shook her head in despair. Would she ever understand the workings of the chronometer and the barometer by the clock? Lisha used to talk about those instruments with the other boys and with father, but she had never listened. They had talked in a foreign language to her. But now those words were taking on real meaning, like chimes of the grandfather clock standing in the hall back home, and the church bells on Sunday mornings and prayer meeting nights. And, oh yes, the school bells.

A thought struck Maria. 'But, John, what do you do when the sun's not out? In stormy weather?'

'In that case we have to work out the exact noon by dead reckoning, and that means guesswork as to winds, drifts, currents, and so forth. Then, when I do have a chance to shoot the sun again, I can set ourselves correct again. But this is not all. To find the longitude I usually shoot the sun soon after breakfast.'

John finished his reckoning, returned to his desk and made an entry into the logbook.

'But now, my dear wife, for some food. I see our half hour has passed,' and taking Maria's hands in his, he pulled her gently out of the little rocker and they hurried toward the saloon. Maria, by now famished, was glad to see that Henry was waiting patiently to serve them. Agrimonte, the third mate, was still eating.

Thistle in Her Hand

'Potato stew today! A good Cape Cod dish,' exclaimed Maria, sniffing the appetizing aroma of a favorite combination of potatoes, onions, and salt pork. 'And biscuits!' She could see that Doc knew his business; he saw to it that all were well fed. And into the noonday meal he put his best effort.

Agrimonte turned to John with a gruff yet knowing look. 'Sir, I hope Mrs. Hamblin don't think the ship is always quiet and we have good meals like this.' Then, turning to her, he said, 'Ma'am, when a whale is raised, there'll be plenty doin' round about. Even the meals will be forgotten. Ain't that so, Captain?' One bell sounded then and the mate hurried away.

'Yes, Mr. Agrimonte,' and John looked at Maria with concern in his eyes. She knew that he was wondering how she would take the days ahead. She had so much to learn; but she'd learn it, she thought with determination. She smiled up at John.

'Anyway, I am learning about the watches, John. Twelve-thirty is one bell and it must be Mr. Agrimonte's watch.'

A flicker of a smile showed John was pleased, relieved at the change taking place in Maria's attitude toward her new life.

'John, what day is today? I wish I had brought an almanac and could check off each day, counting off the days until we come home.'

'It is September ninth. We have been out at sea about sixteen days. But Maria, my beloved, I must give you another lesson. An almanac for you would not help as life on a whale hunt cannot be hurried. But time of day is important, absolutely essential, on shipboard, for, unless watches are carefully observed, there would be disaster. You will soon learn to tell time by the bells.' John ran his hands through his thick sun-bleached golden red hair, a gesture Maria was getting used to. It showed he was thinking deeply or was troubled. 'Maria, clock-watching and calendar-watching can drive men crazy at sea on a whaler.'

In the days that followed, Maria learned that even when nothing unusual was happening, a strict routine was enforced on The Roman. The watches soon became as familiar to her as the information given by the big gold watch John carried in his pocket. At midnight eight bells and at twelve-thirty one bell. At one two bells. At one-thirty three bells. At two four bells. At two-thirty five bells. At three six bells. At three-thirty seven bells. And at four eight bells and end of the first watch. Then started another turn of the bells until eight bells again and the end of the second watch. Even the routine of the dog watch of two hours between six and eight at night, which served to break the routine of the main four-hour watches each day, became understandable. Maria saw that the captain and mates kept their eyes on the time-keeper, the helmsman, to check his precision. He had the ship's clock, also on gimbals, by the compass, to go by.

And Maria learned to her dismay, that when it was pleasant, when the sea was calm, she could walk about easily, but when it was rough, misery returned, seasickness, and she would have to run to the stateroom and bend over the privy in the agony of nausea. She no longer noticed the green waters dashing by below, or the occasional creature, maybe even a shark.

Chapter 10

DELEGATIONS were coming in from the cabins, steerage, and forward for dinner supplies. Doc ladled out food into dishes for the cabins, wooden 'kids' and 'kegs' for the others, fast as they could move.

Just then there was a cheerful jingle of the handbell rung by Henry, the steward. John and Maria went out to the saloon. They sat down on one side of the table and the first mate on the other. Later at the second table would come the third mate and the cabin boy who helped the steward.

Mr. Richards, the first mate, said as he helped himself to another boiled potato and turnips, 'I hope, Captain, the Mrs. doesn't think it is always this peaceful and quiet on the ship.' Then, turning to Maria, he continued, 'When a whale is sighted you'll see and hear plenty of liveliness—and sometimes meals are forgotten—except by Doc. And in stormy weather even he sometimes forgets.'

'Some days are certainly rough on these whalers,' agreed John. He looked at Maria with a troubled expression. He dreaded those times for her; she knew little what they were like.

But before many days had passed she learned. In fact, she began learning the very next Sunday morning.

The trip up to that day had been uneventful. The ship was cruising over whaling grounds near the Bahamas, covering as much water as the wind allowed during the hours of daylight, with one or two men always on watch in the crow's nest. When night came, the whaler remained as stationary as possible under reefed sails, mainyard back. Since they had little work to do at night (there had been no 'trying-out' time) most of the men had been allowed to sleep, with only the necessary night watches. This, however, never altered their vigilance.

'It would not be safe,' John explained to Maria one night, 'because on the sea things happen suddenly and unexpectedly.'

The lookouts on the ship were kept every day from early dawn until four o'clock. After that it would not be safe to send boats, since they could be lost in the darkness.

Even Sunday found the men up on the perch high on the masthead, although Captain John kept Sunday on his ship as a day of rest with no work except that necessary for the care of the ship. No religious service, just a quiet observance of the Sabbath. But, the routine continued as usual as far as watches, meals, and lookouts for the whales were concerned. If whales were sighted there would be the customary chase after them.

Several times that week there had been the call of 'Ah-BLOWSO-OW!' and the captain, never an underling, hailed the crow's nest shouter with the shout of 'Where away?' The answer gave the direction, perhaps a stated number of 'points' off a bow or quarter of the ship, perhaps a guess at the distance away. Then the captain rushed below for the long and powerful

Thistle in Her Hand

spyglass hanging on the cabin wall, took his bearings by a look at the compass, swung into the main rigging, and hurried up the masthead.

Then Maria felt the tense waiting on the deck until his report came down, sometimes a long wait if the spouter was too distant for prompt recognition or if it chanced to sound before showing itself often enough for the necessary study. The verdict had been either 'finback' or 'sulphur bottom' or the name of some other bone whale of no great commercial value, whereat the people of the ship relaxed disappointedly, and glumly resumed the interrupted tenor of the day.

But that Sunday morning, as Maria sat in the stateroom having her own religious service while John hurried upstairs on duty, the call came. Not long afterward Maria heard John's voice, 'sperm whales! sperm whales!' followed by the order, 'Call all hands and get the boats ready.' Then there came an excited rush all over the ship as the watch below was aroused from the forecastle, steerage, and aftercabin by the joyous shouts and poundings.

Maria, heart pounding, lips white, rushed up on deck. John seemed like a different man, taller somehow, powerful, every bit a captain. She looked at him adoringly, but he paid no attention to her. She realized with dismay that at this moment he was not her John; he was the captain of The Roman. The ship turned as he barked staccato orders.

Doc, standing by the galley door, his hands floury, noticed Maria on the afterdeck, alone, bewildered. Wiping his hands on his apron, he joined her and explained what was taking place. Maria listened with gratitude to the kindly seaman.

'Captain's given orders so's the ship's working well to windward of the quarry, if that's possible, partly to give the boats a better working chance, and partly to keep the ship in better position so's the small boats and the whales won't git too far away. When startled those critters always hurry to the windward. Whales seem to know their safest path. They's sure not dumb critters, Mrs. Hamblin, especially that sperm whale; why they have mo' sense than many folks. I know all about 'em big monsters cause you know, Mrs. Hamblin, I was a whaler myself before I got myself crippled and since became a cook.'

'I am sure you were a right fine whaler, Doc. If your whaling was as good as they all say and as good as your cooking, those smart sperm whales are lucky you're up here explaining things to me and not out there hunting them down!'

'Well, Ma'am, I don't know quite about that,' Doc answered slowly, embarrassed by Maria's compliment yet thinking about what she said. What if he were still a whaler, might even be a mate by now or maybe even a captain of a small ship...?

The sails snapped loudly as the deck watch maneuvered them by John's orders. In two's and three's the men from below rushed to prepare the boats for lowering. Maria watched as kegs of water and ship biscuit were put on board, also oars, rowlocks, and small flags. More articles were brought speedily: a compass, lanterns, and other things Maria could not distinguish. Tubs of whale line were unlashed from their canvas coverings on top of the upper deckhouse and put into place in the stern of the boat.

'There's a lot of equipment goes into one of those whaleboats, ma'am. Besides the big things like oars, masts, and sails, there are ship biscuit, a compass, them oil-filled lanterns, matches, flags.' The whaler counted them off on his fingers.

'Flags?' inquired Maria, to keep him talking.

'Those flags are called "waifs" and are put into the dead whale's body in case the men go on after another whale. Later they come back and tow the carcass to the ship—or, more likely, the ship goes to the carcass.'

Maria nodded, trying to imagine the men doing all of these tasks in the cold and dark sea nights in such small boats on the rough sea.

'Now, now look, Mrs. Hamblin!' Doc said, pointing frantically to the stern of the boat where the ends of the lines were carefully being laid forward to the bow. His old eyes shone with excitement as he proudly explained the happenings on deck to the captain's wife. 'There's the boatsteerer...the harpooner...fastening those lines to the irons resting in their crotches...oh, excuse me, ma'am.' Doc reddened, having forgotten he was talking to a lady, then continued, '...the irons resting on holds on the frame of the boat. See how he set up that frame on the starboard side of the bow?'

Maria looked at the deck with the men scrambling about chaotically, all doing something or other. None of it could she understand, hard as she tried to listen to everything Doc was saying '...starboard sides, the this and that part of the frame, boatsteerers and whomever else,' he was speaking so fast and there was so much to see...

'...there you see a first iron and a second iron,' Doc continued without pause, 'for if he missed the first try that second iron would give him another chance. And if he was an extra expert why he might succeed in fastening to the whale with both irons!'

Now Maria saw John desert the mast at last and descend to the deck to supervise the launching of the boats for the chase.

'Clear away the larboard boat!' was the first order as

the ship came to lay, followed by the rush of the crew to their stations. The mate boarded the boat at its stern, the harpooner at the bow, each laying hands on the hoisting blocks that held the boat. Theirs was the responsibility to ensure that there be no twist of the tackle and no danger of the blocks letting go until the precise instant.

'Should this happen,' Doc said gloomily, 'and one end should drop faster than the other, the result would be a spill and probably a ruined boat. But that wouldn't happen as the other men are castin' off the "gripes" that hold the boat steady on the cranes.'

Maria, her hands clasped tightly against her chest in her excitement, saw the men fling aside the cranes. As the boat swung free, held only by the falls, they shouted, 'All clear, sir!'

'Lower away!' was the next order from the captain. With two men at each davit, the boat was dropped to the sea on even keel, the other four men tumbling into the boat from the side of the ship as she touched the water. An instant later all were in their places, oars out, the long steering oar in place, and the boat started away from the ship as the captain shouted final orders on direction.

Maria stared, unbelieving. The whole proceeding had not taken much more than a minute or two. Everything moved with precision.

Now the second boat, in the charge of the second mate, was beginning the same proceeding. Doc turned to Maria, 'Yes, that is the Pirate—a good man and a dang good harpooner. Can't say much for the harpooner in the second boat, that man Portugee. Good harpooner but an evil character if I ever did see one. He's probably escapin' from the law in Brazil or swearing vengeance

Thistle in Her Hand

for murder. The whalin' fo'c'sle is a good hidin' place for them types.'

'John says he was a doctor or surgeon at one time.'

'Captain shipped him on last voyage somewhere near Brazil,' the old seaman said, watching the second boat make its neat landing on the sea.

Curiously, Maria glanced down at the harpooner, a dark man with a heavy black beard. He looked up at her. Quickly she looked away. Ugh! The man's a murderer! Her body shivered at the thought. She had laid eyes upon him before and feared he may indeed have noticed her...and yes, he had. She was frightened.

But then she noticed that Smitty was in the same boat, his hair bleached blond by the sun and his skin rugged and tanned. Her mind was set at peace and her expression became pleasant again.

'Now for the belayin',' Doc exclaimed. Maria looked down at the men left on deck who were quickly making fast the ropes by winding them onto the cleats and pins. As Doc proceeded to rattle off a few yarns, Maria laughed with appreciation. How good it felt to laugh and forget all the thoughts and fears that troubled her mind! She loved Doc for making her laugh. He always made her forget she was on the whaling ship living in tiny, smelly wooden rooms with slits for windows—that she wore plain grey dresses and had no one in whom to confide her fears and troubles, no women to share with. He even made her forget the nagging nausea, always ready to creep up and strike her. She felt strangely comforted by him. Looking around, she noticed that the loosened gear had been 'belayed', as Doc described it, for security and neatness. The crew was working with sails as if the ship was about to put to course again.

'Where's the captain?' Maria asked, looking around the deck. Then she heard him bark out orders which put the ship in order again and watched him return to his high perch to keep a watchful eye on the distant doings. Maria blinked in the afternoon sun as she watched her husband at the masthead with his spyglass to his eye.

'Does he have to stay up there long, Doc?'

'Oh, yes, Mrs. Hamblin. He must never lose run of either boat. Remember the lives of all the men out there are in his care. Small wonder, ma'am, that a day of whaling leaves a captain a bundle of whacked nerves.'

Maria shaded her troubled eyes with her hand and continued to look at John.

'Poor dear—high up in that hot sun,' she murmured. He might be the captain, the 'Old Man' to others, but to her he was her beloved husband. She then noticed that John held the spyglass with his left hand while with his right he raised a long ball-tipped pointer.

'What's he doing now?' she asked.

'He's signalling. You see, Mrs. Hamblin, the boats can't always keep sight of the whale and sometimes they are so far from it they don't know whether it is still on the surface or has sounded. So they look at the ship and from there the captain signals with the pointer. See? The pointer's up. That means the whale is on the surface. Look...the pointer keeps pointing in their direction. If the whale goes down, then the pointer comes down, and the captain doesn't raise it again 'til the whale comes up. Then that black ball points out once more where to look. See! See! He keeps pointing in their direction. They're doin' fine!'

Doc gazed long without speaking. Then he said softly. 'It's dangerous whaling, but there's lots of excitement. I'd do anything to be out there. Here's my spyglass, Mrs. Hamblin, you watch what's going on out there. You can be sure they're mighty quiet in that boat—nobody's speaking, just hand signals. The whale has mighty sharp ears for only having those small holes. Their eardrums are 'bout the size of two big oranges. Notice the men just peak their oars as they git near the creature. Watch the mate. Can you see him?' Maria nodded. 'If he acts crazy-like, that means the whale is near. The harpooner gits ready to plunge his iron. Then the whale may sound—and they wait for it to come up again. Or it may take off and the boat is in for a real Nantucket sleigh ride. If he goes too far, they may cut the rope and say goodbye to the whale. We've caught whales that have two irons in 'em. Some of these tough critters swim all the way down from the Arctic like that in a year!'

'If it doesn't take them too far, what then?'

'The mate, or second mate, changes places with the harpooner and throws a lance right into the middle of the back if he can. The men have to be careful to keep the boat away from those powerful flukes. If not, there's a stove boat. And the men...' the old cook threw up his hands as he started to hobble away.

Maria hurried back to the stateroom and did her chores quickly. Then she combed her hair neatly into a braided roll at the back of her neck, put on her sunbonnet, and went back on deck.

With some difficulty Maria adjusted the spyglass and watched the boats, first one and then the other. Time went by and she found herself getting weary and dizzy from watching the gray-green waves rise and fall. Suddenly the black form of the whale appeared near the second mate's boat. Portugee plunged the iron. Then a high wave obscured the boat from her sight. Doc came limping up fast. He was visibly moved as Maria handed him the spyglass.

'There goes the boat. Whew! No sign of whale. It's sounded—the line's pro'bly flashing out of the boat over the roller at the bow so fast it's smokin'. Yes, they're pouring water over it. That rushing out of rope is a mighty dangerous thing, terrible dangerous. Why once when I was whalin' one of our men was caught in the loop of the flying rope, snatched out of the boat, drawn into the sea and never seen again. Another time one man's leg was burnt off as he fell against the rope and...'

Maria did not listen to the second story. She remembered Eben Robinson, her father's friend in Waquoit, who had lost his leg, burned off by the line rushing out. Now she understood the horror of how it happened. Her thoughts were suddenly of home...of her family...

Doc handed the glass to Maria.

'See...the whale's up, the second mate's changing places!'

After a while Maria could make out the second mate, lance in hand, raising and plunging it into the huge body. There was a terrible thrashing...a mountain of spray...it was hard to distinguish what was going on...how could the men keep the boats above water? Oh! The whale was now spouting...spouting blood!

Maria could stand no more. Poor whale...poor men. She hated it all. She saw over and over in her head the cruel line rushing out. She remembered again the one-legged farmer in Waquoit. Thanking Doc, she handed him back the spyglass and left him at the rail as she quickly found her way to the dark stateroom. She threw herself on the bed, grabbing at the pillow to keep out the awful visions from her head... the rushing rope, the murderous sailor with the heavy black beard, John high up the mast with the sun parching his hair and skin, the strange sound of the whale, audible above the din of the ship activity, the spouting blood, spouting blood, blood... Finally she fell into a sound sleep.

The saloon bell awakened her with a start. The room was totally dark. She felt the bell had been ringing a long time. Hurriedly she washed her face and smoothed her hair. Then she tucked in her waist, tightened her belt and, composed again, went across to the saloon. No one was there but Henry, the steward. 'Where is John?'

'The capt'n won't eat nothing til the men come back, Mrs. Hamblin. He wants yo' to eat.' Henry's dark face was animated; he kept listening for sounds from the deck above.

Maria drank her tea and ate a few bites of hash quickly, then hurried up on deck, feeling that she had failed John somehow. She had overheard that the whale was too large for the boat to tow back to the ship without great difficulty, so the ship was going to the whale. Maria couldn't bear to look at the huge, grotesque creature, fearsome even in death. In the darkness the lamps were burning and the deck buzzing with activity still. Something must have happened. John was at the rail giving the order, 'Get up the flukes chain!' A moment later he issued orders for picking up the boats. From the afterdeck, Maria watched the boats being hauled aboard almost as quickly as they had been lowered. The hunt was over!

Maria sighed with relief. But I must get used to this, she told herself. There will be much more of this ahead, so much more.

The day was almost over. The towline was tossed aboard and the body of the leviathan was drawn into place below the starboard gangway and securely fastened. The cutting gear was brought up from the hold and all was done to make possible an early work start the next morning. The men were too tired and the darkness too near to begin the cutting-in that night.

The captain told the men to relax and enjoy a good supper, with a treat of grog in store for them. The whalemen behaved with the jubilation of hunters, yet they knew that a hard day was coming with the cutting-in and the trying-out, and finally the storing of the 'greasy gold' and the spermacetti riches.

When he finally came to the stateroom, John was no longer the hard captain, but a tired man with raw nerves. Maria gently applied Bay Rum compresses to his temples and wrists as he lay on the gimballed bed.

'How good it is to have you here, my sweet Maria,' he murmured, resting.

Maria bent down and kissed him lightly on the forehead.

'Sleep now, John dear,' she said softly. 'Sleep...'

John was now fast asleep but not so Maria; she lay in bed, wide awake, thinking and listening. How quiet everything was! The ship was standing-to on a serene sea with only now and then a low wave hitting the side of the ship, or was it the dead whale? Maria shuddered at the thought of the monster form, almost as long as the ship.

Poor creature! Just a few hours before he was cavorting happily in the high seas, hurting no one. Now he hung there, dead. And tomorrow the layers of blubber would be peeled off in long blanket strips 'like peeling the skin off of an apple' John described it, the spermacetti from the head baled out like soft wax, and

Thistle in Her Hand

the lower jaw with its massive teeth removed and taken aboard for the men to decorate their 'fancywork.' Then the rest of the carcass would be cut free from the tackles for the sharks and scavenger birds to finish.

'Poor, poor whale!' Maria murmured softly to herself, 'has to lose his life because he carries something so important to mankind...oil for making the brightest light in our lamps...papa's library lamp...and its spermacetti taken from its head...like our brains...taken to make what we all think are the best candles...'

'Someday something more modern in illumination will be discovered,' John had told her the other evening when they stood side by side on the peaceful quarterdeck, watching the fiery ball of sun disappear in the salmon pink and mauve sky. He had talked about how they were experimenting with an earth oil, something called petroleum. They would refine it to make something else, kerosene, that would give a light more bright than even that of the sperm whale. Maybe that is the answer. Maybe it will be cheap enough to manufacture so the world can use it before the sperm whale is hunted down to extinction...if only it could be developed soon and end these whale hunts...all the dangers...having to turn the whale's body, its head...into oil, barrels and barrels and barrels of oil.

Maria fell into a fitful, uneasy sleep.

Chapter 11

BEFORE dawn the morning after the whale hunt, Maria was awakened by the great commotion above. Men moving about, equipment rolling. She could hear John's voice shouting orders, repeated by the mate, then by the three mates. Shouts to arouse the sleepers: 'Tumble-up lively there! No skulking! Cuttin'-in today!'

'Oh dear, the time has come for that awful cutting-in today. It's not right!' Maria muttered, 'that poor monster creature was so happy yesterday and today—' and she muttered some more as she dressed with resignation to go on deck. 'The sea is quiet, I can do it. I must. It will please John.'

Another desire was now becoming uppermost in her thoughts, the desire to move about and to talk to someone. Now that she was conquering walking on the ship without difficulty and her great fear of the sea, she was bothered by inactivity and loneliness. All her life she had been active and had had many friends and relatives to talk with. But now, when John would be gone all day and night, she had no one to talk to, nothing to do after cleaning the stateroom: no one but Henry, little Tim, and of course, Doc.

In one of her talks back in New Bedford, Mrs. Snow had cautioned her against talking to the cabin help too much, or even the mates at meals. For the sake of discipline and authority the captain must lead a lonely life, must keep above the officers, and of course, the crew. As whaler captains understood, familiarity breeds contempt, and they were bound by this understanding with their crew. If there was any conversation, joke telling, and so forth with the men it was the mate who did it, but the captain's wife remained removed. Her place was with the captain.

'Sewing and writing letters can keep me busy,' Maria said aloud as she put on her corset and some underclothing. She combed her hair into a knot at the neck and, looking into the small mirror above the washstand, 'No sense looking like a hag!' she added with a coquettish turn of her head. 'And now my old seersucker dress. "What cannot be cured, must be endured," stepmother would say.' Then she put on her bonnet and hurried to the saloon for a cup of tea and a piece of ship bread for breakfast.

'Henry, I'm going above deck to watch the cutting-in,' she told him, sighing as she thought of the day's operations ahead.

'Ma'am, the cuttin' in and that tryin'-out is some back breakin' and soul tryin' work,' Henry told her, feigning a wince as he served her breakfast. 'That'll sure be a tryin' time fo' yo', Mrs. Hamblin, 'specially fo' this bein' yo' first time.'

She could see that Henry was dreading the cutting-in ordeal, and for her especially.

When Maria finally reached the deck she joined John near the afterhouse. He was looking over the bulkhead and supervising the men standing on the cutting stage.

Thistle in Her Hand

'Good morning, Captain!' Maria said, squeezing his hand, 'mate Maria is ready to learn about the 'cuttin'-in!' She was determined to be cheerful and interested, and also look her best for her husband this morning.

'Well, good morning, my pretty lady! I am glad to see you are looking so well!' He was obviously pleased to see Maria and her growing interest in whaling. It surprised him that in such a relatively short time his landlubber had become not only accustomed to, but interested in his whaling life. He called Timmy and asked him to bring up a folding chair for Mrs. Hamblin.

'Now, Mrs. Hamblin, I will give you your first lesson in the cutting-in of the whale. The beginning of the barrel-filling, which will bring us home full of greasy gold before we know it!'

'Why, yes, my captain...or do I also call you "The Old Man?"' she teased him as she sat down and propped herself up in the folding chair, ready for her lesson.

'We'll begin by having you look over the bulwarks at the men on that wooden platform, what we call in official whale talk, the cutting stage.'

Maria stood up and peered over the bulwarks at the wooden platform suspended by ropes over the ship's side, four feet above the water. There were tackle and other whaling instruments she couldn't distinguish.

'Merciful heaven!' she gasped, bringing her hand to her throat, when she saw that below the platform was the headless carcass of the whale attached with massive chains to the side of the ship. 'Where's the head, John?'

John chuckled at his young wife sounding so much like a little girl seeing something for the first time in school.

'First of all, the head of the whale, sometimes called

leviathan, has already been severed and secured to the ship to be attended to next. You will see why later.'

Maria was glad she did not see the head, that grotesque huge thing with the awful little eyes, floating next to the ship. Maybe she would be fortunate enough not to have to see why later. But she smiled and continued to listen to John's proud explanation of the cutting in.

She looked again and recognized mate Richards and another mate on the platform. They were leaning against the handrail for support while they used the long spades to carve into the carcass. The other men on the platform were hoisting huge strips of blubber on board. It all looked so awful!

John was called away and Doc stepped over to explain. Although the morning was cool, the men on the ship were sweating at the task of hoisting the heavy blubber strips on board and cutting them into sections.

'Those, Ma'am, are the "blanket pieces" and the men are dropping them into the blubber room of the hold. Slippery business down there, Ma'am. You can see those men are jist drippin' with that oil.' Maria grimaced. John even used to do that horrible, hard work!

Doc continued, 'And in that blubber room they really sweat cuttin' the blanket pieces into small pieces about the size of a blanket.'

Papa would certainly call this a 'Herculean task,' thought Maria, wishing that he could see this to understand all the work that men like John went through for their lamps and candles! Doc continued to explain in his usual graphic detail what each man was doing on deck. Maria saw in amazement how hard, yet how efficient, was their work, transforming this huge creature into smaller pieces for their thriving little factory, all on the ship!

She looked back down to the platform and saw that finally the men on the cutting stage had seemingly finished their cutting-in. They unfastened the enormous chain that had held the huge whale and the remains of the carcass drifted off to be devoured by sharks. And to think John had said this was a small whale, only forty-five feet long. And didn't he say that sometimes there would be two whales caught at once? What then?

Doc excused himself to go back to work in the galley. Soon after, John returned, pleased and a little surprised that his wife was still on deck watching the whole process.

'Now, my dear pupil, our lesson will continue. If you look down again at the cutting stage you'll see that the men have finished with the cutting-in of the body and are now getting ready to work on the gold mine of the operation—on the head.'

'John, are all gold mines this grotesque and oily, or just the special ones inside sperm whales?' She kidded her professor, hoping that he did not realize just how disgusting she actually thought the whole ordeal was.

'And an impudent student at that! At least one demerit for you, Miss Maria,' John joked back. 'But watch now, with the head you'll see the men are separating it into two parts.' He continued more seriously as he supervised their activities from above.

'But why, John? Could they not bring the head on the deck instead of doing it down there? They could fall in the water and all of those sharks are swimming around the carcass!'

'Hardly possible, Maria. The head is about fifteen feet long, about one-third the length of the whale's body, eight feet in diameter, and the weight must be close to fifteen tons—thirty thousand pounds! To lift such a weight on such a small vessel as The Roman could buckle the mast and you can guess what the bulk would be across the deck.'

Maria nodded and watched as the men cut the head into two wedged pieces along a line running from just above the mouth back to the top of the whale's head.

'The upper piece where the two spout holes are located contains the "case," a sack filled with pure spermacetti. They bail out this liquid gold with a bucket, as you'll see them doing.

'Maria, I once counted fifteen barrels filled with spermacetti from one case alone.'

'Fifteen! I wonder how many candles the candle factory in Woods Hole would make from that one case?' Maria mused out loud, trying to calculate candles in the thousands.

'Well, Maria,' John responded to her cogitations with a grin, 'I'm sure it is over ten.'

'Oh yes, teacher-captain!' she quipped back and giggled.

'After removing the spermacetti the case is abandoned as useless,' John continued.

'And what happens to the other half of the head?'

'It's called the "junk," and that, my dear, is composed of alternate layers of rich oily blubber which makes very valuable oil. The rest is called "white horse." It is tough membrane and the men just throw it overboard. The teeth and lower jawbone are kept for the making of scrimshaw.'

'Junk and white horses,' Maria laughed.

Eight bells rang out, but the men continued their grueling work. As after storms, lunch, usually salt beef, ship's water, and biscuit would be brought to them and eaten while they worked. All the officers, including John, had not the time to break for lunch either. Maria went down to the saloon alone to eat. Doc and the rest were all busy getting the meals to the men.

Maria felt uncomfortable sitting alone in the saloon and eating with everyone else on the ship toiling so hard. She looked at the food on the table and realized that the cutting-in, seeing the sharks gnaw at the whale's carcass, watching the men bail out the grotesque, fatty, oily head of the whale, seeing the oil gush like water during the cutting-up process, had ruined any type of appetite she may have had before. After a few sips of tea she left the saloon for the cabin to rest and eventually dozed off in her little rocker.

She awoke with a start. The small room was filling with black smoke and the stench was terrible. They must have begun trying-out the oil, she realized with dismay. This was the potent stench that Mrs. Snow had warned her about. She had told her that it sometimes lingers for days with a big whale or a multiple catch. 'Ugh,' Maria uttered, putting her hand, with its slight Bay Rum scent, to her nose.

Reluctantly she put on her sunbonnet and headed up to see what the men were doing. She knew it would be unpleasant, even Doc had warned her of that, but it was better than sitting below in the stench and smoke-filled cabin. She knew John would be up there, maybe waiting and wondering if she would join him and watch the process so important to him and the men—and now to her. It meant they were nearer to home.

When she reached her watching spot close to the afterhouse entrance, Maria had hardly seated herself on the folding chair placed for her by the cabin boy that morning than she saw John striding over to her. His eyes shone with pleasure and surprise; his tired face beamed as he greeted her. Maria decided she was glad for that reason that she had come on deck to watch the horrible ordeal. She hoped that John was not aware of how she detested it all and how the sight of the men, the whale, and now the stench of the trying-out brought on her nausea again.

The deck was covered with pieces of blubber cut up into pieces about eighteen inches long and six inches square. John explained that the men in the hold, the 'blubber room men,' were below squeezing themselves in as best they could between the greasy masses of fat and cutting it into those 'horse pieces' to toss up on deck.

'Being down there doing this you become so saturated with oil, Maria, it's as if you just took a bath in a tank of it! When I was a blubber room boy it was so hard to maintain a footing when the ship rolled that every tumble was right into the blubber running with oil!' John explained to the grimacing Maria.

She was hard pressed to find anything more revolting that she had ever heard tell of at home, and shocked, too, that John had once done these things, that he was at one time one of those men she would only watch from above as the captain's wife, but never deign to speak to! She often felt so pampered and foolish and young when he would tell her of his experiences and when he commanded the ship with such authority.

The men were dragging the horse pieces forward with blubber hooks to the mincing machine near the tryworks. It looked to her somewhat like a chaff cutter, except that the knife wasn't even attached to the machine and it only rose and fell without cutting right through the blubber.

Thistle in Her Hand

'The men only deeply score the pieces instead of cutting them up in small pieces so that although they are sliced thin so as to quickly get the oil out of the blubber, it is more convenient in handling the refuse when there is a thin strip holding the pieces together. This refuse is the only fuel we use for try-pot fires,' explained John. Though she could not understand everything John was explaining she concluded that the whole process was not unlike the way she sliced up pork at home for use in baking beans. John laughed at her analogy. She was indeed seeing his life through very different eyes than his own. Hers were the eyes of a landlubber.

'Those pieces in the tub, called the "book leaves," are now ready to go into the tryworks and have the oil in them boiled out. They are mighty heavy, as you can see.'

Maria recognized the two harpooners attending the trypots. One was the Portugee man, his face and thick arms covered with sweat and his stout frame, like that of the other men, soiled and dripping with oil. The two men were replenishing the try-pots with minced blubber from the hopper at the port side, and bailing out the sufficiently boiled oil into the great cooling tank on the starboard. Another officer superintended the mincing while mate Richards seemed to exercise a general supervision over all.

As one by one the pieces were forked from the tub to the trypots, a smelly, oily smoke filled the air. John fanned vigorously with his cap to keep the smoke from Maria's face. She held her handkerchief to her nose as she watched the pieces dancing around in the huge pots, until, drained of all oil possible, only a crisp curl remained; these remains, about the size of a person's head, were skimmed out by a large ladle and were what

John called the scraps. Even from where she was sitting she could feel heat from the intensely hot fire this fuel made to keep the huge cauldrons boiling. How could the men on deck stand it? And John had done that also!

'It seems like adding insult to injury, doesn't it, John, to first kill the whale and then make him cook himself into oil?' Maria said with a smile.

'But it saves a forest of trees and wood gets very scarce on these ships at sea, Maria, as you will notice before many weeks. Besides, those scraps make a hotter fire than wood.'

This information did not surprise or please her. She knew she would be living with the stench in her hair and her clothes for a long time and she remembered the jokes people used to tell about the putrid smell of whaling folk off the ship. She could hardly believe that she was one of them now. She would wash her clothes in Bay Rum if she had to before she arrived in New Bedford!

Soon a column of black smoke poured out the back arches almost halfway to the mainyard and drifted away on the lee quarter in graceful curves. As she looked about for John, who had had to leave her there, she noticed that no man was at the wheel nor was there a lookout! The vessel was 'hove to' under two close-reefed topsails and foretopmast-staysail, with the wheel lashed hard down. What if someone runs us down, she wondered, but chuckling, realized that the glare of the tryworks fire, to say nothing of the blazing cresset, could have been seen for miles!

Seeing that John was busy on deck, Maria quit her watching post, hoping to escape the rancid, hot air and return to the stateroom to be away from it all. Even though the whale was only a 45 foot male, she heard

Thistle in Her Hand

that the whole business would last into the night. The stench and smoke seemed to pervade everything and everywhere. Her 'home,' the two tiny dark rooms below deck, was unbearable now. Even her charthouse was surely filled with smoke and stench directly from the deck. Nausea gripped her in the heat of the close quarters. Covering her nose and mouth with her handkerchief she ran into the water closet to vomit, but instead began dry heaving uncontrollably.

She moaned. She had not eaten any lunch or breakfast. She collapsed onto the bed with her head in her pillow and cried. She was angry at herself for crying, but it was so awful, so much worse than she had expected. She ought to get up, tidy herself, and go up to the deck to watch the 'horror show' and keep poor John company. He must be at the great cooling tank where, he had explained, oil sufficiently boiled was bailed into a huge hose down to the large casks in the lower hold below. This was the modern method of cooling and stowing oil.

In years past, John had told her, the men used to pour the oil from the tryworks into large casks and then shift and lash the casks to the rails on each side of the quarterdeck.

Maria shivered as she thought about the huge casks filled with oil being shifted about on the greasy deck of the rolling ship. Doc had told her how 'one stumblin' man meant a slide of a ton'n a half of weight and a small heap of corpses somewhere in the lee scuppers.'

John had explained to her that oil cooled that way in the tropics took three days before it could be stowed in the hold.

The smoke seemed to grow intense and Maria, fanning herself vigorously, decided not to go up to the deck but to stay in the cabin and write letters to the folks at home. She would have them ready for when The Roman met a whaler going back to New Bedford. Maria found that writing letters relieved her greatest trial—loneliness.

Today she would write to Milly and tell her of the flying fish that flew on deck the night before.

She wrote on her writing pad:

Dear Milly,
Last night a flying fish flew on the deck and I had a chance to see one close. It is small like a sucker with dark and light spots. It has beautiful wings made of thin skin with a sinewy substance that could close the wings together when not flying.
The little flying fish swim to the surface of the water and skim quite a long way before they duck under water again. A big hug from
Aunt Maria.

Maria, suddenly feeling very tired, stopped writing and put her head on the pillow for a little nap, but slept on until John came down to rest. He awakened her, exhausted but jubilant.

'Maria, the job is over and thirty-five barrels are stowed away! The men are now scrubbing the deck!'

When Maria climbed on deck in the morning she marvelled at how the decks had regained their normal whiteness. Yet the men were still scrubbing the rails, paintwork, and decks.

John was finally resting in the stateroom. The air had cleared and the stench diminished considerably once the try-pot flames had been extinguished. 'Dirty work for clean money,' Doc would say all the time, 'dirty work for clean money.'

Thistle in Her Hand

Yes, it would have been the most unpleasant living she had ever endured had John not been with her whenever he could. Maria inhaled deeply, relishing the sea breeze as it filled her lungs. The ordeal was behind her now. Yes, there would be more to come, many more, but she hoped they would come soon, for they were now thirty-five greasy gold, clean money barrels closer to home.

Chapter 12

THE evening meal was eaten in heavy silence in the saloon that night. The light of the flickering flame from the whale oil lamp on the mizzenmast column at the table end danced across the wooden plates resting solemnly against the fiddles. It was an ample meal of dried beef, potatoes, and turnips with ship bread, and plenty of tea. The two tired men, the captain and mate Richards ate without speaking. Their thoughts were elsewhere. Maria knew where...on the barometer. She could feel the ship beginning to roll more than usual, long, slow rolls. Maria could not eat. Her stomach was tightening and the food was hard to swallow. She, too, listened in silence...and watched.

When the second mate arrived to take mate Richards' place at the table, he reported that the barometer was going down, down, down. John finished his tea with a gulp and hurried on deck. Soon she heard his terse, staccato orders to 'furl the sails' and 'batten down' everything. Maria's uneasiness increased with every passing moment. The Roman's timbers made noises she had not heard before. She tried to finish her dinner, but couldn't; the ship was lurching back and forth too much. She just sat on at the table, fighting against seasickness. The wind whistled and moaned down the companionway. Maria shivered, pulling her wrapper around her.

Now everyone moved fast, purposefully, each intent on his assigned task. The cabin boy and Henry, the steward, came in and cleared the table quickly, then told her the captain advised her to go to the stateroom with them to prepare for the storm. There was a momentary lull and the three worked together. All movable pieces were safely put away into chests clamped to the floor. Maria did the best she could, while battling the worsening nausea, to put away toilet articles and shoes into the chests. Henry, his ebony face sympathetic, handed Maria a small brown vial of smelling salts.

'M's Hamblin, dat's a good thin' to have by yo' in this mean'n rough weather. And yo' 'ad best stay in bed. Yo' not us'd te knockin' about, yo' kin git hurt awful, awful bad.'

Maria thanked Henry and put the smelling salts bottle under her pillow. Finally the boys saw to it that all the drawer locks were firmly clamped down; then they left her. Their disturbed glances full of concern for her in this, her first storm at sea, made her feel even more fearful. The stateroom, divested of familiar things, had a dismal, frowning look in the eerie light of a sunless evening.

Above, the men were strangely silent. There was no swearing or commanding in belligerent tones, only the sound of bare feet running around the deck. And then, everyone seemed to wait. In the total darkness she felt the ship rolling considerably in long, slow rolls. The sea covered the porthole for a while, then it cleared...only,

Thistle in Her Hand

rough water. If only there was a light, but even the light in John's cabin had been extinguished for fear of fire. The dark sea rushing by the portholes portended disaster.

She had to find John. She made her way to the cabin, clutching at the cupboards or walls. Just then a squall hit the ship and sent her reeling toward the captain's chair. She managed to crumple into its stout arms until the ship should right itself again.

There John found her a little later. He picked her up like a child and placed her gently in the bed. His voice was not that of John, her husband, but of a stern, serious man, the captain of the ship, as he commanded her to stay in bed. In no circumstances should she leave it until his return. The boat would soon be pitching and she had to be careful. With that he hurried back up to the deck, leaving her alone in the pitch darkness of the cabin as the boat heaved and rocked.

A mighty squall struck and the ship reeled as if all the demons of hell had been suddenly let loose. The murderous green water crashed up against the dark portholes. The violent waves now pounded the ship relentlessly. The waves broke overboard, wildly tossing and battering the whole frame of The Roman. The ship lurched forward powerfully as the storm gathered fury and intensity.

The stateroom became unbearably hot and close. Maria retched with violence, her stomach thrown into convulsions with every lurch of the ship. She searched for the smelling salts. Her hand felt around the swinging bed for the bottle. She grabbed desperately for the vial which leaned precariously against the corner of the swinging gimbal bed. But the careening ship sent it reeling crazily across the tilted floor.

Maria crawled out of the bed, gripping its sides and

trying not to fall across the room. She must get that precious bottle. At that moment, the ship flung back into position, pitching Maria against the chest of drawers; her lip was cut on the exposed clasp. Another heave threw her against the washstand. Her weak, frail body was thrown about the dark room, just like The Roman in the sea. In desperation, Maria finally retrieved the bottle and somehow got back into the bed. She lay there sobbing and moaning, feeling the blood on her cheek and lips. Her head throbbed. Her stomach knotted. She gasped, inhaling the stinging salts.

'Wretched, wretched sea!' she cried, gripping the bed. The cabin had become stiflingly hot in the darkness. She could feel the sweat and blood on her face and hands. The putrifying smell of the small room closed in on her. Her body languished in pain. 'Wretched, horrible sea!' she cried aloud into her drenched, twisted pillow.

She looked up at the sound of someone entering the cabin. Doc's figure appeared in the doorway. The captain had sent him to see how she was faring in the storm. His large warm eyes surveyed the room and instantly sized up the situation.

'Oh, Mrs. Hamblin, poor lady! I must get you some hamamelis!'

In spite of her pain and misery, Maria watched in amazement as the crippled old whaler made his way into the captain's cabin, then returned, moving with the ship as if he were part of it. He handed her a cloth soaked in hamamelis. Maria felt comforted by the old seaman's presence. She thought back to her father coming in to soothe her and put a chilled cloth to her head when she was a little girl sick with fever.

'Now you had best stay in that bed until this danged

storm is over, Mrs. Hamblin, or the captain's goin' to be right angry with you lest you git hurt agin!' The old man limped toward the door.

'Doc, where is my husband? Where is the captain? Has anything happened to him?' she cried in sudden fear.

'No, ma'am, but these last hours, why he's been at that wheel himself working like the dickens to get the ship out of a trough! He and the helmsman are lashed to that wheel. This is a terr'ble storm, Mrs. Hamblin, a real hurricane. The worst I've seen. But our captain, he's great. If anyone can see us through this one, he can. Now just you lie there and pray to the good Lord to help him.'

With these final words the old seaman balanced his way out of the room. Maria felt strangely comforted. She had great faith in John at the wheel. She prayed earnestly for him up there battling to keep his ship afloat. She prayed as she pressed the soaked cloth against her swelling lips and cheek. She could scarcely move her body. It ached all over. The ship still rocked and lurched in the storm. Thrashing waters pressed against the porthole and then lurched away. She continued to pray.

Thus she lay through the night until the storm began to subside. She finally fell into a deep sleep and did not wake until the sound of meal bells. Startled, she sat up and looked through the porthole. The storm had passed and the sun was shining! Hammering and pounding announced repairs already begun. Otherwise, life on shipboard soon resumed its usual tenor. She could hear John's voice and wondered if he had had any rest.

Painfully she got off the bed and went to the mirror over the washstand. 'What a sorry looking creature!'

was her self appraisal. She had learned her lesson. She would stay in the swaying bed during any subsequent storms. She sighed deeply, thinking of the storms ahead that would be part of her life as a whaling wife. It was all a part of the price she would willingly pay to be with John.

Now what could she use to wash up? Everything had been emptied and stored yesterday. But there was water, a small pitcher of the precious liquid, and beside it a bottle of Bay Rum, the sweet-smelling necessity for all grooming on a whaler. John must have prepared this for her awakening. John! Maria's heart lifted.

Chapter 13

ONE afternoon soon after the whale hunt, John came down to the Big Cabin where Maria was sitting in her little rocking chair making tatting lace.

'Maria, my dear, would you like to go up on deck with me and see the men not on watch making scrimshaw with the teeth of the whale we got?'

'That I want to see,' Maria answered as she put her fancy work in her dress pocket and got up. Together they went up to the deck.

Maria looked in amazement at the group busy at work. Men sprawled out near the waist of the ship. One man was busy at the cooper's bench, removing the teeth from the long, slender, whitish jawbone of the whale caught a few days before.

'This was a large male whale,' said John, 'so there are probably forty-eight teeth in its jawbone. There are always at least twenty on each side in a sperm whale. Each tooth represents about six inches of good ivory.'

'Where's the upper jaw?' asked Maria curiously.

John replied that a sperm whale had no upper teeth, but only depressions in the upper jawbone into which the lower teeth fit.

'How hard they are working to pull those teeth. It's really the job for a giant dentist.' Maria put her hand to her own jaw as she spoke and asked John a question that had been bothering her.

'John, what happens on shipboard if someone gets a bad toothache?'

'Oh, the captain has a pair of forceps just for that purpose. Why, Maria?'

Maria was not yet ready to admit such dire necessity, so she quickly asked, 'What will be done with those whale teeth?'

John was pleased with Maria's interest and answered at once. 'The good ones will be put into the hold; they will bring good money. The small ones and broken ones the men keep for their scrimshaws. Honey, I'll have to go down for a minute; they aren't holding the jaw right.' And he strode down toward the men.

'Scrimshaw,' Maria said aloud. 'Sailor's fancy work to keep them from going crazy from boredom during long periods of no whale chase and great calms.' How often she had heard that explanation in Cape Cod homes, when the elaborately carved pieces were taken off the mantels by admiring or curious visitors.

Mother would not have one, but how she did love her jagged wheel gadget for cutting pie crust! Uncle Asa always said that the knife was the sailor's favorite scrimshaw. About every whaling household had one, Maria reflected. How did that little ivory-horned sea horse head with a much-ridged little wheel between his front hooves come to be called a jagging wheel? 'I must ask John if he knows,' she decided. Her thoughts went back to the many different jagging wheels she had seen. Of them all, none was as handsome as Aunt Eunice's. Uncle Asa had carved it himself. Such minute detail in the spirited horsehead and the tiny hooves and the long undulant fishtail that twined itself in loops.

'It helped me pass many lonely hours,' Uncle Asa had told her. 'Even the captains of whaling ships work on scrimshaws. You know, niece, a captain is lonelier than any of his crew because discipline forbids his mingling with his men friendly like.' Then he had added with a twinkle in his blue eyes, 'What dreams went into this jagging wheel! Dreams of baking days at home and your Aunt Eunice's juicy mince and apple pies that I would enjoy some day, after our ship diet of salt junk and other seafare.'

Maria could see her aunt's capable hands guiding the jagging wheel as it trimmed crusts, joining them neatly when the filling was in, pressing a beautifully crinkly edge. Oh, the swirls and twizzles her aunt could work with her jagging wheel! Maria could still remember what the minister had said when he came to Aunt Eunice's for dinner.

'Really, Mrs. Tobey, this is such a masterpiece of pie crust that it makes one wobble between the urge to bite into its crispness and the desire to just look at it.'

Nostalgia for the familiar past overtook Maria for a moment. The winter holidays without her own dear ones! Oh, she could not bear it. Then the sight of John's figure coming toward her brought her back to the present and her spirits lifted. At least she would be with John and his holidays would not be lonely this year.

She was struck with an idea. She would ask Doc to let her bake a pie for John. There was no mincemeat on the ship, but there were plenty of dried apples in the barrel. She smiled at John as he held out a whale tooth.

'See how heavy this tooth is, Maria. It weighs every

bit of a pound. The weight depends on the size of the hollow inside; some are larger than others.'

'John, what was inside the hollow?' Maria pressed her hand to her cheek. The tooth was paining her again.

'They are filled with a pinkish jelly-like substance. The nerves I suppose. Pity the poor whale when he has a toothache!'

'Oh, John, I can sympathize; I'm sure now this soreness in my jaw is a toothache.'

Whale teeth were forgotten and John hurried Maria down to the main cabin, where laudanum was found in the medicine chest and applied to the offending molar. It gave relief for only a short time, however, and before the afternoon was over John had to tell Maria that the tooth must come out.

With characteristic fortitude and presence of mind, John prepared to perform his duty. As captain of the ship, he was prepared to act as dentist, doctor, even surgeon, counselor, legal and personal, and judge, with power over life and death. A whaling captain was indeed the master of the world of his ship. To perform this duty on his beloved Maria was painful to him, but he set about it methodically.

Pouring a few swallows of brandy in a cup, he handed it to his wife. She sniffed it and protested, 'Oh, John, not that horrid stuff.'

'Take it, Maria; it will dull the pain somewhat.' He looked sternly at his wife, and she obeyed at once. In a short while the tooth was extracted. 'Open your eyes, dear, it's out.'

Maria continued to sit on the quarterdeck whenever the weather permitted, and she felt health and strength returning as the days passed. On some days the ship seemed a hive of industry. The men scrubbed, painted, polished, kept the water barrel filled from the stored casks in the hold, slushed masts and spars, repaired rigging, and attended to a hundred and one details. Maria remarked to John one day that the captain of a ship was one of the most scrupulous housekeepers in the world.

'Have to be, my dear. Only by keeping the crew busy from morning till night am I able to keep the ship spick-and-span and in proper repair. And it is good that it is so, for nothing is worse on a ship than too much idleness. It is certainly the devil's opportunity. That's why we see to it there's always material on hand for scrimshaw work. Wait until you see the pretty things the crew makes from whale teeth and bone, with whatever wood or yarn happens to be on hand. You will see elaborate canes, bags, work baskets, and much more.'

'What could be prettier than the work box you gave me when you were courting me? Such a beautiful thing, made of inlaid brown and black wood, whalebone, and abalone shell.'

'I bought it in New Bedford, Maria,' John confessed. Then, looking grave, he went on. 'I'm afraid I was courting you for a dull and trying life on board an old whaler, so far away from civilization most of the time, dear.'

'John, I am with you, my beloved husband, and I am glad.'

John went on about his duties, and Maria was left to her thoughts of the scrimshaw articles they would take back home to the family. Perhaps they would send them on ahead by some homecoming captain whose ship they might meet soon. For her father, one of those canes, delicately carved with a bird's head and neck for a curved handle. How proudly he would carry it to church or the Lodge meeting. For her mother and aunts, camphor chests.

As Maria mused, she watched two men sitting on the deck floor in the shade of the midwaist whaleboat. They were deeply engrossed in scrimshaw work. Maria smiled with fellow-feeling. They were submerging their loneliness, or homesickness, or just plain boredom in their sailor fancywork. She recognized one of the two as Smitty, the father of the baby born the night before they sailed. The other she realized with a start must be Portugee, the man David had feared. He was dark, foreign-looking, yet handsome in his way.

Well, evidently he was behaving. She had heard of no incidents below and his name had not been mentioned for weeks.

Smitty seemed to be working with slivers of bone. She thought of the long, slender jawbone of the whale. Probably that was the source of these slivers. He was arranging the polished pieces like an open-work basket. No! It was a doll cradle for his little girl. Oh, that would be just the thing for Milly! How happy and surprised she would be to get one like that. She would ask Smitty if he would make one for her Milly.

Carried away with the idea, Maria stepped to the forward deck and spoke to Smitty. She admired the scrimshaw he was making and asked about his baby girl. Smitty's face shone as he talked about his mite of a baby and how he hoped to get a tintype of her in the first letter from his wife.

Then Maria's eyes fell on the object the other man was making. It was a jagging wheel, exquisitely carved; the little horsehead seemed almost alive. What a beautiful gift that would make for Louise. Her face showed her delight as she asked to look at it more closely and buy it if it were for sale.

Thistle in Her Hand

'Why, yes, la-dee,' he spoke softly, drawling his words. 'I will make for you.' He pressed the partly finished object into her hand; his dark, sensual glance swept over her as he sat on the deck floor, then he rose and stepped close to her. Maria started back, suddenly embarrassed, humiliated. Then she quickly handed the ivory piece back to him and turned to go, but as he took it, his brown fingers trailed over her forearm lightly. Horrified, Maria tried to look dignified and calm as she walked away, murmuring something about having the captain discuss the sale with him later. Inwardly she was in turmoil. Oh, what had she done? John and Uncle Asa and her brother Lisha had all cautioned her to keep away from the forward deck and its rough characters. Why had she been so impulsive?

She hurried to her stateroom, her heart palpitating in her breast over her impetuous act. Leaning against the chest of drawers, she tried to think of the best course to take to avoid further trouble. She would not say anything to John, or to anyone. But she would be very careful in the future to keep out of Portugee's sight.

'Maybe it is not so bad. Maybe I am making too much of it,' she consoled herself.

Her eyes fell on her work box on the shelf above. 'That's it. I will get busy with my work, get my mind on something else. I mustn't sit here and brood over something that may be nothing.' But her mind remained troubled.

Chapter 14

'JOHN what is our next stop for supplies?'

Captain Hamblin looked up from his log book, in which he had been entering the latest whale catch, reached for Maria's hand, and held it to his cheek before answering. 'The Cape Verde Islands. But, Maria dear, you mustn't get your heart set on going ashore there. Those rugged islands are constantly swept with high winds and the sea is always rough. A trip ashore in a whaleboat would not be very pleasant for you.'

And as they approached the small town of Furna on the island called Brava of the Cape Verde group, Maria saw that it was as he had said. The mass of volcanic heights, some as much as 10,000 feet above sea level, looked bleak and barren, as though the snarling trade winds had whipped away all signs of vegetation. Maria decided that they must have been named for some explorer whose name they bore, for the only green she could see from the deck of The Roman was in an almost hidden notch in the hills. As she watched, a cloud of smoke and fire spurted from one of the volcanoes. Maria looked about the deck wildly, but no one seemed to be alarmed. Mate Richards nearby saw her fright and joined her at the rail.

'Don't you be worried a bit, ma'am. That's just old Fogo actin' up. Never been by here yet she didn't give me a salute. I 'spose once some of them other peaks were alive too, but Fogo is the only active volcano on the Cape Verdes now.'

As they drew near, the ship tossed in the rough waters and Maria hurried below to the comfort of her gimballed bed, hoping only that the supplies would be taken aboard quickly so that they could get away from there.

When John and mate Richards continued to spend much time at the captain's desk in the cabin, over their charts and instruments, Maria became curious.

'Surely, John, these waters are familiar to you. You've been over them many times. What is it all about?'

Pleased at Maria's interest in his work, John put his left arm about her as he indicated their position on the map with his right hand. 'We're approaching the horse latitudes, often called the doldrums. This section,' he said, pointing, 'abounds in calms, squalls, violent thunderstorms, and light baffling winds.

'It takes very careful planning, for there are shifting zones of equatorial calms. For instance,' John indicated a section of the map with thumb and forefinger, 'in this area, the zone of calms went up to 12 degrees north latitude after the summer solstice, and then down to as far as 1 degree north of the equator.

'But we are watching out for a region between north latitude 4 degrees and 10 degrees and longitude 18 degrees and 23 degrees, that trace of sea called the rainy sea,' continued John, pointing to a section on the map that would be in line with northern South America.

Thistle in Her Hand

'What happens there?' Maria asked.

'Lots of rains. Violent storms with rain falling in streams. Almost no calm weather.'

The mate entered at this moment and, slipping his pipe into his pocket, joined the captain and Maria.

'Yes, Mrs. Hamblin, a ship caught in the rainy seas is trapped. It's hard to get out. I remember when The Orinoco got caught and we stayed there in that stormy hell for twenty days. Our food gave out and two men were killed in fights.'

Maria's face turned chalky white and her eyes widened with fright.

'Maria, we are not going into that region! That's why we're charting so carefully!' John was alarmed at the horrified look in Maria's eyes. The mate looked troubled too.

'Suppose we go on deck and get some fresh air,' John suggested.

'No, oh no! I can't bear to look at the sea,' Maria evaded. 'I'll just lie down a while. I'll be all right.'

Maria walked unsteadily to her bed, fighting the weakness that had suddenly come upon her.

As she lay there thinking of the days ahead, one picture after another presented itself to her troubled mind. She remembered that John had shown during their courtship that he was capable of flashes of jealousy when another man showed special admiration for her. And this was so much worse. She imagined the crew in the doldrums, both physical and mental, their moods growing uglier each day of idleness. She pictured Smitty and Portugee fighting over trifles, the lance poised to strike.

Suppose Portugee and the Pirate fought over the kind of music the Pirate played on his harmonica, or over anything at all? Suppose somehow he gained control of the men and started a mutiny? Suppose he made some other advance on her and John saw it? John would punish him severely, she knew.

But what harm might come to her beloved husband first? Maria stifled a moan in her pillow. She must do something to make sure that at least she was never on deck when Portugee was on duty. She resolved to look in John's log book at his list of the watches so she would always know where he was and keep out of his sight.

A little later John came in and stood looking at his wife.

'Maria,' he said, 'you don't seem like yourself these last few days. You're getting as peaked as a sick kitten. I know you need to get your feet on solid ground and to hear some news from home. You will, too, when we get to Buenos Aires. Or maybe we will speak to a New Bedford ship even before then.'

Maria reached for John's hand and held it to her face. 'Oh, John, I am so glad. And please don't worry about me. I'll be all right.'

After John left, Maria hugged to herself the comforting thought that there might soon be news from home, but presently her mind went back to the more immediate problem. She knew what she would do. She would tell John everything and have him put Portugee off at Buenos Aires. He could get another seaman to take his place at that port.

Maria's relief was short-lived. The black thought came to her that between now and Buenos Aires lay the doldrums! And what if a mistake were made and they got into the rainy seas! Maria slipped to her knees beside the bed and prayed fervently that nothing would happen before they got to Buenos Aires.

When she rose, she was more calm in spirit, but she

still felt physically ill. She sat down again on the bed in deep thought. Perhaps there was another reason for her weakness. Her monthly cramps were late, if not missing.

The good trade winds carried the ship along each day now. Blessed trade winds! Maria remembered studying the winds in her geography lessons. As she sat on John's horsehair sofa, mending a weak spot in one of her husband's shirts, she was back in school again in Miss Sweet's class. How she had drilled them in geography! It had seemed tiresome then to Maria, the memorizing of rivers and seas so difficult!

But now, the world's geography was part of her life. It was as if lamps were being lighted for her on a living map of the world. Just ahead the biggest lamp shone on Buenos Aires, where at last she would be freed from what was becoming a nightmare.

Trade winds and greasy luck were with the ship until they reached the region of the calms. Even then for a while there were some variable winds and Maria rejoiced. Maybe this would be an unusual crossing with easy sailing.

Then the winds died down and the sea became a waveless expanse. The Roman scarcely moved. Its sails flapped loosely. The days were hot and muggy. Maria fancied that even the sun was perspiring, for it looked white and far away. There seemed to be no shade anywhere. Now the captain and mates were more alert to any disorders among the crew than ever before. Work went on relentlessly. Sails were mended or shortened. Worn ropes were spliced and repaired. The decks were kept spotless. New supplies of fine woods, weaving materials, and bone were brought out to discourage idleness which might lead to arguments and fights.

One day it turned foggy hot. A moist, overcast sky hung low; there was no sun, only a terrible, blinding glare. During such days, Maria's favorite spot was the sofa in the captain's cabin. When her household chores were finished, she liked to sit there with her mending or needlework, listening to John if he were talking to one of the men, or questioning him about what was going on when they were alone.

They had a day when there was ear-splitting thunder, sheets of lightning, and rains that fell in torrents. The men rushed to the decks in glee, allowing the water to soak into their hair, their faces, until they were saturated. Maria envied them, but stayed below. She could not take the chance of being seen by Portugee.

One morning when she and mate Richards were alone in the saloon sipping their tea, Maria asked the question that had been worrying her since they had been becalmed.

'How are the men taking this? That nice Tom Layton, what about him?'

Then she had inquired for Smitty, the Pirate, any whose names she had learned. Finally, she mentioned Portugee. But she waited until the mate had left the table for his desk in the cubbyhole, so that he would not see the fear which her face might betray.

'I'm really surprised we're not having trouble with the tough fellow. He could be a dangerous man in a time like this. But he is keeping quiet. Does his work and then goes to his carving. Guess he plans to sell his scrimshaws for fancy prices. But I still don't trust him any further than we sailed today!'

Maria was beginning to hate that word scrimshaw. She was sure that somehow, sometime, Portugee would approach her using a scrimshaw piece as an excuse. She wondered why she had stepped off her quarterdeck that day.

The rainy respite was short. Steaming hours followed. The winds were not directional, but went upward, so the ship made little progress.

'This is the place where the trade winds meet,' John explained to Maria as she sewed on the buttons of his best captain's jacket in preparation for a possible gam ahead.

'The trades from the south meet those from the north. They swoop up, then circle back to their place of origin.'

'Where is that?' Maria asked, looking at John with pride. He knew so much. This was one captain who would not have to do scrimshaw to keep from boredom. John would always have books to read and enjoy or navigation articles to study. She, like Uncle Asa in his young days on a whaler, needed handwork to escape from worry or as a release from boredom. How often these days she wished she had a garden to go to when her mind was troubled! But she must listen. John was answering her question.

'The north trade winds start from the beginning of the tropics north of the equator and the southern trades start from the end of the tropics and move northward. They commence the circle back from here.' John looked at his pupil's perspiring face and saw a faraway look in her soft eyes. He finished his little lecture quickly. 'Everything about this world seems to whirl in circles, ovals, or cycles.'

John knelt before the sofa, pulling Maria close to him. There was a world of concern in his face and voice.

'Maria, my little wife, was I wrong to bring you with me? I know these days are hard on you. They are hard on all of us. But they will pass. We seem to be standing still, but the ship really is moving along a little each day. Soon we will pick up the trade winds again and be in Buenos Aires before you know it.'

He took his handkerchief from his pocket and tried to dry the tears which started from Maria's eyes. Maria longed with all her heart to confide her real trouble, but dared not. She must allow him to think what he would until they reached port.

As John replaced his handkerchief, Maria saw that it was soiled from frequent use in mopping perspiration. She felt a twinge of conscience. She had been neglecting her wifely duties in these days of inertia.

'John, give me that handkerchief,' she said briskly, 'and call Henry and ask him to get my wash tubs ready. It is high time I washed some of our clothes. I am ashamed to have the captain go about without a clean handkerchief.'

Maria closed her work basket with a snap and went quickly to the stateroom to gather things to launder. John looked after her with an amused smile and much relief. 'Everything, yes, everything whirls in cycles.'

As soon as the water was heated and carried to Maria's little deckhouse, she began her task. John stretched a clothesline between there and the afterhouses and helped Maria wring out the heavy pieces and hang them. When the work was done, the clothing Maria was wearing was as wet as that on the line from her exertions, but she felt better. She had worked off some of her fears.

Even the monotonous ship fare tasted good to Maria that evening, and she waited, relaxed, in the cabin for John to finish nightly inspection and take her up for their usual stretch on the upper deck before turning in.

There were still a few of John's heavy things to be taken off the line. The day had been too sultry for quick drying.

As she waited, she heard a sharp crack of thunder. She wondered if there would be another downpour and hoped there would be, for the men's sake. Now she wished John would hurry. It was getting dark too quickly. The sky must be darkening for rain and she did not want her clothes to be wet again and have to clutter the deck another day.

When he did come for her, Maria sensed that something unusual was happening. He hurried her up to the deck and to a place where she could get a clear view of the mainmast. 'Look, Maria, up there on the yardarms and mainmast.'

Maria gasped in amazement and clutched John's arm. He hurried on to explain the weird sight.

'It looks like fire, doesn't it, Maria? But it's just an unusual electrical display. Sailors call it St. Elmo's fire.'

Maria watched the flame-like effect high over their heads. 'Won't it even scorch the wood, John?' she asked, curiously.

At that moment, a flaming bolt seemed to descend from the tip of the mast almost to the deck, lighting the whole ship for a second. Maria became conscious that the deck forward was full of seamen also watching the display. She drew closer to John and begged him to take her below.

The captain held her against him tightly and bade her listen. Her ears caught a low rumbling of men's voices, which mounted with the passing seconds until the sound took on an ominous quality.

'Oh, what is it now?' she cried, with sinking heart.

'Nothing to become upset about, my dear. It's just an

old sailor's superstition. If a bolt of St. Elmo's fire runs down the mast, it betokens disaster of some kind during the week ahead. If it runs upward, then look for good luck.'

John's explanation of the cause of the spectacle made sense. In spite of that, the ethereal display renewed Maria's apprehension and that night she slept uneasily. She wondered at the downward roll of St. Elmo's fire. Nightmares interrupted her rest. John shook her awake from her crying.

'What is it, dear? You must be dreaming. You are safe here in bed with me. Wake up and see.' John stroked her hair and spoke soothingly, trying to bring her back to reality.

When her sobbing ceased and he knew she was awake, he spoke sternly. 'Now, Maria, what is the matter? I know there's something troubling you. You must tell me.'

His tone was commanding and Maria almost told him. Then the image of Portugee's sharp knife stopped her and, instead, she told John of her suspicion that she was pregnant.

John was immensely relieved and delighted with the news. 'That explains everything.' He thought a moment, then added, 'We'll plan to be in Australia, in Albany or Sydney, in plenty of time. They are modern cities with good doctors.'

The next day, the tenth in the doldrums, the sails caught enough breeze finally to push the ship into the trade wind lane and The Roman sailed on. The sight of taut sails again was cause for rejoicing throughout the ship. Even those asleep below decks were awakened by their enthusiastic companions. All sullenness, dissatisfaction, and dark thoughts about the St. Elmo's fire

Thistle in Her Hand

omen of the night before evaporated like fog before the rising sun. The whalemen again sang at their tasks.

Maria, in her little deckhouse, heard the Pirate's harmonica playing a gay tune once more as she applied the sad-iron to her freshly washed clothes. She had had her moment of thankful rejoicing too when the ship had begun to move. At least the danger of fighting below deck was now reduced.

The main thing was for her to keep out of Portugee's sight until Buenos Aires. John's log book was keeping her informed of his whereabouts. She felt reasonably safe and hummed a cheerful song as she worked. Doc was watching her irons on the galley stove, testing them with a moist finger from time to time. Timmy was within calling distance whenever she had a filled basket to be carried to the stateroom.

'Seein' those men takin' soundings reminds me of a story, Mrs. Hamblin. Like to hear it?' and Doc proceeded to tell it without waiting for Maria's assent.

'It's about a Nantucket whaling captain who always wanted to get a sample of the sand when the men took the soundings, so he had some kind of special lead made that sand would stick to when the men made the soundings. He claimed that by tasting the grains he could tell with his eyes closed the region they were in. Well, they were nearin' home once and the men thought to have some fun, so they put dirt from the bottom of a barrel of potatoes bought from Hackett Farm in Nantucket on the lead. The captain, eyes shut, tasted the grains of dirt, and started yellin', "Men, men! Nantucket's sunk! We're going over Ma Hackett's garden!"'

Maria laughed heartily with Doc. It was a good sea story and about home folks, which pleased her most.

'This is the last piece, Doc. You can take my irons off and start your supper now.' Maria quickly pressed a pillowcase, stretching the crocheted edges carefully, then folded it and called Timmy to carry the basket below. She put her ironing board in its place against the side of the deckhouse, saw that it was fastened securely and stepped out on the deck. She glanced around quickly as, out of the corner of her eye, she saw a kneeling seaman working with the scuppers just beyond the quarterdeck. With relief she recognized Tom Layton and turned toward the stern. As she started toward the afterhouse companionway, a dark figure blocked her way. Portugee! Her heart pounding, she heard his low voice.

'Pretty la-dee, I have scrimshaw for you. The likes you have never seen before. When can I give it to you?'

For a second Maria was too dumbfounded to speak. Then she cried fiercely, 'Let me pass. The captain will discuss buying the scrimshaw.'

But Portugee did not move. 'This scrimshaw is jus' for you, la-dee.'

As he stepped toward her, he came into view of Tom Layton, who, sensing that something was wrong, yelled, 'Portugee!' Then Doc burst out of the galley shouting, 'Hey! You there!'

But Maria was not even conscious of the commotion. Her eyes had caught the outline of a knife in Portugee's belt. She could not take her gaze from it, but stood frozen. Suddenly, seeming to come from the thin air, John appeared in back of Portugee, his eyes blazing in anger. The man felt his presence and his hand went instantly to the knife. But Maria's hand was quicker than his. She and the seaman struggled furiously for possession; then, snarling an oath, Portugee tore her

Thistle in Her Hand

hands loose with his nails and whipped out a long, slender knife carved from whale tooth, and turned to face John. Maria screamed. She heard a crash and saw Portugee fall.

She next sensed John over her, forcing something bitter into her mouth. She lay in her bed. Timmy stood nearby with a basin of steaming water in his hands, looking white and frightened. John's face had an expression on it that she had never seen before. She felt confused. Then the whole nightmarish experience came back to her. She closed her eyes thankfully. John was safe. She could rest now.

'I'm all right,' she murmured. 'Just let me sleep a while. I'm so tired.' She raised her hand to touch John in reassurance and saw that her hand was bandaged. She must have cut it in the struggle for the knife. No. Those fingernails had torn into her hands. But it did not matter. John was safe. She slept.

When she awoke, she tried to talk to John about the incident, but he would not discuss it. 'Put it out of your mind, Maria,' he ordered. Maria's curiosity about what happened when she fainted was not satisfied until the next day, when she overheard Henry and Timmy talking about Portugee.

'Did he eat his grub?' Henry was asking.

'Yeah, ate like he was starved. Guess he's figgered out how lucky he is to be alive. Man, if the captain's lady hadn't went out like she did, he sure would have killed Portugee. His fist must be made of iron when he's mad. That long knife didn't scare him a little bit.'

Later Maria insisted that John listen to the story from beginning to end so that she could sweep her mind clean of it. When she finished, he raised her bandaged hand gently and said, 'Poor torn hand, my brave little lady.

Your doing what you did gave me the seconds I needed to get the man.'

He told Maria that The Roman was heading for a Brazilian port where Portugee, now in chains in the steerage, would be put off.

That very next morning they came to the port and arrangements were made for two boats to leave. One, with the mate and some of the crew, carried Portugee. The other carried Agrimonte, the third mate, and some others of the crew who were to fill casks with water and get fruits and vegetables. Limes and oranges were specially ordered to help prevent scurvy.

Maria stayed in the stateroom when the boats left. Later she heard the mate reporting to John in the cabin. 'I put Portugee in the hands of the police and asked them to hold him until after we had sailed to prevent trouble. I told Portugee to get on a foreign vessel, as you were reporting him to the United States government and if he was found escaping from the law, he'd better watch out, as the long arm of the law would get him.'

'Thank you, mate Richards. You did well. Now I want to hear about Agrimonte's boat and the supplies.'

'We came back with both boats loaded with fruit and vegetables and the casks filled with water.'

Maria didn't listen any more. Now that Portugee was off the ship she felt she could rest with a peace of mind she had not enjoyed for many days. She lay down on the bed that was now swinging as the ship sailed out to sea once more. Yet the thought of Portugee reappearing at some distant port lingered in her mind.

Two days later, while Maria was still recovering from her shock, The Roman approached the equator. From her stateroom Maria heard the first mate inquiring of

Thistle in Her Hand

John whether or not he would allow the usual high jinks as the line was crossed.

'If this wind holds,' John answered, 'we may be ready for Old Neptune's visit by nightfall. I'll leave it in your hands, Mr. Richards, to keep the fun within bounds. I don't want any tricks that would disturb Mrs. Hamblin. She isn't too well yet.'

'I'll pass the word along to Rogers and Agrimonte. The green hands are both on their watches.'

'What will they do, the men?' Maria demanded, when John looked in on her before going up to take his daily observations.

'You'll see! A shave and a christening is the usual fare.'

Later, as daylight faded, Maria took the place arranged for her in a secluded spot on the quarterdeck. The men were dipping buckets of sea water and pouring it into a large hogshead set up near the tryworks, upon which the men stood as they emptied their buckets. When all was ready, the first green hand was led blindfolded from below, where he had been detained by his shipmates while the preparations were being made.

Old Neptune suddenly appeared on the forward deck. He wore a ragged pair of trousers that scarcely covered his bony knees and his head was disguised in a wig and beard made of unraveled hemp rope and rowsy oakum. As the blindfolded man was forcibly hurried to the tryworks, Neptune prodded him from the rear with his trident, which Maria recognized as a whaling iron.

Maria could not hear all the conversation, but she saw the men brush his bearded face with some sticky concoction and proceed to shave it with a broad strip of iron from the cooper's chest. Judging by the man's howls, Maria decided that any hair taken came out by the roots. A bucket of water dashed into his face completed the shaving.

While he was still puffing and blowing and confused, the men lifted him to the tryworks and sat him upon a long board which led up to the hogshead. In a twinkling the board was lifted and the hapless sailor doused in the hogshead.

'Man overboard!' was the cry as the water splashed up over the rim. In a moment Maria saw his head appear above the tub. He clung to the edge and tore off the blindfold. She could not join in the laughter that went up as he looked wildly about the hogshead, the men, and Old Neptune himself.

'Now ye be shaved and christened proper and fit to live with your fine shipmates,' declared Old Neptune, in tones that Maria recognized as Rogers' Irish brogue.

'Where is the next recruit?' demanded Neptune.

Maria put her hand on John's arm. 'Please, I've had enough. I want to go below.'

John's face sobered. 'Don't worry, Maria dear, no one is getting hurt. Watch how that fellow's going to enjoy the next show!' But he helped Maria to the cabin and stayed with her until she had relaxed.

With the initiations over, all hands joined in singing and dancing. John persuaded Maria to return above decks. When she saw that the initiates were the gayest of the crew, she was relieved and enjoyed the frolicking until mate Richards declared that the line had been crossed and ordered all hands to return to their bunks except those on watch.

Chapter 15

CAPTAIN Hamblin could not help noticing that Maria spent a great deal more time above deck than before, now that she felt free of the menacing Portugee. Often he found her standing at the quarterdeck rail gazing at the sea. He knew she was looking for a passing whaling ship, longing for news from home. Occasionally a vessel came into view, but the spyglass had revealed only merchant ships thus far. He felt Maria's keen disappointment each time this happened, and his heart ached for her. The lack of news about the mysterious smoke they had seen over New Bedford as The Roman left port was still on his mind. Could it be that the whaling ships in port had caught fire?

One day, to divert Maria's mind, he asked her to help him sort and file the ship's papers. As she sat in the cabin with him, going through the bills, she came upon a baker's bill for $700.00.

'My goodness, John,' she exclaimed, 'how much does it cost to fit a whaling ship like this for a long voyage?'

John laughed. 'About $9,000.00, counting whaling implements and all kinds of tools. There is everything to keep a ship in repair and good working order for months. Let me see that baker's bill.

'Seventy barrels of flour, packed. Ninety barrels of flour, baked. That's hardtack, Maria. One thousand, one hundred gallons of molasses, and two boxes of sugar. That's a lot of food, but only a small part of it. There were 100 bushels of potatoes stored in that slatted pen on the afterdeck when we left New Bedford.'

'Yes,' answered Maria, 'and they are disappearing fast. Will you buy more when we reach Buenos Aires?'

'Yes, and other supplies, such as fresh meat for a treat.'

'And a change from salt beef and pork and ham,' replied Maria with relish.

'And codfish. Here's a bill for 700 pounds of New England cod,' said John with a smile.

'This bill is for rice, peas, beans, and cornmeal. Oh, salt and pepper, too. And here's one for cabin stores of tea, coffee, and spices.'

Maria piled the bills neatly on John's desk. She picked up another. 'One thousand pounds of dried apples! That must be almost an orchard's yield.'

John turned over some other papers. 'Here's a bill for $250.00 for two whaleboats and their fittings. Yes, a whaling voyage is a costly investment for the owners.'

He handed her another paper. 'Here, this is interesting. It's for clothes for the slop chest. There are caps, jackets, pants, peg pumps, brogans, thick shoes, and boots. Just wait until the men go on liberty. You'll see some dressing up then. We're getting close to Buenos Aires.'

'Oh, John, how good that sounds! How wonderful it will be to walk on land, to talk to women. I can't wait to listen to just women's chatter about clothes and children! Well?'

Thistle in Her Hand

John had thrown back his head, laughing.

He explained, 'The women you'll meet in Buenos Aires will look like American women, but they speak Spanish. They say *"si, si"* for yes and *"quien sabe"* for "who knows". I learned those words when we stopped there on my last trip. I'm afraid you won't do much conversing except in sign language. But you'll see some mighty stylish clothes, the latest in French fashions, I am told. They looked strange to me.'

Maria knew that just to see another woman and pretty clothes would be delightful to her. And surely there would be mail waiting for them, sent by clipper ship or steamer, since the shipping office knew they were to stop there.

To prepare Maria for certain possibilities, however, John described the harbor's deficiencies. 'The harbor at Buenos Aires is really the Rio Plata estuary, with shallow water far out to sea. Whaling ships have to stop several miles out and finish the trip to port by whaleboats.'

Last year, he told her, it had been too shallow even for the whaleboats to finish the trip and the seamen had had to transfer to anfibios or high, horse-drawn carts that could go through the axle-high water to the shore. Sometimes the horses would step into a hole and everyone would get a good wetting. 'Now they have extended the pier,' finished John, 'so I am sure we can get there by whaleboat.'

'Why do you want to go to that port especially?'

'I prefer it to Montevideo, the usual stop. It's a great cattle and farm country. We can stock up on the best of meats, vegetables, and fruits. The ship people have good appetites and need to be well fed. This is our last chance to get fresh food for some time.'

'And mail, hopefully.'

Maria forgot everything for a moment, lost in her longing for news about her family, friends, and home. She recalled Aunt Abby's fat molasses cookies. They were always so crisp, fragrant, and full of raisins, and always had a surprise nut in the center. Ever since Maria could remember, those cookies had been Aunt Abby's cure-all for sadness or homesickness or hurt feelings.

John smiled, almost reading Maria's thoughts. 'I hope they send us news of the family, especially of your beloved David. Yes, our beloved David. I feel a blood kinship with that little chap.'

Maria was up at dawn the day after the ship anchored two miles from Buenos Aires. Her chores were done and she was dressed. Everyone was excited, both those leaving and those remaining, for there would be mail from home and good meals ahead with plenty of fresh meat. John had gone up to supervise the lowering of the whaleboats.

Maria waited in the cabin. Her hazel eyes were bright and her cheeks pink with anticipation. Seated primly in her rocker, she wore a fullskirted dress of larkspur blue, with a dark blue cashmere shawl and silk bonnet edged with lace the color of her dress. She looked like a young lady awaiting her beau.

She heard John's footsteps at last on the stairway, but they were not the buoyant steps of his ascent. He was coming down slowly, reluctantly, as a person bringing disappointing news. He came and took Maria's hand.

'Maria dear, a black cloud is forming in the southwest over the Rio Plata region. We are afraid it is a storm cloud. We will wait for a while. Come up on the deck with me while we decide what to do.'

Thistle in Her Hand

'A storm? Why, it's such a lovely day!'

Maria could not hide her vexation. She followed John to the deck, frowning.

They joined mate Richards and Doc at the rails and studied the sky intently. The cook spoke first.

'I'm afraid it looks like a pampero storm. And that can be a mean storm. I've been in one.'

'But the sea looks calm enough,' protested Maria.

She took the spyglass from John and looked toward the city with intensity. She could make out some church spires and distant hills beyond the city. She had so longed for this day on land and could hardly bear the thought of being robbed of it by a storm.

As they watched, the blackness increased in the southwestern sky. Then there came a distinct flash of lightning. The wind, which had been southeast, dropped, and there was a dead calm. The crew rushed to batten down, furl the sails, and take in the flying jib. Maria retreated below and regretfully disrobed and put her pretty things away. Then she hurried to dismantle the room again before the time came for her to take to the safety of the gimballed bed.

The ship, ready now, awaited the storm's attack. A vast mist capped with black clouds came driving toward The Roman. Then the storm struck, bringing a maelstrom sea that tossed the ship about like a toy. Maria became deathly sick. Even some of the seasoned seamen were ill. Once the bed swung so sharply with the lunging ship that she was pitched to the floor. Henry, who had been stationed in the captain's cabin to watch over her, heard her scream and crept into the stateroom on his hands and knees and steadied the bed while she climbed back on it. After that she held on with both hands until at last, as suddenly as it had come, the storm departed. By evening most of the storm damage on The Roman had been repaired.

The sea was still choppy the next morning, but John decided that the two whaleboats should set out. Maria, still feeling squeamish in her stomach, knew without asking that she could not go. But she went up on deck to watch the boats leave.

Maria was amused at the changed appearance of some of the seamen. Out of their sea bags had come a motley array of garments they had purchased weeks ago when the slop chest sale had been held.

Only the Pirate looked the same. He had his clothes and shoes draped around his neck. He was taking no chances on their getting wet! Maria wondered where he would change and what those ladies in Paris gowns would think if they caught a glimpse of him. What a strange group of men made up the fo'c'sle! An involuntary sigh of sheer relief escaped her. They were rid of that menace, Portugee.

'We'll be back before sundown, if no sudden storm blows up,' John had assured her.

Long before his expected return, she waited on the quarterdeck, gazing pensively toward Buenos Aires. She thought of the modern buildings, elaborate theatre, and pink government house that John had described to her. 'Some day,' John had predicted, 'Argentina will make channels in that Rio Plata estuary so ships can come in and Buenos Aires will become one of the great ports of the world.' John knew so much. She was sure that some day she would sail into the port with him and see the sights she was missing today.

Now she no longer cared. All she wanted was to have the boats come back safely. The waves were certainly getting higher.

Thistle in Her Hand

Suddenly she spied two dark blots, then lost them. Then again she saw them. Yes, they were the boats! Up and down the waves they climbed, as if they were keeping time. Probably they were singing.

> *Heigho! Heigho! The waves*
> *higher and higher go—*
> *Heigho! Heigho! We go—We go—We go—*

How music could push a job along! It helped so much on the ship in furling sails, pulling up the anchor, or on the chase. Maria wondered why people didn't use the power of music more when working the land, planting or harvesting. She must discuss that with Lisha sometime.

They were getting nearer. She was sure she could make out John's huge figure. But a mist seemed to be coming down. Oh, how unpredictable the weather was in this part of the world! The boats must get back to the ship before a second storm set in. Maria, grasping the rails, her tendons straining, watched tensely. Others joined her, watching too. Their anxious eyes strained first at the sky, then at the sea.

The mist was not changing. It just hovered, threatening. Finally the boats were well within sight, almost within hailing distance. Maria saw John stand and hold something up in his hands. Letters, she hoped. A sob escaped her lips and she whispered a prayer of thanks. She thought she could not leave the rail. As the rising wind would only blow her hair again, she excused herself. She wished she could go to the spot where the ladder would be lowered to the boat, so as to get the precious letters in her hand sooner. But no, it was wiser to stay on the quarterdeck where she belonged. She must be patient.

First up the ladder, John hurried to his wife's side.

'Back again and with mail,' he smiled. 'I accomplished a great deal today and signed on a new seaman from New England, but my thoughts were back with you, all alone. I wish you could have made the trip.'

Quickly the captain handed out a few pieces of mail to members of the crew, then hurried down to their quarters with Maria. There, in privacy, they could read their own mail.

With trembling fingers, Maria tore open one from Aunt Abby first, and out fell tintypes of the whole family. Brothers David and Lisha. John laughed.

'Look at the date, Maria,' he said. 'Aunt Abby must have had that taken soon after we left to get it off to us in her first letter. Remember, it has been waiting here for us for weeks.'

But Maria was deep in the letter about the family. She could not even take time to read it aloud to John. When she had skimmed through it to make sure that all was well, she handed it to him. 'Please read it aloud to me, so I can really enjoy it.'

When John reached the last paragraph, he stopped, startled. 'What's this, Maria? Did you see what this says?'

Maria looked in his direction, alarmed. John read it aloud. '"I will not take the time to tell you about the awful New Bedford fire for doubtless you will hear it from all the others."'

John tore open a letter from his brother-in-law, Sam. 'Listen to this, Maria,' he said after scanning the first line or two. 'That smoke we saw when we sailed out of the harbor wasn't a wood-burning ship. It was the city!

'Let me read you Sam's letter.

Thistle in Her Hand

My esteemed brother-in-law and his good wife Maria:

I take my pen in hand to inform you that on August 24th of last week our city suffered a great catastrophe in a devastating fire. The only consolation is that The Roman had already sailed, or she might have been enveloped in flames.

The fire started at noon when everyone was at dinner and the streets almost deserted. It broke out in the planing mill of William Wilcox and spread, taking in all the shops, including my own insurance building. A strong wind was blowing along the wharves, allowing the fire to take in its path all the buildings and their contents. The oil stored near the wharf took fire and the ship, John and Edward, lying at the head of the dock—'

'The John and Edward. I was envying them! How terrible,' interrupted Maria, aghast. 'Go on, John,' she commanded.

John, shaking his head as he noted the contents he was about to read, continued.

'The ship was absorbed in the destruction, the flames enveloping the entire vessel and leaping to the top of the masts. The scene was impressive. Oil was burning everywhere and at one time the water for some distance was covered with burning oil, forming a sea of fire. The ships tied to the wharf had to be pushed out into the harbor to save them from destruction.

What you referred to as the hives of industry are now charred ruins. Many of our friends have been ruined. Insurance was small compared to the loss. I need not comment.

Margarita Thompson Diddel

You will be interested to know that the 14,000 barrels of oil we were looking at were saved from destruction when a number of citizens seized big brooms from a nearby store and thrashed out the burning cinders as they fell in great clouds. The heat made this task almost unbearable, yet with great pluck they stood up to their work and thus saved that much.

Once during the fire some stored whaling bomb lances exploded, creating great alarm, for some citzens still remembered the marine attacks of the English during the War of 1812 and were sure it was an enemy attack.

Enclosed is a diagram of the damaged section of the city.'

'John! Tell Smitty no one was killed!' Maria exclaimed, horrified as she remembered that Smitty and some of the other men came from New Bedford.

'Smitty lives in Fairhaven. But some of the others are from New Bedford.' John picked up Sam's letter and the diagram and went out to talk to the New Bedford men.

Maria turned back to the yet unopened letter. There was one from her father and an entertaining letter from Elisha.

'When you get home, I may have surprising news for you. Elisha is engaged to be married as soon as he finishes school and his apprenticeship at the shipyards.' When Maria read this, she smiled. 'It's that little Rosalie Bowman! That little brother of mine can't fool his big sister. He has been in love with her since they were on the McGuffey's readers.'

Dinner that night was festive. There were rich, juicy Argentine steaks, with fresh peas and red beets. French pastries and French coffee topped the banquet.

'Eat well, my hearties,' exclaimed the mate jovially, 'it will be a long time before we get such a repast again.'

In every section of the ship that night the mood was jolly. It was as though everyone were trying to make the most of the moment.

Chapter 16

John had arranged in the city to have the barrels of oil in The Roman's hold shipped back to New Bedford. Whaling captains preferred to go 'clean' around the Horn. Since The Roman was unable to unload the barrels at the wharf, a ship came alongside and the oil was transferred and sent on its way to the home port.

When the operation was finished, sails were set and the voyage southward began again. All aboard knew well that the most dangerous days of their journey were ahead.

Now Maria opened the trunks and took out their winter clothing, for there was added chill in the air each day. The men, too, dressed warmly and stomped about in heavy boots.

Stormy seas were encountered in the 'roaring forties,' the area 40 degrees south of the equator, but fine weather followed for several days and nights before the actual rounding of the Horn began.

Dressed warmly, Maria and John paced the quarterdeck one evening when the air was unusually clear and the stars crowded the sky from horizon to horizon. John paused and pointed to the heavens almost above their heads.

'Look, Maria, see those four bright stars? That's the Southern Cross, one of the brightest constellations in the heavens.'

'The Southern Cross! Oh, John.' For some reason Maria felt strangely moved.

'And see how clear the Magellan Clouds are? Do you remember our astronomy lesson?'

Maria answered, parrot fashion, 'They are not really clouds, but—' and she broke off, partly to tease him and partly to hear the wonder which was close to reverence in his voice as he taught her what he knew about the orderly universe.

'—but misty patches of light caused either by stars too distant to be seen or by masses of gas. Two of those masses look light, but the other looks dark.' John finished the definition.

Maria added, 'The Milky Way back home is like that.'

The next day a whale was sighted, pursued, and caught, then turned into oil to begin the filling of the hold again. The seamen worked fast in the chill air and The Roman was scrubbed and under full sail by noon of the second day.

A little iron stove was brought into the captain's cabin and clamped securely to the floor. It was fed with fuel and carefully watched over by both Henry and Timmy. The galley had the only other stove aboard; the danger of fire was too great on the wooden ship, for the most meticulous scrubbing could not remove the oil that soaked into the wood during the trying-out.

Many times in the next week or two Maria heard the call, 'All hands ahoy!' Often she rushed below to batten down in the stateroom, while the seamen scurried fore

Thistle in Her Hand

and aft and up the masts to prepare for rain, hail, and sleet storms. One morning after such a storm, she found the deck covered with snow. John had the steward give each man a glass of grog as he came off watch or finished reefing topsails. The bitter cold could freeze fingers and the frozen sails could rip off fingernails. Maria marveled to hear the crew singing their sea chanteys as they worked under these adverse conditions.

Maria stayed as long as possible on the quarterdeck when they sailed close to shore, for the new and unusual sights held her in their spell. Bundled to the ears, she stood in her little deckhouse out of the cold winds, gazing at the great rocks of Tierra del Fuego, absorbing the majestic beauty of the high, serrated, ice-laden peaks against white cloud banks and the severe blue of the sea in the foreground. Strange birds followed the ship, swooping and soaring.

Sometimes John joined his wife. Maria learned that he took delight in birds and vicariously flew with them. Once, Maria expressed the wish that she could paint pictures of the Islands of the land of Fuego, saw-like hills rising out of the sea, cold and grim, desolate in their snow-covered solitude, often with conical icebergs around their base.

John said, 'I often wish I could paint, too. And I would have in the painting all those shags, Cape pigeons, albatrosses, and mollyhawks.' Then he mused aloud, 'Perhaps some day men will be flying over all this.'

Maria laughed. 'John, for such a practical navigator, you can think of the most outlandish ideas.'

'You mean "outairish,"' he punned, laughing at himself. Then, serious again, he continued, 'Men are inventing so much. Look at the magnetic telegraph. And the steamboat. Some day man will invent a flying machine. I suppose it will be long after our time.' His blue eyes held a faraway look.

'That doesn't worry me. I'd never ride in one. Give me land I can put my feet on.'

John smiled as he looked down at Maria. 'Still a landlubber at heart. Now you had better go below before you freeze that pretty nose.'

The wind rose to a gale later that day and Maria spent a miserable night. The ship's tossing made her ill and filled her mind with visions of all the ships that had gone down along this dangerous coast. She thought of John, up on the cold deck, alert to every move of the helmsman, every creak of the masts.

John had told her they were not going to heave to, as they had the night before, but were going to beat to windward under close-reefed topsails, balance-reefed trysail, and foremost sail. Maria was beginning to have some knowledge of these ship terms; she knew that a maximum of skill and watchfulness was needed to steer the vessel close-hauled in a heavy gale of wind against a strong head sea. John took no chances that carelessness should let a heavy sea sweep her decks or take a mast out of her.

Toward morning the wind abated and The Roman tossed in a strange calm. Then a dense fog descended and blotted out the rock shoreline. John asked Maria to come up on deck to see what a calm off the Horn was like.

Maria could see nothing but a patch of heaving sea near the ship; they were completely enclosed by the gray fog.

'It is so strange. It isn't like any calm I've ever been in before. Why is it so different?'

'The periods of calm in this area are so short that the

waters have no time to go down, so there is the odd combination of high seas running in a calm. The ship lies like a log upon the water, without command of sails or rudder. That's what you notice.'

'John, am I imagining? I thought I saw a shadowy black body a minute ago,' whispered Maria, peering into the fog. 'Could it be a whale?'

John listened closely. 'Yes, we may be near shoals of sluggish whales and grampuses, but we can't see them for the fog and they can't see us. They may be rising slowly to the surface or perhaps lying out at length, as they do sometimes.'

They moved closer to the rail to see and hear better.

'On a late watch once when I was a seaman, I actually heard the long drawn breaths of the whales.'

Maria kept close to John. It was all so eerie. She could picture the creatures lying supine upon the waters, breathing softly. Or was it the slapping of the great regular swells against the bulwarks?

The cabin with its warmth and familiar furnishings looked homelike to Maria as she returned, cold and damp, from the deck. She took off her wet outer things and hung them where the heat of the stove would dry them. As she crouched near the stove to warm her hands, she felt a pang of pity for the men on the rest of the ship who, during wet weather, lived in damp clothes, even slept in wet clothes at times. John told her that their hard work in storms made them so tired that they could sleep under any conditions—cold, noise, discomfort, danger.

But at least they ate well on this ship, Maria comforted herself. During this part of the voyage, Doc put extra effort into serving hot meals, often making favorites of the sailors, such as skouse, a mess of biscuit pounded fine, salt beef cut in pieces, or beans, with a few potatoes boiled with them, and seasoned with pepper. Another favorite was a 'duff' made from dolphin meat or blackfish, with unleavened dough, all boiled together in a bag. There were always pots of tea at supper, sweetened with molasses. Breakfast was usually corned beef hash, hardtack, or ship's biscuit, and coffee. Other meals included soups—barley, bean, or pea, with a bit of salt beef.

The cabin folks fared somewhat better, having some extra delicacies, such as plum duff, a pudding made with plenty of raisins. This was just, Maria mused, because each of the officers had come up through hard, bitter experiences, with much heartache and backache. And they found it worthwhile, or they would not have endured long enough to arrive on the quarterdeck.

Maria well knew by now that there would be many days during the rounding of the Horn when there would be no meals or even the fire to heat water for tea; or so everyone, from John to Timmy, had told her. John tried to prepare her in every way. She could see he dreaded for her the ordeal of the coming weeks, from the time the ship entered the roaring forties until it crossed into the Pacific.

One morning as John sat at his desk, working on the charts, he called to Maria to come and look at the map. She stood by him, her hand on his shoulder while he traced his finger over the route The Roman would take around the Horn, through the Drake Strait, which separated South America from Antarctica.

'Why don't you sail through Magellan's Strait? It looks a much shorter way,' Maria asked him.

'The Strait, my dear, is too narrow and landlocked for larger sailing vessels like The Roman. The Drake

Strait has more sea room, is ice-free, and the crossing would be easy with one long tack to the southwest, followed by another to the northwest, but the winds are so capricious and likely to bear down on the ship in sudden squalls and fierce storms that a mariner going from the South Atlantic to the South Pacific must usually sail into the teeth of the wind.

'This is possible only by making tacks, if sufficient sail can be carried to keep the ship moving. I have to plan the course from hour to hour. Sometimes for days on end it is impossible, because of the low and heavy clouds, to fix the ship's position. Between the ice fields of the south and the rocky, uninhabited islets clustering close to the Patagonian coast of Chile on the north side of the Strait, there is plenty of need for sea room.'

John stopped and looked up at his wife smiling.

'Don't you worry, Maria,' he assured her. 'I have travelled over this route now six times since my fo'c'sle days. Just bear with me when I'm plagued with worry and fatigue and my temper gets out of control. And take care of yourself; you are especially precious to me now you are carrying our baby.'

'I will,' Maria said, cradling his head in her arms and kissing his cheek. 'I am not afraid sailing with you. I'd sail to the ends of the earth with you in command. But now I'll leave you to your charts.'

And Maria hurried back to the stateroom and the making of the bed, a really cumbersome task.

As she tucked in the covers she thought of what John had said about his temper. She had seldom seen him in a high temper; she marvelled at his ability to keep it under control. Only in unusual circumstances had she seen his eyes blaze with anger when some seaman had acted unseemly, as, for instance, the encounter with

Portugee, or once when the seamen had been careless in coiling the rope in the whaleboat just before a whale chase; a mistake that could have cost the life of one man or more when the iron was sent hurling at the whale. She had never forgotten the look on his face that day.

She hoped she never would do any foolish thing that would cause him to look at her that way; she thought she couldn't stand it. Of course she would never intentionally do anything to bring it on, but she worried about an impetuous, impulsive act—like stepping out onto the deck and talking to Portugee, as she had done when she knew better.

Oh, she would be so careful, especially in the days ahead rounding the Horn, those terrible days ahead she had heard so much about. She would pray a lot, and read from her mother's little Testament. The little Testament in its casing of leather that Lisha had made for her.

Lisha, her beloved brother. She remembered how he had clung to her after their mother had died. Though only twelve, she had felt like a mother to ten-year-old Lisha and five-year-old David.

She still felt that way, always would, Maria thought as she reached into her pocket for a handkerchief and wiped her eyes. A sudden wave of nostalgia came over her now for her home in far-away Cape Cod, for the family she had left behind.

Then she straightened up and briskly finished making the bed.

John had indeed prepared Maria for what was ahead. Sometimes the day would start clear and sunny, really tolerable weather, and the ship would be making headway; then sudden squalls and fierce storms attacked from nowhere. Those seas during a Cape Horn gale would be mountainous, reaching sometimes to fifty feet.

Thistle in Her Hand

Maria got accustomed to the sudden cry, 'All hands on deck!'—first from John, the captain, with the orders echoed by the mates. And then came the orders to take in sail on all masts.

So, to the urging of bellowed commands, the creak of blocks, and the rhythmical chants of 'Haul We Heigh We Ho,' the hard-driven men worked away, pushing themselves to the utmost in the oncoming darkness and storm. All sails were clewed up, except the foresail, the three lower topsails, and a jib.

The men had to work with stiff, wet sails and rigging covered with sleet. They were nearly blinded with the violence of the storm before the vessel's sails were reduced and everything secured on deck. When that was done, there was little the men could do but steer and stand their watches. Between trips to the cold wet decks the crew slept.

Sometimes there were brief calms when the men would clean up the steerage and forecastle and overhaul their wet clothes. The cabin people would do the same. Maria did her share but still found time to make a quick trip to the deck to glimpse the stark beauty of the scenery, so new to her eyes. The albatross, and other strange birds, were always with them.

One morning when the breeze dropped and there was a brief calm, the surface of the water unbroken except for long, heavy swells, Maria spied a white albatross floating asleep upon the water, with his head under his wing, now rising on top of a swell, then falling slowly until he was lost in the hollow between. Suddenly, the noises of the ship roused him and he lifted his head, and looked at the ship with the large staring eyes which gave him such a peculiar appearance. Then, flapping his long wings and trailing his long legs, he took flight.

Maria's reverie was broken by John's commanding

voice. 'Better hurry down, Maria. I am afraid we are in for a real Cape Horn snorter.' Startled, Maria looked and on the far western horizon dense masses of clouds loomed with evil portent. The temperature dropped suddenly, the skies clouded. As she hurried toward the afterhouse entrance she saw that the long, oily-looking swells from the west had a sinister look.

The ship was alive with activity as the men followed the bellowed commands, 'All hands on deck! Clew the royals up!'

Maria stood at the porthole, staring now at the sheet of water below, now at a brief glimpse of the sky as the ship rolled over the crest of each successive advancing sea, then rolled back with a violent jerk into the trough behind it.

'The ship is not moving, not moving into the teeth of the storm that John talked about. She is hove to. Why are the men running about so much?' she said aloud, alarmed.

She could hear the moan of the whimpering breeze in the rigging rise to a top-pitched note, and subside to a sob in an eerie manner, as the top-hawser fell away or was driven up against the wind by the ship's rolling motions.

'Oh!' she screamed as she glimpsed suddenly, in the wall of darkness to the westward, a line of vivid whiteness advancing relentlessly toward the ship. It seemed to Maria as if the surface of the water was being churned by the approaching storm, about a mile away, so that it seethed as though boiling in a gigantic cauldron.

'The oily swells are being transformed into dangerous running seas,' Maria groaned. Without being aware of it

Thistle in Her Hand

she was, like the sailors, now calling the waves 'seas.' 'What is ahead?' She hurriedly prepared the room for the storm.

'Hard up the helm!' Maria heard John shouting. 'Lee forbrace.' And she heard the men moving at a run to obey his command as, with a roar like the voices of ten thousand angry lions, a hurricane-force squall shook the ship.

Maria hurried into the bed. She now could keep on her feet even during a storm, but she was taking no chances of falling and hurting the baby under her heart.

Just as the deluge of rain fell on the ship, Doc appeared at the doorway, his face creased with concern. 'Are you all right, Mrs. Hamblin? Capt'n told me to come down and look in on you.'

'What terrible rain! I never saw anything like it.'

'And you ain't 'ave neither, Ma'am. It's Cape Horn rain. But be glad it ain't August. That's winter down here. It's turrible cold with lots of snow and the rain is a deluge of hail and sleet. Turrible, turrible, turrible.'

'Doc, what's happening on deck?' Maria asked. 'Aren't they scared?'

'Ma'am, they're too busy to be scared. They're up to their bellies in water awashin' on deck as the ship rolls, holding on to the lifelines, to the belaying pins, to the rail, to anything handy, as they unravel the tangle of lines in the cold water, and secure them in the riggin' beyond the reach of the sea. The capt'n and the mates are giving orders and the men are obeying. They know that is the only chance they have to beat the Greybeards of Cape Horn.'

'There's a limit to endurance, Doc. What then?'

'Just take another hitch on the hold on the line and

hang on some more,' Doc said with a grin as he leaned against the doorjamb, his weight on his one good leg. 'But, Ma'am, what kin I get you?' he added. 'I cain't bring you hot tea, as the fires have gone. The men have to keep relighting the sternlight and binnacle lamp and the hand lanterns. What about some cold biscuit and jam to hold you until I can get some water heated for tea?'

'Nothing, thank you, Doc. Just stop the storm,' Maria said, attempting to joke.

'I'll do my best,' chuckled the crippled man as he swayed his way out.

Maria lay in the swinging bed, at times clutching the sides to keep from falling out. She thought of her beloved husband up on deck and what he was enduring. She must do all she could to help him. At least she would spare him any discomfort that would add to his trials.

For one thing, she would not let him know how miserable she felt. She remembered the look of annoyance that would pass over her father's face when he would come home and her stepmother started on her ailments. Aunt Abby used to say, 'Your stepmother does it to get attention.'

She must be careful, while John was under so much strain, not to do anything impulsive that would cause him to look at her with angry eyes. Maria stopped and went over her thoughts. Why did this thought come again? Why did this thought persist? Was her impulsiveness in the Portugee affair still nagging her or was she telling herself that she could act that way again—act without thinking?

For fifteen days and nights the gales continued with intervals of calm in between. The ship jogged along when the winds permitted. Finally, after days of intense hardship, The Roman completed its voyage around the Horn and headed north into the Pacific, favored by the winds.

'It was one of the easiest Cape Horn voyages I have ever made,' John said to Maria. 'As Henry said, you brought us good luck, dear.'

They were having breakfast alone, their first leisurely breakfast for some time. Maria, though still pale and thin from the long ordeal, smiled happily. She was relieved, because the danger of what the great stress would do to John was gone.

He looked so happy, his blue eyes smiling across the table at her. The fear lurking in her mind that she might do something impulsive that would make John angry—cause those eyes to look at her with anger—had vanished, she thought.

Or had it?

Chapter 17

CHRISTMAS Day came, appropriately for the New Englanders, while The Roman still sailed in the cold seas. Doc consented to having his privacy in the galley invaded by Maria, who was intent on baking a raisin pie for John's Christmas dinner. He also promised Maria that he would make an extra rich plum duff for the crew, providing the day turned out to be free of storm, whale chase, or some other unusual occurrence.

When Maria and John went up on deck on Christmas Eve for their usual stretch, the weather was settled; only a brisk breeze ruffled the sea. Maria searched the skies for the brightest star to claim as her Christmas star, but could not decide. Every star in the firmament seemed to her to be glowing with brilliance tonight. She finally chose the Southern Cross as her Christmas symbol.

Husband and wife spoke little. Their minds were with the home folks. The ship was quiet except for the usual ship noises. Even the fo'c'sle tenants seemed subdued tonight. Distantly they heard the Pirate's harmonica seeking a tune a few of the seamen were humming, then, finding it, soaring above their low voices.

Margarita Thompson Diddel

'Listen,' whispered Maria; 'they're trying to make Christmas music—'

To you, in David's town this day,
Is born of David's line,
The Saviour, who is Christ, the Lord,
And this shall be the sign,
And this shall be the sign,

The heavenly Babe you there shall find
To human view displayed,
All meanly wrapped in swathing bands,
And in a manger laid,
And in a manger laid.

Maria sang the words softly, feeling deeply moved.

Now they were trying to find another tune. The harmonica faltered, the humming picked up, and she recognized the little German carol that was becoming such a favorite, 'Silent Night.' The song was repeated and the harmonica began to find the rhythm, adding harmony as the player gained confidence.

Maria did not want to leave the deck while the music lasted, but the cold was beginning to penetrate and John insisted that they return to the heated cabin to warm themselves before turning in. Timmy would have put the last fuel into the iron stove for the night.

The raisin pie turned out to Maria's satisfaction and John's praises were sweet to her ears. He also made much of a pair of socks into which she had knitted his initials with red yarn.

'Now, dear, you sit down in your rocker and close your eyes. I have a surprise for you, too.'

Maria obeyed, wondering how he could have found anything aboard ship. Scrimshaw, perhaps? She heard a drawer in the captain's desk opening and closing and then felt an object, too heavy to be scrimshaw, drop in her lap. She opened her eyes and found a black leather case and a little piece of paper, on which was written in John's fine hand, 'To my beloved little landlubber who is turning into a good sailor, but who is most of all my precious wife.'

The gift proved to be a small spyglass purchased the day he had been ashore at Buenos Aires. Maria was delighted and insisted on putting on her wraps and going to the quarterdeck at once to try it out. Thereafter it was her constant companion.

Whenever the cry, 'Thar-she-blows!' set the ship in action, as happened often in the early days of the new year, 1860, she always hurried to the quarterdeck with the spyglass.

She was sitting one day in her deckhouse, sewing on a long petticoat for the coming baby, a beautifully worked eyelet embroidery making the article a work of art, when a sighting was made. Immediately there was great excitement and apparent confusion on board. But the seeming confusion was really a quick orderly movement of each man to his job.

In response to the captain's query, 'Where away?' the lookout called, 'Two points off the lee bow, sir.'

'How far off?'

'Two miles and a half, sir,' came the answer.

Mate Richards appeared as if by magic, spyglass in hand. John seized it and looked, then shouted in great excitement, 'Sperm whales, sure—at least fifteen—a pod!'

Both men went into immediate action, shouting

orders in rapid succession. 'Haul aback the mainyard! Get the line tubs into the boats.'

By this time Maria was on the lee side of the quarterdeck, peering through her glass in practiced fashion. She gave a low cry of surprise when she located the many black mounds.

'The bushy spouts of vapor tilt forward. That's the mark of the sperm whale.' There was no one nearby to comment on her display of sea knowledge, but Maria felt a sense of satisfaction. Uncle Asa had been right when he told her just before she left home, 'Niece, you will find the sea is a great educator.' She could see him now with that far-off look in his eyes that meant he was thinking of his early whaling days.

Maria continued to watch the lowering of the boats with her eyes, but her mind stayed with the home folks. She wondered what her brothers would say when she came home with a baby. They would love him or her just as she loved her baby brother David, she decided.

A voice startled her. It was Doc, his hands shading his eyes as he looked toward the whales, and he was saying, 'Looks like we're set for a good haul of oil today, Mrs. Hamblin.'

The boats were away now, and to Maria's surprise, each had hoisted a small sail.

'When they get close, you'll see them begin to paddle like a lot of Indians.' And shortly Maria saw this happen. The men sat on the gunwales, paddles dipping into the water without a splash.

'Why, Doc?'

'Ma'am, that's so everything's quiet as possible. Whales have mighty keen hearing, 'specially when they're lying so low in the water. See, their spouts just clear the water. They're taking life easy-like, not gallied a mite.'

Doc handed her the spyglass and she looked again at the whales, spread out over acres of water. Then she said sadly, 'It seems a shame to disturb their peaceful life, to start killing them.' And she handed the glass back to Doc.

The cook leaned far out over the rail, pointing to the boats, 'See ma'am, they're getting nearer; they're going to strike. I expect some boats will get two whales. There's so many.'

'And the whales don't seem to know they are coming,' commented Maria in astonishment, looking once more through the glass.

'Ma'am, if you was out there, you wouldn't hear a sound except the sharp bow of the boat cutting through the water and the whales spouting. The men know that a sudden noise and those black backs would go down like grindstones dropped into water.'

'Doc, oh Doc, will you look? I don't see any whales now.' Maria spoke in a dismayed whisper.

Doc groaned as he looked. 'They're sure gone. Somebody must have sneezed or dropped a paddle. What a pity! I wonder who was the poor devil who did it. The air must be sizzlin' with sulphur curses. And him wishing he was home in the fruit cellar with thick walls.'

'And what will they do now? Wait for the whales to come up?' Maria asked.

'Oh, no, ma'am, not likely. They'll just wait until they get a signal from the ship to start chasing to the windward. And that means long, hard pulling and then maybe the chase is for nothing.

'Funny thing, Mrs. Hamblin, but when the whales get gallied, you know, frightened, they run to the windward. I've myself seen them gallied in a calm and they turn in the direction from which the wind blew last and keep that course for hours.'

'For hours! How can they?'

'Yes, ma'am, keep a straight course and never vary a point of the compass from it. I can't explain it. It's something that's puzzled many a whaleman besides myself.'

Maria saw the boats moving, but Doc knew from the signal on the masthead that the whales had been sighted on the weather beam, or windward direction.

'A long wait they'll have and lots of rowing around; it's hard telling where the gallied whale will turn up. And when he does, he's a mean creature. Lord only knows when they'll be back.'

Doc shook his head and limped back to the galley. Maria felt somewhat faint from standing and watching so long, so she went below to lie down.

The afternoon faded into evening and nothing was heard from the boats. Up on deck signal lamps were hoisted and many watchful eyes peered into the black waters, hoping to see the returning crews.

Maria waited in the cabin, thinking of the black night, starless and blanketed with clouds. And out in it were men in trouble of some kind—men like Smitty, with wives and babies at home, who perhaps at this very moment were rocking and wondering how their men were faring. Maria wiped a tear away, picked up her Bible, and turned to the passages that had comforted her in the past.

At ten o'clock there was a great commotion on deck and Maria hurried up to the quarterdeck in time to see two of the boats, towing a battered one, approaching the port side of the ship. She heard the captain's voice asking questions. Yes, they were all safe; one boat stoven, but most of it saved.

Maria sighed with relief and went below. The night was not so fearful now. She went to the porthole in her stateroom. As she gazed out, she saw the clouds part and the Southern Cross glow in soft radiance. She smiled and said aloud, 'Agnes, your Smitty is back safe and sound. I saw him.' Her own heart was filled with thankfulness that all the men had returned.

She wondered about the whales. Doc had said that sometimes the windward chase was for nothing. This must be one of those times.

Maria was already in bed when John finally came down. He told her the men had eaten supper and gone below to sleep, a tired and glum lot. No, the luck was bad. No whale and a good boat stoven. But it might have been worse; someone might have been killed.

She was sleepy, but curiosity made her ask what scared the whales in the first place.

John replied, 'One of the men in the second mate's boat struck the side of the boat with the edge of his paddle and before the sound had faded, the large school of whales had disappeared. That shows how sharp their sense of hearing is.'

'And didn't they catch even one whale?'

'We'll hear about that tomorrow,' John said. And he extinguished the lamp in the stateroom and dropped his tired body beside Maria.

Next morning the second mate made a full report. The boats were pulling to windward as the signals had ordered and had spotted the whales about a mile away. But suddenly the quarry had disappeared. Still the boats went on, the men thinking the whales would appear ahead later. At last they spied a dark form about twenty feet under the surface of the water, then another and another.

'One was on his side, eyeing us; then, his big mouth wide open, he started for us, lookin' mighty wicked,' a crew member reported.

At that moment the harpooner was poised for a strike at another whale, then came the lightning swiftness of the attack. There was a crash and everyone in the boat was thrown into the water, for the whale's mouth had closed over the end of the boat.

Then a strange thing happened, which probably saved several lives. The attacking whale started back and somehow collided with an oncoming whale.

Chapter 18

JOHN looked up from his charts one day as Maria came into the cabin.

'I have a surprise for you, dear,' he announced. 'I'm going to put in at a Chilean port for supplies before we cross the Pacific. With good luck you can have a few hours ashore.' He showed her where the port of Talcahuano lay on the southern coast of Chile. 'It's just a rough port town,' he said apologetically, 'but you may be able to get some of the sewing things you've been wishing for.'

'Just to walk on land again will be wonderful,' exclaimed Maria. Her spirits rose at once.

Two days later Maria put on a warm brown woolen dress, her bonnet and cloak, and stood at the bulwarks, filled with inner excitement, as The Roman sailed into Talcahuano Bay.

Even from the ship, the town did not look inviting. 'But it is on good, solid land,' she reminded herself.

When the ship had docked, she walked unaided down the gangplank onto the pier. But after only a few steps on land she clung to John's arm.

'Why, I can hardly walk. I feel as though the earth is heaving!' she exclaimed.

John smiled down at her tense face. 'Don't be alarmed,' he told her. 'It will pass. Just hold fast to my arm.'

All the short distance to the hotel, the ground seemed to sway and she was filled with dizziness. She looked fearfully at the passing people. Their faces appeared coarse and cruel, and John's warning that Talcahuano was a city of vice and wickedness came to her mind.

'Perhaps if I knew them, though, they would be just ordinary people, more good than bad,' she reasoned.

The ancient hotel for seafaring folks was weather-beaten on the outside and shabby inside. Still, after the cramped quarters of the ship, it seemed spacious to Maria. The man behind the desk looked like a German, but he addressed them in Spanish. When John asked for a room, he switched at once to English. He led them to a downstairs room off a hall back of the lobby.

The windows of the room faced west. Looking out, Maria saw the familiar masts of The Roman on the horizon.

'Maria, I think you will be all right here while I go to see about supplies,' John told her. 'Why not rest a while until you get the feel of land again?'

She locked the door securely after John left, and spent the rest of the morning alternating between lying on the bed and walking about the room. 'This is so foolish,' she told herself. 'I've waited so long to step on solid ground and now I can't enjoy it.'

By the time her husband returned at noon, she had lost some of her dizziness, but she still felt safe only when holding on to something. They went to the dining room and sat down at a small table. It was some time before the waiter approached them. As he recommended the *Chupe de Mariscos*, a fish chowder, Maria decided that he resembled mate Rogers. She was surprised that he didn't speak with an Irish brogue. Another period of waiting passed before he brought the steaming chowder.

'But it is worth waiting for,' Maria observed after the first careful taste.

'Siesta is observed here,' John told her. 'When the stores open again at three o'clock, if you feel able, I will take you.'

The time consumed in the dining room brought three o'clock around quickly. Maria, rested and with her list in hand, was waiting when John came for her.

The little port city was bustling when they reached the street. Spanish was heard everywhere, although many of the people looked to be of Anglo-Saxon background.

Maria was delighted to find shiny new needles in the little store to which John led her, for the salt air had rusted much of her supply. Warm wool and flannel materials were offered also, and she bought enough to finish the baby's layette, and make herself a couple of plain roomy dresses and a shirt for John.

With John carrying her bundles and Maria clinging to his arm, they walked a little farther up the street. As they passed a saloon, the door opened and they caught a glimpse of several of The Roman's men standing at the bar.

John returned Smitty's greeting and called, 'Remember, we're sailing at sundown!'

One of the drinkers turned. 'We got Smitty with us;

he'll see that we get back in time.'

John nodded, muttering, 'He aims to be captain someday—has to be a tough *hombre*.'

'I'm glad he's not a drinker, a good man,' Maria said in a warm, approving tone.

The dining room was open for tea when the Hamblins reached the hotel. 'Suppose we have a substantial tea now,' John proposed. 'Dinner will be served too late for us.'

The waiter suggested cold sliced beef and they agreed. When it was finally served, the roast beef was accompanied by fresh breads and hot tea. A strange dessert made with pineapple topped off what both declared to have been an excellent meal.

Maria was surprised that she felt normal again when she was back on The Roman. 'I'm getting more used to the sea than land,' she told John as they stood at the rail on the gently swaying ship.

She did not go below until all the crew had returned. Smitty must have had a difficult time getting some of the men safely back on board. A few were noisy, boisterous; others were sullen or stupid from the wine they had consumed. Maria saw the wisdom of allowing only part of the crew shore leave. Smitty was the only one who could have been trusted on the ratlines.

As they sailed out of Talcahuano Bay, Maria was not unhappy to leave the Chilean port behind.

Whaling luck continued bad in the next weeks, but one day the glum atmosphere of the ship dissolved into a spirit of joyous anticipation by the sharp call from the lookout, 'Ship ahoy! Ship ahoy!'

Maria in her deckhouse became instantly alert.

'Where away?' sang out Captain Hamblin.
'On the weather beam.'

Maria knew that was too far away to discern the type of ship, but she put aside her sewing and hurried to the rail of the quarterdeck with her glass.

'Oh, if only it's a whaler from home,' she said over and over as she watched the approaching vessel. And her hope was shared by all.

It seemed long to Maria before they could make out her outline against the blue horizon. At last, though, the square rigging and bluff-bowed outline unmistakably betokened a whaler. Now, if only she had news from home for them!

When the ship was close enough to observe without a glass, The Roman's rails were crowded; eager eyes watched to see whether there would be a gam, a jolly good time in steerage and fo'c'sle, as well as in the cabin.

Finally the whaler was within hailing distance and, through a trumpet, the captain of the approaching ship called, 'Captain James F. Cleaveland of The Seconet, five years out of New Bedford. Mrs. Cleaveland on board.'

'Oh, John,' was all Maria could say. It was a warm day but a chill tingled Maria's scalp, so delighted was she at the thought of meeting another woman there in the trackless sea.

John quickly answered, 'Captain John Hamblin of The Roman, seven months from New Bedford. Mrs. Hamblin on board.'

Maria kept her glass fixed on the approaching ship to get her first glimpse of Mrs. Cleaveland. Finally, the two ships squared sails at a safe distance and Maria glimpsed a feminine figure on the quarterdeck of The

Seconet. The women waved to each other. Quickly, a gam was planned. In view of Maria's pregnancy, it was agreed that Captain and Mrs. Cleaveland should come to The Roman.

Maria watched while her visitor was let down in a bos'n's chair to a waiting whaleboat and was rowed over by willing crewmen.

According to inflexible whaling etiquette, they came in the starboard boat, while, at the same time, mate Richards of The Roman returned the call in the larboard boat. The men who manned the boats visited with the other ship's crew—the steerage men with the steerage folk and the fo'c'sle men with each other.

The cooks on each ship did their best to make the occasion festive; musical instruments were brought out and there followed songs and dances and much merriment. Yarns and whaling adventures were exchanged and any news from home was news worth everyone's close attention.

Mrs. Cleaveland came up over the side in The Roman's gamming chair and Maria saw a lively looking young woman some ten years older than herself with dark hair and eyes. Her whole expression revealed interest and vitality. After an exchange of civilities, the visitors were shown below to the cabin, where Captain Cleaveland handed John a bag of mail.

'It is a stroke of luck that we met a New Bedford whaler headed for the Arctic, for the Bering Sea whaling season, a few days back and they handed your mail to us since we were more likely to gam you,' the visitors informed John.

Maria watched John quickly sort the mail. When he had finished, he handed her a batch of papers and several letters. He went quickly with the crew's mail to distribute it to them. It was always the captain's duty.

When he returned, the visitors gladly excused John and Maria to read their long looked-for mail. They had experienced the same feelings themselves in the time that had elapsed since they had seen their loved ones.

Aunt Abby's letter was opened first and read silently, with John looking over Maria's shoulder as she sat on one of the folding chairs.

David is here visiting us. He is growing like a weed and is getting to look more and more like your dear mother, my beloved sister. He and Amasah talk of nothing but when they go whaling with Captain John Coquin Hamblin. You are their hero, John. I am enclosing a tintype of David with his captain's cap that you gave him.

'Do you have any children?' Maria asked Mrs. Cleaveland, handing her David's tintype to admire.

'Yes, two little girls, both born since we left New Bedford. I didn't bring them with me because the sea is so choppy. I left them with Mr. Wap-Wap, the fourth mate. My elder daughter, Ninita, is so fond of him, and has called him that since she first started to talk.'

Maria looked at her guest in amazement. Two babies born in foreign places and she looked as though she had not a care in the world! Quickly she glanced through her other letters so that she could give her interesting guest her full attention. Her father, somewhat upset by the hard feelings between the North and South, her Uncle Asa, sure that in the coming elections Abe Lincoln would win and be able to patch things up, Lisha, interested in Rosalie Bowman, church affairs, his chances of promotion in the shipyards.

'Oh, that is too bad!' Maria exclaimed and read

aloud, "'Amasah is deviling his mother into letting him go on a whaling ship as soon as he can get a berth. You may meet him at a gam if you stay away three years.'"

Maria glanced quickly up at John's face. He was frowning. She touched his hand resting on her shoulder. She knew without speaking that they shared this disappointment. If Amasah had only been patient a little longer! On John's ship he would have had opportunities for quick advancement. On another ship, under a careless captain, or a cruel captain—Maria's heart ached for what might be ahead for this favorite cousin.

There was nothing more of particular interest in the letters, except that they all held in common an underlying uneasiness about the political situation in the States. After a quick glance at each, Maria put them away until later and turned her full attention to entertaining her guests.

Captain Cleaveland proved to have an inexhaustible store of sea yarns and personal adventures which he related with dash and humor. John did his share of yarning and the cabin rang with merry laughter. Maria inwardly contrasted their visitor's dark eyes, glinting with wit, his well modeled features and black beard, with her own husband's bronzed skin and sunburned hair and thoughtful blue eyes. John looked much more the sea captain; James Cleaveland would have been equally at home in a drawing room, Maria thought.

After a while, Maria took Mrs. Cleaveland into the stateroom to show her the fancywork which had occupied the months at sea and to have her alone for the 'woman talk' which she craved. There were so many questions she wanted to ask about her two babies and about her background, for Maria's ears had discovered that this was not a New Bedford girl, but an Irish girl.

Mary Cleaveland's story was indeed interesting and

Thistle in Her Hand

Maria drank in every word of her account of immigration with her family to Sydney, Australia, her desire to visit America with its great opportunities, her chance meeting with Captain Cleaveland, who had swept her off her feet, and her lonely year in New Bedford with her husband off on a whaling voyage.

'But your babies! Where were they born?' Maria could not wait to know.

Her guest made a grimace. 'One in Talcahuano—an experience I would rather forget; the other at the tiny Peru port of Paita, with few comforts, but among friends. Believe me, that is the most important consideration.'

Maria paled. Who would be a friend in Sydney? John's acquaintances there would be mostly businessmen. Hesitatingly, Maria told her guest of their plans for her to be in Sydney for the birth.

Mrs. Cleaveland's face lighted. 'That will be good. If you have no plans, I can tell you of a sanitarium where you would have the best care possible. It is run by two spinsters. Oh, it's a pretty place with gardens and a wide lawn, right at the end of one of the coves.'

'Tell me more about it,' pleaded Maria. 'Do you think they would take me in?'

'I'm sure of it. I'll give you a note of introduction. Everything will be all right. Don't you worry your heart the least bit.'

And Mary Cleaveland squeezed Maria's hand warmly and turned the conversation to making clothes for herself and the children aboard ship.

While the two young women visited, John and Captain Cleaveland in the cabin or above deck discussed whaling luck and the rising storm cloud on the political horizon at home.

Doc prepared a gala meal, bringing out delicacies

from the captain's special cupboard. The Cleavelands had brought along a jar of crystallized ginger and a special kind of cookies that Mary often made for the little girls when the galley was free.

After the meal, the gamming continued above decks and below. On the forward decks the men were still entertaining each other and their guests. Maria felt great contentment, and the big world of the seven seas grew smaller as she shared experiences with her sea neighbor.

The gam was brought to an abrupt end by a change of weather. Misgivings about the accumulating clouds along the horizon ended when distant rumblings and flashes of lightning warned them of an approaching storm. The goodbyes were said quickly and regretfully. Mary Cleaveland was lowered in The Roman's gamming chair while her husband went down the rope ladder to the waiting boat, and there was much waving of hands as the ships again exchanged boatloads of crew and officers. When all were safely on board again, The Seconet and The Roman set sail at once, hoping to put plenty of distance between the vessels should the storm turn out to be a squall.

The ship was buffeted all night, but somehow Maria did not mind it as much as usual. She had so much to think about —the news from home, the companionship enjoyed with new friends—above all, the feeling of security brought by the knowledge of a refuge in Sydney where her baby might be safely born.

Whaling luck changed now. A day or two after the gam, early in the morning, the lookout raised the welcome cry, 'Thar she blows!' and 'Sperm whale!' And an eighty-barrel whale was caught and brought alongside. The cutting-in was completed before dark and John ordered the trying-out begun at once.

Thistle in Her Hand

Maria looked on a strange scene that night. In addition to the usual deck lamps, blubber burned in a basket made of pieces of hoop iron that swung between the twin chimneys of the tryworks. A 'bug light,' John called it. She shivered in spite of the heat as the blubber sputtered and hissed in the night wind and the forms of the perspiring seamen passing back and forth on the decks cast strange and menacing shadows. Sometimes the thick black smoke from the full blasting tryworks blew back toward the quarterdeck, stinging her eyes and choking her, although she held a handkerchief to her face.

She could not bear to go below while the fires were lit; she had heard of wooden ships, saturated with whale oil, catching fire during a trying-out. She told herself that she must have confidence in John's judgment, his great sense of precaution. She knew the big iron try-pots, their one flat side fitted snugly against the other, were encased in strong bricks and then surrounded with iron plate, well insulated from the deck beneath by a water bath.

But the whole procedure was so much more fearful at night! She paced the quarterdeck until the bells rang out the midnight hour. Then she went below, exhausted, to sleep fitfully until the sounds of the decks being scoured and scrubbed awakened her. The smell of the oil still assaulted Maria's nose everywhere. John, who joined her in the saloon for breakfast, warned her to be extra careful of her footing because there was still a lot of oil about.

'And have you had no sleep, John?' she asked anxiously.

'I had a few catnaps on the sofa. But, never mind, Maria; the sooner the barrels are filled, the sooner we set sail for home.' He finished his tea in one gulp. Then, looking anything but worn out, he told Maria he wanted her to see the pretty amber hue of the oil. It had by now been passed through the cooler to the storage tank between decks and was being run by the watch, with the cooper in charge, through a canvas hose into the bungs of the great casks.

The last of the rigging had not yet been cleaned of its accumulation of soot and grease when the 'Ah—blow!' came again from the masthead. The jubilant seamen forgot their weariness as the whale chase resumed.

By late afternoon, two sperm whales were moored alongside. John considered the weather conditions with care and decided to postpone the cutting-in until dawn so that the men could have a full night's rest before the labor of reducing the great bodies to oil commenced again.

As soon as the eastern skies promised the coming of day, the men were roused and the work began. Maria awoke to the sound of their chanteys as they raised the great strips of blubber with the cutting blocks and falls, and the sharp song of the grindstone against steel as the cooper sharpened the cutting blades.

'Another day of smoke and smell,' thought Maria, but her mood was cheerful. The barrels were filling fast. She found herself humming along with the strains of 'Sally Brown' and 'Whiskey Johnny,' as the voices of the men reached her. The words of many of the chanteys did not make much sense to her, but the rhyme and rhythm pleased her ear.

Later in the morning, chores done, she worked on the coming baby's clothing in the deckhouse. As she finished the long petticoat she had worked on for weeks, she held it to her cheek, thinking of the child who would wear it. Suddenly she sniffed it closely and groaned, 'Whale oil! Even on my baby's clothes!'

Everything would have to be washed after they reached Sydney if their whaling luck continued. Resignedly, she picked up a piece of soft flannel and lay it out on the table to pencil in the scallops for another petticoat, using half of the circle of a spool for a pattern.

Now the men were singing a chantey that had become familiar in the hard days of rounding the Horn. She sang beneath her breath along with the lusty voices of the sailors.

> *A long time, and a very long time to me,*
> *Way-hay-heigho,*
> *A long time, and a very long time,*
> *And a long time ago.*
> *While strolling on the shores,*
> *Way-hay-heigho,*
> *I met a maiden fair as May,*
> *A long time ago.*
> *Around Cape Horn with flying sails,*
> *Way-hay-heigho,*
> *Around Cape Horn to hunt for whales,*
> *A long time ago.*

They must be thinking of home getting nearer, for they sound happy, thought Maria. But what about the wanderers, like the Pirate, who had no home, no place to go back to? Oh, it was good to have a home with folks you loved and who loved you, even if you had to be away from them, and even if the thought of them increased your loneliness. Now they were singing another verse—

Margarita Thompson Diddel

My Bess is fine and fair to view,
Way-hay-heigho,
Her hair is brown and her eyes are blue,
A long time ago.

Maria's eyes wandered away from her work to the sky. What would the baby look like? Would she or he be like Bess with hair of brown and eyes of blue? She wished her ordeal in a strange land were over.

John—would he be able to stay with her? Probably not. As before, he would most likely be away filling the casks with oil. She must hold on to that thought. The sooner the barrels were filled, the sooner they would head for home.

The men must be thinking again of home, too. Over and over they sang the verse:

Around Cape Horn with flying sails,
Way-hay-heigho.

A new song caught her ear.

As I was awalkin' down Paradise Street,
Away, ay, blow the man down.
A flash lookin' packet I chanced for to meet.
Give me some time to blow the man down.
I hailed her in English; she answered me clear,
Away, ay, blow the man down.
I'm from the Black Anchor bound to the Shakespeare.
Give me some time to blow the man down.

Other verses followed, but Maria could not understand the words, for the men sang them indistinctly and with a lot of yipping. When she asked John about it, he laughed and told her the men did not intend for her to understand, for those verses were not fit for a lady's ears. The simple, decent ones were the favorites, however, and the ones the men sang over and over again.

Greasy luck had come to stay, Maria decided. During the next three weeks fires blazed in the try-pots almost constantly, and the decks were hardly ever free of oil. The men snatched their rest whenever they could. Maria seldom saw John except at a distance during the day and sometimes not even at night.

She usually ate her meals alone now. The dark, oily smoke seeped into every corner of the ship. She could not escape it, no matter where she went. She felt it in her hair; she couldn't wash it out. She even imagined she tasted it in her food.

When she thought of John and the men on the slippery decks, trying to fill the casks while the ship rocked and lurched, as it was doing at that very moment, or of the men on the cutting-stage trying to use their sharp spades with the stage bobbing up and down with the waves and only the iron railing running waist high along the platform to keep them from falling into the water, then she could not complain of her lot. Instead she went about her housekeeping affairs on the ship with a laugh and a song and the great hope that the whole messiness would mean they might make this a record voyage and start for home long before the usual time.

Chapter 19

'Oh, no,' scoffed Maria one day as she glanced toward John, who stood on the taffrail with his glass to his eye. She remembered now his words of warning to the redhaired, hot-tempered Irish third mate.

Her attention was now directed toward two of the four men in the mate's boat. One was Chock, a hairy, swarthy, muscular man with an ill-tempered look, and the other was Skinny, the youth who always seemed to be the older man's shadow. She wondered why he was called Skinny. He was slim, about Lisha's build. In a way he reminded her of her brother, not in the face, but in the way he loped along. She hoped the mate, who was known as a harsh, cruel man, would not be too hard on Skinny. And for a moment she felt a stab of nostalgia as she thought of Lisha and home.

Maria's glance returned to the lovely island they approached that day, but still, an uneasy feeling persisted as she watched the long boat with its load of barrels to be filled with enough water and wood to last until they reached Sydney Town.

She saw the men arrive at the shore, pick up two

buckets apiece, and dash into the bush. A hush fell on the ship as all eyes turned toward the land. Even the men sleeping in the fo'c'sle were on deck. She felt fright in the very air.

Suddenly the mate and one of the men ran out from the bushes and headed for the boat. She could hear the mate and another man shouting. But there was no sign of Skinny and Chock. The mate motioned the men to climb in and start rowing, and then Chock and Skinny appeared on the shore. It looked as if the mate meant to go on without them, but then he slowed down and let the two swim to the boat.

Maria turned around at the sound of something strange behind her and saw John and mate Richards handing guns to some of the men. In horror she looked back toward the boat, racing fast for the ship, then beyond the boat to the island. It bristled now with dark men with lances, and some of them were launching native canoes. John shouted commands, echoed by the mates on board, and sails sprang out.

By good fortune a brisk wind had come up, and the ship started collecting her men and their boat and struck out for the open ocean. Maria grasped the rail tightly, weak but relieved. Her relief was short-lived when she saw that John's face was ashen gray with a look of fury she had never expected to see on his face. Smitty, beside him, had much the same look. So did many of the crew, those with guns still clutched in their hands or those tending the sails.

She called to the cabin boy and asked him to help her downstairs. She could just make it to the sofa, where she lay down. Henry, who had followed them, ran to the pantry and made her some hot tea.

'It's all right, Mrs. Hamblin, the ship is sailing at a good clip and we're beyond the divils,' he said, and, his

Thistle in Her Hand

hands still trembling, he closed his eyes and folded them in prayer. 'Praise ye dear Lord for saving us from what lay on the island, especially our little lady,' he mumbled, with a look of grim satisfaction.

'But now comes the reckn'in,' announced Timmy, who had gone up on deck and had hurried down again full of news. 'Seems the men saw some women and started chasing them, then they saw the men.' Timmy reported, 'The captain told the boat's mate to give them the full works. And I never seen the mate so blazing mad. He said to the cap'n, "Aye, Aye, Captain—the whole works and extras."'

Maria sat up wide-eyed and asked, 'Whole works—what do you mean?'

'Hanging by the thumbs and beaten...' His words were stopped by a black hand across his mouth.

'Shet your fool mouth.' Before Henry could stop her she was heading for the deck. In her distraught mind it was Lisha who was to be hung by the thumbs and beaten and she must save him.

'Stop it,' she screamed at John. Then for a fleeting moment Mrs. Snow's words came to her. 'You must never interfere with the captain. Never. Never.' That was the last she knew until she came to in the bed.

She was aware of John's hands moving fast and his voice ordering Smitty to bring him things. Henry was at the door with a pan of steaming water which he handed to Smitty. Then the pains became so intense she thought she was going to die and she clutched at John's shoulders and she heard him say, 'Push, push.' She heard a lot of screaming and then realized it was her own screaming and she couldn't stop it. Then she suddenly heard a baby cry and her pains stopped.

'My baby,' she cried weakly with joy. 'Our baby.'

'Yes, darling,' John said as he smeared grease over

the tiny body. 'Now Smitty, get...Oh my God ...Henry!' he shouted, and, wiping his hands, laid the baby by Maria and leaned over a prostrate Smitty, blood streaming from a cut where he had knocked his forehead on the corner of the chest.

'He's fainted,' he told Henry. 'Take him to the other room and bring him water and call Doc to tend to him.'

Later Smitty sheepishly admitted to his captain that when his baby was born the midwife had sent him out of the house because he turned sick.

'I thought this time I could stand the sight of blood,' he said disgustedly. 'I ain't got no guts.'

John laughed, 'You got guts enough in your work, Smitty. You're a seaman, and a darn good one.'

John never would discuss the matter of her intervention in the captain's disciplinary duties. Doc told her in private that the punishment was stopped when she fainted, to be taken up later. The men were put in the brig. But when soon after the ship stopped for water and wood at an island known to be safe, Chock and Skinny somehow escaped from their detention in the brig and swam ashore. Mr. Richards and his men spent little time looking for them, maybe thinking it wiser to get rid of them, and hired two Kanakas who were experienced seamen.

The baby, named Alice because John liked the song 'Alice Benbolt,' looked like a tiny doll, thin and frail. Maria, too, looked frail. John was anxious to get them to a good doctor and aimed at getting to Sydney as quickly as possible.

Maria declared that she was feeling better each day and insisted on walking about and tending to the baby and preparing for their shore leave.

'The ship will dock at Sydney for a while and I'll stay

on the ship to watch some repairs made and barnacles removed,' he told Maria, 'but I'll come up to see you and Alice every day.'

Maria realized it was the only thing John could do, but she felt depressed that they would be far apart so much of the day. She realized that, bad as it was on the ship, there was great comfort in knowing that John was always so near. Now she would be among strangers and she felt a little timid at the thought of it.

But she brushed the thought aside when she thought of how much good it would do the baby, and the doctor would also hurry her own recovery. She became a little excited at the thought of seeing the city the Cleavelands had talked so much about.

Chapter 20

THE night came when John announced to Maria that the next day they would reach Sydney Town.

'Tomorrow morning we enter Port Jackson Bay, which is really the landlocked harbor of Sydney.'

'My things are all ready; I've packed the trunk and a bag,' Maria answered happily.

'We'll have to do some sailing before we dock, my dear,' John warned her. 'The harbor here is twenty miles long.'

'Twenty miles! But can our ship sail right up those miles to the piers?'

'Yes indeed, and not only our ship, but much larger ones. The water is deep; it's a fine natural harbor.'

Maria sighed with relief. 'Just imagine being able to step down the gangplank onto the pier!' She felt she could not have endured being let down to a boat and rowed ashore.

Next morning while the baby slept, John and Maria stood at the stern rail of the quarterdeck, gazing at the pleasant vistas of a new world on either shore and admiring the magnificent expanse of water they were sailing upon.

'What a harbor! It spreads out from deep water fingers stretching miles up between those wooded banks.'

Maria was more interested in the homes that were coming into view. 'They're made of stone, aren't they?'

'Yes, this is a great sandstone country. You'll see many sandstone quarries. The wharves are of the same stone.'

As soon as the ship made dock, John sent word to the sanitarium of Maria's imminent arrival. When the hack drove up to the homey, two-story house of buff sandstone, surrounded by wide lawns and shrubbery tinged with the first quick brush of fall, the two sisters came out at once to bid them welcome.

'We are delighted to welcome any friends of Captain and Mrs. Cleaveland. What! The baby—'

'Yes, the baby arrived early,' John quickly explained.

'We are so happy to have you, Mrs. Hamblin and Captain Hamblin—and the darling little baby.'

One spoke, then the other. They were just as Mary Cleaveland had described them: Miss Emma, tall and slender, with wings of white scattered through otherwise dusky hair; Miss Essie, small and plump in stature, her hair in puffs and curls of silvery hue. Both sisters had fine textured skin with a touch of pink in their cheeks, and their gray eyes with well defined brows also proclaimed their sisterhood.

Beaming with approval of their guests, the sisters led John and Maria to the room she and the baby were to occupy. Since leaving the boat, Maria had been walking as in a dream, with no sense of reality. The feeling increased as she looked about the airy, cheerful room.

This was the kind of bedroom she had planned before she fell in love with John and became a whaling wife. Dark mahogany furniture, polished like satin; soft carpet; fresh white ruffled curtains, and over all a sweet, fresh scent. She was sure she would awaken and find herself in the gimballed bed which occupied so much of the crowded stateroom she had lived in for almost a year.

Suddenly the feeling of weakness came back again and John, noting her white lips, put his arm around her. Maria crumpled on his shoulder in tears. 'Oh John, why can't I hurry up and feel normal and enjoy being in this charming place, on land?'

John put her on the chaise longue and Miss Emmy plumped the pillows before Maria's troubled head touched them. She covered Maria with her paisley shawl because it was getting chilly. Miss Essie took the now crying baby into her own room. Miss Emmy soon slipped out and left John to comfort Maria.

In a short time the tears ceased, but the feeling of unreality persisted. Presently, John left to return to the ship, insisting that she continue to rest before attempting to walk about.

'It's like getting used to walking on the ship, but in reverse,' he joked as he tilted her chin to give her a goodbye kiss.

Shortly after John had gone, there was a gentle knock and Miss Essie entered, bearing a tea tray which she placed on a small table beside Maria. She lifted the teapot from the lacquered tray and poured the amber fluid into a dainty cup of transparent china and handed it to Maria. The tea and the scone with it revived Maria. Miss Essie suggested that they take a turn about the front yard.

'My sister is looking after the baby,' she reminded her, 'and walking on the grass will really bring you back to terra firma.'

'Oh, Miss Essie, it's what I've dreamed of these many

months,' Maria said, getting up. Drawing the paisley shawl about her shoulders, she stepped out onto the grass on Miss Essie's arm.

'I'm afraid I'm walking like an old sea dog, after being on a ship so many months,' Maria giggled nervously.

'Oh no, my dear; you are doing excellently. Now let us go to the bench under that eucalyptus tree—the one over there on the lawn.'

So Maria once again walked on grass, soft, green grass. She got down and touched it, felt the solid earth under her hands. She touched the bark of the tall tree and sat down on the bench. She felt so strange, so unreal; yet it was her world, the land world. What was the matter with her?

'Just a few months ago, I, an earth person, was learning how to walk, to act in the sea world,' she remarked to Miss Essie. 'It was comical.'

She began to laugh and suddenly found herself crying, remembering vividly how she had tried to thwart punishment of the two seamen; and she thought that John—no, Captain Hamblin—had probably looked at her with eyes of fury. Only she didn't see that look she had dreaded all those months. She had fainted.

'Here's a handkerchief.' And Miss Essie handed her a spotless handkerchief and patted her shoulder with sympathy for a moment. Then she said quietly, 'Tell me about it. Sometimes telling someone about something that is troubling you helps.'

And Maria told her all, and a strange feeling of relief came over her. She sighed: her world had begun to right itself, as the ship had done after the hurricane had passed.

'Now, dear, back home for a nap. Talking about your experience has been an ordeal, but now it is in the past.

Thistle in Her Hand

Don't let it haunt you anymore and retard your recovery. Someday when you are both relaxed, talk to your beloved John about that incident. That will truly put it where it belongs—in your common past.'

Later Maria awakened when the bedroom door opened and the slender sister appeared with a tray. Maria, feeling quite herself again, sat up and enjoyed a bowl of hot chicken soup and a custard dessert. The china again was delicate and pretty, but Maria's eyes were fastened on a strange flower in a vase, a ball of golden fluff, with two silvery fern-like leaves. She touched it with her finger and looked inquiringly at her hostess.

'That's an acacia flower, called "the wattle" here in Australia, and it is here as a welcome to you. There are other varieties, but that pale gold shade is one of my favorites.'

Smiling at herself now, Maria told Miss Emmy how much she had felt like a ship in a storm.

'Why not?' the lady countered. 'We are part of our environment. For so long yours has been a ship, a sturdy ship that has buffeted the ocean storms and brought you here to our Australia.'

'It seems like home here in many ways; yet there is a strangeness about everything—the trees, the colors, the flowers,' said Maria thoughtfully.

'Australia is a land of strange animals and trees that belong to another age. If you visited museums in some of the great cities of the world, you would find fossils of a bygone age that are still living and growing here in Australia, but nowhere else.'

Maria listened entranced to the gentle voice with its clipped English accent tell of the interesting things to be found in her adopted country.

Later, when Miss Emmy and Maria were discussing

the newness of Australia, Miss Emmy pointed out that although it had been so recently settled by Europeans, it was thought by scientists to be the oldest as well as the smallest continent.

'My father and others decided that point at a conference in London years ago. They believed that this was part of a great continent, including South America. Then, at some distant time in the past, all of it submerged except Australia. Other parts of it reappeared as we see them today.'

Maria was puzzled. 'How can they tell that?'

'By the flora and fauna flourishing here and the mountains. You remember I told you that there are animals living here that have become extinct elsewhere in the world.'

'But what about the mountains?' Maria enjoyed drawing out her scientific companion.

'The mountains I refer to are very old, worn down by the elements. The sharper the mountain peaks, the younger the region. Our mountains are so old, their peaks are worn down to nubbins.'

Alice in her world was as content as her mother. The constant attention of three loving and admiring women was only part of the source of her good nature. She gave every promise of being the kind of child that brings delight to those about her. She ate and slept with amazing regularity and, when awake, was good-natured and showed a growing interest in the world about her.

'I'm sure she is going to be musical, Maria,' declared Miss Essie when Alice was almost two months old. 'See how she appears to be listening when I sing.' Miss Essie sang a few lines of 'Comin' Through the Rye' as she walked about the bedroom. The baby's blue eyes followed the sound.

'You must be sure to give her piano lessons when she is old enough.'

Piano lessons. Maria looked troubled. Would the time come when she and John could settle down on land with their children and live like other people? Such a possibility seemed distant indeed.

Maria smiled, 'I'm afraid the whalemen's chanteys will be her music for a long while.'

Nevertheless, as the time drew near for The Roman to return to port, Maria found that she was ready to return to the sea life. All the attractions of living on land did not compensate for being separated from John. And surprisingly, she somehow missed the sea. Her trunk was packed and waiting on the day John returned to take his wife and daughter back to the ship. There were many extra bundles, things for the baby, gifts to take home, including seeds from the sisters' garden. Miss Essie was not too hopeful about their growing on Cape Cod, but Maria was determined to try to raise some of the Australian flowers.

When John saw how well his wife looked, he could not help wondering whether he was asking too much of her to return to the hard life ahead. But Maria dispelled his doubts quickly when she clung to him and cried, 'Oh John, don't ever sail away without me again.'

Chapter 21

THE Roman wore an air of festivity on the day in early July when the captain brought Maria and baby Alice on board. The ship had been painted and the carpenter had rebuilt the tiny deckhouse under the skid beams on which the extra whaleboats were upturned. Maria peeped in and found the same sturdy bench along the wall, with its removable cushion for the times when the bench would hold her washtub. She sighed. It looked so small after the spaciousness of the homes in Sydney.

The narrow work table was piled with gifts from the crew for the new baby. The seamen had carved scrimshaw and wood toys for the time when Alice would be old enough to enjoy them. Chipps had made an elaborate sea chest, brightly painted and with whales and fishes carved on its top and sides. Others had spent many hours rolling hemp into rope for easy looping over the davits and there was a basket full of rope yarn lengths to tie the baby's clothes to the line.

As long as the land was in sight, Maria stayed in the deckhouse. Once John came and took the baby from her, to show to the ship's crew from the tryworks platform. He pushed back the warm shawls to display Alice's golden ringlets. The baby appeared to be interested in everything and everyone and won their hearts.

'She is the ship's angel, and may Mother Mary protect her.' The Pirate crossed himself as he spoke.

The stateroom too, had received special attention. Fresh paint and polish had been used liberally; there was a rack for drying clothes during rainy weather and the improvised crib in the chest of drawers was complete with slats to hold the baby in during rough weather.

In the weeks and months that followed, whaling luck was good and the crew declared that Princess Alice had brought the ship good fortune. Fires blazed often in the try-pots and many barrels of 'greasy gold' were going into the hold.

During this time, little Alice adjusted to sea life with ease, sleeping serenely through squalls and those periods when trying-out made the ship noisy, smelly, and smoky. When she was awake, she was always ready to be entertained and rewarded her entertainers with a dimpled smile or a throaty baby chuckle. All of the quarterdeck, from cabin boy to the dignified captain, vied for her smile or her even-more-to-be-desired laugh.

In these days, Maria's greatest problem was laundering the baby's clothes. More than once the call 'Ah—blow!' came while the davits were strung with lines of baby things. Often the boats had to be lowered so quickly there was no time for her to rescue them and they were tossed to the deck and trampled by hurrying feet. She did not complain; this was part of being a whaling captain's wife. Getting the precious oil was all that mattered and Maria was as eager as any of the crew to fill the hold in record time and start for home.

As the southern winter dwindled, the good whaling came to an end. For a while the decks were cleared of the oily smoke and fumes; the ship was cleaned and scrubbed from bow to stern. John insisted that the men do the same with their own quarters.

Bedding and clothing were washed and aired carefully, for the men knew from experience that their captain would not overlook the shirking of these tasks. Captain Hamblin prided himself on maintaining good health on his ship.

One day, when Maria sat in the deckhouse with mending, John brought his charts and spread them on the narrow table. When his duties did not interfere, he tried to be with his wife, remembering the many days when she hardly saw him. Maria looked lovingly at his bent head as he worked in silence. She never ceased to be proud of her husband's knowledge of the ocean currents, the trade wind routes, the feeding habits of whales in the various seasons, the effect a hurricane or a long period of calm would have on the whales' habits. She knew that he used this accumulated wisdom in charting cruises to good whaling grounds.

'Well, Captain, where do we go next?' Maria laid her work aside and peered at the chart.

'Here's where we are now.' John pointed to a dot on the chart. 'The southern summer is approaching, so we will head north of the equator in the vicinity of the Sandwich Islands. Perhaps we will catch up with a few sperm whales there.'

Maria's eyes held an unspoken question. John laughed as he read her thoughts. 'Yes, dear, you and

Alice should both be able to get ashore there for awhile. And the chances of news from home are good, for often other whalers are in the harbor. But don't begin counting the days. There are many long miles between here and the Sandwich Isles.'

Maria picked up another sock to mend. Yes, she thought, many long miles and perhaps many storms and other bad times to get through. But what news would await them? Would the elections at home be over? Would the new leader, whoever he was, be able to steer the States away from danger?

'Oh, John, if only there were a magnetic telegraph out to the Pacific. If there are not letters or papers when we get there, how much longer will we have to wait to know what is happening back home? Sometimes I feel I can't bear it—not knowing for months when something important is happening.'

John reached across and patted Maria's arm. 'It is hard, dear, I know, but that is part of our life.'

A sharp wail from the awakening baby sent Maria below and the future was obliterated by the present problem of making a teething baby comfortable. Alice stopped crying as she was picked up from her slatted crib, but she made it plain throughout the days that followed that her swollen gums were giving her discomfort.

The Pirate on the forward deck saw Maria pacing the quarterdeck with the fretful child or trying to amuse her in the little pen which the carpenter had built beside the deckhouse door, and went to work on a piece of scrimshaw. A few days later he gave the captain a smooth well-polished ring.

'It's for the little angel's teething,' he said, 'I made rings for my babies long ago. They bite hard and the little teeth come through.'

Thistle in Her Hand

John thanked the sailor for his thoughtfulness, but he found it hard to believe that the picturesque fellow had ever been a family man.

Maria was touched by the Pirate's gift. She scrubbed it well and gave it to the baby. As if recognizing its use at once, Alice put it to her mouth and it quieted her. It was not long before the point of one little tooth emerged and then another and Alice was herself again, smiling and showing the utmost good nature. The Pirate, from a distance, saw that all was well again and showed his pleasure by playing merry tunes on his harmonica. Maria was sure that Alice heard and enjoyed his music.

As The Roman neared the area of the Sandwich Islands, Maria prepared packets of mail and small gifts to give a homeward bound ship in harbor. John assured her that this was most likely as the Arctic hunters would be southbound after their long summer of whaling in the Bering Sea.

Maria adjusted her bonnet to shade her eyes and walked over to the rail as she caught a glimpse of an island mountain rising out of the lonely sea.

Mr. Richards, passing her on his way to the afterhouse companionway, remarked cheerfully, 'We'll be on land soon.'

'I'd say very soon,' Maria answered. 'We can't be more than a few miles from that bleak rock.'

The mate smiled. 'Oh no, Mrs. Hamblin, the island may look close but the sea view on a clear day can be mighty fooling. We are more'n twenty-five miles away.'

As the ship neared the island, Maria saw the barren-looking island gradually take on life and color. Splashes of white against rich greens then turned into lacy waterfalls rippling over chasms and friendly coconut trees waving their branches in welcome.

Now the brilliant tropical flowers unfolded their

colors before Maria's delighted eyes. She longed to put the scene on cloth with her embroidery silks. The water around the ship was indigo and serene, but shoreward great rollers fringed in foaming white thundered over the coral reefs, racing for the sandy beach.

When the harbor came into view, John looked over the ships with his spyglass and reported to Maria that there were two whaleships at anchor. Soon, by whaleship language, Captain Hamblin discovered that one was The Metacom, homeward bound to New Bedford after four years away. The other, The Virginia, was recently from Sag Harbor. The Metacom was sailing almost at once, so the mail packets were hurried to her by whaleboat.

Later, part of the crew was given shore leave, while the remaining men went ashore with John for supplies of fresh fruit, vegetables, meat, water, and wood. As Maria watched several casks of sperm oil lowered into lighters to be taken ashore and exchanged for the supplies, she wondered if the price of these luxuries would be long days of hunting, a delayed home-going.

When the ship's business had been attended to and the rest of the crew given their turn at shore leave, John took Maria and Alice ashore for a holiday in Hilo. He hired a horse and carriage and drove them about the city for an hour, but again Maria had trouble with the land. It heaved for her like the ship in squally weather, and she could not enjoy the ride.

After a while John took her to a hotel where she rested and Alice was fed and napped. Then he ordered a meal sent to their room and they ate on a shady balcony, enjoying the privacy and the distant view of the harbor, with The Roman riding at anchor.

When Maria felt normal again, they descended to the

porch of the hotel. John soon discovered a whaling captain from New England and they pulled their chairs together for an exchange of home news. From time to time Captain Frazier looked admiringly at Maria.

'Mrs. Hamblin, you look more like one of my daughters than you do the wife of an old sea dog like this fellow,' he said, with a hearty slap on John's broad shoulders.

Maria blushed, but was pleased, feeling repaid for the long hot hour she had spent ironing the green sprigged dress which had lain in the bottom of her trunk since she left home.

After a bit of light talk, the conversation turned to conditions on the political scene at home.

'When I left, things were looking worse rather than better,' Captain Frazier said. 'Ever since the Republicans nominated "Honest Abe of the West" there has been a sense of impending doom everywhere. There is fear for the Union. The South will not accept "the black candidate," as they call Lincoln, because he is personally against slavery.'

John interrupted. 'I still think our hope is in Abe Lincoln. He may be able to do the impossible, if he gets to be president.'

'Why shouldn't he?' Maria joined the discussion. 'You know that all the menfolk at home are writing wonderful things about him.'

'Remember, Maria, they are Republicans—and strong abolitionists.'

Maria's hazel eyes reflected the green in her dress as she tossed her head. 'Honest Abe will be our next president and he will talk sense to the rest of our people—those who do not understand that slavery is an abomination in the sight of God.'

Captain Frazier smiled. 'It's not that simple, my dear Mrs. Hamblin. It's more than slavery; it's a question of states' rights. It's a matter of principle.'

John agreed with the captain, but Maria's eyes flashed with indignation. 'John, I'm ashamed of you, in a way. You seem to be standing up for the South. It doesn't have a point in its favor while it holds humans as slaves.'

'Maria, remember there are two sides to every question. I guess we should say there is a third side, the right side; or maybe it's a compromise side. If the states all take the third side, we'll avoid trouble. If not—'

Maria looked so distressed at the thought of the alternative that Captain Frazier changed the subject, asking a question about Alice, who reclined in John's arms, at peace with the world.

Later in the day, Maria asked John what date it was.

'This is November 2nd,' he answered. Then, reading her thoughts, he added, 'Yes, dear, in two more days, November 4th, the die will be cast. I hope the election news reaches us quickly.'

'Where John? Where will we be?'

John looked sober. 'Our best hope is a gam with a ship just recently out. From this area, we will hunt southeast and then across the South Pacific again to New Zealand. We are certain to have news waiting there. And I hope it will be good news that we can start homeward.' John bent and kissed Maria. 'Come now, let's enjoy our holiday. How about another spin with that mare?'

Maria assented and began to prepare Alice for the ride. But suddenly she wished they were back on The Roman and ready to sail on so that they might hear the news more quickly.

Thistle in Her Hand

The next afternoon they set sail. Maria stood at the rail and watched the vivid colors fade again into grayness. A pair of gulls followed the ship, gracefully swaying as they circled the stern. She wondered if gulls were the shorebirds in every ocean. She must remember to ask John. At last the gulls turned back and only the distant mountain on the horizon remained. They were on their way again.

Chapter 22

CAPTAIN Hamblin kept The Roman in the vicinity of the Sandwich Islands for the next two months. Whaling was good and the weather favorable. There was a balmy sweetness in the air that enabled the crew and officers to approach their hard tasks with a relaxed strength which appeared effortless. Maria felt unusually well and accepted her second pregnancy with cheerfulness which approached gaiety.

'This time you'll have nothing to worry about, John dear. We'll all be safe at home when this one comes into the world. But can't you just see the expressions on the faces of our folks when we ride into New Bedford with Alice and another on the way?' And Maria laughed merrily. John pulled her to him so that she would not see his face. Devoutly he prayed that it would be so, but he did not confide his fears to her. It would be time enough when they reached Hobart, where his orders would be waiting.

Baby Alice, too, grew strong and sturdy, although tiny in stature. One by one the little teeth came through with the aid of the Pirate's gift until her smile was a lovely thing, cherished by all.

But the time came when John charted a new course. The Roman would sail southward again across the Line and then proceed through the South Seas westward, hoping to fill the hold before reaching New Zealand.

Maria awoke one morning to the sound of birds, which meant that land was not far off. John had already left the stateroom, so she dressed quickly and followed him up on deck. It was still very early and the lookout was just climbing to his high perch in the crow's nest. Maria could not bring herself to watch his progress. She went to the deckhouse for her glass and waited there for the call which she felt sure was coming.

'Land ho!'

At the call, the ship stirred to life, quickened by the thrill of a sudden landfall on an ocean where there had been nothing for days. Maria felt herself a part of the response. She joined John in the wheelhouse shelter.

'What is it? Another island?'

John was peering through his glass at the brightening horizon. 'Yes, my dear; one lonely little island, Pitcairn by name.'

'Pitcairn! Oh, John, isn't that the island where those awful English mutineers live? I remember Father and Uncle Asa talking about it.'

John lowered his glass. 'Yes, Maria, and if we weren't in need of fresh water and a change in our ship fare we wouldn't go near that unsavory spot. For one thing, I dislike having anything to do with even the descendants of mutineers, and, for another, it takes real seamanship to get a boat ashore on Pitcairn's coast.'

Maria was silent, recalling a winter evening when the family had lingered late around the fire, with Lisha recklessly piling on the wood, although he knew his would be the task of replenishing the woodbox in the morning. How the children had enjoyed the rare times when their father and his brother were carried away with their own eloquence, Uncle Asa with his recollections of the sea and their father with the lore of the printed page.

'Mutiny,' Uncle Asa had said, after telling several stories of mutiny, 'is a word more dreaded on a ship at sea, especially by the captain, than even "ship's afire" or "ship's sinking."'

Mate Richards joined them and John began discussing the hazards of a landing party.

'It will be rough. I was one of the crew who went ashore here once and our boat nearly stove on those rocks. There's only one cove where it's possible to make a fair landing and that's on the northeast side. Pick yourself a dependable crew, Mr. Richards. I'll stay by the wheel until we make the rounding.'

As mate Richards left for this duty, Maria reminded John that they had not yet breakfasted. After checking with the helmsman, they went below, but food held little charm this morning with the prospect of the sight of land, and they returned quickly.

Together they watched until at last the mountain island could be seen without aid of the glass. At first it looked like a single peak, but as the ship, under a good fresh wind, drew rapidly nearer, Maria saw that it was a ridge with a small peak at either end. One peak rose high and sloped gently to the sea; the other was flanked by straight precipices, against which the waves crashed and raised great spouts of water.

'Could there be a more dangerous coastline?' exclaimed Maria. Then she added, 'But it's perfect for the birds that nest on those high rocky places. Nothing can disturb them.'

Clouds of sea fowl passed restlessly this way and that over the island and as far out to sea as The Roman.

Later in the morning, Maria brought Alice to the quarterdeck to watch the birds. Doc joined them as they stood in the shade of the wheelhouse.

'It sure is pretty up in them valleys, ma'am,' he remarked, waving his pipe toward the island.

Maria thought of other islands whose green lushness hid unknown evils. What kind of people could these folk be? What sort of violence could one expect from the hands of descendants of mutineers?

Doc went on, talking half to himself, 'No one could starve on that island with those birds and the eggs. Ha! A bird pie for supper would taste all right. I'll go tell Layton to take a gun when he goes ashore and bring us a batch of birds.'

Without waiting for an answer, he thumped away in a hurry, savory pies for his ship folks in mind.

Now there was the sound of the anchor being dropped. The Roman stopped off a cove, where a feasible landing appeared on a narrow strip of beach, and the sails were clewed up. Maria heard the whaleboat being lowered and, with Alice held tightly in her arms, looked over the bulwarks. She saw the casks being rafted to the bow of the boat and the crew getting in their places. Tom Layton had a gun strapped to his back. Doc would get his birds.

The sea was fairly quiet where The Roman lay, but as the whaleboat approached the shore the waves became tumultuous. Maria stood tensely until the men maneuvered the boat onto a huge wave which swept boat and casks safely to the beach. When she looked again, the men had disappeared among the rocks and trees. All day as she went about her tasks, Maria's

Thistle in Her Hand

thoughts were with the landing party and many anxious glances went toward the home of the mutineers, but there never at any time was a sign to tell her what was happening beyond that verdant hillside.

The men were full of talk when they returned in late afternoon. While the casks of water, bundles of wood, and baskets of fruits and vegetables were unloaded, mate Richards reported their adventures to Captain Hamblin.

'I'm afraid we scared them at first, especially Layton with his gun. Some of the women and children started screaming. But we pointed to the ship and told them it was a whaler and they calmed down; seems whalers have been their good friends.

'We came nigh to findin' that island deserted, Captain. Seems the British government moved 'em all off of this out-of-the-way spot to Norfolk Island to bring them closer to Australia. That was about four years ago. But some didn't like it and a few families ventured back. They've only been here a couple of years—found the island overrun with goats and other livestock gone wild, but they are getting things fixed up real nice—pandanus thatched roofs on their houses and gardens neat and trim. Seemed real nice folks.'

Maria, watching the unloading process, saw the Pirate's head emerge over the bulwarks, a branch of glossy green leaves spotted with white blossoms descending from the knot in his bandana over his back and shoulders. As he reached the deck, he unloosed the branch and sent it by the cabin boy to Maria.

'He said it's for the little angel. A lady on the island sent them,' said Timmy. 'Oh yes, and she called them "high whites" because they grow high on flower trees.'

Maria told Timmy to thank the Pirate and took them

to the stateroom, holding the blossoms against her face for their delicate fragrance. In a moment, the room was filled with sweetness.

When the ship lifted anchor at sunset, most of the officers and crew were at the rail, waving goodbye to a little group of people who had gathered to salute them on a promontory overlooking the cove. Maria watched, too, until the island became a dot on the captain's chart and all was ocean again.

But the memory of unexpected human kindness lingered on long after the fragrance of the high whites had faded from cabin and stateroom.

Chapter 23

THE Roman proceeded slowly westward in the warm seas, with whaling luck holding. Unless there was a need for fresh water or food and wood, they kept away from the many islands that dotted John's charts.

Now Maria measured time by little Alice's signs of growth. When the weather was pleasant and no trying-out was going on, the child spent many of her waking hours in the little pen outside the deckhouse door. Maria kept a wide-brimmed bonnet on her daughter's head for protection from wind and sun, but the quarterdeck people found it hard to pass her without a gentle pull on the bright curls on her neck. Alice usually responded by shaking her head vigorously and dimpling both pink cheeks in a smile.

One morning in May, 1860, Maria put Alice in the pen set high on a platform while she went about her laundry work in the deckhouse. After a while she heard the child chortling over something that amused her. Drying her hands, she went to the door.

To her surprise, she found that Alice had pulled herself up on the railing of the pen and was standing there watching a display of flying fish. As the silvery finny creatures darted from the surface of the sea, Alice's strong little arms shook the railing in glee.

'Oh,' thought Maria, 'she is growing up too fast! So tiny but already almost walking. I must watch her every minute now. The sea is so near, so fearfully near.'

Suddenly Alice lost her balance and, turning, fell into a sitting position. At once, she was on her knees, pulling at the railing until she stood up again. She had found her footing; now Maria realized she would soon be walking, climbing everywhere. They must plan ways to insure her safety in the months ahead.

Not many days later Maria was again warned by Alice's shouts that something unusual was occurring and put her head through the doorway of the deckhouse, to be drawn to the ship's rail by the sight that had amused the baby.

A myriad of sooty black little birds with a bit of white on their wings were everywhere. The choppy blue and white sea was alive with them. They seemed to be dancing from wave to wave, but, as she watched closely, Maria noted that they were skimming the crests of the waves and slapping their feet on the water as they flew along. Others were hovering about the ship, fluttering in apparent excitement.

Maria remembered having seen birds like these before, but never in such numbers. Then it came to her. They were stormy petrels. The sailors called them 'Mother Carey's Chickens,' from the Latin words *Mater Cara*, the name sailors used for the Virgin Mary, the protector of sailors.

As Maria listened she was sure their cries sounded like quick calls of, 'petterel, petterel, petterel' on a high-pitched note.

Thistle in Her Hand

'Frisky little birds, aren't they, darling?' Maria addressed her tiny daughter. 'And their home can't be far away—a nice rocky island with petrel babies, but we'd better keep away from them.'

She recalled hearing that a mother petrel on the nest defended herself by shooting a smelly, oily liquid from her mouth.

'Now we had better go down for a nice bath and nap,' she told Alice. 'Your mummy wants to do a good washing on this nice sunny day.'

At this moment John and the mate came through the afterhouse companionway. As they sighted the birds, the mate exclaimed, 'Oh no!' Then he blurted, 'Drat those stormy petrels!'

John's quick glance went to the ocean and then to the sky. His face was serious. The mate hurriedly checked the telltale compass and the barometer beneath the skylight.

'Not good,' he reported.

Maria knew it meant the dreaded message that the barometer was falling. She lifted Alice from her pen and held her close.

On the forward deck the men were calling to one another in excitement. Maria saw the Pirate lean over the bulwarks and cross himself. She realized that all on board regarded the petrels as a storm warning. Their coming was unwelcome, dreaded, as the coming of bearers of bad news.

'What bad news?' she asked Timmy.

'It means a wreck and drowned sailors, Ma'am,' was his frightened answer.

When the dinner bell rang, it did not produce the usual gay, noisy reaction; everyone went about the business of eating as part of the day's job, to get well fortified for the work ahead. Maria and John, in the saloon, ate silently. John was planning the preparations he would make to ready the ship for a storm. Maria, hoping in her heart that it would pass them by as it sometimes had in the past, was also thinking of all she would have to do to protect herself and Alice in the cabin. John had trained her well. Hope for the best, but prepare for the worst, was one of his favorite maxims. A good one, too, thought Maria, for his ship had weathered storms when some other ships had not.

By mid-afternoon, the long swells of the Pacific had turned into angry looking billows and the temperate air had become raw and chilly. Timmy came to the cabin door to tell Maria that the captain had ordered the decks cleared; he would help her remove her things from the deckhouse. As Maria carried workbasket, toys, and laundry below, she watched the sky grow darker. A ghostly green glare loomed over decks and rigging as the crew labored to furl the sails and make them fast to the spars. While she worked below to make the stateroom safe, she could hear the men battening down the hatches and securing the whaleboats.

John looked around the stateroom when he came down later and smiled at Maria. 'You're well battened down here, too, I see,' he observed. 'Not scared anymore?'

Maria closed a drawer and latched it firmly. 'I'm scared plenty inside, but there's a pair of big blue eyes watching me so I don't dare show it.' She grinned, but her drawn look and agitated movements showed her worry, fright. She was learning to be stoical in the face of danger, like Papa, who always said, 'What can't be cured must be endured cheerfully.' I must make my face more composed, she thought, and quickly passed

Thistle in Her Hand

her hand over her forehead, trying to erase the worry creases.

John went to Alice's slatted crib and picked her up for a moment. He glanced at Maria, concern in his eyes. 'That's right, little one; you keep your eyes on mummy when I'm not here.' He kissed her warm cheek and returned her to the crib. 'Maria, you have guts, thank God,' he said as he left.

Alice was asleep when the storm struck a few hours later and, despite the crashing and thumping of the waves and the howling of the wind, she slept on. Above, on deck, the crew battled the weather, shouting and stamping their sea boots.

Several hours passed and there was no decrease in the storm's fury. When John opened the hatch to come below, Maria heard the water pour down; the light in the cabin flickered and almost went out. Some dishes in the steward's pantry fell with a crash and Alice awoke, crying.

John was soaking wet beneath his oilskins and his face was set in worried lines. Maria longed to do something, anything, to help him. 'I wish I could get you a cup of hot tea,' she cried in distress.

'Don't worry, dear, Doc is managing to keep a fire going and has his kettle of water to have tea ready when we have time for it. I just wanted to see if you and Alice are all right. You stay in bed and keep her with you until morning. We are in for bad seas. Even your sea legs won't keep you from falling.'

He picked up the whimpering child and placed her on the gimballed bed beside Maria, and she became quiet at once in her mother's arms.

Before she could question him further about the storm, John turned and left. An hour later the wind seemed to reach its peak of wrath and there was a crashing of glass and the sound of water coming in the skylight. Maria did not dare to leave the baby to investigate. Soon the water stopped pouring in, so she surmised someone must have patched the spot with sailcloth and wooden slats. What could have caused it, Maria wondered?

'My poor geranium—Milly's geranium,' she sighed. Then a sickening thought came to her. 'Merciful heavens,' she groaned aloud. 'If something would crash the whole skylight, these quarters would be deluged, then the whole ship and we'd drown like rats in a trap. Wrecked ship and drowned sailors...could there be truth to the superstition?'

And, holding the sleeping baby close to her, the mother lay on the swinging bed, eyes closed, tears streaming down her cheeks. 'Merciful Lord, help us,' she prayed.

She abruptly stopped crying and opened her eyes as a thought struck her. How disgusted John will be if he finds me crying over something that has not happened and may never happen. I must get those terrible thoughts out of my mind and think of something pleasant—like those darling porpoises we watched, John with Alice in his arms and I beside him at the quarterdeck bulwarks, when we were nearing Hilo.

How Alice laughed as those five-foot-long black bodies with blunt, rounded snouts frolicked about the ship, sometimes swimming under the bow, and without apparent effort keeping with the stem of the ship as it gently parted the water, as though they were escorting her into the harbor. Maria, remembering, felt calmer and more human. Soon she dozed off into a fitful sleep.

When she awoke later the storm had at last worn

itself out and she caught a glimpse of stars as the side of the ship heaved out of the sea. Then the storm was back, with the sea rushing past the porthole, foaming and churning. There were no sails to hold the wind, so the ship tossed about like a log on the ocean.

Suddenly she listed to the port side. Then something hit the porthole. It was the phosphorescent, livid white belly of a shark. As Maria screamed in shock, it passed in a flash and was gone.

Maria's scream awoke Alice into frightened crying. While the young mother busied herself pacifying her little daughter, her mind dwelt on the frightful apparition at the porthole. Oh, those sharks, those ferocious sea brutes that followed the ship days on end, cruising tirelessly round and round with sinister power, waiting for parts of the whale carcass at cuttin' in times, at other times waiting for morsels of garbage from the galley, or for a man overboard.

Or for the people on the ship, if it sank in a storm like this. Always they were there whenever she looked at the sea, and always she looked upon the sleek monsters with loathing and horror. And the sailors did, too, and never lost an opportunity to catch and kill them.

Fortunately the baby kept Maria so busy for a while that she had no time to let her imagination run wild. At last, emotionally exhausted, she and Alice fell asleep.

Maria awoke with a start when at dawn Timmy knocked on the partition. 'Mrs. Hamblin, I have tea for you and hardtack for Alice to gnaw on until Henry can get something from the galley. Doc is tryin' to get a fire going. The sea is still kicking something awful and the cap'n wants you and Alice to stay in bed until it gets calmer.'

Margarita Thompson Diddel

It was almost noon before John appeared below. That meant the danger was over and she could go on deck now for a breath of fresh air and see the havoc wrought by the storm. John dropped on the bed and slept almost immediately from exhaustion.

Maria, with Alice in her arms, climbed the stairs slowly, almost afraid to look. The mate, refreshed by an early morning nap, was in charge. He pointed to the skylight and told her it had been broken by a falling spar in spite of the protective lengths of wood that had been nailed across it. The masts were erect, though, and Mr. Richards said, with feeling, 'It's a miracle how those Oregon boles stood the storm.'

Maria breathed with relief. There were ragged strips hanging from the reefed sails and the galley roof had been blown askew, but there appeared to be no damage that cooper and carpenter and sailmaker could not repair. They were lucky to have come off so well, with a hold heavy with barrels of sperm oil.

'Well, Mr. Richards, Mother Carey's Chickens surely foretold the storm, and God be thanked, there was no wreck and drowned sailors.'

'Almost was a wreck,' the officer said, grimly, pointing leeward to a break in the far horizon that looked like a peak of jagged rocks. 'The Roman nearly left her bones there last night. We saw the rock pile when the sky cleared suddenly and the late moon appeared. There was a lively time here on deck. The captain and I both made for the wheel like streaks of lightnin' to steer the ship away, but without sail the wind kept blowin' us toward the rocks. But just as we thought we were losin', the wind shifted and dropped, thank God.'

Maria's hand shook as she shaded her eyes to look at

the point of danger being left behind. 'That must be the home of the petrels, the ones that came to warn us.'

'Probably,' answered the mate.

'Sweet little birds. Yes, sweet little birds!' Maria felt almost childish in her intense gratitude for their deliverance from shipwreck, from drowning.

For the next few days the ship was under repair. The cooper and the carpenter, with the help of some of the crew, were busy rebuilding while others cleaned and cleared. The sailmaker meanwhile made new sails. Again the ship was ready to continue the whale chase as she headed toward the region around Three Kings, near New Zealand.

The greasy luck was so good that John declared that just three eighty-barrel whales would finish filling the hold.

Chapter 24

ALTHOUGH the southern summer was on the wane, John turned the nose of The Roman toward the New Zealand whaling grounds, reputed to be good hunting water. The hold was so nearly full that he did not wish to pursue whales into areas too distant from Hobart and the news he hoped would be waiting there.

For a month they cruised in the area of Three Kings, a trio of volcanic islands about twenty miles northwest of New Zealand. Whaling was disappointing, but the island waters proved to abound in fish. As they sailed, Maria often saw groups of canoes paddled by tall, golden-brown natives. John told her they were the Maoris, natives of New Zealand.

'They are superior, I would say, to the other natives around here, more self-reliant and courageous. I'd like some on my crew, but they stay very much to themselves.'

Maria watched a group of canoes leave the nearby mainland early one morning for the distant waters. She thought, 'They're just folks like ourselves, loving their homes as we love ours, but leaving them behind to hunt food for their families.'

Margarita Thompson Diddel

While cruising thus, The Roman spoke to a whaler from New Bedford and there was a short gam and letters from home. All had been written previous to the election day, so the news for which they hungered was still denied them.

However, The Roman's officers and crew had to wait only a few days longer before they at last spoke to a vessel that had the news. The Minerva, under Captain Hathaway, had left Albany, Australia, not many days before and had learned that Mr. Lincoln had been elected President in November, so that now in March he was already established as head of the ship of state.

The gam turned into a celebration, that lasted far into the night. Doc dipped into his dwindling stores to produce the best possible supper for the crew and their visitors.

As darkness fell, cresset lights hung from masts and davits. One of the visiting seamen had a fiddle, so a dance was called for. Maria, with wide-awake Alice in her arms, joined the two Yankee captains on the deck to watch the festivities.

On the forward deck the seamen sat or stood in a circle, clapping hands or stomping heavy boots as the dancing progressed. One after another the men performed the traditional sailor's hornpipe or some other folk dance picked up in their travels. The Pirate's harmonica was added to the fiddle music and hearty songs of the sea rose to the stars.

Captain Hathaway looked at Alice and smiled, 'A new experience for the little, un, eh? A celebratin' gam.'

'And she is in a gay mood, like the rest of us, with all the wonderful news you brought!'

'Mrs. Hamblin, your husband and I were agreeing that, along with this festivity, we should do a lot of praying for the brave man who's taking over the captaincy of our ship of state, about to sail into uncharted seas.'

The captain looked grave and Maria saw that John was quietly interlacing his strong, tanned fingers and she knew he, too, was deeply worried. Her spirits sank for a moment, then rose again as she reflected that these troubled men might be wrong in their dour thoughts of things to come.

'Captain Hathaway, in my father's last letter he said that if Mr. Lincoln were elected, the country would settle down to peaceful living again. He will persuade Congress to offer to pay the slave owners for their slaves and they will realize that slavery is an abomination in the eyes of the Lord and settle for the slaves. Why, right here in my pocket is a newspaper piece my father sent us that tells about a man, a William Hickman of Henry, Kentucky, who has freed his slaves.'

Maria extracted the clipping from her pocket and handed it to the captain as she continued, 'The slaves insist on staying on as before but, of course, they are now free men.'

It was late when the crews returned to their respective ships, tired but happy after the jolly gamming session.

The crew on The Roman was jubilant for another reason. Captain Hamblin announced that two more good sized whales would see the hold filled and they would start for Hobart.

Even Maria scanned the ocean whenever she was on deck, lest somehow the last two whales they still needed should elude the watchful man on the crow's nest.

Shortly after the memorable gam that celebrated the election of Abraham Lincoln, Maria prepared to launder the accumulated baby clothes. While Doc heated the rain water, she stretched her line between the davits. She was aware of something unusual in the appearance of the sky. As she studied it, she decided that the greenish glow came from the action of the veiled sun on the emerald waters, which rose and fell in long sluggish swells. Confident that the sun would soon dispel the mist, she proceeded with her work and was about to hang up the first article when she was startled by a warning shout from the lookout above.

'Waterspout!'

Following the direction of the watcher's gestures, Maria saw, about a third of a mile distant, an inky cloud hanging over the sea, its sagging point dipping toward the churning ocean beneath. As she stared at the portentous cloud directly ahead of The Roman, the sea rose into a conical point. It met the heavy cloud above and began to whirl. Slowly the column of water grew thicker, darker, taller. Then, to her horrified eyes, it began to move in the direction of the ship, with a rushing, roaring noise that rose to a thunderous pitch. All around her, she was conscious of movement.

John and the mate barked the order, 'Hard aport!' The crew swarmed up the rigging, shifting sails. But Maria could not take her eyes from the advancing menace. It reminded her of the deliberate, sinuous movement of a snake. At last the wind caught the sails and the ship veered slowly out of the direct path of the waterspout.

But suppose it turns this way? she thought, wildly. It was not a quarter of a mile away now. Suddenly, it broke at its ocean base and gradually disintegrated. With unbelief, she saw the sky-high column of cloud slowly spread out and disappear. Her sigh of relief came like a sob and was echoed over the ship as tense seamen relaxed with an explosive, 'Well!'

John left the wheel and stood beside Maria, wiping

the sweat from his face. She laid a trembling hand on his arm.

'What would have happened if it had been night?' she asked, shuddering.

'Just be thankful, dear, that it wasn't.'

Maria bowed her head and murmured in a slightly trembling voice, 'We thank thee, Oh Lord, for our deliverance from danger.'

'Amen,' John added huskily, touching her arm, and then left to consult with the mate.

For a few minutes Maria stood pensively, gazing into space. Her thoughts returned to the joyful expectation that they would soon go home. First a stop at the branch of the home office in Hobart for the necessary clearance, and then, Hallelujah, The Roman would turn its prow homeward. John and the mate calculated it would be August when the welcoming cannon would announce the arrival of The Roman. Yes, in record time, two years, and with all casks filled with greasy gold—sperm oil! And in time for the baby to be born at home, a September baby.

Maria cut short her reverie and returned to her laundry duties. Her slim fingers worked fast, as if in tune with the gay ditty in her thoughts, 'We are going home soon, soon, soon, hooray.'

Whaling resumed with vigor, and within a short time the order came, 'All hands, get the ship under way for Hobart.' Jubilantly the men cleaned and painted the ship to the tune of 'Mobile Bay,' 'Off She Goes,' and other chanteys. Their songs floated over the waves and reechoed from the rocky banks of nearby islands, making the uninhabited isles seem alive.

On the Saturday before Easter, The Roman, led by the pilot sloop, entered the Tasmanian port. Maria, too happy to speak, stood at the deckrail and gazed at the approaching city, delighted with everything she saw. Hobart was spread out over low hills at the foot of a great mountain, towering and majestic. Mt. Wellington reminded Maria of a sentinel, God's own sentinel standing guard over the city.

The ship sailed easily into the deep, ample harbor. While the docking operations went on, Maria went below to dress herself and Alice for a leisurely turn about the city. John did not expect the shipping offices to be open until Monday.

Not long after, John came to the stateroom, beaming smiles. Mr. Thomas, one of the owners of the shipping office and a friend of John's, had sent an invitation to the Hamblin family to spend that night and the Easter holiday with them. Mr. and Mrs. Thomas would drive down soon to conduct them personally to the Thomas home.

'I know you will enjoy the stay at their home,' John told his wife. 'I was there for dinner on a former trip. Such charming people. And you will love their garden—a regular English garden.'

Maria hummed a gay tune as she packed a bag and then dressed Alice in a dainty ruffled white dress and a blue coat and bonnet that matched the little girl's eyes. Her own red merino dress hung ready to put on; she had mended worn places with care and had pressed the wide skirt with its yards of black rickrack braid.

It was a favorite of John's, but Maria eyed it with some misgiving. She had noticed a new trend in fashions on that day ashore at Hilo. Well, she would have to wear her old clothes until after the baby was born, anyway, so she would not allow styles to disturb her holiday ashore.

Meanwhile, John had changed into his port clothes.

Thistle in Her Hand

Maria thought how distinguished he looked in his black coat, elaborately embroidered white vest, and pin-striped trousers.

'John, I hope this baby will be a boy and will grow to be just like you in every way.' Maria's voice was full of love and pride. John bent and kissed her tenderly.

The Thomases were waiting as they had promised. Maria at once liked the spare, clear-skinned couple, whose complexion and sandy hair made them look so much alike. Clothes and fashions were altogether forgotten as she scanned with delighted interest the pleasant homes, huddled together in the fashion of the English in the territories. Each had its hawthorn-hedged garden, its owners' private bit of England abroad.

Some homes had a Dutch look. Mrs. Thomas explained that the Dutch also had settled there, and that they, too, were trying to make their surroundings as much like home as possible.

The drive had hardly begun when Maria experienced the same old difficulty in adjusting to solid ground. While she tried to see everything, she held tightly to the side of the carriage and to John's arm. From time to time she glanced at Alice, wondering if the child felt the change; but Alice was wide-eyed. The lively horse attracted her attention and she stood on John's knees to watch the animal.

Presently the carriage stopped before a two-story home with casement windows. Beyond the hedges Maria caught a glimpse of flower beds, extravagant in their late summer blooming, and a few small fruit trees against the garden wall. Before she had time to satisfy her longing to walk in the garden, however, Maria's hostess had whisked her through the formal, velvet-draped parlor upstairs to the guest room. She was followed by John with Alice.

In that austere but pleasant room, Maria quickly settled their few belongings. Then, while John went downstairs, she rocked Alice until she fell asleep.

For a long while she stood at the window, gazing down at the wealth of color in the garden below. Some of the flowers were strange, but somehow the sight of a garden brought her close to home.

'This is what I will see when we get home in late summer,' she thought, 'if only the shipping office allows us to return now.' How wonderful to be at home, to have her baby born at home, to have the folks all together again.

There was a light tap and John entered the room, bearing a baby crib that had served the Thomas children. 'We'll put Alice in it and then she will be safe. Then you must come down. It is time for dinner.'

He lowered his voice and added, 'Only they call it high tea here.'

At tea, Maria found herself laughing and talking as she had done at social gatherings back home. John, too, was enjoying a carefree day. Tomorrow they would go to church with the Thomases. It was almost like being at home.

In spite of the pleasant surroundings and good company, Sunday seemed endless to Maria and John. Both tried to put the future out of their minds, but without success. So much depended upon the letters awaiting them!

Monday arrived at last and John left early with Mr. Thomas for the shipping office. The morning passed pleasantly as the two women took care of Alice and exchanged ideas about housekeeping problems. At noon a messenger brought a note from John saying that he would be detained until tea time.

Thistle in Her Hand

How strange, thought Maria, that he would not make a great effort to bring her the mail, knowing how anxious she was. Disquieting thoughts intruded as the afternoon wore on. At last, she excused herself and took Alice to the bedroom. There she sat by a window facing the street, watching for John's return until it was time to dress for tea.

Maria was downstairs and tea was being served when John entered with Mr. Thomas. Her first glance at her husband told her something was wrong. John's face was tired and drawn. He did not look directly at her, but accepted his tea and drank it as though grateful for its warmth. Mrs. Thomas sensed that her guests needed to be alone and served the tea with dispatch.

'Now, my dears, I know you have something to talk over, so we will excuse you to go to your room. Leave Alice here with me.' Without waiting for a reply, Mrs. Thomas picked Alice up from the floor and left the room.

John looked at Maria and nodded and slowly they climbed the stairs together. When they reached their room, John dropped into the nearest chair and put his head down, pushing his hair back in a troubled way. He was not yet able to meet her eyes.

Maria stood beside her husband. 'John, you have some troubling news,' she said. 'Tell me; I am ready to hear it.' She spoke in a quiet, firm voice; but inwardly she trembled.

John took Maria's hand and held it to his face. 'I hate to tell you,' he said. 'Yes, I have only bad news. There's no mail from home. But that isn't the worst.

'Maria, we are not sailing for home. The New Bedford office has ordered me to send the oil home by the first ship that can take it, and to keep on whaling and sending the oil home until further notice. The orders said that war is imminent and the sperm oil is much needed by the government.'

Maria sat down on the edge of the bed, her eyes blank, mind confused. She tried to realize the import of John's words, but all she could recall was, 'We are not sailing for home.'

Why? With the hold filled with oil, why couldn't they go home?

'John, I don't understand. Say it again, slowly.'

John repeated the message. Now he was on his feet, walking restlessly about the room. Maria's mind cleared and she stood.

'Let's go back to the ship, John; we can think better there.'

John looked at his wife in surprise and relief, then he took her in his arms and held her close.

'Oh, my darling, I hated so to tell you, to bring you this terrible disappointment. All the way home I talked to Mr. Thomas about the possibility of sending you home by clipper ship, or leaving you here in Hobart while I sail again. I was afraid you might never want to step foot on The Roman again.'

Maria looked up at him. 'It doesn't really matter where I am, just so I am with you, John.'

When they reached The Roman, the crew had already heard the news and were in tumult. Some talked of quitting, of taking the first ship home. John had his hands full for a while, and Maria was able to relieve her feelings with a good cry in the privacy of her stateroom. After that she felt better, and could show John a cheerful face.

When The Roman sailed out of the harbor some days later, the same crew was on board as before. One by one they had returned. Maria was grateful for John's sake and for her own. These men knew her; with new ones there might be a problem. Maria shivered as she remembered her experience with Portugee.

The ship had been refitted and reprovisioned for sailing, just as it had been when they left New Bedford. Barrels of sperm oil had paid for everything; the rest of the oil was already on the way to the United States. No one knew, now, how long it would be before The Roman could follow.

Maria stood in the stern, gazing pensively at the vast expanse of ocean around her. She thought of all that had happened since they had entered Hobart so short a time before—their joyful anticipation of going home and seeing loved ones, then the dashing of all those hopes and dreams. But there had been the happy moment just before they sailed when John came dashing down the stairway with a packet of mail from home.

And she would hold fast to the memory of several delightful days with the Thomases. Mrs. Thomas had come for her in the carriage, insisting that she and Alice spend a few more days on terra firma if John was too busy to leave the vessel.

What a time they had had shopping! Gifts to be sent home for the folks, materials for clothing to last another several years.

How difficult it had been to anticipate Alice's needs! She was so tiny now, but she showed every sign of walking soon. Maria bought several pairs of soft but sturdy little shoes, hoping they would fit her when needed.

She glanced at the skylight frame, where a row of potted plants had been securely fastened. She had brought a bit of garden to the ship—geraniums in reds, pinks, and whites.

Then her thoughts went back to the news in the

letters from home. There had been an undercurrent of fear in all of them, although the written words were full of hope that, with Mr. Lincoln as President, serious trouble could be avoided.

A tiny shadow of fear came into her own heart about the future. Where now would her baby be born? John had spoken hopefully of returning to Sydney, but there were many weeks before her and so much could happen. She felt beset with problems, big and little, pricking like so many sharp points.

A deep sigh escaped her. Then, with forced determination, she closed her fingers firmly, telling herself, 'This is the time to hold the thistle tight in my hand.'

Chapter 25

CAPTAIN Hamblin cruised the Great Australian Bight in search of whales, with moderate success, as long as the weather held. At times he dipped close to the fringe of the Antarctic. Trunks and sea chests yielded up their warm clothing, and the cabin stove was brought up again to make the captain's quarters comfortable for Maria and little Alice.

On pleasant days, Maria brought the child on deck to play in her little pen while she did the laundry. When Alice tired of her pen, Maria walked her about the confines of the quarterdeck, holding firmly to the ends of a little harness she had devised for the child's safety as she learned to walk. Alice had developed a gait adjusted to the roll of the ship, in true sailor fashion, and she relished these frequent excursions.

By late April, 1862, The Roman made ready to leave the Australian Bight to return to whaling on the Line. First the ship headed for the Bay of Islands, a port on the northeast end of New Zealand.

'This is a good resort for whaleships to get recruits, wood, and water, and to give liberty and paint the ship,'

John told Maria as the ship made her way from the sea to the harbor some ten or twelve miles inland.

The captain and his wife were standing at the deckrail, admiring scenery pleasing to the eye as the vessel wound in and out, now by green-clad islets, then by reefs of rock, and then by woodlands on the main island. Here and there were to be seen the white cottages of the settlers, with cattle roaming at will among them.

'It's sort of English-looking,' Maria remarked. 'I thought this was a Maori settlement.'

'Oh, no. Not right here. It's mostly English, descendants of the missionaries that came in the early part of the century. I've been told the chiefs, Maori chiefs, in gratitude for what the missionaries did for the natives, gave them large tracts of land and they settled here. We'll get off sometime during our stay at the port and you'll meet some very friendly English people.'

Maria shook her head and sighed happily. She had come to accept the good and the bad with equal quiet.

Under all sail with a fine breeze, the ship passed a high bluff of land and entered a deep bay which was nearly circular and about five miles across, the land sloping to the shore around it. Now the yards of the ship were braced sharp up and she turned toward a sandy beach, in back of which a row of houses extended to right and left for a mile or more.

'This port is quite a town,' Maria said in surprise. The houses were obviously English-style, square, cement-built, with sloping gabled roofs and gardens fenced in with stone or hedge.

The ship lay in the harbor for more than a week, taking on board some three hundred barrels of water and an ample supply of wood, as well as vegetables and fruit. Barrels of potatoes, cabbages, and onions were brought aboard by the whaleboats, since the ship could not anchor close to the wharf.

Maria knew that John would see to it that the crew had plenty of onions and citrus fruits, since he was a firm believer that such foods would do much to prevent scurvy. She and John ate raw onions as one would an apple.

Each watch was given two days liberty. John watched them go, a worried expression on his face, as one by one they slipped over the rail and down the rope into the waiting boat. 'Most of them will come back drunk, and some even sick,' he told Maria. 'The English tavern-keepers here are very generous with their drink.'

She and the child had their day on shore. She held Alice on her lap as they were lowered in the bos'n's chair and into the boat. This was always a time of furrowed brow and nervousness for Maria, but to Alice it was a great adventure and she wore a big smile during the whole proceeding.

As usual, Maria staggered under the unaccustomed feel of firm ground. Alice walked with a distinct sailor roll, giving those watching her a good laugh.

On former visits to this port, John had made friends on shore and now the family had warm invitations to come to several homes. Maria especially enjoyed a stay in the home of the Summervilles, descendants of missionaries. While the women chatted, Alice, now walking, played hide and seek and other games loved by children the world over with the flaxen-haired little Summerville daughters.

Maria listened with interest to talk about the island. Some day David, Lisha, Amasah, and others would ask her about these strange, faraway places. Her own curiosity was provoked by the account of the huge and powerful Moa bird that once roamed in New Zealand, but was now extinct. Judging from the bones found, her New Zealand friends told her, the Moa bird must have had legs about the size of a horse's legs.

One afternoon Maria and the children were taken to visit the Maoris' settlement. They travelled by a wagon resembling an American buckboard. It was hard to believe that the peaceful, brown-skinned Maoris, busy about their farms and small businesses, had once been a warlike race and that the English had had some bloody fights with them. In many of these fights, too, the English had suffered more losses than the Maoris.

At the end of the stay in the Bay of Islands, the ship hove up anchor and with a fine northwest wind set sail. Standing out of the bay, she rounded the bluff, running with a leading wind through the channel. Soon she had the broad Pacific before her.

As The Roman sailed past a rocky bit of coastline near the tip of New Zealand, Maria stood in the stern for a last look at that favorite country of whalemen away from home. John, coming up the deck, looked at his wife. Later he told her what a pretty picture she made as she stood at the rail, drinking in the clean, bracing air and watching the changing scenery about her.

Something about the proud tilt of her head had reminded him of the day he had met her, standing among the marigolds and zinnias, garden shears in hand. Only she was a young girl then. Now she had become a young woman, a mature and lovely woman. Maria had turned to him then just as she was turning now, her hazel eyes warm and smiling.

'John, do come and look at all these birds—thousands of them. And the water is the most beautiful blue.'

Thistle in Her Hand

John picked up Alice and together they watched the wake of the whaleship, cutting into the ruffled blue sheet of the southern waters, and the rugged coastline with its rocky promontories contending for the teeming bird life. As they drew closer they saw that birds were everywhere, on the high ledges, on the rocks below, in the sand and the water.

'There are so many more birds here than I remember seeing in the tropical waters,' Maria said. 'Remember how we'd go for days without seeing a bird, and when we did it was only a booby?'

'Quite true,' John answered, watching a seabird with heavy white wings and cream-colored beak circle slowly about the ship. 'Gulls and gannets, like this one above us, and many other seabirds seek those high rocky places exposed to the elements. I suppose they are freer from other dangers up there.'

Maria watched the movement of the gannet. 'It looks so well fed and lazy,' she remarked.

'A gannet lazy? I should say not. He is forever hunting the ocean for dark schools of small fish. His eyes are sharp as needles. He's the fisherman's friend, for wherever a gannet dives there's a school of small fish and that means there will be big fish there, too, going after the little fish.'

'So they are useful and important, as well as graceful and charming against that blue sky,' Maria mused, watching a group of gannets dip and turn this way and that.

Alice suddenly began to babble in her own special language, pointing excitedly to a school of porpoises cavorting like lively boys just released to their play.

'Those porpoises are probably waiting for the gannets

to dive, so they, too, can go after small fish dinners. The gannets show them where their dinners are,' John told Maria.

'And don't tell me those dreary-looking birds over there are waiting for the gannets to dive!' Maria pointed to some large grayish birds perched on the rocks.

'Yes, those mutton birds are waiting to see where to dive for fish. And those gulls, too.' John nodded toward the gulls yawking across the wake of the ship.

'Well,' said Maria decidedly, 'I hope nothing happens to the gannets.' Then she added slowly, 'It seems the Lord has chosen some beings to be very important in the bird world as well as among us humans. At this moment, while the other birds watch the gannets, we humans are watching President Lincoln, depending so much on him—all of us Americans, even us out here.'

John agreed and for a long moment the two stood watching the birds while anxious thoughts raced through their minds. What was happening at home? Had Lincoln been accepted? What was the state of the nation? They could only wait in patient and prayerful hope for the answers. But even now, the uppermost thing in their minds was personal—Maria's pregnancy.

Soon John began spending many hours in the cabin, charting the ship's course for the next four months. They were heading northward toward the Line and warmer waters, for the southern winter was turning stormy and dangerous. John hoped for good whaling along the Line before Maria's condition urged them to return to Australian waters, so that she and Alice could be left at the sanitarium in Sydney in plenty of time for the birth.

Maria joined her husband in the cabin and prepared to write a letter home. 'John, will you draw a rough chart of our voyage from now to Sydney time? I want to send it to Aunt Abby. She liked the one I sent her so much and asked for more, remember?'

'Very well, dear.'

He took a sheet of paper and ruler and scaled the dimensions to size and began drawing in precise fashion. She watched admiringly as he drew in the islands, beginning with Tasmania that looked like a heart lurching in the waters south of Australia. He carefully penned the names of the waters around the island. Bass Straits between Tasmania and Australia, the Indian Ocean on one side and the Tasman Sea on the New Zealand side.

'How nicely John letters,' thought Maria as he drew in New Zealand and then made arrows toward the northern point of New Zealand, straight up into the Coral Sea, then on to the Solomons and up around the Line. Now the arrows pointed back to the Coral Sea and straight to Sydney.

Next John put in comical faces, showing the wind blowing, and took out his whale stamp and stamped whales in the waters where he hoped to find them. Below the finished chart he wrote in fine script, 'For Alice from her father, Capt. John C. Hamblin, May 25, 1862.'

On the passage to the Line, many islands were sighted, bits of green surrounded by waters of mingling greens and blues. But there were no whales. One morning, though, the dull crew was electrified by a call from the masthead, 'A sunfish in sight—to lee of ship.'

Maria joined the crew and officers at the deck rail in time to see a dorsal fin sticking out of the water. She heard John speak to the mate.

'Mr. Richards, would you like to go after it in your boat?'

'Why not, sir? It would mean half a cask of liver oil

for softening fine leather and for rheumatism medicine. Yes, I'll go.'

Maria watched the mate and his men lower the boat in lively fashion and pondered again the impulse that sent men to sea for a living. 'Doc, what is it that attracts men to this hard, dangerous life?'

Doc puffed silently on his pipe a moment, then began to chuckle. She knew a yarn was forthcoming.

'Mrs. Hamblin, ma'am, I don't rightly know, but I spect salt gets in their blood. Why, when I was a lad in Nantucket, every mother's son in the town aimed to go to sea first chance he got. Reminds me of a story, and this is a true yarn, ma'am.'

Maria smiled encouragingly, and the cook cleared his throat and went on.

'One day a neighbor of my mom's sent her boy to fetch a bucket of water from the well. Just as he got there, he looked out over the bay and saw a ship readyin' to sail. He set the bucket down and ran all the way to the wharf and signed on.

'Five years later the ship returned and he headed for his mom's house. When he passed the well, he saw a bucket standin' there and he filled it and carried it home with him. When he went in the kitchen door, his mom was cookin' over the stove same as when he left. He just walked in and said, "Here's your water, mom."'

'Oh, Doc, that can't be true!' laughed Maria.

'Ma'am, my mom'd never make up a story like that. I know it's true.' And Doc pretended to be offended.

In a short time Mr. Richards' boat returned with the odd-looking fish. One darting iron had finished the creature without a fight. The tackles were lowered and the sunfish hauled aboard. Maria gasped as she looked at the catch. It lay on the deck, a gray oval nearly six feet across, with skin like a shark.

'It's like a funny picture in a book, or one of Elisha's drawings,' thought Maria. The body was flat, more so as it neared the tail, where the hind part was pinched off, leaving a thin ragged edge almost straight up and down. Its mouth was a puckered protuberance, found midway in the pancake shape of the forward part of the body, and the small eyes were a short distance back of the mouth on either side.

Doc joined Maria, eager to talk about any part of whaling life that interested the captain's wife.

'It feeds on flimsy food like jellyfish and the Portuguese man-o'-war. That critter has no bones, and cuttin' into the body is like cuttin' a chunk out of a candle. If the chunk is rolled into a ball, I'm told it can bounce like rubber, but I never tried it.'

The men proceeded to cut out the liver, which they dumped into a tub. Then the carcass was tumbled overboard and the deck washed down. Maria held her handkerchief to her nose during this process. Even after the deck was scrubbed, the strong fishy smell remained.

'How disagreeable,' thought Maria. 'This is worse than a try-out.'

The open tub with the liver, enough to fill a bushel basket, was left on the deck to rot since only when the liver was putrid was the oil released. Only then could it be poured off.

'It's a stinking mess,' John admitted to Maria, 'but it's the only way to extract that fine oil.'

Maria kept as far from the tub as possible. The weather added another woe, for as they reached the Line it grew hotter daily. Then came a day when the wind gave out altogether and The Roman floated on a liquid glass sea that scarcely heaved.

A strange silence engulfed the vessel, so slight was the touch of the sea against the ship's sides. Instinctively the seamen lowered their voices and the sound of the bells in the stillness startled them. Pitch bubbled out of the seams of the ship and ran down its sides, and its smell was added to that of the rotting liver.

The decks were kept wet and the men on watch darted from shade to shade, except for the man at the masthead. He had to stand and swelter until relieved. Whaleship duty was hard.

'It's no place for weaklings,' Maria thought as she lay on the bed, panting. At the same time she tried to fan Alice, who was cutting a molar and was slightly feverish.

The cabin and steerage were uncomfortable enough with all the doors and portholes wide open. What must it be like in the forecastle where the watch below were trying to sleep? It must be suffocating, thought Maria. Poor men. Life was trying to them all.

John had a sail awning stretched over the deck for Maria's comfort, but the smell of the sunfish remained and the stench of the putrefying liver was borne from the forward deck on any vagrant breeze. Maria could not stand it for long. Nauseated, she retreated to the stateroom.

After sunset the ship came alive. One could almost hear the sigh of relief that went up when the sun slipped below the horizon. Then sounds of talking, even laughter, came to Maria's ears from the forward deck and she was glad.

'How odd the ship looks in a calm,' said Maria to John as they took a turn about the quarterdeck one night. The Roman seemed resting on air, her sails hanging flat up and down from the masts and squareyards.

'You think the ship is standing still, but if you could

watch the compass you'd see that sometimes she turns completely around,' John informed her.

'What! Completely around? What causes it?'

'The action of the current, which is setting us westward at least twenty or thirty miles every twenty-four hours,' answered John as he lifted a tendril of soft brown hair which had escaped from the snug coil on the top of Maria's head.

The next morning started out the same as the last. The sun rose like a red-hot ball of fire, looking twice its usual size. Maria saw it from the porthole of the stateroom. 'Another hot, calm day,' she thought, 'another day of tepid water starting to spoil even in the filter.'

But the decks had hardly been scrubbed and the masthead manned when came the call, 'Th-a-r-r- she bl-oo-oo-os! Sperm whale!' Heat was forgotten and the ship galvanized into action. There was the sound of running bare feet, of boats being lowered, of John's voice issuing orders.

Maria lay limply on the bed, imagining the men straining at the oars in the heat, with the mirror-like ocean reflecting the sun's hot rays, reddening their eyes. And John, standing on the tryworks or taffrail, watching, signalling the men, his eyes, too, tortured by the glare.

And what was ahead? Battle with a terrible bull whale, a stoven boat, or perhaps a life lost? A man sunk into the deep—gone forever, soon forgotten except by a few in the forecastle? Certainly never given a thought by those who enjoyed the lamps and candles that gave comfort to their homes and cheerfulness to their gatherings.

Maria's thoughts were bitter as she lay beside the

sleeping Alice. The society people who enjoyed the particular brilliance sperm oil lamps lent to their social functions, did they ever take time to reflect on the hazards of the long whaling voyages which gave them light?

Later that morning she was looking through her glass at the whaleboats, which had become almost dots to the naked eye, when she saw a strange sight. The black form of a huge sperm whale leaped upwards, completely out of the water. Excitedly, Maria called to Doc, asked him what the action meant.

Doc walked slowly to her side, his sharp eyes fixed on the horizon. 'Ma'am, whales do that sometimes. Maybe there's a pod nearby and he's signalling.'

Maria marvelled again at the powerful creatures that could lift their two-ton bulk right out of the water.

When the boats came back, they towed a large whale—a good one-hundred-barrel one. Early next morning the officers set the stage for the cutting-in to start. The men were spirited in spite of the heat and made the old windlass roll to the cry of 'Board oh!' One blanket piece after another was swung over the gangway. For the first time in many days, Maria heard them singing the chanteys that made work light and she smiled as she listened. Alice clapped her hands with delight, swaying against the rail of her pen in time to the beat of the music.

That night the trypots blazed and Maria fled below, wondering how the men could stand that inferno on a night that was already stifling.

As if rewarding their efforts, the wind picked up at dawn, the ship moved, and life became bearable again.

John turned the ship at once for one of the many atoll

islands, coral islands having the form of a ring of coral surrounding a core of blue water. Maria was beginning to recognize them from a distance. At first only the feathery fronds of the coconut palms were seen. Then, just three or four feet above sea level, low-lying islands appeared. John had told her that these islands were thought to have been made by a coral insect which probably started building on the rims of sunken volcanic craters.

The atoll they were approaching had a navigable lagoon, open to the sea. Before entering the lagoon John had soundings taken. The crewman ran out a hundred fathoms (about 600 feet) and no bottom was found.

'It is often that way with an atoll, and even this lagoon is deep enough for a good-sized vessel,' John told Maria, as The Roman sailed into the island lake.

There were huts along the shore among the coconut trees. John said that he had stopped there before and knew the people. Before a boat could be launched to take the casks ashore for fresh water, the ship was surrounded by canoes filled with dark-skinned natives selling coconuts and finely woven mats and hats. John made known his need for wood and vegetables, fruit and chickens, and the canoes soon returned with plenty of everything requested.

Meanwhile, mate Richards went ashore with a few of the crew and returned with the much needed fresh water. Maria thought nothing on earth had ever tasted better and Alice drank greedily from her little mug.

At first Maria was fearful when John allowed the natives to board the ship with their wares, and even more alarmed when one of the men cleft a coconut with one sharp thrust of his knife. She kept herself and Alice out of sight in the safety of the deckhouse under the skids. From there she watched every movement of the strange men until they had finished their trading.

'I noticed you bartered tobacco for everything,' Maria said as she joined John at the wheelhouse.

'Yes, they don't want money or oil. They want tobacco or liquor. And a little pays for much here.'

As the sails were set to move out of the lagoon, John ordered the decks scrubbed clean of the debris of coconuts, wood, and the litter left by the natives. With fresh water and a change of diet in store, the crew worked with a will.

One morning, shortly after the island stop, a sail was reported from the masthead, two points on the lee bow. Since The Roman and the stranger were on opposite tacks, they soon came abreast of each other. The approaching ship went four points to the lee and hauled up her mainsail. Maria, watching from the rail, knew it meant a gam and heard John give the order to haul up The Roman's mainsail to show that the offer was accepted.

'What ship can it be? Is it outbound from home or does it come from Australia with news from home?' Maria asked herself as she grasped the top of the deck rail. The Roman stood alone until the other ship bore about two points forward of The Roman's lee, then she heard John giving commands to put the wheel hard up and square the yards.

Soon the two ships were within speaking distance. The captain megaphoned that he was New Bedford bound. The ship was going home!

Maria hurried below to prepare the packet of letters and small gifts to send back home. She added a drawing of the lagoon that they had recently visited to the chart

Thistle in Her Hand

of the voyage that John had made for David, and carefully sealed the letter. She kissed the letters, tied them into a packet, and then put a fresh dress on Alice before going up on deck.

Just then she heard voices, John's and a deep, booming voice. The two captains were in the cabin. Maria stepped in to meet Captain Mellon of The Levi Starbuck, a short, stocky, dark-bearded man about John's age, a jolly man full of jokes and gallant phrases. He was homeward bound to Nantucket by way of the Cape.

All too soon the gam came to an end, for the visitors knew that darkness in the tropics comes suddenly, like the dropping of a dark blue velvet curtain.

'Mrs. Hamblin,' the affable captain promised, 'you may rest assured these letters will get into your aunt's hands as soon as I can get to Pocasset. I'll give them first-hand information about you folks.'

By the sound of his booming voice, Maria followed the captain's progress up the companionway and finally into the whaleboat. A little later she called Timmy to carry Alice up the steps and they stood together, watching the visitor's ship, all sails set, heading for home. By nightfall her topgallant sails dropped below the horizon, leaving The Roman's people alone to continue their wearisome cruise.

'Don't you wish that was us there?' asked the cabin boy.

'Yes, Timmy, I do,' Maria answered yearningly.

Chapter 26

TIME passed quickly now for everyone on board ship, except Maria. The weather was favourable and whaling good for the most part throughout June and July. In early August, John set his course toward Sydney, with plenty of time for a leisurely trip to the Australian current which would carry them swiftly to their destination. He planned to leave Maria and Alice at the sanitarium of the English sisters several weeks before the baby was expected, and to continue whaling nearby until it was time to return to be with Maria.

Maria's needle flew and a drawerful of baby clothes accumulated. Then, without warning, her peaceful, orderly world was turned topsy-turvy. Before dawn one morning a freakish storm swung abruptly upon them. The scurrying men on watch barely had time to batten down the hatches and furl the sails before wind and rain exploded from the darkened skies in a demonical blast. Throughout the morning it raged, spinning the ship like a child's toy.

John ordered Timmy to look after Maria's needs and Maria to remain in the gimballed bed with Alice no matter what happened. Maria remained calm, certain that The Roman would ride out this storm as it had so many others. But in mid-morning there was a terrible sound from the deck, the sound of ripping and crashing, followed by the shouts of the men and then the sound of ax blows. Maria, sick with fright and foreboding, clutched Alice to her side. Even without Timmy's quick report, she knew that one of the masts must have gone.

'If the masts and the hatches hold, we are all right.' How often she had heard John say that.

'It's the mainmast that went. The men are cuttin' it away,' Timmy informed her through chattering teeth from the doorway.

A cold chill swept over Maria, although the stateroom was stifling, and she could not answer the boy. She held Alice more tightly and prayed. Soon the howling of the wind lessened; but there was a new sound, one that Maria had never before heard on The Roman.

'What is it?' she called hoarsely to Timmy, who had pried his thin body between a chest of drawers and John's big trunk as though expecting the ship to turn completely over.

At that moment John came in the room, water running from his thick reddish hair and dripping from his clothes. 'It's the pumps, dear,' he answered Maria. 'We've sprung a leak. The men will have to pump until we make port.'

In spite of her fear, Maria felt a deep pang of sympathy for John. He looked ten years older, with deep lines etching his face.

'Sydney?' Maria questioned.

'No. We must find a nearer port. We have been blown so far westward that we must be near Norfolk Island. As soon as the sun comes out and I get our bearings, I can tell definitely.' John went on describing the havoc wrought by the storm. The deck was a shambles, some of the boats gone.

'The deckhouse?'

'Yes, gone, too, and everything in it. We had no time to save small things.'

Maria started to cry out at the remembrance of all her small treasures: spyglass, sewing box, the pots of geraniums, now all swept into the sea. Then she remembered the fury of the storm and felt grateful that they were still alive.

When the storm subsided at last, John set the few remaining sails for Norfolk Island and for three long days and nights the crippled ship made its tortuous way across the sea. Day and night the men pumped, in back-breaking shifts of work.

'The harbor here is too shallow for The Roman,' John told Maria as the small bleak island came into view. 'As soon as we drop anchor, I am going to take you and Alice ashore in a whaleboat.'

There was a new note in her husband's voice. As Maria watched his face, she saw that the drawn look that had been its constant feature since the morning of the storm, was leaving, as if a great weight of worry were lifting.

'He must have thought we would not make it,' thought Maria with compassion. 'And he never told me.'

John's silence in the face of his despair gave Maria courage to descend into the waiting whaleboat by way of the bo'sun's chair with outward calm, although she never made the descent without trepidation. She was conscious now of her bulky figure and sat awkwardly, holding Alice to her shoulder.

'This used to be quite a rendezvous for whaling

ships,' John said as the men rowed shoreward. Maria shivered under her wool shawl as a chilly wind helped them toward the island. That piece of land was not inviting.

'What a dreary sight!' thought Maria, gazing at the browned hills and shallow ravines, relieved with the occasional green of Norfolk pines.

'Such grim looking buildings! Oh, over there—gallows.'

John nodded. 'Remember, this was once an English penal colony. Those stone and cement houses were mostly built in that period. Later, the government transferred the colony to Australia. Now the Pitcairn people are here—all except the ones who returned to the island.'

For a fleeting second Maria could smell the haunting fragrance of the Pitcairn flowers. High whites, the Pirate had called them in presenting the gift of the kindly islanders.

'Look, Maria.' John pointed shoreward to a group of somberly dressed people standing on the wharf, waving.

At once Maria's spirits began to rise, like a pinioned bird released. She had been conscious of this phenomenon at other times—at the sight of a beautiful color, or a white tern against the blue sky, upon seeing someone do a kind act or on reading a pretty phrase. The lift now was caused by the scene before her—people raising their hands in friendly welcome. Maria waved back, smiling.

Helping hands lifted Maria and Alice from the whaleboat with a gentle greeting. Alice was picked up by a dark young woman. She opened her blue eyes in alarm, but, seeing her parents relaxed, she quickly lost her fears.

A tall elderly man came forward, greeted John, and

introduced himself as George Hun Nobbs, minister, doctor, and teacher of the Norfolk people. John explained their dilemma and the minister-doctor called aside a couple whom he introduced as the Rossiters. After a short conference, John told Maria that the Rossiters had an extra room in their cottage and would take them in. Maria was relieved; she liked the looks of the amiable couple who were part English, part Tahitian.

The Rossiter home was nearby, with others grouped about it in a clearing. The houses were plain, with whitewashed walls outside and in, and with thatched roofs. Maria noted with pleasure that there were still hardy annuals blooming around the house, as yet untouched by frost.

The room to which Mrs. Rossiter showed them was fresh and clean, although sparsely furnished. A patchwork quilt on the bed gave color to the room; a picture of the young Queen Victoria and her prince consort furnished the only wall decoration. Later, a child's bed, borrowed from a neighbor, was brought in for little Alice.

Alice was soon the center of a group of children, for the island children flocked to the Rossiter home to see the visitors. A half-grown girl, Amelia Young, took charge of Alice with Maria's permission. Maria watched from her window until she saw that these descendants of the mutineers and their Tahitian wives were gentle and well-behaved. She walked about, trying to get accustomed to the steadiness of the land, while John returned to the ship to bring the clothing and bedding which would be needed ashore while The Roman was under repair.

When he knew Maria was comfortable, John gave his attention to the battered ship. In a few days, it was beached on the other side of the island. The casks in the hold were unloaded and the ship was hove on her side with keel above water's edge and hatches well battened down to keep out the water. John took his wife to see the ship one afternoon.

'Oh John, will she ever be fit for the sea again?' Maria asked in consternation. The crew and some men recruited on the island were scraping the barnacles and sea growths that had attached themselves to the bottom of the ship. Before John could answer, Maria asked the question he had been dreading.

'How long will it take, John? Will we able to get to Sydney in time?'

John took Maria's hand between his warm palms before he answered slowly, 'I'm afraid it will be weeks before the ship is seaworthy and fitted out for further voyaging. We have to get a new mast from Sydney, I'm afraid.'

'Oh dear, dear!' wailed Maria softly. 'Then the baby will be born here.' Her heart sank within her.

'It could be worse, Maria. These people from Pitcairn are good, kind people. Be brave, dear.'

Maria managed a tremulous smile. 'Yes, Captain.'

The days slipped by pleasantly enough. Although John was gone much of the day, Maria did not have time to be lonely, for the people on the island made frequent informal calls and she soon knew many of them by name. When she learned that Mrs. Rossiter was occasionally called upon to act as midwife and the elderly Mr. Nobbs was quite capable of delivering a baby, she faced the future with confidence.

On sunny days, John took her to the beach to show her the progress being made on The Roman. First, the copper sheathing had been removed and the planks scraped. 'The seaworms play havoc with the hull of a

Thistle in Her Hand

ship in tropical waters. Even the copper sheath couldn't keep them out. In colder waters, the worm doesn't do much damage,' John told her.

'What a lot of work!' sighed Maria.

'Tomorrow the seams will be caulked with oakum,' John explained, pointing to a pile of loose hemp fiber, 'and coated with tar. They'll use paint brushes for that.'

Maria leaned against the piled up casks of oil and looked at the sooty old ship.

'After that, pine sheathing will be nailed over the planks and then the copper sheathing replaced. The Roman will get on her keel again and the masts and jib boom will get a going over. We're having a new mainmast made. Oh, there is much work ahead before the dressing up with paint starts.'

Before the mainmast was in place, Maria had learned a great deal about the history of the islanders. Bit by bit, the story of the terrible days that preceded the mutiny on the ship, Bounty, was told her by the Rossiters and two of their close friends, Hannah Adams and Dorcas Young. The appalling acts of cruelty, the malevolence that grew in Captain Bligh's heart like a poisonous growth, made it appear that the mate, Fletcher Christian, was justified in leading the mutiny.

'Many was the time,' Mr. Rossiter informed Maria, 'when I heard Thursday October Christian, his son, say, 'No one knows what would have happened to my father and many others if the voyage had continued under Captain Bligh.'

Maria smiled when she heard the odd name. 'I wonder if he was born on a Thursday in October, or if his Tahitian mother thought it had a pretty sound?' she mused.

When they were alone in their room, Maria told John of her conversations with the islanders. Captain

Hamblin did not hold these descendants responsible for the acts of their forebears, but still the connotation of the word 'mutiny' to a sea captain was such that she had little expectation of winning full sympathy for the plight of the inhabitants of Pitcairn and Norfolk. By the end of the third week of their stay, however, John was willing to admit that the population that had survived the early struggles had been well trained.

'Imagine, John!' Maria exclaimed at the end of one of their discussions, 'John Adams, the sole survivor of the mutineers, a man with little education, a sinful man at one time, and, with only the Bible and an English prayer book to aid him, somehow taught these people to be quiet, God-fearing, and industrious.'

'And to be happy and still have a strict morality,' added John, thinking of the virtues of the men who were working with the crew to repair The Roman.

In their turn, the Norfolk people plied Maria with questions about the places she had visited. The brief stop at Pitcairn Island was reviewed over and over again. The crew members who had gone ashore that day were extremely popular with the Norfolk people.

'Many others were talking of returning,' Mr. Nobbs told John. 'Some of the old people find Norfolk too chilly. They are homesick, too, for the tropical beauty of Pitcairn.'

As the days passed, Maria went out less and less. The almost carefree life and the temptations of appetizing land foods had caused her to gain considerable weight. Often she was short of breath, and various small ailments afflicted her. It was pleasanter to sit by the kitchen fire and sew and talk now than to walk awkwardly about.

Her world had become small on the little out-of-the-way island and, for the moment at least, Maria had no concerns ruffling her serene days. When the time came for the birth, Mr. Nobbs would be doctor, along with his helper, Mrs. Rossiter. Alice was put into the temporary care of Dolly Dinah, a dedicated young woman planning to be a missionary.

Even when an unexpected blow struck their well-laid plans, Maria was not greatly disturbed. Mr. Nobbs fell and broke his leg. John assisted in caring for the injured limb, and Mr. Nobbs assured him that he would advise Mrs. Rossiter, but that she was quite capable of handling a natural birth alone.

'I only hope the Lord will see fit to deliver the child soon,' said Mr. Nobbs thoughtfully. 'This baby may not be as tiny as your wife tells me her first child was.'

John watched Maria anxiously after that, but another week slipped away without incident.

One day, however, the islanders awoke to find another vessel approaching the harbor. It was the first since the week of The Roman's arrival, when fortunately a whaler Sydney-bound had stopped for a few repairs and had taken a message from John to his shipping office. There was a touch of spring in the air that September day as John hurried to the wharf, expecting a message from Sydney, if not other mail.

He was not disappointed. The ship's captain put a bundle of papers and letters into his hands. There would be rejoicing among the crew and officers, for it had been months since any mail had reached them.

John hurried to the Rossiter home. News from home would cheer Maria. She had been uneasy when he left her, unlike her usual self.

'Look here, Maria. We've news from home.' John tossed the bundle of letters on the bed and took out his pocketknife to cut the bindings.

Maria's face brightened and she picked up a loose

paper with an old date some months past, while John carefully cut the precious length of cord that bound the ship's letters together.

'Oh, *The New York Times*!' Mechanically, without sensing its meaning at first, Maria read aloud the headline.

'Fort Sumter attacked. President Lincoln declares War...'

'What?' exclaimed John, turning quickly. He was in time to see Maria's face turn ashen as she repeated, 'declares war, war, war—' then heard her give a low moan, like a wounded animal, that rose into a scream.

He sprang to her, tried to gather her to him, saying over and over, 'Don't Maria. Don't take on this way.' But Maria, her eyes glassy, lips white, continued to scream.

Mrs. Rossiter burst into the room without ceremony and immediately took charge. 'There, there, my lamb, it'll soon be over. Just take it easy-like.'

To John she said, 'Her time has come. I'll get her in bed while you go for George Nobbs.'

By evening, when the whale oil lamps were lit, the news had swept the island that the American lady was in a bad way, that her life was despaired of. Mrs. Rossiter and Dorcas Young had used every art they knew to bring the baby into the world, with Mr. Nobbs watching Maria's condition closely. Still the birth had not occurred.

In the big rooms of what had once been the prison, the gallows still standing, the crew slept fitfully. Several times during the night Smitty, the Pirate, or Tom Layton left their quarters to go to the Rossiters' for news.

A thunderstorm came in from the ocean during the

night, and as the thunder rumbled and the rain beat noisily upon the roof, Maria in delirium cried out, 'The cannons! They've hit the masts!' Then, 'The mainmast is gone! We're sinking!'

Shortly after midnight, it was the minister-doctor who assisted a lusty big baby boy into the world. The crippled man, held up on either side by the willing hands of the two women, prayed and worked quickly for some agonized minutes. Then his efforts succeeded and Harry Hamblin was born. Maria faced a long convalescence, but she would recover.

The mating songs of the island birds had changed into the anxious, quarrelsome twitters of nesting days before both Maria and The Roman were ready to sail again. Harry was a strong child and gave her no trouble. John purchased a cow to provide Harry's milk, for the doctor would not permit Maria to nurse this child. A place was made on the deck of The Roman beyond the tryworks for the cow, as well as the nanny goat, chickens, and some small pigs. 'If we are going to carry a cow, we might as well have the whole farm,' laughed John.

On a fair day in December, The Roman put to sea again, amid tears and promises of future meetings. That night Maria, looking out on the ocean from the porthole, saw only the roll of the empty sea under the moon.

'But it isn't an empty sea really,' she thought, 'for somewhere out there is Norfolk Island and the good folks on it—our friends.'

Chapter 27

As Captain Hamblin set his course again for summer whaling in the cool South Pacific region, Maria whirled in a domestic world of her own. With two children to care for, her days were filled to the brim. The ship's carpenter, in rebuilding the little deckhouse under the skids, had exercised every trick of his trade to add conveniences for Maria's housekeeping. In the stateroom, baby Harry usurped his sister's bed in the chest and a slatted bunk was now Alice's sleeping place.

The addition of fresh eggs and milk to the diet of the captain's family proved its worth; Maria and the babies filled out and grew rosy with health. Indeed, Maria had to let out the seams of her dresses and adjust them to a more mature figure.

Early in the year, 1862, The Roman gammed with the ship Thomas Pope of New Bedford. The captain, Charles Robbins, brought the ship folks letters from home dating back to October, 1859. Although the news was old, it was welcomed joyfully. Maria's father wrote at length of John Brown's fateful raid. 'He accomplished nothing but trouble for himself and eventual death by hanging,' Elisha Tobey wrote.

Margarita Thompson Diddel

Twice in the Australian Bight that season, gamming ships brought later news from home.

'How awful it would be without you kind whaling postmasters,' Maria said to short, stocky Captain William H. Vinal of The Bark Waverley of New Bedford. Captain Vinal had been given the packet by the captain of another ship recently from New Bedford and heading for the North Pacific. The captain of the northbound vessel had decided that the passing Bark Waverly was more likely to meet The Roman.

The letters were disturbing, with news of events that had led up to the declaration of war. One told of the secession, in February, 1861, of the states of Mississippi, Florida, Alabama, Georgia, and Louisiana, and the founding of the Confederacy with Jefferson Davis as provisional president.

'He is from Kentucky, just the same as President Lincoln,' wrote Uncle Asa. He was confident that there would be no conflict, because a large part of the North was in sympathy with the South over the question of states' rights.

'President Lincoln, though personally opposed to slavery, is more concerned now with preserving the Union than in abolishing slavery. So I am confident we shall not have war,' wrote John's sister.

'But war is raging,' said Maria sadly to John. 'How little we can tell what is ahead of us!'

Aunt Abby's letter contained the news they had been dreading to learn. 'Amasah enlisted at the first call for volunteers,' she wrote. 'Elisha was going to, but was needed at the shipyards because of the ships that are blockading the southern ports. He still feels he should be carrying a musket, and probably will yet.'

Maria's father wrote, 'David is bound and determined

to go to sea. He thinks if he goes now he can catch up with you and get transferred to your ship. Maybe it will be good for him to get a taste of whaling now and get the notion out of his system. We are considering the idea.'

As Maria read this part to John, he jumped to his feet and began to pace the cabin floor, saying, 'No! No! This is no time. The South is sure to retaliate against our shipping. I shall write to the home office to send a message to the family to wait until we come home and to tell David I promise to take him on my next voyage. Oh, my dear...'

Maria scarcely heard what John said. Face buried in her hands, she wept for the folks at home in these times of trial, for the boys, near and dear, and the sons of friends who were going to war, for herself and John.

John put his hand on her shoulder as he said quietly, 'Maria, regardless of what the home office says, we are going home just as soon as the barrels are all filled.'

He spoke with determination, and Maria knew he would keep his promise. It still would be many months, maybe a year, before they could sail for home, but Maria was comforted.

The search for whales went on with renewed energy, with the knowledge that The Roman would head for home when the casks were filled.

One morning, when the familiar cry, 'Thar she blo-o-ows,' was answered by the captain's voice, 'Where away?' there came the answer from the loft, 'On the lee four points.' Then came the words the men had been longing to hear, 'Sperm whale. Prepare the boats.'

Maria, lingering over her breakfast tea, noted that the ship was quietly humming, all sounds muted. This meant the quarry was not far away and must not be frightened. The baby awakened with a lusty cry, and Maria went to him quickly to quiet him. She heard the boats being lowered and John's staccato orders. She smiled as she detected the note of exultation in his voice, knowing it was echoed in the hearts of all on board.

At the same time, the old dread came into her heart; these men were going out to danger, to an uncertain fate. Then would follow the cutting-in, with John taking his turn with the men, standing on those swaying planks, wielding those razor-sharp knives.

She shut her eyes for a moment, then opened them with determination. 'It's part of our business,' she scolded herself.

As soon as the children were dressed and breakfasted, they went up to the afterdeck and Maria scanned the horizon for the boats. Doc joined her at the rail, pointing at the direction the boats had taken. There was no sign of a whale then, but as they watched the great black creature emerged, close to one of the boats.

'It's Mr. Richard's boat,' Doc whispered, as if fearful the whale would hear his voice.

Maria saw the iron thrown and then the whale reared up and started off. Doc was living the chase as he talked.

'They're lettin' out the line fast. See, they're pourin' water on. I'll bet the rope's just sizzlin'. It must be a strong bull. See, see, it's making off! Oh, oh! The boat's in for a Nantucket sleigh ride!'

Maria watched in consternation as the boat was pulled farther and farther away until it disappeared over the horizon. Two other boats followed in the direction of the first boat. John, part way up the mast, was giving directions, and soon she felt the ship moving toward the boats.

Doc stared as if his eyes would leave his face and follow the boats. His hands were clenched white against the rail. The crippled man was no longer the galley cook; he was a whaler again, glorying in the chase.

The hours passed. Doc had returned to his cooking and Maria to her motherly duties. When she had free time, she usually spent it on her fancy work—at this moment, exquisite rickrack to adorn a dress for Alice to wear when she reached home. Otherwise she was at the deckrail, scanning the horizon for a prayed-for glimpse of the boats.

All over the ship, anxious glances went seaward; the glances became anxious as the hours passed. The most anxious person aboard, Maria well knew, was John; and she knew also as she watched his tense face that his concern was not for the whale catching, but for the men out there.

Now the ship was no longer moving. John explained that whales sometimes took strange notions and veered in other directions, so there was nothing to do but hove the ship and wait. Late in the afternoon the other two boats returned with the sad report that the mate's boat was nowhere in sight, although they had scoured the sea.

Dusk came briefly and night descended, a moonless night. Maria thought she had never seen the night so black. The lanterns set high on the masts threw out their feeble lights to guide the wandering boat home. The men moved about their tasks in silence. A pall of horror was on the spirits of all.

Maria put the children to bed and joined John as he

went down to a late meal. He ate in silence and when he answered her, he did so in tones of great weariness and sadness. His thoughts were out there where the mate and his men were struggling to survive, if they were still on the ocean in the boat.

As night wore on the sea roughened and it began to rain. Maria heard the men walking about on deck. She knew John would remain up there most of the night, with perhaps brief naps on the cushioned bench in the deckhouse. Finally she fell into a troubled sleep.

When morning came she dressed quietly and went up on deck, leaving the children asleep. It was a drizzly morning and the men on that watch were solemnly going about their duties. John was standing on the tryworks, spyglass glued to his eye. The ship's sails were now set to sail about cautiously, slowly.

Toward eight bells the rain stopped and the sun shone. Maria went up on deck with a heavy heart. Still no sign of the boat! The grim-faced crew performed their tasks, but from time to time raised their eyes toward the ocean, glancing sometimes in one direction, sometimes in another.

Maria was filled with wonder. To these veteran whalers hope was not dead; the men could still be living. As she watched John, sextant to his eyes as he shot the sun to take the ship's bearings, she saw that he was white-lipped, the pallor visible under his tan. Could he still have hope?

How can he, after all this time? she thought dully, as she went to the deckhouse to wash the baby's clothes while the children napped. She removed the cushion from the bench, turning the latter into her worktable, and she felt grateful for tasks that would keep her from standing at the deckrail. Her head ached from so much peering.

Thistle in Her Hand

She had not been at her work long when the quiet was pierced by a shrill call from the masthead, 'Boat ahoy! Boat ahoy!' Instantly the ship came alive with the sound of excited voices and running feet. John bolted from the afterhouse companionway, spyglass in hand. Maria, wiping soapy hands on her apron, was already at the deckrail.

'God be thanked. God be thanked,' she repeated, tears of gratitude running down her cheeks. Soon she saw, afar off, a speck that grew rapidly to become a whaleboat!

It moved so slowly! It must be the mate's. Or could it be from some other whaler, another boat taken on a long Nantucket sleigh ride?

Maria recalled hearing of such an incident. She had thought it just a yarn then, but she had sailed enough by now to know reports of strange occurrences were frequently true. How often she had heard her father say, 'Truth is stranger than fiction.' And she was finding he was right.

With relief she saw the boat gradually take on the identity of The Roman's whaleboat. What terrible dangers men face in the course of a day's work, she thought, on sea, on land! Suddenly her thoughts were with her homeland and what was happening in that once peaceful country.

This frightful experience they were going through here had happened because men went out in the line of duty. But at home this horror of war, this killing of fellow Americans—internecine warfare, her father had called it—was the result of men's stupid thinking. If men acted like the thoughtful humans God meant them to be, then peace could be in America.

'Daughter,' her father had written in so many letters lately, 'I hope you will see the day when men will settle their differences like men, not like bulls with a red flag in front of them. If this war wakes people up to the error of their ways, it will not have been in vain.'

Tears ran down her cheeks as she thought of Lisha, and Amasah, as dear to her as a brother, fighting, perhaps wounded—no! She must not think that. She hurried back to her washing, scrubbing with energy to stave off these sad thoughts.

After what seemed a long time, she heard John shouting into the speaking trumpet, 'Everybody safe?'

'Aye, aye,' came the mate's voice, as willing hands helped the exhausted men aboard.

Maria heard the children's voices in the stateroom; she could not stop to learn what the men would say. A few minutes later, however, the mate and two other men were helped down to the captain's cabin, for they needed aid from the medicine chest for their badly lacerated hands. Maria heard through the curtained doorway the mate's account of their experiences.

'We just sleighrode and there was no stoppin'. T'was a fine big bull, a good hundred barreler, and the men wouldn't hear of my cuttin' the rope. I guess we lost track of distance because when he come up and I sent the lance and he finally turned fins up, we found we couldn't see nothing of the other boats or the ship.

'We waited, fightin' the sharks from eatin' the whale. I've never seen so many hungry sharks in my born days. After we killed some they stopped botherin' much and went after the new carcasses.

'We didn't know what to do; we reckoned we had veered west of ship but weren't sure, so we waited. Night came on mighty soon an' we just had to wait it out, usin' the lanterns to scare away the sharks. I can just see them white bellies and jaws, too near to us for comfort.

Thistle in Her Hand

'We ate our rations. Ouch! Sir! That's too much!' And the brawny mate wilted under the application of John's remedy. Maria in the next room smiled to herself as she heard him and the other two seamen in turn moan and groan as the medication was applied. Brave, heroic men in their terrible ordeal were now acting like little boys when they were having their hands treated.

The mate continued his story. 'And drank the water we had with us and kept bailing when it began to rain. When morning came with all the rain and mist, we couldn't see a yard in front of us. The sharks was keepin' us plenty of company, eatin' at that whale when they could. The men yelled at them so much it helped keep the critters away and pass the time.

'Then, when the rain stopped and the sun came, we saw those topgallant masts. And how good they looked! You never heard such cheerin' and yellin'. It sure scared the sharks off. We put two waifs on the carcass and started rowin'. That's all, Sir.'

John thanked the mate for his report and gave orders to start The Roman after what was left of the whale.

The tired men went below and slept the rest of the day. That night Doc had plum duff in celebration of the men's safe return. Meanwhile, the ship sailed to the whale and rescued the remainder of it. Late that afternoon there was a cutting-in and trying-out, yielding thirty barrels of oil and two barrels of spermacetti.

'All's well that ends well,' Maria said to John that night as they were preparing for bed. She was tired from the long hours of emotional excitement, of waiting. She asked, 'John, why do men choose the life of whaling? Why? Why?'

John did not answer. He was sound asleep. Maria bent over and kissed him on the forehead.

Chapter 28

By the time Harry was a year old there were 2,000 barrels of oil in the hold. Maria, who watched the figures grow in the record book, knew it would not be long before The Roman would be able to point its blunt nose toward Hobart in Tasmania, and thence head westward toward home, completing an around-the-world voyage.

Despite anxieties about the strife at home, between the hardships and adventures of whale-catching and storms there were many days of quiet peace and contentment as the ship sailed the tropical sea. On such a morning Maria stood with her husband at the rail as they approached one of the Gilbert Islands. Maria had been watching since the first tips of the coconut palms had appeared on the horizon, reminding her of a cornfield.

Now they could see the low green isle with a native settlement of thatch-roofed houses among the trees.

'This is an open atoll with a navigable channel. It's a good place to get water and wood,' John told her as she gazed down at the ever-changing greens, yellows, and purples of the lagoon waters, enraptured with the delicacy of the colorings. When her eyes tired of the reflection of the sun on the waters, she raised them for relief to the fringe of lush green along the shores.

Suddenly the lagoon was filled with canoes, their occupants clamoring to barter coconuts and chickens, which they held up for appraisal by the ship folks. Maria knew they would ask for tobacco or liquor in return for their offerings. When in early afternoon the whaleboats returned with water and wood, John gave orders to seek the safety of the open sea, for the southern sky was banked with heavy clouds.

That evening Doc gave the entire ship a treat of chicken stew made with coconut milk, a delicacy he had learned to prepare from the islanders. The coconut meats would be used later with his duff puddings.

Later, when the children were asleep, Maria went up on deck to savor the balmy softness of the night air. She tried to think what it felt like as it caressed her cheek. If velvet could be made by the fairies, that would be it, she decided.

Waiting for John to finish some duties in the forward part of the ship, she looked down into the translucent waters at the phosphorescent swarms of sea life.

As always, she marveled at the delicate traceries of cold fire, then looked above to the gem-studded canopy of the southern skies. The threatening cloud banks had disappeared with the setting sun and the sails fluttered almost without sound so that the whispering surge of the waves against the sides of the boat could be heard.

Maria sighed deeply as she turned to speak to her approaching husband. 'What a peaceful existence one must enjoy on the Gilbert Islands!'

'Not when hurricanes come. It's really bad on these low-lying islands,' John answered, taking her hand for

Thistle in Her Hand

their brisk evening constitutional about the quiet ship. The day was over; tomorrow would bring its own cares or pleasures. Now the whaling people must rest.

Only a few days passed before the masthead lookout raised a sperm whale right after breakfast. The usual excitement followed the call, and the boats were being lowered when Maria and the children reached the rail. She held the baby while Alice stood on an upturned tub. Together the three of them watched the men jump into the waiting boats, take their places, and dip their oars.

The Pirate was one of the last to get into a boat and Maria laughed at his resemblance to a scarecrow, in his ragged clothing and bizarre red turban. Alice stood on tiptoes, waving her hand and laughing gleefully. Glancing up at the sound, the Pirate waved back with a long skinny arm.

As Maria looked eastward, she caught a glimpse of the whale that was their quarry—a monstrous black creature, arching his back as he plunged toward the depths of the sea, his powerful tail remaining high in the air for a few seconds. She knew the men were straining to arrive in his vicinity when he was due to come up again for air, meanwhile forcing up that diagonal spray that is the distinctive bushy spout of the sperm whale. Maria did not wait for the kill; she took the children to the deckhouse to play while she sewed.

Suddenly she was startled by an unusual increase in the commotion of a whale sighting. Alarmed, she looked out of the doorway and saw John charging toward the wheelhouse. At the same time Doc, wild of eye, was making for the lee rail in a limping run. Maria snatched up the baby and hurried little Alice by the hand after Doc. Even before they reached the rail she saw the huge whale charging directly at the ship. Like a monstrous black devil, she thought, suddenly weak and trembling so that she had to put the heavy child down.

Doc turned with amazing alacrity, picked up the little boy, and said sharply, 'You and Alice come with me.' In a moment they were back in the deckhouse. Maria sat on the cushioned bench, a child pressed to either side, while the old seaman-cook stood at the doorway as if on guard. He held on to the doorjamb, waiting, waiting for something appalling to happen.

At the wheel, John was adding his great strength to that of the helmsman as they labored to veer the course of the ship away from the monster's path. The deck watch had sprung to the masts, fighting to turn the sails with their bare hands.

Such an enormous creature could sink a small ship like The Roman. Maria had heard of such instances. She clutched the children to her, praying silently. She wanted to speak to the children but her vocal cords seemed paralyzed and she could only moan.

There was a shout, and Doc left on his limping run. Before Maria could disentangle herself from the frightened children, John ran past, signalling to the men at sea.

Then Doc returned, shouting, 'The whale's turned back—seems to be going toward the boats.' Doc was clearly relieved; but he had a strange look about his face, as though he could not believe they were safe.

By the time Maria and Doc reached the rail the whale had disappeared. Suddenly to their anguished eyes, the great black back reappeared, and the next instant one of the boats was tossed high in the air, breaking in two. Maria saw the figures of men falling, then a dreadful confusion of churning waters, pieces of boat wreckage, and men flailing about with their arms and legs.

Thistle in Her Hand

'Oh no!' she wailed, putting her face against Harry's sturdy back. She felt like screaming to relieve her pent-up emotions; it was too much to bear in silence. She hurried back to the deckhouse, sobbing. Alice put her head in her mother's lap and cried in sympathy. The mystified baby tried to wriggle from his mother's arms toward a toy on the floor.

When she had gained a measure of control, Maria took the children below to the stateroom, thankful that the others were so absorbed in their concern for what was taking place that her near-hysteria had gone unnoticed.

In the privacy of the tiny room, Maria prepared the children for an early nap. Then she gave herself over to the homely task of scrubbing every inch of the small area of floor not covered by nailed-down furniture or trunks. Calmed at last, she prepared to go above again when she heard Timmy's quick steps come down the companionway and go into the captain's cabin.

'What is it?' she called through the doorway.

'Captain wants I ask you for the medicine chest. He needs it on deck. Smitty's hurt bad. And—'

Maria would not let him finish. She handed him the wooden chest, saying, 'Tell me later. Hurry now. And be careful with the chest.'

When he had gone, she sank into her rocker, torn with fear and pity. 'Smitty hurt bad and—' What further griefs would this day hold? Her thoughts went to Smitty's young wife and daughter at home, and she reached for the worn black leather Bible that was her altar, her church-home.

'O Father in heaven, spare Smitty. Return him safe to him family,' she prayed.

Later, Henry knocked on the partition near the

curtained doorway and called gently, 'Mrs. Hamblin, Captain wants you should eat lunch now. He cain't come yet. A real nice lunch is ready, ma'am.'

Maria arose from the rocker stiffly. How long had she sat there, her thoughts hovering between earth and heaven?

'Yes, Henry. Thank you. We'll come shortly.'

Maria washed her face with the tepid water and then wakened the children and dressed them quickly.

In the saloon, Henry served them hot pea soup followed by corned beef and potatoes. A dessert of cut-up oranges and dried coconut was an unexpected treat. Doc seemed to try his best to get up good meals in times of stress, thought Maria. Bless him for it.

During the meal, Henry kept up a lively chatter with the children as he hovered solicitously about the saloon. The children responded with delight; but their distraught mother sat in somber silence. She knew the steward was trying to keep her from asking questions.

When the children had finished a hearty meal and were teasing each other with good humor across the table, Maria turned to Henry and said quietly, 'Now I am ready to hear the sad news. What is it?'

'Yes'm, it is bad news. Smitty's leg was awful lookin' but the cap'n feels it ain't hurt too bad. But the third mate, Monty, cap'n thinks his back is broken.'

Maria gasped; her hand went to her throat.

Henry's eyes were full of pain as he went on, 'And that ain't the worst. The Pirate, he never did come back, ma'am. Them's as think he was carried down with the bow of the boat when the whale sounded. Men's out in the boats lookin' for him, but...' Henry broke off, tears choking his soft voice.

Maria's tears followed. 'The Pirate, gone, carried off

by the whale. Oh, how awful.' The kindly Pirate, Alice's devoted friend!

She wept again later when John told her that, when the whale was rushing the ship, the Pirate was heard to pray, crossing himself devoutly, 'Mother Mary, protect the little angel and her folks.'

For two long days the ship sailed around slowly with a faint hope of finding the Pirate, perhaps clinging to a board. But at last the search was abandoned and the ship sailed on, sadness in the hearts of all aboard.

'We're heading for the nearest port—Suva of the Fiji Islands,' John informed Maria. 'I want the missionary there to see Agrimonte and Smitty. It looks as though Smitty may be hurt inside, too. And I need to get recruits; we are short-handed now.'

Maria's eyes widened with horror at the mention of the Fiji Islands. 'Those cannibal islands! John, you can't mean it.'

John smiled and patted Maria's hand. 'The people are changing. With the coming of the English and the missionaries, things are different. There are no cannibals in the town part. I don't know about the interior, back in the mountains. But we are not going there.'

Maria's mind was uneasy after that. No matter what John said, she resolved she would never leave her two plump little children alone after the Fiji seamen came on board, not even when they were napping.

In a few days they neared the Fijis. It was late in the afternoon when the call came, 'Land ho!' Maria's eyes showed a mixture of fear and curiosity as she searched the horizon for the first glimpse of the islands.

In the distance they appeared only a mass of grey-green upon the violet and blue waters. Then, as they neared them at twilight, they looked like patches of fleshy violet on the clouded blue of sea and sky. Night came and the ship hove to until morning when they could enter the harbor of Suva on the island of Viti Levu.

Soon after dawn the ship made ready to sail into the harbor. Maria and the children rose early and went up on deck. The violet patches on the sea had turned into an enormous landscape of mountains about a fine harbor, a symphony of greens and blues.

By the time they had breakfasted, the ship was at anchor and John made ready to descend the rope ladder into the boat that would take him ashore to make arrangements for the missionary to come aboard, as well as to recruit three crewmen, Fiji natives if there were no others.

A few hours later Missionary Edwards came aboard. A tall, thin Englishman, he had had medical training for his work on the islands, although he was not a doctor. He examined Agrimonte and agreed with John's opinion that his back had been broken. After some discussion, it was agreed that the third mate should be taken ashore in a litter, which would be securely fastened to two native boats. The missionary promised to make him as comfortable as possible for the short time he might live.

Smitty's case presented a different aspect. Although the visitor advised that he also be taken ashore so that his leg wounds could be given careful attention and his general condition watched for internal injuries, Smitty would not agree.

'No, Sir, not on that heathen island. No tellin' when they'd take a notion to eat us up.'

And Smitty was so upset that the plan had to be abandoned and the injured man moved to the third mate's cubby-hole bunk so his injuries could be better cared for. Maria sympathized with him and resolved to redouble her efforts to see that Smitty was made comfortable.

As Mr. Edwards was leaving, Maria noticed three Fijis on the forward deck. They were tall, muscular men, almost black, with a fuzzy mass of hair that they occasionally bushed out with their hands. As Maria stared, the missionary said, 'They are very proud of their mop of hair.'

Turning to John with a smile, he added, 'You'll find them amiable and childlike, but without the slightest ambition.'

Maria wanted to ask about their cannibalism, but somehow it did not seem to be the right thing to ask of people living among them.

The afternoon before The Roman sailed, the Rev. Edwards brought his wife aboard for a farewell tea. Maria was happy to meet the tiny courageous woman and listen to her cultured English tones and ready wit. As they sat taking their tea and the dainty wafers that the Hamblins kept in tins for special occasions such as this, they talked of home: England and Cape Cod. Maria could speak of home with more serenity now since they were soon going there, but her eyes filled when they talked of the war.

When she expressed her fears for her brothers, cousins, and other young men, and for possible attacks from the sea on New England's whaling ports, the English lady interrupted her, patting her knee and speaking earnestly, as if to impress a truth on Maria's troubled mind.

'My dear, don't grieve; there is no use torturing ourselves about what may never happen.'

Maria was silent, thinking over this advice—sensible advice from a truly brave woman. Then, lifting her eyes to meet those of her guest, she said, 'I am grateful to you for those words.'

At sunset The Roman sailed out of the harbor into the open sea. The captain and his wife stood at the bulwarks enjoying the silver-toned Pacific twilight. Even the pinks and rose, the mauve and violet of the highest clouds in the eastern sky were enclosed with silvery grey.

Maria looked back toward Viti Levu, now a long, faintly violet cloud in the distance.

'What brave people those missionaries are! And what good, dear folks,' she said, deep feeling in her voice. 'I'll never again think as I used to when I hear the name Fiji Islands. I know now that, mixed with all the bad we hear about, there is all this beauty, and our good friends Mr. and Mrs. Edwards as well.'

'And Agrimonte,' John added sadly.

'They will be good to him.'

'Yes, I'm sure of that,' John sighed. 'He was a good third mate. Never had much to say, but he always kept his word and the men respected him for it. The Portuguese people have been great seamen from way back.'

Agrimonte from the quarterdeck, the Pirate from the forward deck—both would leave a void in the ship life. They would be missed and mourned as long as this voyage lasted. Afterwards they would join the long list of men lost at sea and forgotten.

Chapter 29

For the next few weeks Maria kept a cautious sentinel eye on the Fiji Islanders and a warm maternal eye on Smitty. Each day when the captain or Doc finished dressing the seaman's wounds, Maria managed to appear with a cup of fresh milk or some tidbit from the quarterdeck fare, which was a treat for the fo'c'sle hand.

At first the crew grumbled at having the Fijis as their intimate bunkmates, and Maria was sympathetic. Suppose, she thought, one of them reverted to his early standards! She shuddered at the thought of a strong man with cannibalistic background in the close quarters below decks.

One evening John and Maria were pacing the confines of the quarterdeck before turning in, enjoying the tropical scent of opening coconut pods brought to them on a breeze passing over a nearby island. The ship seemed unusually quiet. Since the Pirate's tragic death there had been no one to start a tune and set the men singing.

Now as the Hamblins rounded the afterhouse and walked toward the lee rail, they heard a voice singing faintly, hesitantly, as if not sure of its reception. Then, as though encouraged, the notes grew stronger, rounder.

'Why John, that's an old English hymn tune I know!' She hummed along with the unseen singer, trying to recall the words, then broke off.

'Now I know! It's an old Charles Wesley hymn. It goes like this—' And Maria sang softly as the seaman began another verse.

> *Depth of mercy! Can there be*
> *Mercy still reserved for me?*
> *Can my God His wrath forbear?*
> *Me, the chief of sinners spare?*

'It must be one of the Fijis,' John remarked. 'There's no one else on board with such a rich voice. Listen. Do you know this tune, Maria?'

'Oh, yes; Father loves that hymn.' Maria broke off and joined in the next verse.

> *Come ye disconsolate, where're ye languish,*
> *Come to the mercy-seat, fervently kneel;*
> *Here bring your wounded hearts, here tell your anguish;*
> *Earth has no sorrow that heaven cannot heal.*

'Oh, John, if you knew the awful thoughts I have had about those Fijis,' said Maria contritely, 'and here I am singing hymns with one of them. Can't I do something to show them I am glad they are on board now?'

John pulled Maria closer and laughed a bit. 'Now, now, dear, don't let your kind heart get you in trouble again. They're still rough seamen and part of the crew.

I'll find a way to let the singer know we enjoyed his songs.'

Her cheeks burned. She would keep to her quarterdeck. She never wanted to go through another episode like the one with Portugee.

As she fell asleep that night, with a lighter heart than she had borne for days, the words of the missionary echoed in her mind, 'Don't torture yourself with what may never happen.' And as the days went on she learned that the missionaries had taught the Fijis many virtues.

The barrels in the hold filled with sperm oil and spermacetti, The Roman again set her sails southward for the port of Hobart, Tasmania. Several ships were gammed, but only one had letters for them and they proved to be a year old, answering none of the questions gnawing at their hearts. As John read a letter from his brother-in-law, Sam Holman, dated November 15, 1861, he suddenly exclaimed, 'Listen to this, Maria!'

And he read:

Today I saw a strange sight. A fleet of twenty-four whaling ships sailed out of New Bedford harbor, their destination in sealed orders to be opened at sea.

All this fall the government has been buying up ships and whaling vessels, which from their peculiar model, seemed well adapted to the purpose. These twenty-four, with many others, have been loaded with stone and refuse granite. Some farmers found it profitable to sell their stone walls at fifty cents a ton.

Preparations of the ships were under the supervision of Messrs. Ivory H. Bartlett & Sons. It is rumored, and I think with good authority, that these stone-laden vessels will be sunk in the harbors of southern ports to prevent blockade-running.

'That must have been a sad sight, John! All those good ships going out to be sunk!'
'Not sad at all, Maria. Listen to this.' And he read on.

Clark's Point was crowded with citizens who sped the parting fleet with cheers and waving handkerchiefs. I attach a list of the New Bedford ships, many of which you will recognize.

John read the list silently for a moment, then exclaimed, 'The Bark Garland, The Harvest, The Herald! I know their captains. They were good ships. What a pity! And The Frances Henrietta.'
Maria shook her head sympathetically. 'What terrible things war demands of us.'
John finished reading the long list, then spoke slowly. 'I am wondering how this shortage of ships is going to affect us.'
'You think they might ask you to stay out longer, John?' Maria's voice trembled.
John folded the letter and put it in a cubbyhole in his desk. He turned to his wife with a reassuring smile.
'No matter what they ask, I'm taking The Roman home.'
There were so many questions that could only be answered when Hobart was reached! Maria's mind was busy with them.
Was their country still at war? Had John's message reached home in time to prevent young David from shipping out in the hope of meeting The Roman at sea?

Had Amasah seen any action? And what of steadfast Lisha? Was he still safe at home, working in the shipyards? Or had the call to defend his convictions been too strong to keep him there?

One day as Maria was caring for her children, she remembered the handsome twins, the sons of Sam's southern cousin. Cordelia's jewels! How awful it would be, she thought miserably, if Amasah and one of the twins met on a battlefield!

So it was with subdued excitement made up of hope and dread that Maria stood at the rails on the summery day in December when The Roman was piloted into the harbor of Hobart again.

John decided that Maria and the children should remain on the ship while he reported to the shipping office. When he returned, he brought an invitation from the Thomases to stay at their home while in port and a large packet of mail for the ship.

Maria selected Aunt Abby's letter to read first. Surely there would be nothing but good news about the family in it.

But the first paragraph brought a cry of dismay from Maria's lips.

'What is it?' Is anything wrong?' John leaped to his feet and peered at the letter over Maria's shoulder, as they sat in the cabin.

Maria pointed silently to the words, her throat too choked to speak.

John read, '...such sad news I must tell you. Amasah, our beloved only child, was killed in battle. Uncle Josiah grieves. David visits us often now, as if trying to make up for Amasah's not being here. But he talks of going to the war next year when he is sixteen if he doesn't go to sea. Even Lisha feels that he should ask to be relieved at the shipyards to take Amasah's place in the ranks.'

Each of the letters from home told again the tragic news of Amasah's death. When the last one was read, Maria tied them together with a piece of her yarn and soberly put them away and prepared to go ashore.

The genial Thomases welcomed the Hamblin family again to their home. Alice revelled in the attention given her, but Harry found it all very difficult and clung to his parents.

On the second day in the harbor, Captain Hamblin had Smitty brought ashore and examined by a doctor. The medical man complimented John on Smitty's general condition. 'Not a sign of gangrene,' he declared. 'Some of the tendons have been permanently injured so that the leg will not be as useful as before, but there is no reason to believe this man will not be able to work anywhere except aloft on the ship within a few weeks.'

Maria and John received this assurance with varying emotions. John felt pity that Smitty would have to give up the sea, his dream of being a captain, and become a seaman who could not go aloft, could never sign on a sailing vessel. Maria realized this, too, but her heart rejoiced that this young man's future need no longer mean years of separation from his family, with all the worries such absences meant for them and him.

John spent many hours at the shipping office. Maria never knew whether or not the home office raised objections to his resolution to proceed home. All preparations were made for the long journey home, and only enough barrels of sperm oil were sold to provision The Roman for it. The cow was exchanged for a goat so that the children's milk needs could be met without the burden of large quantities of fodder, and a number of laying hens were added to their diminished flock.

Christmas Day arrived before The Roman was ready to sail, and the Hamblins had the pleasure of selecting a new toy for Alice and Harry. Apples, oranges, and nuts, as well as several useful pieces of clothing, were among the children's other surprises.

One day John returned from the shipping office with strange news. Maria saw at once that he was troubled and put aside the petit point she was starting under Helen Thomas's tutelage.

'What is it, John?' she consciously braced herself to hear it.

'Bad news, dear, brought by a merchant ship that arrived today. The South has started raiding northern shipping in earnest. Whaleships are their special target. Many have been sunk already. The Alabama, a ship under both steam and sail, is the most feared. Its captain was formerly in the U.S. Navy and it is a fast runner. Whaleships have little chance against it.'

'Oh, John, it can't be!'

'I'm afraid it is all too true, Maria. This merchant ship had picked up a couple of seamen whose ship had been blown up by the raider. The Alabama is ranging the South Atlantic, hunting homeward-bound whalers especially. Loss of oil would hurt the North badly. Maria, dear, we must consider whether you and the children shouldn't remain here in Hobart while this terrible danger exists.'

John dropped into a chair and put his head in his hands, his shoulders sagging.

For a moment Maria was silent, her mind filled with visions of ships being blown to bits, of helpless survivors tossing about in stormy seas, of John running into these dangers while she and the children were half-way around the world from him.

'No, no,' she answered with determination. 'We are going home—all of us. We'll take our chances together.'

Chapter 30

AFTER two weeks in Hobart, The Roman, now in good condition and well-provisioned for the long journey home, was about to sail. Home! Home! Home! The words ran through the ship as the pilot shouted, 'Mr. Richards, are you ready?'

'All ready sir,' answered the first mate.

'Then heave ahead.'

'Aye, aye, sir. Man the windlass.'

The hawser was passed from the tug and made fast to The Roman. The windlass groaned and creaked as it began to turn, and the heavy chains rattled. It was music to Maria's ears, for it meant they were starting for home. She stood on the deck and with a light heart watched the proceedings.

They were going home! The holds were filled almost to the brim with good sperm oil and spermacetti and just one big whale or two small ones on the way home would make up for what had been sold at Hobart to fit out the ship. The Roman would enter New Bedford Harbor with a full load of liquid gold indeed.

'What a glorious homecoming,' Maria thought.

'Heave up anchor,' the pilot ordered. Maria had to guess at words spoken in the Tasmanian English accent; British, but with a twang of its own.

'All away, sir.'

Slowly, like a great gull preparing for flight, The Roman swung around and headed seaward. At the top mast flew Old Glory and the blue peter flag still fluttered at the fore, calling all crew back and announcing that the ship was ready to sail.

'Let fall sheets of tops'ls and top gal'n sails,' the pilot shouted.

The men sprang to the ratlines. The broad sheets of canvas flapped as they caught the wind. With these new wings The Roman glided along, gracefully cutting the sunlit waters of the current into furrows of creamy foam. The men sang chanteys as they sailed.

After a day's sailing, with the ship's routine well established, John summoned the crew to the deck.

'Men, you have all heard about the raiders the South is sending out to get northern shipping, and you know that whalers are on the list. I hope we do not meet them, especially The Alabama. But if we do, I will expect every man of you to do his duty, to carry out instructions. I know I can count on each of you to act quickly and coolly. That's all, men.'

Maria, in the deckhouse with the children, heard the men's quick, firm answer, 'Aye, aye, sir.' They were aware of what might be in store for them and they were ready to act.

In the days that followed, the lookouts scanned the sea for unfamiliar ships as well as for whales.

Before many weeks had passed The Roman's barrels were again filled with the valuable sperm oil, spermacetti, and whale oil, replacing that given in exchange for the refitting of the ship at Hobart.

Thistle in Her Hand

Maria watched John one morning as he worked over the charts with mate Richards.

'We'll pass St. Paul,' he said, pointing to a single dot in the Indian Ocean, 'and give a day or two to fishing there, and then we should have enough provisions to get us to Port Elizabeth. From there we sail around the Cape of Good Hope. A stop for wood and water at St. Helena and the Cape Verde Islands should see us through, barring any misadventures.'

Later Maria asked John about the island of St. Paul.

'No one lives there, dear. Too many earthquake shocks, sudden and bad, to attract anyone. It's the home of sea birds, seals, crawfish, and other kinds of fish. I'll send a couple of boats in for fish; the harbor is too shallow for our ship.'

As they approached the bleak volcanic island, Maria saw that John was right. St. Paul's steep cliffs, rising abruptly from the sea, were alive with sea birds, swooping and darting from rocks to sea and back. Avoiding the side of the island where the waves dashed mast-high against the cliffs, The Roman hove to, and two whaleboats put out under sail.

'It's impossible to row on account of immense beds of kelp around the island. Sometimes it's several feet deep,' John explained as the boats glided over the masses of brown weed like sleds over snow.

Maria saw that the fish were caught easily, taking the bait as fast as the lines were thrown overboard. 'We'll have enough for everybody tonight,' she thought with satisfaction.

When the men returned laden, all hands turned to cleaning the fish and soon Doc had the fires going and the fish treat under way. The next morning John sent other crew members to fish, and when they returned, boats loaded almost to the thwarts, again all hands fell to and cleaned the catch. This supply was packed away in salt for the future.

Now The Roman, under as full sail as the winds and weather permitted, ploughed across the Indian Ocean toward Port Elizabeth and the Cape of Good Hope.

At the South African port, Captain Hamblin declared shore leave and everyone on the ship in turn had a day in that strange and alluring country.

'It will be good for all of us,' said John. 'From here until New Bedford's reached, there will be only hard work and worry.'

'And strict discipline,' added mate Richards to the first group as they prepared to man the whaleboats.

Maria, looking shoreward at the heavy breakers on the beaches, wavered momentarily. Dared she risk the bo'sun's chair and the boat ride to the beach with the two children?

'The worst you would get is a wetting, Maria, and some oilskins will help there. I think you need this holiday, too.'

Ashore, Maria was glad that John had insisted. As they drove about the port city in a hired rig, she feasted her eyes on hosts of blooms new to her sight, as well as some whose acquaintance she had made on tropical islands. Everywhere she turned there was a profusion of bougainvillea, camelias, cannas, roses, dahlias, and exotics she could not name.

'I must remember all of this,' murmured Maria as she gazed at the riot of color against the flawless blue African sky and breathed the heady fragrance carried on the warm breezes.

When the children tired of riding about the hilly streets, John stopped at a green park, and he and Maria sat on the oilskins on the grass while Alice and Harry romped to their hearts' content. When they were hungry, John took them to a pleasant restaurant for a meal of roast mutton, English muffins, and tropical fruit conserves.

'Excuse me, sir, but aren't you a New Englander?' The question came from an adjoining table, where a hearty, red-faced man sat with an obviously ill woman.

The Hamblins turned quickly at the sound of the familiar Cape Cod twang. Standing politely, John introduced himself and his family and learned that his interrogator was Captain Worth of The Gazelle and his wife, Jane.

John plied them with questions. Captain Worth told them they were three months out of New Bedford. No, they had no mail for The Roman.

'Sendin' mail by whalers is discouragin' business these days. So many ships have been captured or sunk, or reported lost, that the home folks probably fear to put their worries into writin'.'

When the Worths were told that The Roman was headed for home, Jane Worth spoke for the first time. 'I envy you. I've been sick since we left port.' With a thin white hand, she brushed a strand of dull hair under the side of the black bonnet.

Maria expressed her sympathy. 'Perhaps you will feel better now that you have reached the Indian Ocean and milder weather.'

For a few moments the two women exchanged confidences while their husbands talked of the war, the state of the country.

'We were lucky coming across the Atlantic,' said Captain Worth. 'By providential grace, we didn't even see an unfriendly sail. I was especially fearful in the Fayal area, but we had to stop for wood and water no matter what the risk of raiders. I counted myself lucky indeed when I learned that The Golden Eagle, also out of New Bedford a short time, had been captured by The Alabama just off of Fayal.'

Maria picked up her ears at the name Golden Eagle. 'Why that was the ship of one of Uncle Asa's old friends. How awful!'

'And how did the captain and crew fare? Did you hear?' John wanted to know.

'Accounts are not certain. I heard that a bad storm came up and many of the men who put out in boats were lost. You can be sure there was nothing good at the hands of the rascal Semmes. The devil get him— Hell is too good for him.'

And the captain choked back an oath because of the presence of the women, while his face took on a deeper red.

The waiter approached with the delicacies they had ordered and Maria and John gave their attention to the children. By the time the tempting foods were before them, the Worths had finished their meal and were preparing to leave to seek a doctor's office for relief for Jane Worth's illness.

When the Hamblin family was alone again, Maria and John found that the disturbing news of yet another victim of the raiders had taken their appetite. Each tried to conjecture what lay ahead in the Atlantic.

By noon of the next day, with staples for the larder, wood, and a supply of water, The Roman headed for the Cape. Maria sighed as she said to John at breakfast, 'Cape of Good Hope sounds so nice and pleasant, but I remember in school we read that early explorers also called it the Cape of Storms. I hope the storms will not be so violent as those when we rounded the Horn.'

Maria shivered as she recalled the rough rounding of the Horn. 'That was three years ago, December, 1859!' she exclaimed in astonishment.

'The Horn rounding is worse, but this can be stormy enough. Since it is the southern summer, perhaps the storms will not be so violent,' John answered. And he added with a smile, 'I sure hope you can see the tablecloth floating on the mountain top.'

'Tablecloth on the mountain?' Maria asked, laughing. And Alice repeated her mother's question.

John laughed and refused to elaborate. 'Just wait and see,' he said as he hurried up the companionway.

The rounding was unusually calm and Maria and the children were able to go up on deck and gaze on the majestic Table Mountain rising from the shores of Table Bay, Capetown. When the southeast winds blew, a whitish-gray cloud rose from the summit, giving the illusion of a tablecloth floating.

'The tablecloth,' shrilled Alice in excitement. And John with Harry in his arms, and Maria holding Alice, stood at the bulwarks and marvelled at the beauty of the phenomenon before them and for the moment all worries were forgotten.

One morning a few days later John came to the stateroom and said, 'We are now in the Atlantic, the South Atlantic.' For a moment Maria was elated.

'South Atlantic Ocean! Really headed for home. How good that sounds!'

But the thought that they were approaching the prowling grounds of the dreaded Alabama sobered her at once.

Chapter 31

FROM the day The Roman rounded the Cape of Good Hope, John ordered two men on watch from earliest dawn till dark, and Maria noted that either John or one of the mates was usually on deck with spyglass to his eye. She tried to submerge her fears in the petit point she was making for a hassock, a hassock for the home she hoped was to be theirs when this nightmare was over and they were safely home. But as her quick fingers selected the colors for the rose buds, violets, and shaded green leaves that were appearing on the black background, she could not keep her eyes from searching the horizon through the porthole or the door of the deckhouse. At night when she closed her eyes there was always a black cloud advancing toward her, as menacing as the approach of the monstrous whale or the threatening waterspout.

A day or two before the planned stop at the island of St. Helena, the mate reported a lowering barometer. That meant a storm. Maria, hearing the report, hurried to the deckhouse with sinking heart to gather her things and take them to safety below. John sent Henry to help her with the heavier articles. As they worked together she noticed that the black man's hands shook, and she chided him.

'Why, Henry, this is not the first storm we've been through. What's the matter?'

The steward tried to smile, but did not succeed. 'Ma'am, 'tain't the storm I fears. It's—it's what might be waitin' for us any mornin' when the sun comes up.'

Poor Henry, thought Maria, he looks as though he has not slept for many nights. Perhaps if they talked it out his fears could be allayed.

'Henry, this is a great wide ocean; even the islands look like tiny dots on the map. Think how many weeks often pass without our meeting a single ship—'

'Yes'm, but this here raider is huntin' for us, not mindin' his business like a whaler.' And Henry shook his head dolefully.

'Well then, Henry, let's put it this way. For almost four years you have shared the dangers of the sea with the rest of us. Remember the storm when the mainmast went? You weren't as scared then as you are now. I just don't understand it.'

Maria snapped a drawer shut and fastened it securely, then turned to face the man.

'Ma'am,' said Henry slowly, 'even if the raiders was pirates like the mens in the fo'c'sle tells about, I wouldn't be scared—leastways, not much—but ma'am, I don't never tell this before, but I run'd away frum a man just like that Cap'n Semmes. I know what he'd do to me if he found this black man on a ship he captured! Look here, ma'am.'

With a twist, Henry pulled his jersey up across his shoulders and turned his back to expose the ugly scars of a brutal beating. 'That's from the fust time I run'd away.'

Thistle in Her Hand

'Oh Henry,' gasped Maria, sick at heart.

'Ma'am, I is sorry; I shouldn't have showed you.' His sad eyes filled with tears for Maria's distress.

In the silence that followed the pair regarded each other with compassion. But they were suddenly conscious that the usual commotion of battening down had increased to a tumultuous pitch above decks. Was that cry 'Ship ahoy'? Maria and Henry eyed each other in consternation, and then turned and ran for the companionway.

When they reached the deck, everyone was looking toward the bow of the boat, beyond the bow—they were looking far out to sea, straining, straining. Maria saw John in the lower rigging, glass trained on that distant speck, saw the two men in the crow's nest pointing and waving their arms.

John beckoned to the mate, and Mr. Richards swung up the rigging as if he had wings. He took the glass from John. Maria moved closer.

'Do you make out a black ship?' John asked in quick and brittle tones.

'Yes sir, long narrow ship, two smokestacks, two long yardarms, two long black boats amidship on cranes ...yes, looks like The Alabama.'

Without a word, John dropped to the deck and began barking out orders. Instantly, all hands on deck swarmed up the masts and yardarms and the sails that had been furled for the approaching storm were let to the winds. The helmsman leaned all his weight on the wheel and Mr. Richards sprang to his aid. The Roman wheeled about and beat her way into the wind, toward the lowering clouds in the southwest.

Maria stood, almost paralyzed, watching the preparations, watching John's face. This was a new face, the resolute face of an unyielding general on the eye of battle.

Suddenly Maria was conscious of the children in the play yard. They were laughing and talking together in a language both seemed to understand. A moan rose to Maria's lips. Those little ones! How could she protect them?

She longed to have the comfort of John's advice, to feel him close to her and the children. But he did not even look her way. She knew every fiber of his being was straining to captain his ship out of gunshot of that dreaded raider. She would have to manage alone.

Quickly she drew Harry out of the play yard and admonished Alice to climb over the rail at once and follow her below. Alice started to protest, but seeing her mother's strained expression, the well-trained child obeyed. When she saw the gimballed bed was their destination, she opened her blue eyes wide and asked, 'Mommy, will it rain, rain, rain, and blow, blow, blow?'

'Yes darling, I'm afraid it will, and mother still has work to do, so this will be the safest place for you and brother.'

Alice turned to Harry and began to invent a game, as Maria hurried abovedeck to make further preparations.

As she strove to make her working tools secure in the deckhouse, she listened intently to the voices of the officers. She knew The Alabama could overtake The Roman easily; the slow-going blubber hunters were easy prey for the vessel that had both sail and steam power.

The sun was still shining, although the wind had picked up and choppy waves were hurtling against the bulwarks. As she watched, sharp streaks of lightning tore at the blackening horizon.

Thistle in Her Hand

The Irish second mate's keen eye was now pressed to the glass as he clung to the rigging. 'She's gainin' on us,' he shouted.

Yes, Maria could see the vessel now, still an undistinguishable speck to the naked eye, but certainly closer than a half hour ago. As she strained toward the black mote, she envisioned it assuming the proportions of the thunderous ebony clouds toward which The Roman was racing. Almost with relief, she faced about in that direction. Those sable clouds no longer brought terror; they were a part of nature's majesty on the face of the deep. To lose in the battle with those forces was not ignoble. But to go down a victim of the sinister wrath of the war cloud, that would be defeat indeed. Maria leaned to the wind as if to push The Roman with her own weight toward the fast-approaching storm.

Timmy and Henry rushed past, carrying the noonday food to the hard-working crew. There would be no lining up with bowls and skids today. They would do with hardtack and salt beef, eaten on the run. Captain Hamblin himself would not touch food until the ship was out of danger. He walked about the decks constantly, shouting orders, echoed by mate Richards and the third mate, to shift a sail here or there, to take advantage of the wind against which they were pushing.

Could they make the cover of the storm before being overtaken by the raider? That was the question. To be enfolded by the raging elements was the prayer in every heart aboard The Roman.

Maria divided her time and strength between the children in the stateroom and the grim race to be watched from the quarterdeck. Henry brought goat's milk and biscuits for the children and hot tea for Maria and they all sat on the edge of the gimballed bed so that the lurching of the ship would not make them spill the liquids. Henry's face was a mixture of fear and concern for his charges and, in spite of her own misgivings, Maria's heart ached for the former slave. Before he left with the cups, Maria put her hand on his cold brown hand and spoke earnestly to him.

'Henry, do you remember the missionary lady at Suva?' As Henry acknowledged that he did, she went on, 'She gave me a bit of advice that I think will help you, too, Henry. She said, "Don't torture yourself about what may never happen." That's good advice, I've found. Let's follow it now, Henry.'

'Yes'm.' The answer came dully and she knew that she had not reached his demoralized spirit.

His arms swung dejectedly as he left to answer a call from Doc. Maria turned to the stern porthole and gazed unseeingly at the rising waves. Suddenly, as the ship rose to the top of a swell, she saw distinctly the outline of The Alabama, as the mate had described it—a black ship, long and narrow, with two smokestacks. Then The Roman dipped into a trough and she could see it no more. She turned quickly. The children had stretched out and were napping. Holding to any stationary object, she made her way above. She must see John. She must know what was happening.

The wind bit into her face as she left the shelter of the afterhouse and she felt the first spatter of rain on her face. At the same moment, she almost ran into John as he moved swiftly toward the wheel to speak to the helmsman.

Clinging to her husband, she cried, 'John, I saw it—from the porthole! Tell me. Tell me what will happen.'

Thistle in Her Hand

John did not stop. Tearing her hands from his coat, he strode on toward the helmsman, barking an order as soon as he was within hearing distance. Then he turned back to his wife and for a fleeting second the hard-set expression left his face. He pulled her toward the shelter of the afterhouse, held her close for a moment, and in a strained voice said, 'Maria, at this moment only God knows what is going to happen. All I can tell you is that the storm is upon us now. The Alabama's guns will be useless in this heavy sea. Now you get back to the safety of the bed and pray that when the storm passes we will have lost the raider.'

With firm hands he urged her toward the companionway and Maria heard the thud of the hatch as he made it secure against the wash of the rising sea.

In the stateroom Maria prepared expertly for the only storm she had ever welcomed. Folding her strongest sheet diagonally, she slipped it across the bed under the sleeping children, leaving the ends free to bring around them and tie securely when the need arose. The Roman was pitching more and more as the wind strengthened, and through the creaking old timbers she could hear the whistling, snapping noises of the sails. John would crowd each sail until disaster threatened in his effort to lose the raider in the storm.

Before getting on the bed with the children, Maria fell on her knees and prayed with fervor that no one would be swept from the rigging as the sails were maneuvered by the captain, that the two ships would be separated in the storm, that the end of the storm or the dawn of tomorrow would reveal no menacing war cloud.

Then she put her workbasket on the bed, climbed in, and all that afternoon worked industriously on the petit point or amused the children.

Margarita Thompson Diddel

As the hours wore on without the storm increasing to hurricane proportions, Maria's mind was as busy as her needle. She remembered scenes and events from her childhood that had not crossed her mind for years. The little white steepled church. The Lees and the Hibbards in their pews. The hats the Hibbard twins had worn at Easter, flower garden hats. Her father, standing beside her, singing hymns in the tenor voice of which she had been so proud. Maria hummed a bit, then sang the hymns aloud to the children, her voice rising and falling through the clamor of the storm.

Timmy came late in the afternoon with more milk and hot tea. Maria asked how the men were faring above and listened with grave respect to his tale of the courage and hardihood of both captain and crew. Every possible stratagem was being tried to take advantage of the storm and elude the pursuer, the boy assured her.

In the safety of the bed, she wished she could be standing with John, adding her strength and courage to his. She thought of Doc, once so agile, now stumping around in pain, attending to the needs of the men. She longed to talk again to Henry, to reassure him that all would be well. She felt as one with all the crew, even the once feared Fijis, who were risking their lives now in a situation they could not even be expected to understand.

The early coming of nightfall brought some relief from the anxieties of the chase, but none from the storm. There was a gradual increase of wind intensity, tipping The Roman until Maria thought it must turn over on its beam ends.

Lying in the swinging bed, she was attacked by her old enemy of seasickness; she gave thanks for the apparent immunity of the children to that weakness.

Thistle in Her Hand

Alice wakened occasionally and stretched her small limbs for release from the cramped position in which the tightly wound sheet held her to Maria; but little Harry slept on, unmindful of the elements or his present situation.

Toward morning the wind moderated but the rain still fell in torrents. Maria rose with caution and lifted Alice from the bed and put her in her slatted bunk. Then she waited a while. When there was no sign of increased wind violence, she put Harry also in his own bed and returned to catch a few moments of sleep.

She was dozing off when the thought struck her that The Roman must be far off her course. She tried to recall the chart John had been working on after they rounded the Cape.

Suddenly she saw it, as if it were before her now. What had John said about those five little dots to the west of their course? She remembered. They were the rockbound islands of Tristan de Cunha, avoided by whalers except in dire emergency because of their stormy waters. The graveyard of ships, they were called.

Maria's heart jumped, then pounded. What if the ship, scudding along in the darkness, ran into those awful rocky shores? She slipped out of bed and felt her way to the porthole; she watched as the ship lifted and fell in the great swells, but could not distinguish between sea and sky. Could John, could anyone, avoid danger in that inky blackness?

She heard the door to the cabin open and felt John's presence. He did not come into the stateroom, however, but threw himself on the horsehair couch in the cabin. By the time Maria reached him he was fast asleep, exhausted. She sat beside him a while, smoothing his furrowed brow lightly. His hair and his clothing were damp. After a while she returned to the stateroom. She was sure she had not dozed before she heard the first mate awakening him. 'Captain, you wanted I should call you, sir.'

In a moment she heard John putting on his oilskins and leaving the cabin. She fell into a troubled sleep as The Roman sped on through the night.

Chapter 32

THE cheerful conversation of the awakened children roused Maria and she sprang to the porthole to scan the sea for The Alabama. The empty sea stretched behind the ship as far as she could see, but the waters still rose in great swells, like undulating hills, screening the horizon from view. Without stopping to speak to the children or to freshen her rumpled appearance, she threw a shawl about her and hurried above.

Glancing about quickly, she saw no signs of relaxed vigilance. Most of the crew was on deck or in the rigging. John was giving instructions about the sails, grim-faced and weary.

The chase was not over, then. Maria knew despair at that moment and turned to go below. Before she reached the end of the companionway, Henry came clattering down the steps. To her amazement, his face was cheerful again, almost beaming.

'Mis' Hamblin, ma'am,' he called, 'the captain says you have breakfast and don't wait for him. He's too busy turnin' and twistin' them sails, makin' old ship go thisaway and thataway, so old devil-ship can't find us.'

'Can't find us?' Maria repeated, bewildered.

'Yes, ma'am. All night long he have the ship turn and turn and turn. Now nobody know where we are, specially that old black ship. The captain, he save us, ma'am; he sure did.'

When Maria saw that Henry's confidence in John's seamanship had restored him from the cringing runaway slave to his usual happy, cheerful self, even though he knew they were not out of danger yet, she felt ashamed of her moment of despair. John had never failed yet to see them through. He would bring them all home safely.

The Roman kept on her zig-zag course all that day, taking advantage of the continuing brisk winds. The seamen worked until they were completely exhausted, then were given a short relief while the ship held its course. In due time, John or the first mate would call all hands on deck and the sails would be set anew.

The men climbed and pulled at the ropes and sails until their muscles were sore and their fingers bleeding, but no one complained. Doc took no rest; he could not climb or set a sail, but he could keep the stomachs of the men warm and satisfied. Henry and Timmy peeled potatoes and turnips and carried food and drink to the men all day long.

It was mid-afternoon before Maria had an opportunity to say more than a few words to John. She had kept the children below all day, out of the path of the hustling crew. In the little deckhouse, John rested and told Maria of the night's adventures.

'If the storm hadn't come when it did, we would have been easy prey to that pirate,' he told her. 'He was gaining on us steadily, and in another two hours we would have been within gunshot.

Thistle in Her Hand

'It was risky running The Roman so hard in that wind, but the raider kept coming on under steam power. I had to take that risk.'

Maria interrupted: 'Those rocky islands, John! I kept thinking of them while we sailed on in the darkness.'

John looked thoughtful. 'You may believe I gave them some thought, too, Maria! But there was no time to study charts. I had to do my charting in my head. And when I shot the sun today we were just about where I had figured—several hundred miles north of Tristan de Cunha.'

'Which proves what a splendid navigator you are, John,' said his wife with pride.

'The men were wonderful, Maria—every last one of them. I am going to recommend a bonus for each if we reach home safely.'

'If? Oh, John!'

'Remember, my dear, The Alabama is not the only raider abroad in these waters. Some of the ships Semmes captured have been forced into service as privateers. They may not be as fast-moving as The Alabama, but they are armed.'

John stood up. 'Now I must get back,' he said. 'We are still altering our course at intervals.'

Hardly had John disappeared before Maria heard the call 'Ship ahoy!' from the lookout. By the time she reached the deck outside, John, glass to eye, was giving orders to turn the ship and run under full sail. The vessel observed was at such distance that no one could tell what it was, but John took no chances. They would keep their lonely distance from all ships hereafter. There would be no gamming at sea on the voyage home.

Whether the ship was friend or foe no one ever knew. The Roman lost it within the hour. John posted a lookout in the bow and another in the stern of the ship until sundown. The two in the masthead watch were given shorter duty, so that sharp eyes would be watching at all times. Again that night, The Roman sailed with only the covered binnacle lamp, though not in the headlong flight of the previous evening.

By the next morning, all signs of the storm had vanished, and the ship was left to the mercies of an unfavorable wind direction as it headed north again. The captain and mate recharted their course for home with extreme care, using all their accumulated sea knowledge to keep off the usual route of whalers yet avoid the worst of the doldrums when they neared the equatorial regions.

Day after day the alert crew worked and watched, then rested and watched or worked again. The faces of the men grew haggard with the strain, and nerves were ready to snap.

Maria sighed for the peaceful days when the watch was only for whales, landfalls, and other sails. Then officers and crew met the vicissitudes of whaling life with a certain cheerful resignation. Now there was deep, burning fury against this sea-scourge, Semmes, who was one of their own countrymen, and a Northerner at that.

In spite of careful charting, the day came when Maria knew they had reached the dreaded doldrums. Instead of around a hundred miles a day, The Roman made a bare twenty or less. The heat, the severe electrical storms, the sure knowledge that they had no avenue of escape now from a steam-propelled vessel were even more onerous than the labors of keeping the ship in flight.

Maria laid aside her petit point because the feel of the

Thistle in Her Hand

wool threads was unbearable. She was thankful that the children could adjust themselves quickly to changes of weather. In spite of the heat they played contentedly under the sailcloth awning or on the floor of the tiny stateroom when the sun was high above. When she put them to sleep, she sat long minutes fanning them with the big palm leaf fan John had brought her from one of the islands.

To add to their irritations, Doc reported that the water supply was dangerously low. Maria had to use salt water to wash the children and their clothes for several days until temporary relief came with a shower. Whenever a dark cloud appeared, Doc set out his pots and pans beside the ever ready casks, open to catch the rain. Thirst was ever present, a nagging discomfort, another rasp for taut nerves. Doc became irritable. He snapped at the steward and cabin boy when they brought back bowls of half-eaten food from the crew. It was not his fault. How could he cook without adequate water?

Finally, after more than a week, the wind filled The Roman's sails again and the long voyage homeward was resumed. Day after day they pushed on toward the Northern Hemisphere, with growing relief from the heat.

Stops had to be made at two islands for water, wood, vegetables, and fruit. The stops were made as short as possible, with the eyes of all on the ship peeled for the sight of a raider.

A series of storms from the northeast plagued The Roman as she reached the North Atlantic and sent Maria to her gimballed bed with seasickness. As the pangs of nausea beset her, she thought of the first days of this voyage, when she had been so ill she had thought she must die, and of the times without number when stormy weather had sent her to bed in misery.

Will I ever get over being seasick? she wondered.

Twice during the crossing, distant sails were sighted. John decided they were innocent whalers or merchant ships, for they appeared just as eager to be lonely and apart.

One evening, Maria felt well enough to take a short stroll about the quarterdeck with her husband. The stormy skies had cleared and the stars burned in the blackness of a moonless night. Maria lifted her eyes and gasped in sudden realization.

'Why John, there's the Dipper and the North Star! We're home!'

John laughed heartily and Maria's heart warmed at the sound. She could not recall when she had heard him laugh last.

'We've been sailing by the North Star for weeks, Maria. You just haven't looked up.'

Maria was silent a moment, then said slowly, 'No. I've been too frightened and miserable to look up, but all the time you were using it as your guide. I am so proud of you, John. I don't think there was ever a better navigator. Or a better husband.' And she pressed against him in the darkness.

'These have been four wonderful years, dear. There have been bad times—the loss of Agrimonte and the Pirate, Smitty's accident, that awful night on Norfolk Island before Harry was born.'

'And Portugee and his insolence,' added Maria.

'But beyond all that there have been times when I could not ask for more. A good ship under my command and you by my side.'

And that's the way it will always be for him, thought

Thistle in Her Hand

Maria. But she put the thought of future voyages out of her mind and began talking about their homecoming as they left the deck for their stateroom.

As The Roman neared the end of her journey, she ran into great fog banks and for two days the ship was bound in its cottony thickness, fearing collision with a friendly ship more than pursuit of a raider.

Then at last Maria's dreams began to be fulfilled. On a brisk spring morning in May, 1863, The Roman passed Woods Hole, bells clanging.

Maria and the children stood at the bulwarks, waving hands at the beloved shores. She could almost hear the electric telegraph ticking the news of their arrival to Boston and back to New Bedford. And the flags would be going up on Telegraph Hill and Uncle Asa would see them first and jubilantly spread the news that The Roman had arrived.

Now probably the family would be getting ready to come to the wharf to meet them, Maria thought as she eagerly scanned the skyline of her beloved homeland. As John joined her at the rail, she said, 'Just as soon as you can get away, will you drive us to Louise's and you can come back and finish your reports?'

'Yes dear, I will. You are home at last, my darling.'

'The folks will be surprised to see Alice. What a surprise for all! Milly will love her. And our husky little Harry. Oh, John, it is all so wonderful I can hardly breathe. And I am in a hurry to be home. It seems so long ago that we left to get married.'

'And you're still not sorry?' he asked with a grin as he put his hand over hers.

'You don't need my answer, but I'll give it. I love you more than ever, ever, ever.' And for a moment tears came to her eyes.

John left hurriedly as the sailboat from Nashong

brought the pilot who was to take the wheel the rest of the journey. Later he came back looking troubled.

'The pilot thought The Roman was a phantom ship as he was sure The Roman had gone the way of the other whalers from the South Atlantic as reports were that The Alabama was down there. I wonder if others think so? If so, our folks will not be expecting us. The moment we dock I'll send a messenger to your folks and mine. We'd better stay at the Holmans all night to rest up and give your family and mine a chance to get over the shock of our being alive and well.'

'You are right, John,' Maria said as she turned to go down to the sleeping children. She took out her beloved Bible and read her father's favorite Psalm, the 121st, and got down on her knees in prayer for their deliverance.

'John, we'll see many changes around the wharves after that big fire, won't we? I expect everything will be grand and new.'

Her husband assented, but seemed preoccupied, troubled inwardly. Maria prattled on to keep from serious thoughts. She, too, was apprehensive. All the mail they had received had been more than a year old. She knew that many ships carrying mail to or from them must have been sunk or burned by that buccaneer Semmes. But surely New Bedford and the little towns around Buzzards Bay could not have been affected by the battling armies.

When she asked John about this, he said, 'New Bedford's a whaling town and the raiders have destroyed many whaling ships. It can't help but affect the town some.'

After what seemed an interminable time to Maria, The Roman was at last docked. While the lines were

Thistle in Her Hand

being expertly tied, Maria searched the crowd on the wharf for a familiar face. There was none!

She tried to comfort herself with the thought that the flags on Telegraph Hill had gone unnoticed, or that the electric telegraph might have failed to work. But the men from the shipping office were there, shaking hands with John and the first mate. Anxiety returned to her heart.

Where was Uncle Josiah? Maria remembered he had said, 'Niece, we in the marine business get wind when a whaler is coming in. I'll be there to greet you. Probably many others—your folks and friends.'

And where were her father and brothers? David, especially.

John returned to help her ashore with the children.

'Maria, The Roman was indeed given up for lost! The office had word that The Alabama was raiding in the sea lanes of whalers homecoming from the Indian Ocean. And reports had it that The Roman was lost.

'Listen to this, the one that has refused to give up hope was your father. The men tell me that he and one of his sons have been coming often to find out when we were coming. He has had absolute faith that we were coming, that the Lord would answer his prayers and he has kept the rest of the family hopeful. They came just two days ago! And Maria, I have just sent a messenger to your folks at Monument Beach to tell them we are home and will see them tomorrow.'

Maria was crying tears of joy. 'Remember, we promised Louise that we would go there and she told the family to come to her house when they heard we were coming. They are probably on the way. I don't understand why Sam is not here. Probably he is out of town and Louise and Milly are waiting for us at the house. Remember, Milly said she was going to put bouquets of flowers all around our room.'

'I don't know, dear, but we'll find out just as soon as I can leave.'

As they went ashore with the children, Maria was greeted with emotion by people who were strangers to her. The sight of one ship and its company that had escaped the raiders was the cause of much blowing of noses and turning away of heads to hide feelings.

So many whalers had been lost in both oceans! The office was almost deserted; the owners were away and only a few office workers were there.

At last John was ready to drive the family to the Holman home. 'Mr. Richards, take over. I'll come back later to make my final reports,' he told the mate.

A buckboard badly in need of paint awaited them. John took the reins adeptly and soon they were in the residential part of New Bedford.

Maria stared in dismay. What had happened to the charming lawns and gardens she had carried in her memory all these years? Such gardens as there were seemed to be planted with vegetables; lawns and shrubbery looked neglected. Many houses were in need of paint. On some the paint on the trim of the houses was peeling.

Maria looked around wide-eyed with surprise. 'What's happened to New Bedford, John? Why, it looks actually shabby, rundown, like a person just getting over the ague! What a difference from the New Bedford we sailed from four years ago! Oh, what's done it?'

'There have been terrible hardships at home, too. First, the big wharf fire, then the war, taking the young men, then the loss of all those whaleships for the blockade the folks wrote about, then the loss of all those destroyed by the raiders.' John shook his head.

Thistle in Her Hand

'We'll soon hear about it all from Sam. Thank goodness we are almost there.' Maria sighed with relief; then she cried out, 'Look John, the shutters are closed! I can see it from here! What can that mean?'

As they approached, there was no sign of a garden. The perennials looked ragged, uncared for; the grass was high. Only the arching elms looked the same.

'I can't imagine what's happened, but I'll soon find out.' John sprang from the surrey, drew the reins through the ring of the hitching post, and hurried to the house next door.

There was a look of shock, sorrow, on his face when he returned. 'They're in Washington—government work. Went down in January.'

'John, what is it? You are holding something back,' Maria said softly so as not to alarm Alice who was looking around expectantly, her face all smiles and eyes alight.

'Mama, where's Milly? I want to see Milly.'

'Maria,' and for the first time there was a look of tears being held back in John's eyes, 'Milly died in November. Scarlet fever.' He turned to Alice and said simply, 'The family has gone away to Washington to help President Lincoln.'

'Let's go to Washington to see them, but first I want to see David—Uncle David that's still a boy.'

While the little girl prattled, Maria sat with her hands to her mouth fighting back the sobs, trying to get control of herself and keep poised in front of the children. The experiences of these past four years had done much to help her discipline her emotions now. She stared dry-eyed at the house, trying to comprehend John's news.

John climbed into the buckboard but did not start the horse. He looked at Maria and the children. 'Maria, it's

Margarita Thompson Diddel

a long drive to your folks at Monument Beach. Too long for you and the horse. We'll take the schooner ferry across Buzzards Bay. I heard one leaves at one. It'll save time and tomorrow we'll drive on to your folks at Pocasset and Monument Beach. It's better to break the trip,' John said firmly.

Maria swallowed hard. Back on a ship so soon. But John knew best. The family knew they were coming tomorrow or would know it when the messenger J hn sent reached them. Probably they'll send word to the others and all would be awaiting them. And Maria's aching heart was soothed with the thought of seeing her loved ones. It would be good to spend the night at Uncle Asa's—plenty of room and the children would be tired. Oh, but going on the ship! She sighed unhappily, but she said only, 'You are right. The quickest way—' Her heart began to hammer in her chest, but her face was resolute.

John snapped the whip and the horse broke into a trot. John stopped at the office to notify them of the change of plans. 'If I remember rightly, there's a crossing in the next hour.'

Little Alice had absorbed everything without comment until now. She looked at her mother, saying, 'I want to see your little brother, David.'

Maria pulled the child closer. 'And so you shall, very soon, dear. David will be a big boy now.' She herself could hardly wait to see her brothers, David and Lisha, see her father's and Uncle Asa's faces when they saw the children! She glanced at Harry's face. He was growing sleepy. Coming home had no meaning for him.

Maria knew she would never forget that ride across Buzzards Bay. She fought every moment not to show her fears. How John would laugh to know that she was

Thistle in Her Hand

more frightened now than when they had sailed round the Horn. The schooner seemed to be moving without purpose, tossing lightly in the choppy bay. The whaleship had by comparison seemed solid, substantial, dependable.

She sat with Harry asleep in her arms, thankful for something to hold on to. John, with Alice by the hand, wandered about the ship, talking to other passengers. At a counter he bought milk and crackers for the family lunch.

Time dragged for Maria as she waged her silent battle to keep from being seasick, to hide her fright. She wondered who the captain was. If only John were guiding the ship across, it wouldn't be half as bad.

But at last they reached Woods Hole and, with trembling limbs, Maria followed the crowd of people leaving the schooner. She carried her portmanteau, now battered and worn, while John managed the two children.

As they waited for a span of horses to be hitched up to a surrey for them, Maria said with a contented sigh, 'I am glad we are taking this way home, as we can stop a moment to see Uncle Asa and Aunt Eunice and take a turn to Sippewisset to see your aunts. How happy they will be to see us!'

'It must be only a minute, dear, because we have a long ride before us to Pocasset to your Aunt Abby's, and on to Monument Beach to your family,' John said as he touched the spirited roans with a whip. Maria had forgotten how well John handled the horses. She remembered hearing that whaling men liked driving horses and she smiled. The children sat open-eyed with amazement.

Maria looked around at the familiar scenes as they

passed through Falmouth and into West Falmouth. She was troubled because there was a rundown look everywhere. More than ever she was eager to get to Uncle Asa's, because he and Aunt Eunice would never let their place have that uncared-for look. Oh, those colorful petunias lining the walk, everything so fresh.

But when they reached the Capt. Asa Tobey's home, Maria and John were in for a shock. There were no young plants growing along the walk that led to the front door. The gate sagged on its hinges. The yellow paint hadn't been freshened that spring. The curtains at the window were not Aunt Eunice's usual starched stiff lace curtains.

'Alice, you sit here with Harry,' said Maria apprehensively as she followed John down from the carriage. He tethered the reins to the familiar iron horsehead post.

Their knock was answered by a strange face. A Portuguese woman, thought Maria.

'Captain Tobey? Is he here? And Mrs. Tobey?' John asked the woman.

She shook her head, then looked at them searchingly with her dark eyes. 'You must be the relatives she worried so much about,' she said sympathetically. 'She went to live with her sister in Maine a while after her husband died.'

'Captain Tobey—dead?'

'Yes, last September. Pneumonia, it was.' She lowered her voice and crossed herself. 'The night he died a nor'easter hit the Cape and the next morning his whaleboat in the marshes was gone—gone out to sea—some say the good man's spirit was in it, for everyone knew he loved the sea.'

Maria put her hand on John's arm. He thanked the

Thistle in Her Hand

woman and turned back to the carriage, holding tightly to Maria's hand. Her face was white and her eyes wide with fright. She moaned as she climbed into the carriage.

'Oh John, what has happened to our country? Have death and devastation taken our land? What has happened to our folks?'

Alice, frightened, began to cry and the baby to scream. Maria composed herself then and quieted the children.

John said quietly, 'We are driving to Pocasset. I'll go to Sippewisset tomorrow.'

Maria tried to put aside her feelings of sorrow and apprehension, to make the ride pleasant for the children. Small Harry soon went to sleep again, lulled by the steady beat of the horse's hoofs, and Maria stretched him across their laps.

Alice looked at everything in this new world which was to become her home. That the little girl could not comprehend much of what she told her, Maria knew, for until now she had been a child of the sea, her brief visits on land soon forgotten in the monotony of ship life.

As they drove through the little villages and open country, Maria's spirits rose. Here and there the same familiar silvery-gray shingled cottages, the well-tended flower and vegetable gardens, the warm smell of spring touched with the spice of the salty sea breeze.

Pocasset looked the same. And so did Aunt Abby's Cape Cod cottage, with its rose-lined walk from the gate of the white fence to the door. Her heart beating with fearful anticipation, Maria handed the children down to John and then was helped to the ground herself. This house was not closed. There were pink geraniums at the windows and a wisp of friendly smoke drifted from the kitchen chimney.

John reached for the brass knocker and Uncle Josiah opened the door then gave a shout, 'Abby, Abby, they are here—Maria and John.'

Aunt Abby appeared, looking as if she could not believe her eyes. Uncle Josiah stood still muttering, 'God be thanked. Oh, God be thanked for His mercy!'

Aunt Abby touched Maria and then John, as if still unconvinced of their reality, and the tears started from her eyes. Several times she tried to speak but couldn't, and held Maria to herself instead.

'We were worried when no one came to the wharf—no one of the family. We've had no news for many months, you know,' Maria said gently.

'Oh, my dears, everyone thought—' Abby couldn't go on, but stood holding Maria's hand.

'We found that out at the docks,' said John. 'We had a brush with The Alabama, but were fortunate, more fortunate than others.'

'Aye,' answered Uncle Josiah sadly. 'These are terrible times.'

Maria repeated that they had heard no news for a year or more. 'Please tell me about everyone.'

John added, 'We stopped at West Falmouth and learned of Uncle Asa's death. We hope there's no more bad news.'

The two, Abby and Josiah Godfrey, looked at each other for a moment without speaking, and tears gathered in their eyes. Maria's heart ached. She wished she could ask someone else for the news—it must be sad. John put his free arm about Maria as if to sustain her, while he held the bewildered Harry by the other.

Thistle in Her Hand

Alice, her face woebegone and lips quivering, held on to her mother's skirts saying softly, 'Why are they crying, Mummie?'

'Lisha?' asked Maria, a catch in her voice.

Uncle Josiah answered. 'He's home with your folks. Didn't get to go to war yet. Expected to enlist this spring, but got typhoid fever. He was mighty sick, but your stepmother took fine care of him and now he's over it, but ailing and puny. Now you're home safe, maybe he'll get well—have a wanting to live. He thought he'd lost you, too. We all did. Thought the pirates had taken The Roman, too.'

'Something terrible happened. I know it.' And Maria's heart began to beat wildly. 'Aunt Abby! Uncle! Lost who else?'

It was Josiah's turn to choke. His wife patted his arm as she wiped her eyes and forced herself to speak calmly.

'Davey. He insisted on going to sea and catch up with you in the Indian Ocean. That was after we heard you were not coming home but going whaling again. The folks finally gave in. Let him go on The Golden Eagle. The captain was such a good friend of your Uncle Asa's.'

Maria turned to John, sobbing. 'Davey! On The Golden Eagle.' John bowed his head over Maria's, holding her close. Both could hear the words of Captain Worth, '...I learned that The Golden Eagle also out of New Bedford a short time had been captured by The Alabama just off Fayal. Accounts are uncertain. I heard there was a bad storm and many of the men who put out in boats were lost.'

'We've been hoping and praying that he might have

been one of those who made the shore—that we would see him come bounding in with his merry greeting, but time has passed.'

'Oh, Aunt Abby, maybe he will yet,' and hope flared in Maria's heart. 'Maybe he is on one of those islands and can't get off it. That can be. Isn't that so, John?'

John nodded slowly as if holding little hope. 'Strange things happen to men at sea.'

Aunt Abby suddenly said, 'Land sakes alive, my dears, we've kept you standing here in the middle of the room! Do sit down. And let me have that fine baby. Maria, I do believe he looks like your mother. And I want to look at Alice, a little golden girl she is, God bless her.'

In a moment Aunt Abby had seated herself with Harry on her lap and he was already exploring the jet buttons of her black dress, while her arms held Alice close to her. Then Maria asked about the rest of the family.

'Your folks are as well as could be expected with what the terrible war has done to us. Your father's faith in his prayer to the Lord to bring you back has helped to keep them going—and us, maybe, too.' And tears began to roll down her cheeks.

Alice touched her cheek gently and asked, 'Have you any fat molasses cookies Mummie used to eat, with raisins in the middle?'

Aunt Abby suddenly wiped her tears and laughed, 'Land sakes child, I just made a fresh batch of them this morning. Must have sensed you were coming. Let me get a plateful and tea for you folks. I know it is late and you are in a hurry to get home, Maria and John, but this will stay you until then.'

'Aunt Abby, we feel we're at home now,' Maria said, smiling through her tearful eyes, 'but we must get going as the folks in Monument Beach will be waiting for us. I hope John's message got to them.'

Soon the span of horses was pulling the surrey along the dusty white road with pine trees bordering the highway to Monument Beach. Little Harry was asleep on his mother's lap and Alice, snuggled beside her father, was prattling about what she was seeing. All was so foreign to the three-year old who was used to a tubby whaler on the South Pacific or the Indian Ocean.

'The pretty brown horses, Papa.'

'Yes, Alice, and they are tired and hungry now. I will take care of them the first thing when we get home.'

Just then, Maria whispered ecstatically to John, 'We are home. People are waving handkerchiefs to us. Papa must have received your message and told. There's Papa on the porch. He must have seen us coming—he is waving.'

Willing hands took charge of the horses, letting John go into the house with his family where a joyful, teary meeting was taking place. The stepmother, with an arm around the thin, ailing Lisha, now smiling broadly, said to John, 'Since your message arrived, John, Lisha has been getting better. He now has the will to live.'

Chapter 33

Now, after almost four years of marriage, Maria's hope chest was opened and the colorful pieces and fine linens made gay and homelike the two-story yellow house with white shutters which John bought for his growing family in West Falmouth. It was on a rise of ground on the main highway.

For the first time, Maria felt settled. The war and its demands receded for the time being, and satisfying family life became the pattern. There was still time to plant a late spring vegetable garden, and Maria soon had a flourishing flower garden under way from slips and seedlings provided by friends and relatives.

She felt sure they would remain in West Falmouth for some time. The ship owners had decided that no more whaling vessels would leave port until the danger was past. With The Alabama eluding U. S. Navy ships so successfully, John saw little likelihood of returning to his chosen work in the near future.

Before long he bought a pair of fine horses and a light wagon. Cape Cod housewives, peeping from behind their lace curtains, were often treated to the sight of the handsome captain dashing by behind his swift span of horses.

As summer advanced, he was pressed into raising funds for the war-chest. John had no liking for speaking, but when he vividly described the destruction wrought by the raiders as he had heard it from other captains, when he outlined the losses of oil and ships, as well as men, and then told of his own narrow escape from The Alabama, the subscriptions flowed into the war funds.

While he was thus occupied, Maria gave her full attention to making the kind of home she had dreamed of. With a mother's helper to assist in the children's care and a village man to help in the garden and stable, she soon had a well-ordered household.

Satisfied at last with her hearth, she gave some thought to herself. 'I must do something to reduce my weight,' she told Lisha one day in the garden.

'Why don't you try horseback riding, Sis? They say it's a good reducer.'

Maria laughed, but she thought about it for several days and at length told John that she would like to ride with him if he would find a saddle for her. John complied at once, and one late June morning when the breezes brought a tang of salt from over Buzzards Bay, Maria and John started out for her first ride.

She made a pretty picture, seated on the shiny new side-saddle on the roan horse. The train of her dark brown skirt hung gracefully over her feet and the high-crowned hat with its short veil gave her height. But as she picked up the reins in her small gloved hands, she looked at the ground so far below her and cried, 'Oh, John, I'm up so high!'

John clicked and the horses started on an easy walk,

Thistle in Her Hand

with John riding close and encouraging Maria at every step. The strange movement of the muscular animal was frightening. Seeing a delectable bit of grass at the roadside and feeling the slack reins of his rider, Maria's horse bent his head to nibble. Maria grasped the saddle in sudden fear. There seemed to be nothing in front of her except the faraway ground. She turned pale and cried, 'I can't, John. I can't.'

A few minutes later a surprised household saw the pair back again. John helped Maria carefully off her steed, holding her close a moment until she regained her balance. Laughing a little at her chagrin, he murmured in her ear, 'Still my little landlubber wife.' So ended Maria's attempt at flesh reducing.

Soon afterward Maria realized she was pregnant again and confined her exercise to strolling, or to playing croquet, a popular new game, on their lawn, and to her gardening. With immense content she looked toward the coming of their third child the following spring.

Always, however, her happiness was tempered with anguished moments over David's absence, and with grief over the destruction and casualties of the bitter war. In early fall a letter came from Sam Holman, still in Washington, giving family news of himself and Louise, John's sister. He wrote that he had learned recently of the bad fortunes attending the family of his cousin, Cordelia Vandelier, who the Hamblins had met in New Bedford at the time of The Roman's sailing.

The twins, Carl and Charles, enlisted soon after the outbreak of war, and one after another met death in battle. Their father died of heart failure soon after. Poor Cordelia is being cared for by friends in Charleston. Her condition is considered grave, both physically and mentally, following

Margarita Thompson Diddel

privation and mistreatment by Union soldiers while she was on their isolated home plantation during the battles that raged around Charleston.

John sat long in thought when he had finished the letter. Later Maria talked it over with her father.

'War takes away the veneer of civilization from man,' said Elisha Tobey, sadly.

When the last chrysanthemum had been taken by the frost and the rosebeds mulched down for the winter, Maria devoted herself to making the inside of the house as comfortable as possible. In the sunny windows she placed pots of red and pink geraniums, fuchsias, heliotrope, and begonias. She subscribed to 'Graham's Magazine' and 'Godey's Lady's Book' for herself and women callers; for the growing children and neighbors' children there were always books borrowed from her father's shelves. For young and old there were 'Youth's Companion' and 'Harper's Weekly.' She kept the home scrupulously clean, but never objected to the slight disorder of an overturned book, marking the place of an interested reader, a puzzle left for another time, a pink shell or a bit of scrimshaw taken from its place on a shelf. It was all part of good living, and Maria was consciously enjoying every hour of this interlude from whaling voyages and endeavoring to make these months memorable for all of her family.

It was a winter of deep cold and long-lasting snows. In the Hamblin home the fires burned brightly and there were evenings of roasting chestnuts, popping corn, and storytelling. Sea stories were seldom told. Maria's life at sea was not of great interest to her Cape Cod neighbors. She scarcely ever mentioned it. The present was all-absorbing.

Thistle in Her Hand

So, with great serenity, Maria prepared for the coming of her third child in April.

One late afternoon she stood at the windows of the dining room, watching her children playing in the snow in the side yard. She was thinking how beautiful the snow appeared from the warm comfort of home, when she saw her husband approaching with a long narrow package. Another surprise, thought Maria. I wonder who this is for.

The children followed their father in, stamping the snow from their boots, their cheeks ablaze with good health.

John set his package carefully upright on the checkered cloth of the kitchen table and removed his fur cap and heavy jacket, while Maria helped the impatient children with their snowy wraps.

'Papa, is it a doll for me?' Alice could wait no longer to ask.

'This is something for Mother and all of us,' replied John, looking at Maria with a twinkle in his eyes, 'but I'll open it so it won't be broken.'

And he proceeded to take off the many wrappings to disclose a tall copper lamp.

'Oh, oh,' exclaimed Maria in delight, 'it is one of those new kerosene lamps. I've heard they give a wonderful light.'

While the short winter day darkened, John made the new lamp ready and as they sat around the supper table they talked of nothing but the fine light it gave.

'This lamp marks the beginning of a new age and the end of the whale oil period,' lectured John.

'Oh, John,' interrupted Maria breathlessly, 'does that mean there'll be no more whaling?'

John laughed heartily. 'No, Maria, it does not. Whale

oil lamps will be used for a long while yet. Kerosene is too dear. Whalers will go out again many times before substitutes are found for all the many uses of a whale.'

'Nevertheless,' he continued in his lecture manner to impress the children, 'when a new fuel is found which improves on the old, it is a new era, and, wonderful as this kerosene lamp seems to us now, there should be improvements even on this light. And perhaps new uses found for the fuel itself.'

Maria shook her head as she looked at the single wick lamp casting such a fine glow over the table. How could it be improved upon? When the meal was over, John carried the glass lamp to the sitting room and Maria took away one of the whale oil lamps. Tomorrow she would clean it and ask John to put it in the attic.

Nature conspired with Maria to make ideal the time of the birth of her second son. The sap was stirring the maples to new green life, the first robins sang their jubilate, the sweet spring air sent the blood surging through young and old. Maria was in excellent health and spirits and the baby arrived just when the doctor predicted. He was a long slender baby, resembling John even at birth, so that Maria insisted he be called after his father.

So the matchless year at home with her whole family flowed toward its inevitable end. Maria was in her garden that July afternoon, pulling a weed here, tying up a heavy-headed flower there, clipping, tidying up the flowerbeds. She had stooped to pull a thistle weed when John cantered up on his favorite horse, dismounted quickly and approached her, waving a newspaper. She sensed at once that her husband was tremendously excited over the news he was bringing and she shivered in the warm sunshine as she stood up and waited.

Thistle in Her Hand

'Look here, Maria,' John exulted, 'The Alabama's been captured by the S. S. Kearsage and the other raiders are taking to cover.'

Tears stung Maria's eyes. 'Read it to me, dear.'

As John avidly read the account of its capture and sinking, Maria thought of young David, whom the family now mourned as dead, of the many captains and crews sent to their death by the cruel Semmes. It was well that the sea was rid of the scourge, but it did not bring the loved ones back.

John threw the paper on the ground and grasped her by the shoulders.

'I have other news from New Bedford, dear.' He looked at her soberly. There was a glint in his eyes that Maria had seen once before and she knew before he spoke that he was going to sea again. Her heart contracted.

He spoke slowly. 'There is a great shortage of oil products. The Islander, this time, will be ready to sail in a fortnight. Maria, will you come with me? Can you leave all this?'

He nodded toward the house, with the sound of the children's voices at play on the shady vine-covered porch.

Suddenly Maria realized that unconsciously she had been preparing for this moment. There had been a discussion with young Lisha about her home. They had agreed that if the time came when she would go with John again it would be good to know that the home was there, cared for by the family, waiting for her return. Her father had talked about the children, asking that the little children not be separated but left with him. How often her gaze had turned toward Buzzards Bay and the sea beyond and her mind had contemplated its hardships, its terrors. Again and again her inner self had been torn 'betwixt and between,' as her father called it. At times she could bear least the thought of separation from John; at other times, with her happy children about her, she felt she could not leave them. She knew she could not take more than two away with her. This time it would have to be the baby John. And yet—

A picture of The Roman leaving the harbor with John at the bulwarks waving farewell to her and the children came to her mind, and it was as if an icy hand had touched her heart.

'Maria?' John was waiting for her answer.

Yes, she would go with him. Her little trunk would come down from the the attic. Suddenly she was aware of a prickling sensation in her palm and looked down. She still held the thistle in her hand. Closing her fingers firmly on it, she looked at John with a tremulous smile.

'I'll be ready to go with you, dear.'

Margarita Thompson Diddel

ABOUT THE AUTHOR

Margarita Thompson Diddel was born November 12, 1891 in Merida, Yucatan. One of eight children of Henrietta Hamblin and renowned Mayan archeologist, Colonel Edward H. Thompson, The American Counsul in Yucatan, Mexico.

Magarita primarily spoke Spanish and Mayan when she arrived in West Falmouth, Massachusetts at the age of eleven. The Thompson children were schooled in Cambridge, Mass. For the first three years they were placed in the care of their grandmother, Maria Tobey Hamblin, and their Aunt Nella Hamblin while their mother returned to the Yucatan to join their father.

It was here that Margarita first heard the tales of her grandmother's experiences at sea as the whaling wife of Captain John C. Hamblin. These stories and others heard in the Cape Cod area inspired her lifelong interest in the trying times of the whaling wives in that period of American history.

After graduating from Cambridge Latin School and attending Radcliffe College, she married Andrew Glenn Diddel in 1917 and lived in Indianapolis, Indiana. During World War II, Mrs. Diddel, now widowed, moved to Miami, Florida, to work for the Censorship Bureau. In 1946 she completed her education at the University of Miami, graduating with a Bachelor of Education degree.

She retired from teaching in public schools in 1963 and pursued her interest in writing. It was at this time Mrs. Diddel wrote from memory, imagination, and research her romantic novel, *THISTLE IN HER HAND*, about her grandmother and life aboard the whaling ship, *The Roman*.

DATE DUE

MAY 3 '69			
APR 25 '70			
OCT 1 1 '75			
OCT 1 1 '76			